4 WEEKS

P9-DMU-853

WITHDRAWN

CONCORD FREE
CONCORD
MA
PUBLIC LIBRARY

DEATH SQUAD LONDON

Jack Gerson

St. Martin's Press
New York

DEATH SQUAD LONDON. Copyright © 1989 by Jack Gerson. All rights reserved. Printed in the United States of America. No part of this book may be used or reproduced in any manner whatsoever without written permission except in the case of brief quotations embodied in critical articles or reviews. For information, address St. Martin's Press, 175 Fifth Avenue, New York, N.Y. 10010

Library of Congress Cataloging-in-Publication Data

Gerson, Jack.
      Death squad London / Jack Gerson.
          p.   cm.
      "A Thomas Dunne book."
      ISBN 0-312-03981-6
      I. Title.
PR6057.E72D39   1990
823'.914—dc20   89-24091
                                          CIP

First published in Great Brtain by W. H. Allen & Co. Plc.

First U.S. Edition
10 9 8 7 6 5 4 3 2 1

For my friends, Jean and Robert Urquhart.

DEATH SQUAD
LONDON

PROLOGUE

The woman running.

At the edge of the water, she ran. Stumbling over the mud flats at the edge of the river, lungs straining to bursting point, mouth open, fighting for air.

She knew there were three men, one somewhere behind her, the other two coming to join him . . . She had become aware of two of them on the embankment beyond Tower Bridge. The message had been to meet the man at Puddock's Wharf and she had gone to the rendezvous without thinking. 'New information', he'd said, something that would blow the whole thing wide open. It had sounded like Rennie's voice too. The same high tones, even the slight stammer. But now she knew it hadn't been Rennie. Too perfect an imitation. And then she'd realised she was being followed. She had moved quickly, turning off the embankment, hoping to shake them off, afraid more for Rennie than for herself. And she had thought she'd shaken them off.

At Puddock's Wharf, under an ancient cracked wooden sign, 'Boats for Hire', she'd waited. Thinking, no one had hired boats from this wharf for the last fifty years. Only the sign survived, paint-blistered and fading. Underfoot the planks were rotting and filthy. A broken-down shed, the door hanging on rusting hinges, stood at the edge of the wharf surrounded by the refuse of time.

No one in sight at first. She'd begun to think then, why here? Why so far from the West End? And at nine o'clock in the morning?

There was a mist coming up the river, a threat of fog to come. She'd shivered, waiting as nine o'clock became nine ten, nine fifteen. No sign of Rennie. No sign of anyone. Except a figure on a barge moving slowly up river. Then the first of the men had appeared at the end of the wharf. A large man, broad-shouldered, hatless, with a bullet-shaped head. Wearing a black polo-necked sweater and black trousers. It had to be one of them. One of the others. The followers had found her again. The man moved towards her with a slow, rolling gait. As he came closer she could see his face, a grinning mouth under a scarred nose. She was sure then she'd seen him before and that he was one of them.

She started to walk quickly away from him, heading for the east end of the wharf. He followed.

The second man appeared from a narrow lane behind her and joined his companion. She kept moving, looking over her shoulder. The man with the scarred nose said something to the new arrival and he ran back up the lane, out of sight. Going round to cut off her retreat.

She'd thought then how ridiculous it was. In broad daylight in the morning, being pursued by two strangers. Someone had to appear and they would do nothing. Perhaps they only intended to frighten her. To warn her off. The moment she got back onto the street they would disappear into the crowd. Letting her know they were aware of what she was doing. That would be surely their first move.

She moved even faster now until she was running. Thank God she'd worn flat shoes. She searched for another alley leading off the wharf up to the street. There was no other alley. Only a high fence behind which was the scarred, soot-begrimed wall of an old warehouse. The end of the wharf was coming up fast.

The planking ended. With a drop of four or five feet down to a narrow stone stairway that led down to the mud flats and the water's edge. At high tide the water would lap the lowest steps, but now they disappeared into the Thames mud.

She dropped down onto the steps. Turned and started to climb upwards. They must lead eventually to the street. Once there she would be safe. She knew these East End streets like the back of her hand, spent her childhood playing on them, exploring them.

She'd reached the top of the steps and had a clear view of the alley. The second man was coming down the alley towards her.

2

There was another figure just behind him. She sighed with relief. A police constable, the high helmet of the City force on his head.

She ran towards the uniformed figure. And then stopped.

The second man was smiling, saying something to the man in uniform and pointing towards her. The police constable grinned back, a crooked, lop-sided grin. He came towards her, side by side with the second man and she knew there was no help there. The police constable was one of them.

She ran back down the steps and onto the mud flats. Sinking in to her ankles. And forcing herself forward. There must be more steps further along, leading from the mud back up to streets, and people, and the safety of crowds. Or someone must see her, the rare figure of a woman struggling across the mud.

Woman running. Rather, stumbling. Twice she fell on the mud. Now too afraid to be disgusted by the filth that matted her clothes, smeared her hands. Only aware she had to keep moving.

They caught up with her. It was inevitable.

She felt only one blow. To the back of her head. She was only semi-stunned. Aware of hands gripping her body. Of being carried.

A voice saying, 'That's the beginning of the deep water channel . . .'

Then the hands let go and the water swirled around her, closed over her face and she was trying to struggle but the mud was heavy on her clothes and something, a foot, kept pushing her head down and under the blackness until she felt the strength ebbing from her and the cold blackness became strangely soothing and there was no need to keep struggling any longer . . .

ONE

There were still fogs in London in 1936. Pea-soupers, or as Dickens called them, London Particulars. Mist, coming in from the sea, crept over the Essex marshes, drifted up river to the city where it merged with the smoke from a million chimneys and fell to the streets, a dense veil of grime and sulphur dioxide. It was not until 1952 that the government of the time instituted smokeless zones and banished the thickest of fogs from the city with a smug satisfaction that ignored the fact that the poisonous sulphur dioxide was still pouring out into the atmosphere, now invisible to the naked eye but still dangerous to human lungs.

But, for now, it is late September, 1936. Edward VIII is on the throne – as yet uncrowned. And never to be so, by his own choice. The rumblings of that crisis are already heard, and growing louder. Stanley Baldwin resides in Downing Street, looking more like a gentleman-farmer than a Prime Minister. He nurses his briar pipe, creating the image of a stout and reliable John Bull; perhaps successfuly dissipating the older picture of a hard-eyed Tory politician who had master-minded the breaking of a General Strike, ensuring the City and the profiteers of the World War retained their profits. The Great Depression still blights the country. Thin, hollow-eyed men are, even yet, marching and meeting in protest against their own hunger. And elements have arisen under the influence of alien philosophies to use such protests in their own interests.

The world abroad is supposedly at peace. Yet in Africa, Mussolini's armies are massacring Abyssinian tribesmen – rifle, machine-gun, howitzer and bombing plane against the simple spear. The Japanese, having conquered Manchuria are looking avariciously towards China. The Germany of Adolf Hitler's National Socialist Party is remilitarising the Rhineland. In

Spain, a junta of generals has risen against a legally elected socialist government. In Russia, Stalin has instituted a reign of terror, mutilating his own country and people. And the would-be saviour of the world, the League of Nations, is making ineffectual noises.

And London, in September, is shrouded in fog.

The old man trod warily along Leman Street. The unseen bulk of large buildings towered above him, the showrooms of the Co-operative Wholesale Society. The blue lamp outside Leman Street Police Station was barely visible, wreathed in fog. Somewhere ahead, a gas flare penetrated the unnatural darkness, giving the old man some sense of direction.

He was dressed in an ancient serge coat, threadbare around the edges but, by its very weight, giving warmth. A black homburg came down almost to his ears. A woollen scarf concealed the stiff starched collar. The silk cravat, slightly stained, was as old as the man, of another era, an adornment to which he was accustomed.

He was well over seventy, hair under the bowler sparse and white. His skin was lined like parchment, his thin hands, gloveless, were mottled with liver-spots. His shoulders were hunched forward as if his spine had supported him for too long. Which it had. His eyes were red-rimmed but that was attributable to the fog. He walked close to the railings outside the police station and when he came to the end of these, he moved inwards to find the wall of the next building. He crossed a side road with infinite care. Passing along Leman Street, a car crept slowly forward, on his right, headlamps useless against the enveloping darkness. A fellow pedestrian, moving in the opposite direction, brushed against the old man, grunted in irritation and passed on into the black void.

The old man politely muttered, 'Please excuse,' and shrugged at the absence of reply. Who can expect good manners in such weather?

Finally his slow progress brought him to his destination. The lights of Aldgate East Underground Station suddenly rose up in front of him. He stopped under the lights, took a gold hunter from an inside pocket with much delving and searching under the serge coat, and peered at its face. Five thirty. He was in

6

time. He sighed with relief. Not to be late for his daughter, that was the important thing. He moved into the entrance of the underground station, felt the warmth of the lights on his face, replaced the watch, and leant against a pillar. A flood of passengers came from the lifts, moved quickly outwards, hesitating momentarily when faced with the blackness of Aldgate and the Whitechapel Road. They visibly braced themselves before moving forward to be devoured by the intimidating blackness.

The old man stared after them. It was as if God had lifted his leg and covered the city with a kind of disgust. So? *He* had his reasons. Who were we to question? If *He* existed. But, on such a night, he must escort Beth to his home. It was Thursday and every Thursday Beth would come to visit. Normally no need to meet her at the Underground. But, on such a night, no female should be permitted to walk alone. Especially here, in the East End. Still, the old man thought, he should be grateful. He was grateful. Regularly, she came. But maybe this night, she might have telephoned to tell him the fog was too thick. She had insisted he have the telephone for such emergencies. Practically the only telephone machine in Cable Street, it was. He should still insist in living in the small house in that street . . . they called it the worst street in London, some people did, then a telephone he must have. For forty years, since he had arrived in London, he had lived there. He had seen his wife die there. Why should he move away from all that he was accustomed to? It would be a desertion of his late wife's memory. Taken by influenza after the first war. It should have been him, he always said. Hannah had been so much stronger than he. In every way except physically. Also God had been so unfair to take her, leaving him with a ten-year-old daughter. That was when he had determined to spite God by ceasing to believe in him, to abandon synagogue and rabbi. So! Not without a little reluctance.

'Evening, Mr Kovel!'

A large man in the uniform of the London Transport Authority.

'Good evening, Mr Hoskins.' Harry Hoskins, a nice man in his fifties, Maurice Kovel knew. A *goy* but a good neighbour.

7

'You shouldn't be out on a filthy night like this, mate,' Hoskins said. 'Not good for the old lungs.'

'I should let my daughter walk through darkness alone? To Cable Street? No, no, not at all . . .'

'So you stand here breathing in that muck. Could make you ill, Mr Kovel.'

'What's ill? At my age, one expects to be ill. At my age, illness allows one to do nothing with a clear conscience.'

Hoskins laughed.

'Tell you what! I'll wait for her. I'm off duty in half an hour and then I can walk her to your house. It's on my way and you can hurry home just now. Before this gets worse.'

Maurice Kovel was tempted. Standing here breathing in *dreck* was definitely not a pleasure. And he could have the meal ready for Beth. Also Hoskins was a solid citizen, one of the good people in Cable Street. He took a deep breath which at once induced a spasm of coughing. That decided him. He cleared phlegm from the back of his throat and spoke hoarsely.

'She is coming from Fleet Street . . .' he muttered, as if it was important he should know from where she would be commencing her journey. 'You would be able to walk her to my house?'

'Right to the door,' Hoskins assured him.

'Such a night. If she had phoned today I would have told her not to come. But she phones yesterday . . . "coming as usual", she says, so who am I to argue? She should never have left home . . .'

'She's a grown woman with a career, Mr Kovel. Can't expect her to stay with her father all her life.'

'Why not? Thirty-five she may be, but unmarried. A good Jewish girl should stay with her parents until she marries.'

Hoskins gave an amused shrug. 'Wouldn't be doing as well as she is . . .'

Maurice looked up, irritated. 'How well is she doing? Working on a newspaper? Writing a column. What does that mean? Not even a whole page. One column indeed. To hear her, you'd think she was writing the Torah. Who reads a column?'

'You'd be surprised. The *Daily Dispatch*. Over a million

8

readers. That's what they say. Over a million. Reading your daughter . . .'

'Ach, they read the football page. The rest is for toilet paper. I send her to university to be a teacher and she ends up a newspaper writer. That's a job for a female?'

'Pays better than a teacher, they tell me. Bet it pays better than working for London Transport.'

Maurice crooked his head to one side. 'You got a steady job. Be grateful. Money isn't damn all. Ask me, I tell you, it's damn nothing. When I ran the delicatessen I made good money. So my wife died of influenza, my daughter to whom I give an education, she moves away, and my house is kept by my *meshuggeneh* of a sister.'

'I reckon Mrs Jacobs does you proud.'

'What else should she do? Where else should she go? A widow with two sons. I let them run the delicatessen now. Pay them good money. More than I get out of it. The least she can do is look after her brother. Family is family.'

'You've told me it all before, Mr Kovel.'

'So? A man's life story isn't worth hearing more than once?'

'Not with this bloody fog getting at your tonsils. Mrs Jacobs'll be nursing you with the 'flu if you don't get out of it now. Go on, go home. I'll walk Beth to the house when she gets here.'

Maurice nodded with a surly gratitude. 'Is another thing, too,' he said. 'We christen her Rebecca. Becky is all right. But she has to become Beth at school. And later, with the newspaper, she calls herself Coverley now. I ask you? Is she ashamed of our name?'

'Go home, Mr Kovel.'

There was a quality in Harry Hoskins' voice that signified an end to the conversation. The trouble with *goys*, Maurice told himself, they had no relish for conversation. Pulling up his collar, he stepped out of the warmth and light of the underground station and turned into the blackness of Leman Street. Five, six hundred yards and he'd be home. Making sure Sophie Jacobs had the meal ready for Beth. He should still think of her as Becky, but she would insist otherwise. Women! Stubborn. Like her mother. *It isn't the influenza, Maurie. Just a*

9

cold in the nose. And she goes and dies. Adding years to a man's age. Taking years off his life. He could wish it were so. To be with her in Golders Green. It would come in God's good time. If he only could still believe in God.

The fog seemed thicker. He kept one hand on the wall to his right and one hand in front of him. And walked slowly, so very slowly, and with care. Last year, in another fog, Abe Abrahams had fallen and broken his hip. They said he would be in bed for years, and he still was in bed. Was no life for a man, and Abrahams was not old, well maybe seventy-nine, eighty.

There were a few passers-by; moving like snails, some coughing, some trying to stop themselves from breathing in the particles of fog. Some had torches which were of little value, some moved like figures swimming in mud. Some searched for doorways that were no longer where they should be. It was as if a black shroud had descended on the streets of the East End. Not only the East End. It had spread through the City and beyond, to West One and further. Always following the twists and turns of the river. And rising to swirl around chimneys that served to add their own effluvia to the pervading darkness.

Maurice Kovel was passing the police station again when the figure came up behind him.

'Is that you, Mister Kovel?'

Maurice peered through the darkness. The face came closer.

'Joseph Kahn?'

Joseph Kahn, it was. Grinned. A blue face under the lamp above the entrance to the police station. He was in his middle thirties, a small man, barely five foot five, black hair receding to give him a high forehead above dark, intelligent eyes. He had a thick woollen muffler wrapped around his neck, and, below the muffler, an old, military-style trench coat buttoned up to muffler and neck.

'It's me, Mister Kovel.'

'I see that.'

'You're going home?'

'On such a night, where else?'

'Good!' Kahn fell into line beside him. 'Four eyes are better than two in this muck.'

10

Maurice Kovel frowned. The frown was invisible to Joe Kahn in the fog.

'You don't live in Cable Street,' Maurice said.

'No, but you do. And that's where I'm going. Beth phoned last night. Said to be at your place tonight. Something she wanted to talk to me about.'

They were walking with extreme care in the direction of Cable Street.

'She said nothing to me,' said Maruice.

'No? Well, she did phone me.'

'She hasn't arrived yet. I went to the underground to meet her.'

'Not there?'

'Not yet. Mr Hoskins said he'd be good enough to walk her to my house.'

'Good of Mr Hoskins. It's a filthy night.'

'All it needs is a visit from the Cossacks.'

'The only ones in London are a dance troupe.'

'They should have something to dance about.'

They walked on in silence. To the end of Leman Street and then into Cable Street. Passing the chalked graffiti they could barely see on the wall of a house –

YIDS GET OUT!

'We got our own Cossacks in London,' Joe Kahn said, breaking the silence.

'*Shmeck*!' the old man replied contemptuously.

They reached his front door, the *mezuzah* on the lintel. It was one of a row of what the Victorians had called 'artisans' homes'. Some of them had fallen into disrepair, windows broken or boarded up. The occupants of others struggled to keep them liveable and clean. Maurice Kovel's home served as an example, but one which few could attain. He had, some years before, installed a bathroom and an indoor toilet, a luxury unheard of in Cable Street. The friendlier of his neighbours had shrugged and wished him luck. After all the old man had worked hard until he was seventy, at his tiny delicatessen shop in Whitechapel Road. Others, those with particular prejudices, had scowled and said, 'the Jews, they got all the money, they got all the big ideas.'

11

Joe Kahn waited while the old man fumbled for his key. But before he could find it, the door opened and Sophia Jacobs stared out at them.

If Maurice Kovel's natural expression was mournful, on his sister's face was etched the sorrows of the world. Deep lines scored thin cheeks under grey hair untidily pulled back into a bun. The mouth, without effort, turned downwards. The eyes, short-sighted, peered narrowly out into the fog. She refused to wear glasses, saying 'If the Lord had meant us to wear glass he would have put window panes over our eyes.' Despite almost a lifetime in London, she still had an accent much thicker than her brother's. And the accent came out in a high-pitched, whining tone.

'You back?'

'Can't you see I'm back?'

'Wisitors, you got. Who should know what you've done? The police are here. Vill not talk to me. Only you, they say. Me, I'm cooking over a hot stove until I'm *oysgematert*, and the police come.'

Maurice peered at Joe Kahn, seemed about to ask him to go, and then changed his mind.

'You may as well come in, Joe Kahn. You have more experience with policemen than a respectable man like me.'

Joe Kahn smiled. It was true he'd had experience with the police. A deal of experience. Questions about Labour rallies, anti-Fascist demonstrations; in the eyes of the police he was a dangerous, left-wing radical. Also he was editor of a local socialist newspaper, the *Whitechapel Worker*. Enough to label him in the eyes of the law as a Red agitator. Also there was a time Maurice Kovel had blamed him for Beth going into journalism. He would have been proud to have taken the blame, but it wasn't true. She'd done it under her own steam, he'd often said, and gone fast from London University to Fleet Street. Joe admired her achievement, perhaps not without a trace of envy.

He followed Maurice into the narrow hall. In the air was a distinct smell of cabbage and gefüllte fish. The wallpaper was a drab plum colour and had been so ever since Joe, as a small boy, had first been invited into the Kovels' home. Those were

12

the days during the war, when a small East End Jewish kid was always hungry, and the late Mrs Kovel kept a supply of hot bagels for such diminutive visitors as her young daughter might bring home from *shul*.

There was only ever one piece of furniture in the hall, a hatstand on which there were now two homburgs identical to the one Maurice was wearing, and a bowler, which, for some obscure reason, the old man only wore when he paid one of his infrequent visits to his delicatessen.

'The policeman is in the living-room,' said Sophie Jacobs. 'Vhatever it is, I don't vant to know. I got the food ready in the kitchen. Vhere's Becky?'

'You blind, woman? She's not arrived yet.'

'She's late.'

Maurice glared at his sister. 'She's entitled. She's working for a living.'

The old woman made a face and disappeared along the hall with one last riposte.

'So the supper will turn into icicles!'

The living-room door was on the right. Maurice hesitated.

'So what can I have done to be so honoured?' he said and, taking off his coat, he placed it on a peg on the hatstand and beckoned Joe Kahn to follow him. They went in.

A fire burned brightly in the grate of the living-room. It was a neat comfortably furnished room with two deep, if battered, armchairs and a large sofa. There were small tables on each side of the fireplace, on one, a large radio with an illuminated dial. The other contained a solitary ashtray on which was a pipe. The room was lit by a standard lamp by the window, and a centre-light hanging from the ceiling enclosed in a circular lampshade.

There were two of them in the room, large men in soft hats and belted raincoats. With their hats still on, which was nothing to do with being in a Jewish household, but merely the arrogance of the law.

Joe Kahn recognised the larger, older of the two men. Detective Sergeant Brundage, Leman Street Station. At least they hadn't had far to come.

'Evening, Mr Kovel,' said Brundage who prided himself on

13

knowing every prominent local face on his patch. Brundage was in his early forties, with a broken nose and a reputation for breaking heads, irrespective of guilt or innocence on the part of those whose heads were broken. He had come into the police force after the war, where he had served as a sergeant-major in the Military Police. He had a reputation for disliking Negroes, Jews, Scotsmen and Welshmen, and East-Enders, roughly in that order. However on this occasion he seemed in a subdued mood.

'Detective Sergeant Brundage,' he went on. 'And this is Constable Horsham.'

His companion, a fresh-faced young man, nodded awkwardly, eyes studying the carpet design.

'I know you, Mister Brundage. And you will know Mister Kahn,' said Maurice.

An undisguised contempt. 'Oh, yes, I know Mister Kahn.'

Joe nodded with a small smile. To his surprise, Brundage looked quickly away from him, and the policeman's face flushed. There was an awkwardness in his manner which Joe Kahn had not seen before.

'You have a daughter, Mister Kovel. Known professionally as Beth Coverley?' Brundage said.

'I have a daughter, Becky. Who has taken such a foolish name for what she calls professional reasons. She is a journalist.'

Brundage looked down at his feet, moving them in a nervous shuffle. Then a thought occurred to him and unexpectedly he took off his hat.

'I'm sorry to have to bring you bad news.' He took a deep breath. 'Your daughter is dead.'

There was a silence. Nobody moved. Joe Kahn felt suddenly sick.

Maurice Kovel said evenly: 'That is not so. We are waiting for her to come to supper.'

'Her body was found floating in the Thames this afternoon.' Brundage said and looked quickly towards the fireplace. Anywhere but at Maurice Kovel.

There was now an edge of panic in Kovel's voice. 'No! A mistake. How would you know her?'

Brundage half turned to his companion. Detective Constable

14

Horsham drew from under his coat something which had once been a handbag and was now a damp, shapeless lump of leather. Nervously he placed it on the table beside the ashtray. He then produced a transparent envelope and emptied the contents beside the handbag. These consisted of a powder compact, a purse and a number of sodden papers.

'There are letters there with her address on them. Also a trade union card for the National Union of Journalists.' He indicated a small damp document. It was curled up and part of it, where there should have been a signature, was blurred where the ink had run. But a name was typewritten above this blur, that of Beth Coverley.

Maurice Kovel stared at this damp pile for a moment. And turning, he stared bleakly at Joe Kahn, as if seeking some kind of help or reassurance. Then he gave a loud cry compounded of raw agony. The kind of sound Joe was sure had echoed through centuries of suffering of so many of his race.

Later, some short but unestimated time later, Maurice Kovel sat facing the fireplace in silence, face streaked with tears but now set in an expressionless stare. Custom had caused him – with one swift movement, some moments before – to tear the lapel of his jacket. He now seemed, to Joe Kahn, to be in a state of shock.

Joe Kahn went with the two departing officers to the hall.

'The old man'll have to come around to Leman Street and identify the body,' Brundage said. 'You'll tell him?'

'I'll tell him. But there's something I'd like to know. How did Becky . . . Beth get in the river?'

Brundage glanced at his companion and then back to Kahn.

'We're of course still conducting an investigation. Of course, I wouldn't say it to the old Jew yet, but . . . eh, floaters are usually jumpers. Suicide, more'n likely.'

Joe Kahn shook his head vehemently. 'Not Beth! No, not her.'

'You know her well?'

'Enough to know she's not suicidal.'

'Seen much of her recently?'

'Well, no, but . . . she was coming here specially to see me

15

tonight. Asked me to be here. She had some kind of problem . . .'

'Maybe you just answered your own question. Some kind of problem. See you around, Kahn.'

They left, Brundage looking smug.

Joe Kahn went into the kitchen. Sophie Jacobs had also to be informed of the death of her niece. As with her brother she, at first, refused to believe it. When finally she did understand that Beth was dead, she gave one agonising shriek and collapsed, moaning, on the kitchen floor. Maurice Kovel, hearing this, roused himself sufficiently to ask Kahn to bring in a neighbour from the adjoining house, one Mrs Liebermann, who took over with an efficiency born of much expertise in dealing with such tragedies. She put Mrs Jacobs to bed and then produced large mugs of hot, sweet tea for the two men.

By this time Maurice Kovel seemed to be recovering from his initial shock.

'There is no need for you to stay, Mister Kahn. You have been of help. Mrs Liebermann will do all that is necessary. And I . . . I am . . . contained now. At my age, after the first horror, one should be able to show how familiar one is with death.'

'It's all right. I . . . I don't mind staying,' Kahn took a deep breath. 'I . . . I want to say how deeply sorry I am.'

'What else? You were *kinder* together. She . . . she liked you. You have been most helpful. But it is time I went round to the police station . . . to . . . to identify Becky.' His voice broke momentarily and then with an effort he managed to pull himself together.

'You can leave that until the morning,' Kahn suggested.

'No! It would be terrible if . . . if it was not Becky and some poor father did not know his daughter was dead.'

'If you're determined to go tonight, then I'd like to come with you.'

The old man shrugged. 'So. Come.'

Kahn rubbed a hand wearily across his forehead. 'I'd . . . I'd like to know how Beth came to be in the river.'

Maurice looked up, his brow furrowed. 'How . . . ? Yes! How? And why? I hadn't thought . . . an accident, yes, maybe. In the street, a motorcar perhaps? But . . . in the river?'

16

He rose from his chair. 'We go now. I'm glad, Joseph Kahn, you are coming with me.'

The density of the fog had not lessened. The fog reached the front desk of the police station and was visible in the glare of the electric light, twisting filaments of mist throughout the room.

The desk sergeant summoned Brundage, who seemed surprised at Maurice Kovel appearing so soon. He ushered Kahn into an interview room and took the old man to the rear of the building which served as a makeshift mortuary.

They returned some minutes later, Maurice Kovel ashen-faced, cheeks streaked with tears, hands trembling. More than this, his eyes seemed to be staring, not outwards, but inwards, as if he might be contemplating a part of himself which had died. As if he had been touched by some destructive force which had taken part of him away. And indeed it must be so, Kahn thought. Unable to speak the old man looked at Kahn, shrugged and, in that shrug there was a perceptible, if inadequate, indication of the depth of his loss. Joe Kahn knew the identification had been positive.

Kahn asked the question: 'How did Beth Coverley get in the river?'

Brundage cleared his throat authoritatively. 'We have some further information on that.'

He was addressing himself to Kovel now. 'It appears one of our constables saw a woman who may have been your daughter jump from Puddock's Wharf into the river some time this morning. He did raise an alarm but, at that time the river patrol could find no sign of a body.'

'No!' The words seemed to be wrenched from deep within Kovel. 'Not Becky.'

'I'm afraid it was, Mr Kovel. Later in the afternoon, they recovered the body. And you *have* identified it.'

Brundage seemed so definite, Kahn thought, and yet there was something, a nervousness about the policeman's insistence he could not define.

'She would not jump!' Kovel gasped hoarsely.

'There may have been facts of which you were not aware, sir,' Brundage said, starting to pace the interview room. We sent two men to her . . . her apartment flat in Chelsea. She did live there?'

'She lived there,' Kahn assured him.

'A note was found.'

'What note?'

'I'm afraid we have to retain it as evidence for the inquest. It was very short. It just said, "I'm sorry but I can't go on." No further explanation. She must have thought that would be enough . . .'

'It was in her handwriting?' Kahn asked.

'It was typewritten. Still in the typewriter when our men found it.'

'That was all she had written?' Kovel said.

'That was all.'

Brundage now began to show signs of impatience. 'I'm afraid I have a great deal of work to do . . .'

'I will not believe it!' Kovel said, almost whispering.

'You will of course be asked to come to the inquest. But I'm afraid we are satisfied.'

'Satisfied? Satisfied? What does that mean?'

'It means they aren't going to do anything about Beth's death,' said Joe Kahn. 'They . . . believe it was suicide.'

'And if I don't?' Maurice Kovel's eyes sought Kahn's. As if he was pleading.

'They still do nothing.'

Brundage scowled at Kahn and addressed Kovel. 'I have to go . . . I'll ask a constable to bring you a cup of tea before you go, Mister Kovel. There's no hurry . . .'

He went out. Maurice Kovel turned to Joe Kahn.

'I don't believe it. Becky would not kill herself. For no reason. For any reason. She would not do it.'

'I don't think she would either,' said Kahn.

'Perhaps I am wrong. Perhaps it isn't her.'

'You know it is, Mister Kovel.'

'Then they must do something. They are detectives. Let them detect!'

'They'll do nothing.'

'Someone must do something. Me. Or you, Joseph Kahn.'

'Would we know where to start?'

'Someone . . .'

A thought came to Joe Kahn. He said: 'I know a man . . .'

18

TWO

The man Joe Kahn knew sat at a corner table in a room on the fifth floor of a building just off Old Compton Street. The entire floor of this building was given up to the 'Gog and Magog' Club. As a club, the Gog and Magog was utterly unlike the imposing edifices in St James's which were considered clubs for gentlemen. The Gog and Magog never presumed to the status or elegance of such establishments. Rather, it was a refuge for artists, writers, musicians – with a leavening of persons displaced from other countries and alien cultures. It was also a drinking club.

The time was twelve noon, the next day. A clear day with little trace of the previous night's fog, due to a strong breeze which had blown in from the English Channel.

The man was Ernst Lohmann, former inspector in the city of Berlin's Criminal Police. He was now a refugee from that city and that country, and had been for two years. The first of those years had been spent in Paris with his young daughter, Anna. He was a widower, his wife having been killed in a motor accident some years before.

Lohmann had not liked Paris. The city itself had always charmed him, but the atmosphere in nineteen thirty-five had been not unlike that of Germany just before the National Socialist Party had taken over. The political scene had seemed ominous, and distinctly disturbing. He had, in his rather irregular flight over the border, been able to take with him a sum of money which represented his life's savings. This had been sufficient to allow him to send Anna to a cousin in the United States, Boston to be exact, where it had been arranged that she would go to school.

It had also enabled him, through the good offices of an old professional acquaintance of pre-Nazi days, who happened to

19

be the Assistant Commissioner, Crime, at New Scotland Yard, to be admitted as a political refugee to the United Kingdom. He had arrived in London a year ago faced with the problem of earning a living for himself. His reputation as one of the best criminal detectives in Berlin became meaningless in another place at another time. As an alien, be could not follow his profession in London. Also it was doubtful whether he wanted to follow it, after his experiences in Germany where a high Nazi official had been involved in a murder case.

So Lohmann was in London. He had, fortunately, a fluent command of the English language and had obtained some work as a translator, working mostly for a publisher. It was hardly a very satisfying occupation, translating women's romantic novels into German. At least translating German classics into English – which he did between the romantic novels – gave him some small satisfaction. It also allowed him to re-read Goethe, Hegel and others. This, however, induced a sad nostalgia for a Germany that was gone, a nostalgia that drove him to the Gog and Magog and, for the first time in his life, an overindulgence in Scotch whisky, and the reminiscences of fellow refugees. One of those, Traubel, sat facing him across the table now.

'We are only the beginning of the flood, Herr Lohmann,' said Traubel, a small dark balding man, in his fifties. 'Einstein is in America. So is Thomas Mann. Two great men. A genius in physics, Germany's greatest living novelist. Forced out of Germany. You, a great detective, me, the best furrier in Leipzig. Think of such losses.'

'I've thought of them,' Lohmann replied. He was a tall figure with lank, dark hair greying at the temples. He was wearing a leather coat brought out of Germany and now wrinkled as if with worry. It was thrown open to show a crumpled sports jacket and flannels.

'What a loss to Germany,' Traubel went on. 'Do you know, all the best Junker families, when they were in Leipzig, would come to me for fur coats for their wives. Even . . . even Ernst Rohm, head of the SA, bought a fur jacket from me. For one of his boyfriends. Of course he didn't know I was Jewish.'

'Didn't do him much good in the end.' Lohmann looked

20

around the room. A young Englishman, short hair hanging over his forehead, sitting across the room, nodded to him. They'd had the same nodding acquaintance in Berlin some years before. A writer, probably homosexual. Not that it mattered to Lohmann. He'd always had an understanding of human deviations. What was it the English actress, Mrs Patrick Campbell had said?'

'Don't care what they do, as long as they don't do it in the streets and frighten the horses!'

An unorthodox thought for a policeman. No, an ex-policeman, he had to continually remind himself of that.

Traubel was still talking. 'All that is needed is enough capital and I start my business here. But where do I get the capital? Is always a problem. Being a refugee is not good.'

Being a refugee is not good. Traubel was a master of the understatement. Being a refugee was like living alone in a dark city. A city of narrow winding streets, the buildings at strange angles and on distorted planes. An architecture born of loneliness and nightmare. The alien in the alien city. No one really wanted to know the refugee. He was an embarrassment, a reminder of man's ability to exclude those of his fellow beings who were considered different. *Foreigners, Jews, Strangers.* The personification of man's inhumanity to man. *And why should they be here, in my country?* No one wants to know and the buildings close in, the streets narrow. *There are ghettos for such people.* Not the ghettos of Eastern Europe, not quite beyond the Pale, after all this is a civilised city. But they have their place, if they have to be here. Either alone, in drab rooms, or in certain areas, like the East End, let them start there and prove they are worthy of consideration.

Traubel talked on but Lohmann was lost in his thoughts and in his whisky. He took a gulp, feeling its warmth. There was always that kind of warmth.

Joe Kahn came into the clubroom.

He stood in the doorway looking around. The Gog and Magog was busy. Too many faces, too much smoke. And the noise of conversation above all. Kahn's eyes searched the room and finally settled on Lohmann. He came over.

'Inspector Lohmann . . .'

'Mister Lohmann, Mister Kahn. I try not to live in the past.'

'Could I have a word with you? Alone.' A look at Traubel who stood up quickly.

'Have my seat, sir.' Traubel glanced at his watch. 'I have said all I have to say. And I have an appointment with a furrier. At least if I don't have a business, I might yet obtain a job.'

He shook hands with Lohmann and departed, leaving Kahn to take his seat. The two men had met some months before in the Gog and Magog when Kahn had heard something of the story of Lohmann's departure from Germany and wanted to run it as a feature in the *Whitehapel Worker*. Lohmann had not been enthusiastic.

'Too many people still in Germany who might suffer. Also it would only be officially denied.'

Kahn had accepted this with reluctance. But Lohmann still interested him. Most of the refugees in London were Jews and had been small business men in Germany before the Nazis took over. Here was Lohmann, a Lutheran, and a police official of some rank and reputation who had left Germany of his own choice. Who was, moreover, anti-Nazi, when many others like him, although uncomfortable with the Hitler regime, had taken no sides and were content to collaborate. Kahn too had learned something of Lohmann's reputation. David Conway, an American journalist, who had been bureau chief for the *New York Post Enquirer*, had told him of 'the best detective in Berlin. Maybe in Germany'. Also known as the man 'instrumental in arresting Peter Kurten, the Düsseldorf mass-murderer.'

'What can I do for you, Mister Kahn?' Lohmann said.

'First of all, let me buy you a drink?'

'Thank you. But I think I have had enough for now. The danger of being a solitary refugee in a foreign city is that one has so much time on one's hands. The possibility of becoming an alcoholic is always present. And I have yet to eat today.'

'Then have lunch with me . . .'

'That was not intended as a hint, Mister Kahn. Merely a statement of fact. However, if you do want to talk, a restaurant might be quieter.'

They lunched in a small inexpensive Hungarian restaurant in Wardour Street. Lohmann insisted on paying for himself.

'Now, Mister Kahn, this word with me you want. Please proceed.'

Joe Kahn told him of the events of the previous night, of the death of Beth Coverley, née Kovel. Lohmann listened without comment until Kahn had finished.

'. . . and there is no way we can believe that Beth killed herself . . .'

Lohmann paused for a moment, tugged his ear thoughtfully, and then spoke. 'I don't see what I can do.'

'You could find the truth.'

'And I could say to you, the truth is different things to different people. The girl's father cannot accept that his daughter may have killed herself. Possibly because she *is* his daughter . . .'

'I can't believe she killed herself.'

'Because you are a close friend. The girl had left home some time ago. She lived her own life away from her father. There may be many reasons why she might take her own life.'

'She wasn't the type.'

'There's no such thing as a suicidal type. I think it was Oscar Wilde who said that the only thing one knows about human nature is that it is always changing. Miss Coverley may have experienced such events as might drive her to such a terminal act.'

'But only the day before, she'd phoned me to come to her father's house. She wanted to see me urgently. And while it was urgent, there was no kind of suicidal desperation in her voice or attitude.'

Lohmann gave a small shrug. 'Whether it is so or not, what can I do?'

'Investigate.'

'I have no authority to investigate.'

'You could do it privately.'

'It is a matter for your police.'

'They've already made up their minds.'

Lohmann gave a deep sigh. 'Even if that were so, it does not mean they are wrong. Nor does it mean I should investigate such a matter.'

Kahn rubbed his forehead. 'The old man will not let it lie. Not that I blame him. She is . . . she was his only child.'

'There are private investigators.'

'Not with your experience. Look, Lohmann, you'd be paid for anything you did.'

The former police inspector shifted uncomfortably in his seat. There was, within him, a kind of temptation. To be back on the trail, that was indeed of interest. He had always enjoyed the hunt. Not so much the apprehension of the perpetrator, but the hunt itself. And in a city that he knew, street by street, a city that had a network of informers, that had so many familiar faces of minor and major criminals. With a large organisation behind him. With his old sergeant, Reiner, now himself a refugee in America; Reiner, who could almost read his mind, who knew Berlin almost as well as he himself did. But then that had been in the past, in conditions that no longer existed.

'I do not think I can help you,' he said, but the reluctance must have been there in his voice.

Kahn picked it up. 'At least come and see the old man, Mr Kovel. Come to the inquest. See for yourself before you say no.'

'Yes. I will come to the inquest. And meet your Herr Kovel. But if I agree with the verdict of the inquest, I will tell you so and that will be an end to it . . .'

'Agreed!'

'And if I do not agree, then I will possibly still turn you down. Because I do not know whether I can do anything.'

'The inquest is the day after tomorrow . . . I've written down the address . . . the Magistrates' Court in Whitechapel.'

Lohmann nodded. 'I will be there. But I also want to take some advice in this matter . . .'

Kahn looked puzzled. 'What kind of advice?'

'I have a friend here in a position of authority. And I am, after all, a guest in this country. I wish to know the official attitude to any such investigation I may undertake.'

Twenty-four hours later, another lunch in another place. A club but vastly different from the Gog and Magog. It was in St James's and had been there for several hundred years. A club for gentlemen of power and influence. A century ago, fortunes had been lost and won at card tables in the club; estates and been gambled away as had other great business enterprises. But

24

that was in the past. Gaming, beyond bridge, was forbidden today. A member could sleep quietly in the reading-room. He could dine well in the dining-room. He could pass the night in a comfortable bedroom, should he fall out with his lady. And he could entertain his guests to a splendiferous lunch.

Lohmann was the guest. His host was Charles Emerson, Assistant Commissioner, Crime, at New Scotland Yard. Emerson was a tall slim figure in his early fifties. Sleek black hair, temples greying, he could have passed for Lohmann's elder brother. And, indeed, the two men had been friends since 1932 when Emerson had come to Berlin by invitation to study German police methods. Emerson had spent some days with Lohmann on his current investigations and Lohmann had later shown Emerson the underside of the city. The Englishman had then been forced to meet government officials and Weimar politicians . . . the Nazis were still a year from power . . . and he'd been relieved to spend his last day with Lohmann. Emerson had reciprocated this hospitality some years later when he had arranged to sponsor Lohmann's admittance into the United Kingdom as a refugee. And now, after Lohmann's request for a meeting, had invited him to lunch at his club.

'Interesting place this,' Emerson said, as they sipped aperitifs. 'Pitt the Younger, and Charles Fox used to glare at each other over the gaming tables in the old days. Today, at least half the Cabinet are members.'

Lohmann looked around the bar self-consciously. He was wearing the one suit he had brought out of Berlin, heavy tweed, off-the-peg tailoring, contrasting with the immaculate dark greys of Savile Row. And, even in this day and age, a number of frock-coats, striped trousers and wing collars, worn by the elder members.

'Sometimes I wonder how I got in myself,' Emerson went on. 'After all, we English are the most snobbish and class-conscious bunch in the world . . .'

'With the exception of the Prussians,' Lohmann interposed.

'Possibly. But, y'know, I do marvel how I, a mere policeman, wasn't black-balled. Probably because some idiot thought I had a half-decent war record. So perhaps, in a way, I owe my membership here to your lot.'

Emerson, Lohmann knew, had joined the army in 1914 as a private, received a field commission and ended up one of the youngest acting-brigadiers in the army.

'Sam Hoare over there.' Emerson indicated a new arrival, a tall, smooth figure, in tailcoat and striped trousers. 'Foreign Secretary. Too clever by half. Take your glass and we'll go into lunch.'

They were seated at a corner table by an unctuous head waiter. Emerson nodded to a small, neat, inoffensive little man at a nearby table. 'G.E. Stevens. You've heard of him?'

Lohmann hadn't.

'Arabist. Worked during the war side by side with T.E. Lawrence. Lawrence of Arabia. Lawrence got all the limelight. Stevens did a lot of the work.' Emerson suddenly smiled, an expansive grin. 'Sorry, Lohmann. I'm an incorrigible name-dropper. My part in the snobbery of the nation. Now, to your story. But before you start I can recommend the *Sole Bonne Femme*.'

They both ordered the sole and Emerson selected a Chablis to go with it.

'Now,' he repeated.

Lohmann recounted all that Joe Kahn had told him the day before. Emerson listened politely and only spoke when Lohmann had finished.

'They want you to investigate this girl's death?'

'I told Kahn I had no authority. Also I have no desire to step on official toes, as you might say. I am, after all, a guest in your country.'

Emerson smiled again. He had a series of smiles; tolerant, understanding, compassionate, humorous, even tender; something suitable for every occasion.

'I did think, when you first came over a year ago, you might start a private enquiry agency. Indeed I think I suggested it to you. You never thought about it?'

Lohmann looked down at the sparse remnants of the *Sole Bonne Femme*.

'I thought of it. But, remember, Charles, I was accustomed to tracking down murderers, or thieves. Of some distinction, you might say. But what does your private detective do? He

26

follows Mister X or Mrs Y, to see that they are not jumping into the wrong bed. The bed in which one finds Mister or Madame Z. The only crime committed is against a morality I am not certain I even agree with. Also, what right have I to intrude upon these people? They do not harm society. Only each other. They may even be doing each other a favour.'

'Private enquiry people occasionally deal with crime,' Emerson said. 'Would you like a dessert?'

'Coffee only, please. Black. Oh, yes, on occasion they are employed to harass shop-lifters. Or recover stolen property. By agreement with insurance companies. I don't like agreements, even with petty thieves. No, it was never for me, this private detective business. But I do understand you English sometimes really believe there was a Sherlock Holmes. Just as you believe there is a Santa Claus in Germany called Adolf Hitler who will deliver you from the Bolsheviks.'

Another smile from the Assistant Commissioner. Of the tolerant variety. 'You must allow us our whimsies.'

The *Sole Bonne Femme* disappeared and the coffee was served. Emerson became serious.

'I have read the incident report on the death of Beth Coverley. Came on my desk this morning. She was quite an up-and-coming journalist. I don't know why it came to me. But it seemed all above board, policeman saw her jump . . .'

'Your policeman saw somebody jump.'

'Yes, well, later they found the body. Her body. And I believe she left a note . . .'

'Typewritten. Not by hand. Anyone can type a note.'

Emerson shifted awkwardly in his seat. 'That would imply conspiracy to murder.'

'If it were so, that someone else had typed the note.'

'There will be an inquest.'

'Tomorrow. I shall go.'

'You're going to take on this investigation then?'

Lohmann shook his head. 'I did not say so. I want to hear the evidence.'

'And if the verdict is suicide?'

'If I believe it to be a correct verdict, I will inform Mister Kahn and have nothing more to do with the business.'

Emerson sipped his coffee. 'And, if you don't believe it's the correct verdict?'

'Then I should be tempted to investigate. Provided you had no objection.'

The Emerson smile again. Mona Lisa variety. 'And if I objected?'

Lohmann rubbed his jaw. He had shaved in a hurry that morning and could feel the stubble on his chin. 'That would be a problem. I am a refugee, I owe this country something. And I am getting very selfish. I think of myself and my own welfare even more than I used to.'

'Look, old man, from the police report I received, it certainly looks like a simple suicide. And, if the verdict matches that, I can't afford policemen in the East End going off on wild-goose chases. Especially with the trouble we've got there. Mosley's Blackshirts are threatening another march in Whitechapel and we need every man we have just to keep the peace.'

'Why do you allow it? The Blackshirts are little different from the SA in Germany. To permit them to march through a predominantly Jewish area is surely provocation.'

Emerson shrugged. 'You have to understand, Lohmann, this is England . . . we are a free country.'

Lohmann thought, every country taken over by the Fascists starts off as a free country. Were the English so arrogant as to believe they were different?

Emerson went on. 'If we ban the Blackshirt march, Mosley will scream, "Where's your free country now?" And he has influential friends. So we have to rely on my people to keep the peace. But that's hardly relevant to your problem. Look, if you still feel, after the inquest, that there's something not right about this girl's death, go ahead and see what you can find out.'

'Even if the verdict is suicide, and I do not agree with that verdict?'

'Yes. You might be saving us from making a mistake. We don't like making mistakes. Creates problems. Makes awkward publicity. And if it is suicide, then all you'd be doing is wasting your time. I hope, getting paid for it.'

Lohmann's turn for a small smile. 'It has been mentioned. But I only take the case if I believe it is not suicide.'

'Understood.' Emerson glanced briefly at his wrist-watch. It was a signal their meeting was over.

'Time I was back at my desk. Crime doesn't stop for lunch,' Emerson went on.

'One other thing, Charles?'

'Ask me.'

'If I start an investigation, would it be possible to have access to police reports?'

Emerson now raised an eyebrow. 'That's tricky. Let's say, within certain limits, which will have to be defined by me, I may be able to arrange something. But that depends on what you ask for. I may have to refuse you. And you will have to accept that.'

Lohmann nodded. He could ask for little more. 'I accept it.'

'Then let me know if you decide to go ahead.'

They left the dining-room and in the hall encountered the small man called G.E. Stevens. Emerson introduced him to Lohmann.

'Nice to meet you, Herr Lohmann. I understand things are pretty bleak in Germany.'

The English understatement, thought Lohmann.

'They are not good,' Lohmann replied.

'Not good anywhere,' Stevens said. 'Makes me want to get back to the desert. Something very cleansing about sand and sun, away from so-called civilisation.'

'I can imagine,' Lohmann responded politely. He couldn't imagine. Was that German hypocrisy?

'Thought you were just back,' Emerson said.

'From Palestine. This time, talking to Weizmann and the Jewish leaders. I like Chaim but we've laid up so much trouble for ourselves. Between Lawrence promising the Arabs heaven and all the Middle East and Balfour promising the Jews Palestine, we've created a powder-barrel. Someday it'll blow up in our faces.'

'Your worry, old man. Mine is the Metropolitan Police area. And that is quite enough for me.'

They left Stevens heading for the library, and went out into St James's. On the steps of the club, Emerson turned to say goodbye to Lohmann.

'You'll be in touch, Ernst?'

Lohmann hated being called Ernst. Until now, Emerson had called him Lohmann. He could only suppose the Assistant Commissioner was underlining their friendship.

'I shall be in touch, Charles. Oh, one point of interest...' He was aware he was straining the friendship. Emerson was now imperceptibly showing small signs of his impatience.

'And that is...'

'The constable who claims he saw the girl jump? From some place called Puddock's Wharf.'

'Yes?'

'Both Kahn and the newspaper report this morning say that a policeman saw a girl jump from the wharf into the water...'

'So I read in the report.'

'I went to Puddock's Wharf,' Lohmann said. 'This morning. And I checked the tides two days ago. The tide was out. It must have been difficult for the girl to jump into the water.'

'What do you mean?'

'When the tide is out below Puddock's Wharf, there are fifteen yards of mud before you reach the water's edge.'

THREE

Another morning. On the Whitechapel Road. Lohmann was walking towards the Magistrates' Court. An urchin, bullet-headed, with a tattered pullover, ragged short trousers and scuffed heavy boots, ran by, chanting.

Who's this comin' down the street?
Mrs Simpson wiv her sweet...

This is the street comment on the love affair of the day, Lohmann thought. Or the crisis of the year. Whichever, it was typical. The world was falling apart around them and the British were concerned about their King and an American divorcée. Men and women were fighting and dying in Spain for what might just be a rehearsal for World War and the British had just learned their king had a mistress. Wasn't that the prerogative of monarchs throughout history?'

He walked by the local cinema. Advertising *Devil Dogs of The Air* starring James Cagney and Pat O'Brien. Second feature, Joan Blondell in *The Travelling Saleslady*. Both of greater import than the still falling-apart world. And there was a smell of hot bagels in the air.

It was a grey morning. The interior of the Magistrates' Court was even greyer. In the entrance hall, Joe Kahn was waiting with an old man whom Lohmann guessed would be the girl's father. And a young man in a plaid shirt, plum-coloured tie and crumpled checked suit.

Kahn effected the introductions. First to Maurice Kovel who did not look at Lohmann but stared into space over his shoulder. The old man's eyes were red-rimmed and vague.

'She . . . she should . . . should have been buried yesterday,' he muttered, more to himself than his companions.

'It is the Jewish custom, you understand,' Kahn explained. 'The body should be buried within twenty-four hours. And of course the police won't release it until after the inquest.'

'I understand,' Lohmann replied. 'I have . . . I had many Jewish friends.'

Kahn turned to the young man in the plaid shirt and checked suit. This is Sammy Jacobs. He is my solicitor.'

To Lohmann, Jacobs looked like a boy, dressed in a over-large man's suit. A wary boy, not altogether friendly, he also seemed to read Lohmann's mind.

'Qualified, I assure you, Mister Lohmann. Two years ago. London University.'

'I didn't question . . .'

'That's okay. You don't look like a policeman.'

Lohmann shrugged. 'I'm not. I'm a refugee. Also a translator of books in German into English, and books in English into German.'

'But you . . . you were a policeman?'

'That's gone, two years gone.'

Joe Kahn interrupted them. 'I've asked Sammy to represent

31

Mister Kovel. In case anything comes up during the inquest. The coroner has agreed to his representing the old man.'

Three large men came into the building. Two of them were in police uniform.

'That's Brundage,' Kahn said to Lohmann, indicating the plain clothes man. 'Detective Sergeant Brundage. I think one of the men in uniform is the officer who claims to have seen Beth jump.'

Some way behind the two policemen, a small neat man in a well-cut grey suit came in. Lohmann looked questioningly at Kahn who shrugged. 'No one I know.'

The inquest was to be held in one of the court-rooms. The walls and the fittings were of brown wood upon which was a thin veneer of dust. The electric lights were on, bulbs concealed in globes, circumferences of light. From the windows high on the walls the grey morning cast a feeble light into the room. The coroner, a small, grey man in a wing-collar had chosen to avoid the high seat of the magistrate and was seated at a table below the bench. His balding head gleamed under the electric light bulbs. Beside him was his clerk. A chair had been placed to the right of the table to accommodate the testifying witness. A jury of twelve, all men, had been empanelled and sat in the jury-box. They were an assorted collection of middle-aged business men and traders from the district. The well of the court was for witnesses and interested parties. And the public. The public consisted of two men in cloth caps and another youngish man, in a polo-necked sweater, head bare, plump features marred by a long scar running down one cheek.

'Anyone can come in,' Joe Kahn said. 'Justice must be seen to be done. In fact, they're probably out of work. They come in for the heat.'

'There is not much of it,' Lohmann said. 'Mister Jacobs, may I speak to you?'

'Of course.'

Lohmann took the young lawyer by the arm and drew him to the side of the door, away from the others.

'I am not entirely sure of the procedure at your inquests. You can ask questions?'

'That's why I'm here.'

'And there will be medical evidence?'

'Yes. The forensic expert should be here.'

'Good. Then may I suggest a few questions you might ask?'

Jacobs nodded. 'Yes, of course. If they're relevant. But I don't want to upset Mister Kovel any more than I have to. I told Joe Kahn I'd be happy to represent the old man but, from what I've read of the business, it seems a pretty straightforward case of suicide.'

'You think so?'

'Look, Mister Lohmann, you don't know me and I don't know you. Beyond what Joe Kahn has told me. You were a big wheel in the German police. Right?'

'It was so.'

'Well, I don't know why you fell out with them, but, in my book, I'm pretty suspicious of Krauts. All of them I've met, apart from the Jewish refugees, seem to think Adolf Hitler is a pretty good thing for Germany. Well, I'm a member of the ILP . . . that's the Independent Labour Party which means I'm a socialist. And I don't like Fascists or Nazis or whatever you choose to call them. Also I don't like liberties being taken with an old Jewish gentleman who's suffering a personal tragedy. So if you have any idea of exploiting this business for any reason, put it out of your mind.'

Lohmann scratched his chin thoughtfully. 'You don't like Krauts?'

''I said it!'

'So you are racially prejudiced, Mister Jacobs?'

'No, of course not . . .'

'Then you will please remember, all Germans are not National Socialists. And all Germans do not think Hitler is a "pretty good thing". I have met the Reichschancellor and I know what he is. Which is why I am here in London. Which is why if I were not here in London, I would be . . . dead. They have cellars in the building on the Prinz Albrechtstrasse where people like myself can be shot . . . or garrotted. The latter is less noisy, but equally effective.'

Sammy Jacobs stared up at the older man. And was the first to look away.

'Maybe you're right, Mister Lohmann. I suppose I should

33

apologise. But we have our own homegrown Fascists around here just now. I don't want to see any more. I get suspicious too easily. What are the questions you'd like me to ask?'

Lohmann handed him a slip of paper. 'I have written them. One to the police surgeon, one to the police officer and one other.'

Jacobs took the slip of paper from him. A high-pitched voice, the coroner's clerk, called them to order. And the coroner formally opened the inquest by thanking 'in anticipation' as he put it, the jurors for responding at such short notice. They had, in fact been called for jury duty in the next-door Magistrates' Court, and siphoned away for the inquest. By this time a number of assorted individuals had come into the court and the first witness, a constable of the River Police, was called. He described finding the body of a woman floating in the Thames, as if, to him, it was an everyday occurrence, which perhaps it was.

When the constable had finished, Sammy Jacobs stood up. The coroner frowned.

'I understand, Mister Jacobs, you are representing the family of the deceased. However I fail to see how you can question the . . . the finding of the body. We are, after all, anxious to get this matter over as speedily as possible.'

'I appreciate that, sir, but I do have one question. We are, I believe going to have police evidence that the deceased was seen jumping into the river some four hours before the body was recovered.'

'You are anticipating, Mister Jacobs, but I believe that is so.'

Jacobs stared for a moment at the slip of paper Lohmann had given him.

'I would like to ask the officer if it is not a fact that a body usually takes more than four hours to rise to the surface after the initial immersion?'

The river policeman, a middle-aged man, nodded. 'That would normally be so. And when we found the body it was still under water. But it had floated onto a shallow mudbank. That's when we spotted it.'

'Off Puddock's Wharf?'

'About a hundred yards downstream.'

'Thank you.' Jacobs sat down.

The next witness was PC Ordish who described being on his beat at ten minutes past nine on the morning of the drowning when he saw a woman on Puddock's Wharf. He delivered this information in stiff formal tones, those of a man accustomed to giving evidence without emotion.

'The wharf as been out of use since the twenties and so I thought it unusual that anyone should be on it. Especially a well-dressed woman. I was at the end of a lane leading to the wharf and some fifty yards from the woman. I saw her go to the edge of the wharf and look down at the river. And then she jumped.'

'You were too far away to do anything?' The coroner asked.

'I shouted to her, sir.'

'And what did you shout?'

The constable shuffled his feet. 'I . . . I called out . . . "what the . . . the dickens do you think you're doing?" Well something like that. But she went ahead and jumped.'

'And what did you do next?'

'I ran to the edge of the wharf and looked down. But I could see no sign of the woman. I then went to the nearest police box. On the road at the other end of the lane. Phoned the station and informed the duty sergeant that there was a . . . a jumper in the river. He said he would inform the river police.'

'And that was all you could do?' the coroner asked, sympathetically.

'I went back to the wharf but there was still no sign of the woman. Later that evening when the body found by the river police was brought to the morgue, Detective Sergeant Brundage asked me to have a look at it. To see if it was the woman I'd seen jump.'

'And . . . ?'

'I was a distance away from the woman, couldn't see her face proper, like, but it looked like the same woman. So I informed the sergeant . . .'

The coroner nodded. 'Thank you, Constable Ordish. You are excused . . .'

Sammy Jacobs was on his feet at once. 'Sir, I have a question for the witness.'

The coroner did not attempt to conceal his irritation. 'Mister Jacobs, the constable's evidence has been very straightforward. I can't see how you can question it. I admit he has not positively identified the woman but then we can hardly expect . . .'

Taking a deep breath, Jacobs interrupted him. 'It is not to do with the identification. There is another pertinent point . . .'

A reluctant sigh. 'Very well. Ask your question.'

Jacobs addressed Ordish. 'You say the woman jumped and you went to the edge of the wharf to see if you could see her in the water?'

'That's it.'

'But the woman wouldn't be in the water, Constable. At ten past nine that morning the river was at low tide. At that time there are something like fifteen yards of mud flats below the wharf before one reaches the water.'

Constable Ordish flushed. His hand went to his collar as if it was too tight around his neck.

'Well, Constable Ordish?'

'That is correct, sir. But by the time I reached the edge of the wharf the woman must have reached the water.'

'But wouldn't that only have been a matter of seconds?' Jacobs pressed him.

'All I know is, there was no sign of the woman. She . . . might have sunk into the mud . . .'

'It wasn't quicksand, was it? Certainly one might sink to one's knees but not much deeper.' Jacobs turned to the coroner. 'We have ascertained this is so, sir.'

That was from Lohmann's slip of paper. Jacobs prayed Lohmann had got his facts right. He glanced at the German who was sitting listening, his face expressionless.

He went on. 'If she had struggled to the water's edge, it would have taken at least a minute, if not longer. And she would have left deep tracks in the mud. Was there any sign of such tracks?'

Ordish glanced towards Brundage who was sitting in the body of the court. As if asking for help, Lohmann thought. None was forthcoming.

'I did not notice any tracks. But then, as I have said, I was

36

some fifty yards from the woman. Of course she might have hidden under the wharf for a short time.'

'And then walked to the water's edge and jumped in?'

'That is possible, sir.'

'Then it is a pity you didn't yourself go down onto the mud and look for the woman. Surely that would have been the thing to do? To prevent her from going to the water's edge and jumping.'

Ordish did not reply. Instead the coroner took over.

'It may be that the constable was remiss in not considering all the circumstances. Nonetheless, since the woman's body was found drowned, it would appear that she did go into the river. Would you not agree with that, Mr Jacobs?' The edge of sarcasm was obvious.

'That Miss Coverley was found drowned, no question,' Jacobs replied smoothly. 'Whether she was the woman Constable Ordish saw, we can't say. Since his identification is uncertain, by his own admission, and he did not see the woman actually jump into the river.'

'Miss Coverley's body was recovered nearby,' the coroner said, trying to suppress an inclination to scowl at Jacobs. 'There is no doubt of that. And, shall we say, a woman resembling her was seen . . . making her way towards the water. By jumping or trudging through your fifteen yards of mud. Other evidence will doubtless assist us to ascertain the . . . the exact truth. Thank you, Mister Jacobs.'

Brundage was the next to give evidence. He viewed the body, he explained, and the contents of a purse slung from the woman's arm gave him a name. He then described visiting the father, Maurice Kovel, and later Kovel's identification of his daughter.

'There was no note in the purse, no indication of why the girl might have taken her own life?'

'Not at that point in time, sir. I did however obtain from the papers in the purse her address, an apartment in Chelsea. I sent Detective Constable Mason and a uniformed officer, Constable Jones to Chelsea, and with a key found in the handbag they entered the apartment. Mason will testify as to the note he found there.'

Jacobs had no questions. Detective Constable Mason was called. He had round, almost cherubic, features and, to Lohmann, looked like a child. What was it the English said? You know you're getting on, when the policemen start looking younger. But not like children surely.

Mason testified that he, in the company of PC Jones, had entered the Chelsea flat and found a note in a typewriter.

'The note said "*I'm sorry, I can't go on.*"'

'Nothing more?'

'Nothing more, sir.'

The note was handed to the coroner. Detective Constable Mason was excused. The coroner, looking directly at Sammy Jacobs, announced that there would be only two more witnesses.

The first of these was the forensic expert, who duly identified himself as Alexander Laidlaw, a Home Office pathologist.

The coroner, upon hearing the words *Home Office* adopted a rather fawning tone of voice. 'Will you tell us, in your own words, Mister Laidlaw, the results of your examination of the body?'

Laidlaw cleared his throat. 'The body was that of a woman aged between thirty-two and . . . thirty-seven. Death was caused by drowning. The water in the lungs was Thames river water, there is no doubt of that.'

Jacobs was on his feet.

The coroner glowered again. 'You will allow Mister Laidlaw to complete his evidence, Mister Jacobs.'

'I have completed it, sir,' said Laidlaw blandly.

The coroner was nonplussed. 'Oh, I see. Then may I congratulate you on the conciseness of your evidence.' And then wearily, 'You have a question, Mister Jacobs?'

Jacobs addressed the forensic expert but the question was from Lohmann's slip of paper.

'Was there any sign of bruising or other injuries on the body?'

Laidlaw hesitated for a moment, then spoke. 'There was a small bruise on the right arm above the elbow. Very slight and commensurate possibly with a bump against furniture. Nothing untoward. And I saw nothing else.'

Lohmann scribbled on another scrap of paper and pushed it under Jacobs' eye. He glanced down.

'Could the bruising on the arm have been caused by someone gripping the arm?'

'It's possible. But I would be unable to differentiate between the various ways the bruise could have been caused.'

Sammy Jacobs looked down again, at Lohmann's original list of questions.

'Mister Laidlaw, I presume you examined the contents of the dead woman's stomach?'

'I did.'

'Had she eaten recently?'

'I don't see the necessity . . .' said the coroner, but Jacobs cut in on him.

'The point will become clear when Mister Laidlaw answers.'

Laidlaw nodded. 'The woman had certainly had breakfast . . . There was a quantity of egg . . . probably scrambled . . . tomato and some kind of cereal. Also fruit . . . grapefruit. And bread.'

The coroner smiled at the Home Office expert. 'Most thorough, sir.' He turned to Jacobs, 'I still see no point, Mister Jacobs . . .'

'The point is, sir, that I find it difficult to believe that someone contemplating suicide should eat such a large breakfast.'

The coroner attempted a smile. 'Hardly relevant. After all there is an old saying, ''The condemned man ate a hearty breakfast.'' '

This did not go down well with the jury, some of whom stirred uneasily, obviously seeing in the remark a lack of good taste. Aware of this, the coroner at once removed his smile, blinked uneasily and pressed on in a more serious vein. 'Are you implying that, despite the evidence of the woman jumping, she did not commit suicide? Are you saying she perhaps accidentally stumbled?'

'I am merely trying to get at the facts,' Jacobs said, almost smugly. This did not go down well with the coroner.

'That is what we are all here for, Mister Jacobs. The only other alternative, is that she might have had an accident. But, as you have pointed out yourself, the tide was out. Had she accidentally fallen from the wharf, she would hardly have then stumbled fifteen yards to drown herself *accidentally*.'

'Perhaps . . .' said Jacobs, taking a deep breath, his face at once drained of colour, '. . . she could have been dragged those fifteen yards.'

The colour lost by the young solicitor might well have drained into the coroner. His face reddened.

'Sir, there has so far been no evidence at all of foul play. Your suggestion is without basis in fact. I would remind you that Constable Ordish saw the woman fall. No one else was present. I have to say that I find your remarks offensive, in that you are attempting to introduce a kind of sensationalism into this unfortunate business. I would remind you that you represent the parent of the woman who drowned and your remarks cannot but cause him distress.'

He looked towards Maurice Kovel who sat slumped, head down, revealing nothing of his thoughts or showing any reaction to anything. Maurice Kovel was elsewhere, in a world of private grief. Or so it seemed.

Alexander Laidlaw was dismissed and the final witness was called. Christopher Gaunt sat in the witness's chair. He was in his forties, dark hair greying slightly at the temples. He was wearing a well-cut, double breasted suit.

Joe Kahn, sitting beside Lohmann, straightened up.

'What the hell can Chris Gaunt tell them?' he whispered to Lohmann.

'Who is Mister Gaunt?' said Lohmann.

He was answered by the reply to the coroner's first question.

'I'm the Features Editor of the *Daily Dispatch*. As such, I was Beth Coverley's immediate superior.'

'You knew Miss Coverley well, Mister Gaunt?' asked the coroner.

'Very well for the last three years, when she worked directly for me. For four years before that I knew her slightly as a news reporter. She always wanted to work on Features, and eventually she attained her ambition.'

'So you knew her through working closely with her?'

'Yes. I knew her and I liked her. She was good at her job.

Indeed she was one of the first women to tackle subjects which the paper had, until then, given to men. She was well-informed on politics and had quite a grasp of foreign affairs. We were considering her as a possible foreign correspondent.'

'I'm sure her father will be pleased at the obvious esteem in which you held Miss Coverley. But now I must ask you, was she, in your opinion, a suicidal type?'

The suggestion of a smile appeared momentarily on Gaunt's lips. 'I'm afraid I don't know what a suicidal type is, sir. But, regarding Beth Coverley, I would have thought it out of the question.'

'What are they bringing him on for?' Joe Kahn whispered to Lohmann. 'Up until now the coroner's been hell-bent on proving suicide. Gaunt's not helping him . . .'

'Yet,' said Lohmann.

'You still think that, Mister Gaunt?' the coroner went on.

Gaunt straightened up in his chair, threw a fleeting glance at Maurice Kovel, still with his head low, and then replied.

'Eh . . . no.'

'Will you tell us why?'

Another look towards Maurice Kovel. Lohmann thought the man seemed uncomfortable.

'I became aware some months ago that Miss Coverley had developed a . . . a friendship with the journalist who was holding down our foreign desk. Graham Jordan. These things happen when people work in close proximity. Relationships . . . eh, they grow . . .'

Maurice Kovel had raised his head and was staring intently at the witness.

'Often they end in marriage,' Gaunt went on, still ill at ease. 'Unfortunately Graham Jordan was married. Happily married. Jordan came to me and requested he go back to his old job. He had been a foreign correspondent. I pointed out he had been overseas for some twelve years and, indeed, had requested a post in London, having been away from his family for such a long time. He then explained to me . . . in confidence that he had developed a . . . a liaison with Miss Coverley.'

Maurice Kovel was leaning forward, shaking his head.

Gaunt was now staring away from the old man. 'Graham

41

freely admitted he had been unwise and, for the sake of his marriage, and Miss Coverley, he should go abroad for a time. The Managing Editor was consulted and agreed. In fact we were rather glad . . . he's a good man . . . and he is now in Vienna.'

'This had an effect on Miss Coverley?'

'She was definitely unhappy . . . depressed if you like . . . we did think she was getting over Graham's departure . . . but obviously, now, I can see she wasn't. Getting over it, I mean. The note would seem to confirm that.'

'Thank you, Mister Gaunt,' said the coroner and looked across at Sammy Jacobs.

'Have you any questions, Mister Jacobs?'

'Yes,' Sammy Jacobs was on his feet. 'How long ago was it since Graham Jordan went to Vienna?'

'I think . . . two and a half months ago.'

'So it took two and a half months before Miss Coverley decided to take her own life?'

'She certainly brooded on it. I think she hoped Graham would write her. But, as far as I know, he didn't.'

Sammy Jacobs sat down. The coroner proceeded to address the jury.

'You have now heard all the witnesses with information pertinent to the sad death of the young woman. I have to now instruct you as to the possible verdicts you may bring in . . .'

Lohmann noted Maurice Kovel had subsided into his seat, head shaking. He muttered something to Kahn who whispered to Lohmann.

'He's only concerned about the funeral. So he says. Twenty-four hours, it should have been.'

The coroner went on. There seemed, he told the jury, no evidence of foul play. That did not exclude their right to bring in an open verdict. However it would appear that they were faced with the greater likelihood of a verdict of either accidental death or suicide. He went through the evidence briefly but concisely. Lohmann had to admit it was a fair summing up. The coroner ended by instructing the jury to withdraw and deliberate. The twelve men filed out.

The coroner then turned to the court.

'It is now midday. I propose we have lunch and return at two o'clock when we may have a verdict.'

Outside the court, Lohmann came face to face with the man with the scar.

'You are interested in inquests?' he said to the man.

The scarred face looked surprised at being thus addressed. 'Oh, I'm interested in many things.'

The voice was slightly high-pitched with a trace of Irish in the accent. The man stepped around Lohmann. His face flushed, the scar a white streak.

'You'll excuse me . . . he said, and walked swiftly away.

Joe Kahn came up beside Lohmann.

'Find out who he was?'

'No.'

'Probably like the others. Out of work and in for the heat.'

'I don't think so.'

'Thought we might go for a quick pub lunch. Sammy and the old man. Join us.'

'Thank you, I will.'

The lunch was an almost silent occasion. Maurice Kovel neither ate nor drank. He only spoke once and that was to repeat his previous concern.

'She must be buried. It should have been done by now.'

Lohmann joined the two younger men in ordering a half pint of beer. There was a melancholy air around the four of them.

'Thanks for your questions,' Sammy Jacobs said to Lohmann.

'The answers were interesting,' Lohmann replied in a non-committal tone.

'I'm afraid that bloke, Gaunt, might just make the difference. Until he testified, there was no motive for . . .' A look towards Maurice, and Sammy dropped his voice, '. . . for the girl's suicide. But he's provided that, all right.'

'Perhaps.'

They were back in the court-room at two o'clock, when the coroner returned.

'The jury have reached their verdict,' the coroner said portentously. As if he was a High Court judge about to hear a murder verdict.

The jury were brought in and the clerk received a note containing the verdict, which he passed to the coroner, who cleared his throat noisily before reading from the note.

'The findings of this coroner's court are that Beth Coverley, also known as Becky Kovel, took her own life while the balance of her mind was disturbed.'

He looked up and stared directly at Maurice.

The old man shook his head suddenly and violently and whispered, more to himself than to anyone else, one word.

'No!'

The coroner did not appear to hear this. 'I must say that I can only agree with the jury,' he went on. 'It is the only possible verdict. However, I would like to extend the court's sympathy to the girl's father for whom this must have been extremely painful. The verdict is, however, now registered and this court is adjourned.'

Joe Kahn came out of the court, his hand firmly gripping Maurice Kovel's arm. He turned to Lohmann.

'The police will release the body now. We made tentative funeral arrangements for four o'clock at Golders Green. So we'll have to go directly to Leman Street. I . . . I suppose, with that verdict, you'll not wish to go any further. Not . . . not much point . . .'

Lohmann stared at Kahn for a moment and then at the old man.

'On the contrary,' he said. 'I am sure this was no suicide. And I would wish to undertake an investigation.'

FOUR

Lohmann's undertaking to investigate Beth Coverley's death produced a predictable reaction in Joe Kahn.

'Any help I can give you, you only have to ask,' he said, grinning and turning to Maurice Kovel. 'There! Mr Kovel, he will help.'

But the old man's reaction was bleak. 'What's to help? She's dead. And still not yet buried.'

'You believe the verdict of the inquest?' Kahn demanded of him. 'You believe she killed herself?'

Maurice Kovel shrugged. 'If not, then what?'

'It's possible she was . . . murdered,' said Kahn, hesitantly. 'Would you want her murderer to walk away?'

The old man's red-rimmed eyes stared at him. 'It won't bring her back.'

'You agreed I should speak to Mister Lohmann.'

'Yes, I agreed. But it seems . . . so unimportant.' He glanced at Lohmann. 'You can't raise the dead, Mister Lohmann?'

'I can't raise the dead, Mister Kovel. But I might be able to find out who killed your daughter. And people who kill once can kill again. They have to be stopped.'

'Yes. Yes, I suppose so. If you can do this, then do it. But just now, I have to bury my daughter.'

'I understand. But I need a little help. I would like to see your daughter's apartment in Chelsea. With your permission, to examine it.'

The old man sighed. 'Examine, examine . . .'

'I need her keys.'

'The police have them. Come to Leman Street and we'll get them for you. We're going now to make the funeral arrangements. Golders Green at four thirty.'

Lohmann nodded. 'You'll excuse me if I don't go to the funeral. But I would like to see her apartment as soon as possible.'

The old man shrugged. 'You didn't know Becky. Why should you come? We have a *minyan*, Joseph?'

'We have a *minyan*, Mister Kovel.' Kahn had organised the *minyan*, the previous day, the ten male Jews who would chant the prayers at the graveside.

'*Gut!*' said the old man.

They fell silent now as they walked down a crowded Whitechapel Road towards Aldgate. Lohmann was considering the investigation he was about to undertake. It would be different from any previous murder enquiry he had ever conducted. It was two years since his last case, and that had been in Berlin, a city he knew better than any place in the world. This investigation would be in a strange city. After a year in London, he must still count himself a stranger.

And there were other differences. In Berlin, he'd had the backing of a large and efficient modern police force – at least until the Nazis had taken over. He'd had the help of able aides headed by his sergeant, Reiner. He'd have trusted Reiner with his life, indeed had done so on several occasions. Reiner, the film fan, with his awful imitations of movie stars. Difficult to distinguish his Emil Jannings from his Laurel and Hardy. But always a good detective. And at least now, safe in America. At this time, he would have wished Reiner in London.

No, for this affair, Lohmann was on his own. Beyond what reports Charles Emerson could filter through to him, he had no access to police records, no official standing. He was less than a private citizen, merely an alien. In Berlin too, he'd had sources of information, contacts with the underworld, informers only too willing to ingratiate themselves with the great and important Inspector Lohmann. In London, there was no one. Except perhaps . . . a memory stirred within him. Erwin Müller had maintained connections in London.

Erwin Müller! Until Hitler came to power, Müller had been a force among Berlin's criminals. 'The tsar of the city's underworld', the more sensational of Berlin's press had called him. Until, as Müller said himself, the bigger criminals had taken over. Müller had tried to get out of Germany. Reiner, it was, who found his body, garrotted, dead in an empty elevator, surrounded by dollar bills, pound notes, Swiss francs . . . anything but marks.

Of course he'd been a true internationalist, had Müller. Connections throughout the world. Friend of the Mafiosi in Sicily, the Corsicans in Marseille, the 'Mob' in America. And a man in London. What was his name? An Italian name? Or Maltese?

Sabini! That was it. Sabini.

So now Lohmann had two connections. An Assistant Commissioner at New Scotland Yard and a crook called Sabini. Not that Sabini would necessarily know anything about the killing of Beth Coverley. But people like him would have ears all over London.

They were nearing Aldgate East Underground station when the man approached them. Youngish, with a plump face; well dressed, perhaps too well dressed; a trifle flashy.

'How are you, Mister Kovel?' the man enquired politely.

Maurice Kovel shrugged without looking at the speaker. Deliberately avoiding the man's eyes. Moving on.

'I'm sorry for your trouble, sir,' the man said, and looked to Joe Kahn. 'We're all sorry, Joe. If there's anything the boys can do . . .'

'I know, Jack. Thanks,' Kahn replied quietly.

'Anybody troubles Mister Kovel, you tell me, Joe,' the man called Jack went on. 'We got respect for him. Anything we can do would be in *mechaieh*. A pleasure, I tell you.'

He nodded at Kovel's receding figure, glanced briefly at Lohmann, and then gave Kahn another nod and moved away, disappearing into the crowd.

They walked on.

'Jack Comer,' Joe Kahn explained. 'Also known as Jack Spot. A *Yiddisha* boy. Also a bookmaker. And maybe a little bit bent. Which is why they call him "The King of the Underworld".'

'I've met the type before.'

Kahn shrugged. 'An entrepreneur, shall we say? But with respect for Maurice Kovel. They all have respect for the old man. Maurice lives in a place with a reputation as the worst street in London. One of the roughest places in the city. But nobody touches the old man. I think . . . I think they need him. Like an unofficial rabbi. Someone they can talk to . . . bring their troubles to. Now he's got his own, they rally round.'

'This Jack Comer . . . he might be useful.'

'How?'

'People like him. They know things. They hear things.'

'He won't speak to the police . . .'

'But, since I'm no longer police, he might speak to me,' said Lohmann.

They reached Leman Street and went into the police station. Brundage was in front of the duty sergeant's desk, waiting for them.

'Mister Kovel,' he nodded curtly. 'I've made arrangements here. The mortuary will hand over the body to the funeral people whenever they arrive.'

'I would like to wait with . . . with my daughter,' Maurice Kovel said, staring at the floor.

'I'll get somebody to take you down,' Brundage replied and called over a constable from behind the desk. 'Take the old man down to the ice room.'

Joe Kahn glowered at the sergeant. 'What about Miss Coverley's belongings?'

'Got 'em here.' Brundage produced a large envelope and thrust it at Maurice Kovel.

The old man shook his head. 'Give it to Mister Kahn and Mister Lohmann.'

Brundage seemed suddenly to stiffen. He looked across at Lohmann.

'You're Lohmann?'

'I'm Lohmann.'

Maurice Kovel followed the police constable through a door into the depths of the station.

Kahn called after him, 'I'll see you at Golders Green, Mister Kovel.'

The old man disappeared, giving no indication that he had heard. Brundage was still staring at Lohmann.

'You got influence, mister?'

'Have I?' Lohmann replied.

'We got a memo about you from Scotland Yard. Signed by the Assistant Commissioner no less.'

'It's possible.'

'We're to give you every facility.'

'Good of you. Just now you could give me that envelope.'

Brundage handed the envelope to Lohmann. 'You somebody special then, mister?'

'I am . . . an interested party.'

Joe Kahn could not contain himself. 'Inspector Lohmann was with the Berlin Criminal Police.'

Brundage gave a smile that verged on being a sneer. 'That so? A German peeler, eh?'

'I was a policeman,' Lohmann acknowledged reluctantly.

He wished Kahn had kept quiet.

'You *was* a policeman? But you ain't one now. That so?'

'It is so!'

'No authority either way. Not here. This is England.'

'Only the authority of your letter from the Assistant Commissioner.'

Brundage's lips seemed to have become damp. He wiped the back of his sleeve across them, still managing to keep smiling.

'Yeah, yeah, sure. What does the AC say? *Every aid and facility.* Oh, we'll give you that, Lohmann. Depending on what it's all about.'

Kahn said: 'He's looking into the death of Beth Coverley!'

Lohmann shot a glance at Kahn. A prayer for him to keep his mouth shut. Something of this must have been communicated to Kahn who flushed nervously.

'Not much of a job, that,' Brundage said. 'You heard the coroner's verdict. Suicide. Done herself in. Stupid thing to do. But then you never know what the Yids'll do around here. You a Yid, Lohmann?'

'I have no religion.'

'Could still be a Yid. But I don't think you are. So why go messing about in their . . . their messes?'

'Oh, I should think for the same reason you must have, Sergeant. To find the truth. Isn't that what you, as a policeman, do?'

The Sergeant flushed. 'Yeah, yeah, suppose you're right. Find the truth, eh? My job. All the time.'

'Of course you will know there are many truths, Sergeant. Your truth might be different from . . . someone else's truth. Isn't that so?'

'In my book, the truth's the truth,' Brundage said defensively.

The smile had gone from his face and it was Lohmann who was smiling now.

'That makes everything so much easier. Meeting a man so sure of himself. And of the truth. I'm sure you'll be able to help me, when I need help.'

Brundage shuffled awkwardly. 'Sure. Just have to ask. Now I got work to do. See you!' He turned away quickly and went behind the counter and over to a desk. He seemed to busy himself taking up some papers and appearing to read them.

Lohmann handed the envelope to Kahn. 'You had better take care of this. But would you be good enough to give me the key to her apartment. And, if there is a diary or address book, I would appreciate that.'

Joe Kahn opened the envelope and ruffled through its contents. 'No notebook or diary.' He produced a set of keys attached to a gold fob. 'These'll be her keys. Don't know which is which. Except for the big one. That's the duplicate key to the old man's house in Cable Street. Don't know which of the others'll be for her place in Chelsea.'

He threw the keys to Lohmann.

'Want me to come with you?' Kahn said.

'You have a funeral to go to. And I will be better on my own. I shall go this evening. You have the address?'

Kahn wrote the address on a scrap of paper and gave it to Lohmann.

'I visited her there once. Nice little place. But cold. Be colder now.'

Lohmann took the underground to Holborn. From there, he walked to his bedsitter in Museum Street. He had found the bedsitter when he had first arrived in London and taken it at once. Its main attraction was that it was cheap.

It was also tiny. On the top floor of a conversion, the four-storey building had once consisted of several large thin houses, each self-contained. However, eventually each house had been divided into bed-sitting rooms. In the case of Lohmann's room this was an exaggerated description. The room was more like a cell. The solitary window looked down on the British Museum. A single bed took up a third of the space in the room. A card-table under the window served as desk, dressing and dining-table. A chair stood in front of the card-table, the only chair. If Lohmann had a visitor, he had to sit on the bed.

There was also a tall thin wardrobe in which he kept his clothes; with shelves for shirts and underwear, and three hangers for suits and sports clothes. Next to the wardrobe was a gas fire and, in the small area in front of this, two gas rings for

50

cooking. At the side of the fire was a drawer for cutlery and two shelves. On one of these were two dinner-plates, two cups and saucers, two dessert-plates, and two odd cracked side-plates. The top shelf contained a few books, some novels and a German-English dictionary. Behind the door was a peg on which Lohmann hung his raincoat and a dish-towel.

On the card-table was the typewriter and a box of typing paper which he used when working on his translations. Next to the typewriter was a solitary glass and a bottle of whisky, three-quarters full.

It was to this that Lohmann returned, climbing the narrow staircase with a weariness born of habit. Like climbing the Alps, he told himself. Surrounded by walls painted a depressingly dark, plum colour by the caretaker, himself a depressingly drab young man called Bates, who lived in the basement with his mother, an aging matriarch never seen and reputed to be bedridden.

Lohmann returned with a thirst. Indeed that was the reason for his return. The bottle on the card-table. Of course he could have gone to a pub for a drink but there was a perennial shortage of cash. Nothing more had been mentioned yet about a fee for the investigation. Still, he had just agreed to go ahead, and doubtless the fee would come. It was only important for his day-to-day living expenses. He might well have agreed to investigate the death of Beth Coverley without a fee. As something to do. Something he was able to do. A return to his old vocation, two years gone.

A long two years. The first, in Paris, and when his daughter was with him, everything had been well. Only when he had decided – for her education and even more, for her safety – to send her to America, had the drinking started. To pass the time and ease the loneliness. Not that he had started drinking at once. That had been a gradual progression. And there had been other things; women in shabby hotel rooms, professional ladies who brought a kind of solace without involvement. As a refugee, he'd long decided on no involvements. The last one, in Germany, had ended with a painful parting. Also, the memory of his dead wife still recurred, still caused him pain. There were too, evenings at tables in cafés with fellow-refugees. Much talk,

51

and all of it a reverie on the past, on the country they had lost, it would seem for ever. There was also the weekly reporting to the local gendarmerie, where the feeling was always one of barely endured toleration by the French police. At one time, visiting Paris, he had been treated as a respected colleague. That had changed. He had been glad when permission to settle in London had been given, thanks to the good offices of Charles Emerson.

In London he had felt safer, more secure. Further from Germany, the English Channel between himself and the sufferings and upheavals of Europe. Also he was lonelier. It was not easy to make friends in a country that had not forgotten that, only eighteen years before, he had been the enemy.

The Gog and Magog had saved him from the deeper depression. There, he had met a few of his fellow refugees; the emigrants and sons of emigrants of previous decades; and a number of the younger English artists and intellectuals who were at once sympathetic and interested. Not that he liked or wanted their sympathy. But the interest came from young anti-Fascists in whom he found a degree of fellow-feeling. And they were all heavy drinkers. Thus the habit grew.

His work in translating was sporadic. Enough to keep him alive and send a little to America. And to pay for his drinking. Which had increased to half a bottle a day. Not that, in Germany, he had been a drinker. But in London it assuaged his loneliness, gave him something to do in this solitary life.

So he came back to the room in Museum Street. Lay on the bed, poured himself a whisky and contemplated the morning and the inquest. He was amazed at the verdict. It was as if the coroner had been primed to direct the jury to such a verdict. Yet he could see that a verdict of murder was unlikely. There was little direct evidence of murder. Yet, with the questions raised, he would have thought the inquest should have produced . . . what was it they called it? . . . an open verdict. Not that the police wanted such a verdict. It would have left them with an investigation on their hands. But a good detective, a concerned police officer, would surely have been interested in such a verdict. It was their job to be interested.

Of course it would have thrown doubt on the evidence of

Constable Ordish. The man who had seen the woman jump, yet, on seeing the fifteen yards of mud, had not bothered to go down to see what had happened to her. Ordish should have been questioned by his own superiors. There had also been the phone call to Joe Kahn the night before. Kahn had not been called to give evidence of that phone call. Beth Coverley had wanted very much to see him on a matter of importance. Yet within a few hours was she supposed to have forgotten this matter of importance and killed herself? Over a love affair, nearly three months dead?

It was there within Lohmann, the old stirrings of interest, the old excitement engendered by curiosity and, as in the old days, tinged with anger. The anger that a life had been thrown away without care or concern, through some personal motivation. There was no motivation that justified murder. He had another thought then. He himself had killed more than once. The last time, a certain Freiherr von Glauber, who had tried to kill Lohmann and had already butchered a number of youths. Lohmann had killed von Glauber in self-defence. Killing the man had not worried him. But there had been an edge of satisfaction in doing so, and that had concerned him. It was dangerous to have such feelings. One came too close to feeling as a murderer felt. One of the reasons why he had taken to drinking the half bottle a day?

He forced the thought from him and laid aside the whisky and glass. The chase, the investigation, that was his vocation and one that excited him. The disposal of the criminal was not his problem, never had been. Except when his own life had been threatened.

Now all he wanted to know was why Beth Coverley had died. He forced himself up, off the bed, made himself put the cork back in the whisky bottle. He took a towel and went out of the room onto the landing and over to the small bathroom on the other side of the landing. Here he washed his face and hands in cold water, dried himself and returned to his room. He squinted, focusing on his wrist-watch. Four o'clock in the afternoon. Why was he wasting time? He could go now to Beth Coverley's apartment in Chelsea. He would make a start. Outside it had started to rain.

The apartment was in a quiet square off the King's Road. Lohmann had been a guest in another house in the square. A writer he'd met in the Gog and Magog. Name of Sitwell. That had been months ago.

Beth Coverley's address was on the other side of the square. Another house-conversion, but a larger house and the conversion had been not into bedsitters but self-contained flats. Beth Coverley's took up the first floor, probably made up of a hall, two bedrooms, living-room, kitchen and bathroom. A wide staircase led to the door of the flat. Lohmann felt a trace of envy.

It took Lohmann two minutes, standing on the doormat, before he found the right key on the dead woman's key-fob. As he put the key in the lock, he looked over his shoulder; and thought it was like the guilty look of a housebreaker.

The hall was large and pleasant with cream-coloured walls, all air and light. Two doors in front of him and a door on either side. He closed the main door and stood for a moment determining which door would lead to the living-room.

Somewhere something creaked. The house settling?

It creaked again. Lohmann knew then he was not alone in the apartment.

FIVE

So often before. Into strange rooms in strange houses, not knowing whether or not somebody would be waiting. It brought back the past, the job, his job as it had been once. Always, he was alert, always nervous, but never showing it; never allowing it to dominate him. And, for reassurance, the Mauser pistol in his pocket. But not this time, which didn't help.

The sound came from behind the door in front of him, the sound of a drawer being slammed shut. He took a deep breath, the kind that fills the lungs to distract attention away from the nervous system. His foot twitched, about to move. Usual method of entry in this situation. Kick the door in. He had to stop himself. He was no longer Inspector Lohmann, no longer the man in charge. He no longer carried his Mauser pistol.

He opened the door and went in.

The living-room. It was a large room with bow windows stretching from floor to picture rail. With cream-coloured walls, as in the hall. The furniture was modern, *art deco*, a lampshade on the table like a semi-nude dancer staring up at the ceiling, looking for non-existent cobwebs. A deep sofa and two armchairs that looked as if they might be comfortable and probably weren't; a coal fire reduced to ashes, but tidy ashes; a mantelpiece with some ornaments, expensive and in only the best of taste; a framed photograph of Maurice Kovel, looking twenty years younger; a side-table with a decanter (empty) and a number of tumblers; ashtrays shaped like fat people lying down, and an inset bookcase to the right of the fire, filled with books. The wall opposite the fireplace was adorned by a number of old theatre posters in black frames.

The area beneath the window was different. Her work area. A large, flat desk, a space in the middle, and drawers down the sides; with a typewriter, *the* typewriter where the last message had surely been found. An old inspector back in Düsseldorf, Metterstein, once told him you could always tell the character of a man (or presumably a woman) by the state of their work area. The desk was neat, the typewriter cover folded by the side of the machine; beside a telephone, a wire-tray for letters and work in progress, containing two sheets of paper. Also a heavy wooden ebony ruler, an ashtray (clean) and a desk-lamp under which was a holder for pens and pencils (three of each).

One desk-drawer was open and the man was standing over it, head down, going through the contents. When Lohmann entered, he seemed to freeze. Then slowly his head turned and he stared at the new arrival. And tried to smile. The result was a sickly look, a half grin, twisted to one side.

Lohmann stared at him, taking everything in with a practised eye. Five feet nine or ten, age, probably in his early forties, a fat sallow face. Like a bloated loaf of bread, with brown spots on the surface, pumpernickel, but not fresh. The forehead was broad, the hair, where there was hair, thin and plastered across the scalp in streaks. He was well-dressed, white shirt and dark-blue tie under a dark suit, well cut. It had to be, to encompass the layers of fat.

'Who are you?' Lohmann said quietly.

The man looked from left to right and then back again. Seeking an answer or a way of escape. But Lohmann was between him and the door. He opened his mouth, a fish out of water, gasping.

Lohmann repeated his question.

'I . . . my name is . . .' The man squinted at the wall opposite the fireplace. '. . . Irving,' he said. 'John Irving.'

The man was lying. Lohmann's eyes had followed his glance at the wall. The nearest theatrical poster was of Henry Irving in *The Bells*. Not very original, he thought, and with little imagination. Still, play it his way just now.

'And what are you doing here, Mister Irving?'

'I came to . . . to collect . . . to find something I lent to Miss Coverley.'

'You mean, you broke in?'

The man who called himself Irving was sweating even more profusely now.

'Anyway, who . . . who are you? What are *you* doing here?'

'I was given the keys by Miss Coverley's father. My presence is quite legal. But yours . . . ? I think the police might call it breaking and entering. Or simple burglary. Shall we try them?' Lohmann took a step towards the desk and the telephone.

'No, please! I can explain.'

'Do so, Mister . . . Irving.'

The man slid the open drawer shut. Lohmann took note of two inches of white shirt cuff. With black cufflinks with a gold monogram, the letters 'ER' interwined.

'Souvenirs?' Lohmann indicated the cufflinks.

The man looked confused. 'I beg your pardon?'

'The cufflinks? Coronation souvenirs. "ER". Edward Rex. Very patriotic.'

The man stared bleakly at the cufflinks and then nodded.

'Yes, yes. Souvenirs. Of the coronation. If ever there is going to be a coronation.'

'Yes indeed,' said Lohmann. 'Now you were going to explain the reason for your presence here.'

The head nodding again. Like the head of the dummy at a fun-fair. Only the dummy laughed as well as nodded. The intruder was not laughing. He was, Lohmann determined, searching for a reason for his being in the flat. And if he had to search for a reason, then whatever it was would be a lie.

'You know Miss . . . Miss Coverley was . . . was a journalist?'

'I knew that.'

'I run a small private news agency. I was supplying her with some information. Documents. Regarding a . . . a large company and its . . . its manipulations. Confidential stuff, you understand? Industrial spying, you might say. When I read of her death, I wanted to get these documents back. If they were found here and traced to me, then it could be embarrassing. To my . . . my news agency. You understand?'

It wasn't a bad story, Lohmann told himself, considering it was almost certainly made up on the spot.

'I understand,' said Lohmann with assumed affability. 'Perhaps we can find your documents together. Shall we look?'

The man's face went blank. It was an unexpected offer.

'Perhaps I should come back another time. I wouldn't want to bother you . . .' There was an element of growing panic in his voice.

'No bother, Mister Irving.' Lohmann stepped forward and, easing the man away from the desk, reached down and reopened the drawer in which Irving had been looking.

As he did so, he realised at once he was being careless. Back in Berlin, Reiner would have been there to back him up. But now he was on his own and, in reaching down to open the drawer, he realised too late he had left himself in a vulnerable position. He should have known better, especially as he had recognised the mounting panic in the man.

Out of the corner of his eye, he saw the movement, the arm reaching down to the desk; and rising again, the ebony ruler in the hand. He half turned but was too late. The heavy implement struck him on the back of the neck and he fell forward, his forehead striking the desk.

He wasn't knocked out. It's never easy, he thought, to render a man unconscious unless trained to do so. But he was momentarily dazed. He heard the ruler clatter to the floor and was aware of the man running to the door. As the door slammed, Lohmann pulled himself onto his elbows. He should have been ready, should have been expecting something like this.

God, how easy it was to forget the lessons of a lifetime.

He heard the front door slam. Straightening up he gingerly felt the back of his head. A tender spot, no more than that, a painful area above the nape of his neck. He lurched over to the window and stared down into the quiet square. It was still raining and the man, coatless, came running out from the doorway that would be below the window. In the centre of the road, he stopped, looking from side to side. Then his arm went up and a tax-cab drew up beside him. In a moment that cab and the man who called himself Irving were out of sight.

Lohmann turned back and contemplated the room. The raincoat was lying curled up on the sofa, a Burberry, expensive and fairly new. Deserted in a panic by its owner. A man whose name was certainly not Irving, and who was also certainly not used to violence. The blow had been painful but could have been harder. Could even have split Lohmann's skull.

He lifted the raincoat and went through the pockets. A twenty-packet of cigarettes, Du Maurier, now containing only six cigarettes. An underground ticket issued at Westminster Station. Nothing else. He looked for a name-tag on the collar. There was none. Only initials. 'E.R.' As on the cufflinks. He was the kind who would have his monogram on his underwear. Lohmann smiled. That was carrying patriotism too far. At least, if he didn't know the intruder's real name, he knew his initials.

He dropped the coat back onto the sofa and turned to the rest of the room. He knew what he would now be looking for; some indication of the story Beth Coverley had been so anxious to talk to Joe Kahn about; also being a meticulous lady journalist, an address book or diary which might give him some idea of the woman's contacts.

He started with the desk.

He went through it with meticulous care. Born of experience, he thought. He was back doing what he was best at doing. He found little. A file of clippings of old stories by Beth Coverley. The Stavisky scandal and what it meant in England. An anti-Nazi piece on the 'Night of the Long Knives' with which he could sympathise despite certain inaccuracies of detail. She had omitted any reference to Rohm's known homosexuality, or it had been cut by her editor. The British did not write about such things in their newspapers. The nearest they came to it was references to scoutmasters in the *News of the World*. Everybody in this strange country had conveniently forgotten what had destroyed Oscar Wilde.

The only other item of interest was a letter, in neat handwriting.

Dear Beth,

Tried to contact you at the paper but you were out. How about dinner on Thursday. Eight o'clock at the usual place. Let me know.

The letter was signed *Roger*. And dated two months ago. Who was Roger? What was the name of the journalist she'd had the affair with? It wasn't Roger. Graham Jordan.

There was nothing else of interest in the desk. he looked around the rest of the room. There was a drawer under the drinks table. It was empty.

He searched the first of the two bedrooms. Her bedroom. A woman's room. Feminine but not excessively so. No frills. A double bed, with sensible cotton sheets and two large, soft pillows. A dressing-table with a bowl of powder, hairbrushes and a bottle of Chanel. No rouge, but in a drawer, some lipsticks, all the same light-pink colour.

Her clothes, in a roomy wardrobe, were reasonably but not excessively expensive. As far as he could judge. An area of detection with which he was not overly familiar. Two evening gowns, two cocktail dresses, four tailored jackets and skirts. More skirts and blouses and pullovers. Drawers holding underwear which looked and probably was expensive . . . she indulged when it came to underwear and silk stockings . . . a large number of silk stockings, suspenders and suspender belts.

There was no address book or diary.

The second bedroom locked, the key in the lock. He turned it and went in. It was sparsely furnished. A single bed, not made up, a small wardrobe, empty as was the dressing-table. There was a film of dust over everything. The room hadn't been used for some time. Why should it be, Lohmann told himself? If she had a lover he would hardly be relegated to the spare room.

He went through the kitchen and bathroom. Both were modern and tidy, almost sterile. The bathroom yielded one luxury, a big, expensive bottle of bath-salts, half empty and smelling strongly of mimosa. Also large, soft bath towels on a rail. The bath was deep and roomy. There was a thought. Why drown yourself in the filth of the Thames when you could do so in this large comfortable bath? Beth Coverley had been, from the state of the apartment, a scrupulously clean individual. Yet she supposedly had scrambled through mud to kill herself.

Again he found no address book or diary.

Yet someone who was so meticulous . . . the word kept coming back to him in connection with Beth Coverley . . . would surely have an address book. And must have notes on the story she was working on.

He went back into the living-room. Outside it was still raining, the rain carving deltas of moisture down the window. The day was dying, the room dull. He switched on the electric light and stared around. Unless she kept the book in her office in Fleet Street, it should be here. A woman doesn't surely keep an address book in her office, not a personal one. And it might seem unlikely that, if she had notes on the important story she was working on, she would keep them there too, where they could easily be found by her colleagues. He thought about that. He could be wrong, maybe that's just where she would keep the notes.

He dismissed the thought. They were here, notes, diary, address-book, whatever. If the story was so important . . . important enough to have her killed? . . . then it should be here in her apartment. Where she could work on it, where she could contact people. But where, in the apartment?

An old memory came back. From his childhood. Reading

detective stories. Sherlock Holmes and the strange incident of the dog in the night. 'The dog did nothing in the night, Holmes.' 'That was the strange incident!' No, it wasn't that. Something else. Not Holmes. Dupin? Edgar Allan Poe. *The Purloined Letter*. Where was the letter hidden? In a stack of other letters. Where would a clever woman hide the diary? A book, among books.

He turned to the bookshelves.

It took him five minutes to find the book. Going along shelf by shelf. It was at the far end of the shelves, at waist-level near the desk. Between John Reed's *Ten Days That Shook The World* and J.B. Priestley's *Angel Pavement*. It was a leather-bound volume, but without a title and when he opened it, he knew at once it was what he was looking for; there were addresses at the back and, at the front, notes on the *Night of the Long Knives*, in some detail, followed by other notes, incomplete it would seem, and much more recent. These started off with some jottings on Sir Oswald Mosley and below that familiar name, more names, half-scribbled sentences, even what at a brief glance looked like diagrams. He shut the book and put it in his pocket. To be read later and with care.

He locked up the apartment and went down into the rain.

Lohmann had walked some way along the Kings Road before the feeling came to him that he was being followed. He dawdled, stopped, looked around several times but could identify no one in the busy thoroughfare. If he was being followed it was by a professional. Finally and quickly he stepped to the kerb and flagged down a cab. From the rear window he looked back again but could see no activity. He was perhaps getting overly nervous.

It took the cab nearly three quarters of an hour to get to Fleet Street and the offices of the *Daily Dispatch*. It was the rush-hour and tramcars and buses clogged the streets of the City of Westminster. Mentally Lohmann cursed his circumstances. Back in Berlin, two years ago, he would have only had to call for a car and it would have been waiting, with or without his personal driver. Now he had such petty considerations as the price of the taxi.

A uniformed commissionaire stopped him in the entrance hall of the building.

'Can I help you, sir?'

'I wish to see the Features Editor, Mister Christopher Gaunt.'

'You have an appointment?'

'No, but . . .'

'You can't just walk in here and ask to see an editor. They're very busy people. A sub-editor, I can get for you but an editor . . .'

Lohmann took out his wallet and extracted from it a card. It was an old card, one of the few he had left. On it were printed the words –

E. LOHMANN
INSPECTOR- CRIMINAL POLICE
BERLIN.

It was over two years old. He handed it to the commissionaire.

'Please give him this.'

The commissionaire read the card, a frown appearing on his face. Despite the frown, his manner changed, became more respectful. He went across to a desk and lifted a phone. Two minutes later Lohmann was directed to one of the elevators, having been instructed to go to the eighth floor. It was a high building for London. He noted in the lift there were ten floors.

On the eighth floor, he was met by a female secretary.

'Mister Lohmann? If you'll follow me . . .'

He was taken along a corridor, into a large room filled with desks, men and one or two women working behind each desk.

'Newsroom!' said his escort, as if she was giving him a conducted tour.

At the far end of this room were a number of cubicles, small offices for the more senior members of the newsroom. He was ushered into one of these. The man he had seen in court that morning rose to greet him.

'Herr Lohmann, you're a little out of your jurisdicition,' said Christopher Gaunt, indicating he take a seat. He did so.

'I'm afraid I am guilty of a small deception, Mister Gaunt.

That card is out of date. I *was* an official in the Berlin Police until two years ago. I am now a refugee.'

Gaunt's brow furrowed. 'Why the deception?'

'It is important that you see me.'

'Important for who? You or me?' Gaunt was studying a document on his desk as he spoke.

'For the late Beth Coverley.'

The editor looked up. 'I've seen you before . . .'

'At the inquest this morning.'

'Yes. Well, this is a morning paper. We're about to start work on tomorrow's edition. I can give you five minutes and then I have a conference. What has Beth Coverley's death to do with you?'

'I have been asked to investigate her death by her father.'

'The inquest said she committed suicide. What is there to investigate?' Gaunt sounded tetchy.

'Do you believe she committed suicide?'

The tetchy look turned wary. 'Does that matter? The inquest believed it.'

'Was she the suicidal type?'

'What is the suicidal type?'

'Mister Gaunt, you brought up a six-month-old love-affair as her motive for suicide. Do you believe she was the type to wait six months and then kill herself over an affair?'

The reply was grudgingly given. 'Well . . . no, possibly not. But it might have been so. She seemed to shrug off the business with Graham Jordan. But who knows?'

Lohmann cleared his throat noisily and changed the subject. 'What was she working on just now?'

The editor shrugged. 'She had some story of her own. Said it would be big. I trusted her so I told her to go ahead. But if I needed her for something else, she'd have to leave her story alone.'

'She didn't tell you what it was, this story?'

'She muttered something about political dynamite. I've heard reporters use such clichés before. But she was good, so I gave her her head. I . . . I did say this whole business with the King and the American woman was going to blow up any day now and I'd want her to cover it from the woman's angle. She said she'd do that whenever I wanted it. Otherwise ... I left her on her own. But she wouldn't tell me what she was on about ... said she'd only tell me when she had the whole story tied up and all the ... the evidence. Yes, that was the word. The *evidence*.'

Lohmann nodded. And changed the subject again. 'Do you know any friend of hers called Roger?'

'Roger? Roger who?'

'I have only the first name.'

Gaunt shook his head. 'Can't help you. Don't know anyone called Roger.'

Lohmann rose to his feet. 'Thank you for seeing me, Mister Gaunt.'

'That's okay. You really were a policeman in Berlin?'

'Until I fell out with the authorities.'

'You wouldn't like to write about it?'

'Perhaps. Sometime. Not now.'

Gaunt gave a small smile. 'Pity. Look, if you find out for sure that Beth didn't commit suicide, I want to know. Because if somebody killed one of our people, this paper will go all out to get that person.'

Lohmann inclined his head. 'I shall remember that, sir. Good day!'

He crossed the newsroom, conscious that eyes were following him, as if assessing his newsworthiness. He went out into the corridor and walked towards the elevators. He pressed the 'Down' button and waited. The elevator finally arrived with a clanking sound and he entered, closing the meshed metal door behind him. He pressed the button for the ground floor. The elevator ignored this and with another clanking sound proceeded to climb upwards.

Lohmann waited. Presumably someone above had pressed an upper button before him.

The elevator rattled past the ninth floor still climbing. One more floor, the tenth.

It finally and noisily rose and rattled towards the tenth floor. No wide landing here but simply a small, square area. But the first thing he saw through the bars of the elevator was a brown boot. And then a second brown boot. Then the door facing the elevator.

The wearer of the brown boots said, 'Welcome to the top of the house!'

He was a small man, not young, with a wide grin on a wizened face. The brown boots were wrong since he wore a dark suit. This was topped by a wing collar and a crumpled kind of cravat. On his head was a skipped black cap with a shiny peak. Above the peak, the words '*DAILY DISPATCH*' in silver letters. The cap labelled him an employee of the paper, perhaps some kind of messenger.

A plump hand saluted Lohmann.

'Nice to have a customer,' the man said.

'Customer?' Lohmann looked puzzled.

'Don't get too many. Pity. Best view in London. Paper says they want to show it off. But they don't advertise it enough. Just a small sign you can hardly see in the foyer. "*Panoramic view of the City*" it says, but who notices it. I ask you. Mebbe one in fifty comes up here to see it. That's you, sir.'

Lohmann shrugged. 'I regret, but I was trying to go down to ground level.'

'Don't say that, sir! Makes me feel the job's nothing more than . . . than . . . what's the word? A sinecure. That's it. A sinecure for an old soldier. Like an act of charity. Whereas I really like showing people the view. See for miles, you can. When it's clear. It's late today but it's still clear . . .'

'I'm sorry but . . .'

'And even in the dark, the lights of the city are something very special. From up here, they look like a thousand fairy lights. All down the side of the river. Worth seeing, that is. Why don't you just step out and let me show you, sir? Won't take more than a few minutes. Bird's eye view of the greatest city in the world. You sound like a foreigner, sir. Appreciate it all the more.'

Lohmann hesitated. The man had the elevator gate open so that it would not descend. And a vaguely pleading look on his face. Lohmann thought, a refugee in a foreign city should be polite to the people of the city. And there was, in him, still the element of the tourist and sightseer.

'Just for a few moments then,' he said, and stepped out of the elevator cage.

'You'll not regret it, sir,' said the small man in the brown boots. 'Name of Rowley, sir. Me. Official guide to the *Dispatch* building and especially the panoramic view . . .'

He waved a hand in the direction of the door. 'Just through here, sir, and we're on the roof of one of the tallest buildings in Fleet Street.'

They went through the door.

It was true. There was a superb view of London. They stepped onto a narrow catwalk and Rowley squeezed past Lohmann leading the way.

'Just along the catwalk, sir. We get to the flat roof.'

The catwalk ran alongside a sloping wall for about ten yards to two steps, which did indeed lead onto a flat roof. With London spread out below them.

The lights were coming on in the city below, hundreds of pinpoints of light stretching in all directions. The dome of St. Paul's dominated the scene and seemed very close as it rose above all other buildings. To the south-east, Lohmann could see the river winding through the city, a crooked twisting spine . . . he could even see it widening as it flowed past the Pool of London and onwards, the river becoming an estuary, flowing towards the sea.

'When it's real clear you can practically see the Sussex Downs,' Rowley said.

The flat roof was surrounded, at the edges, by a three-foot-high wall, if wall it could be called. A section of it, to Lohmann's right, was under repair, a row of large cement squares were lined up to be cemented to the part of the wall which had broken off.

Rowley followed Lohmann's gaze. 'Get that now and then. Kind of erosion, you might say. Soot an' all takes its toll. Eats away at the stone. Got to be careful. Still the roof'll not collapse under you. Trust Rowley.'

He drew level with Lohmann who felt compelled to say something.

'It is a magnificent view.'

'Told you,' said Rowley. 'Have a look. Over there. By the repairs. Can see the Monument. And get a bird's eye view of Fleet Street.'

Lohmann dutifully moved towards the cement squares at the edge of the roof. Telling himself, one look and then he could go, without offending the little man.

He was now some two, three feet from the edge. Where the wall had been eroded. He looked politely towards Wren's Monument, the pillar that serves as memorial to the Great Fire of London.

There was a scuffling sound behind him, and he half turned as a hand grasped his arm and pulled him to one side.

He saw Rowley, eyes wide as half crowns, running towards him, arms outstretched, palms of hands open.

SIX

Later, some time later, Lohmann told that part of the story to a man he was introduced to in the Gog and Magog. The man, very fat, with a round face, his name was Alfred something or other, he was something to do with the cinema, shook his head furiously.

'No! No . . .'

'You don't believe me?' Lohmann said, feeling the man was being rather ill-mannered.

'Oh, I believe you. But I wouldn't set it in Fleet Street. Now, the tower of Westminster Cathedral, that would be the place!'

But that was a year or two later. For now, it was in Fleet Street, on top of the *Dispatch* building. And Lohmann could see clearly the look on Rowley's face. Bland, smoothed out, as if the wrinkles had been suddenly ironed away. And the eyes, the eyes were cold and without expression.

The hand on his arm pulled Lohmann firmly to one side. Rowley, propelled forward under his own impetus, stumbled over a cement block, as Lohmann had been meant to do, and went over the side. With one short, sharp scream.

'You're out of practice, Inspector Lohmann,' said the tall

man who had seemingly appeared from nowhere to grab his arm.

Lohmann found himself shaking. Cold perspiration seemed to have erupted from every pore in his body.

'Who . . . who are you?'

'Charlie! Charlie Newton. D.S. Newton. Detective Sergeant, that is.'

'How did you get here?'

'Followed you. From Chelsea. Wasn't the only one.' Charlie Newton nodded towards the parapet. 'He followed you too. I was behind him. We were both following you.'

'I . . . I felt I was being followed.'

'Well, you would, wouldn't you? Sign of a pro. Knowing he's being followed. 'Course I'm good so you wouldn't see me. Him? He *was* good. But it'd be him you'd feel.'

Questions were rotating around Lohmann's head.

'But how did you get here? I never heard you. Or the . . . the elevator.'

'Followed you to the eighth floor. When you went up in the elevator, I went up the stairs. See, I knew Rowley had come into the building. Top of the stairs, I found this messenger . . . works for the paper . . . unconscious . . . blow to the head, and minus his skipped cap. So I kind of figured Rowley was getting you up here for a reason. And most of that little bastard's reasons are unhealthy. Came right up the stairs.'

'I didn't hear you!'

'It's the training. And the shoes. Very light shoes. And me, light on me feet. Saw what he was up to, and moved fast.'

Lohmann stared at the edge of the roof. Where Rowley had gone over.

'Who was he?'

'Wouldn't waste much sympathy on Rowley. Nasty piece, that one. Slit his grandmother's throat for her Co-op dividend, he would. Professional killer. Known but not recorded, you might say. Except once. During the war . . .' Newton grinned. Did he tell you he was an old soldier?"

'Yes, he did.'

'Like hell. For three weeks. Spent the rest of the war on the moor. Dartmoor Prison. GBH. Grievous Bodily Harm. To his sergeant-major.'

'But why . . . why was he trying to kill me? And why were you following me?'

'Look, sir, Rowley'll have made a mess of part of Fleet Street. They just might come up here to see the spot he jumped from. Which is what it'll be reckoned. You and me, we should go down. By the stairs, I think. Go and have a coffee an' a little chat. How about that?'

Ten flights of stairs had Lohmann breathless and grateful to go for a coffee. They crossed Fleet Street, avoiding the crowd that had gathered around what remained of Rowley, and went into a small coffee house. It was a dim, old-fashioned place, rows of cubicles along each wall. Newton chose a cubicle at the far end of the shop away from other customers. He ordered a coffee for Lohmann and a hot chocolate for himself.

'Don't like coffee myself. Caffeine. A drug. Chocolate, now that's wholesome. If fattening. Now we can talk some more.'

'Why was . . . Rowley . . . why was he trying to kill me?' Lohmann asked.

'Now you'd maybe know that better yourself, sir. Maybe something to do with the inquest this morning.'

'You were there? I did not see you.' Difficult not to see him, Lohmann thought. He's well over six feet tall.

Newton grinned. 'Now when you was in Berlin, sir, and you didn't want to be seen, did anybody ever see you?'

'No. I see what you mean.'

'I was asked to go to the inquest. A watching brief, you might say. If I was a lawyer, which I'm not. It was . . . politic . . . that's the word . . . not to be seen. See, it wasn't really our job. Local police. Brundage and his people. So my chief didn't want me to be seen to intrude. Or even be interested. Of course I saw you there.'

'And Rowley, was he there?'

'No. Reckon he was contacted later. Now I don't know for sure why you was there, sir. But it's my guess the girl's family weren't too happy with the suicide verdict. So they asked you to look into it. Right?'

'That is correct.'

69

'Apart from me, another interested party heard about this and decided they didn't want you snooping . . . no, detecting around, shall we say? So they got in touch with Rowley, it being his nasty profession to . . . to kill people. Can you think of all the people who would know what you were up to?'

'Maurice Kovel of course. And Joe Kahn . . . he contacted me.'

'Anyone else?'

'Unless Joe Kahn told anyone, I can't think . . . Oh, yes, Charles Emerson knew. I asked his advice . . .'

'The Assistant Commissioner? Well, I hardly think he would employ someone like Rowley to kill you.' The sergeant suddenly laughed. 'More like someone like me, he'd employ.'

'That's why you were following me? Emerson had sent you . . . ?'

'Eh, no. Not the Assistant Commissioner. Shall we say another interested party. But who else knew you were looking into this business?'

Lohmann thought for a moment, remembered, in the police station, when he was getting the keys to Beth Coverley's apartment.

'There was Sergeant Brundage. He heard enough . . .'

'Brundage, eh?' The big man's brow furrowed and his eyes narrowed. 'Well, maybe your friend, Mister Kahn, could have told a few people as well. We know about Mister Kahn. He's on record. Member of the Communist Party.'

'I think I knew that,' said Lohmann and went on. 'So you followed me from the inquest . . .'

'Oh, no, sir. Just noted you were there. I followed you from Miss Coverley's apartment. Y'see, I was . . . keeping an eye on that apartment. My orders. When you turned up, I followed you.'

'Why me? Why not the other man in the apartment?'

Newton was suddenly alert. 'What other man? See, I got there just a few minutes before you left. Thought I'd follow you, having seen you at the inquest. Then I noticed Rowley on your tail too. But you say there was another man.'

'Called himself Irving. But I think he made that name up,' Lohmann said.

70

'Interesting. And if you say he made up the name, then I believe you.'

Lohmann decided to keep the monogrammed cufflinks to himself. For the time being. There was so much more he wanted to know about Detective Sergeant Newton.

'Who are you working for, sergeant, if it's not Emerson? What branch of the British police do you come from?'

'Scotland Yard, sir. Special Branch. I can tell you that.'

'And who ordered you to watch Beth Coverley's apartment? I could go to Charles Emerson and ask him . . .'

'Yes, you could, sir. And I suppose he'd give you the name of my chief. So I suppose I can tell you. I work for Detective Superintendent Thornhill.'

'Why is your Superintendent Thornhill so interested in the death of Beth Coverley?'

'Now that's difficult, Mister Lohmann. Interested party, I'd say. But that's all I could say. And, on account of the fact that I may just have saved your life some moments ago with Rowley, you'd have to believe me. Anyway it is the truth.'

Lohmann stared hard at him. 'You saved my life. I have to thank you for that, Sergeant Newton. But now I shall have to speak to Superintendent Thornhill.'

'Out of town, sir. For the time being.'

'When will he be back?'

Newton grimaced. 'A day, a week, can't say for sure. But when he's back, I'm sure he'll see you.'

'I shall go to Scotland Yard and ask for him. Special Branch, you say?'

'Special Branch. Detective Superintendent Roger Thornhill. When he gets back from wherever he's at.'

Lohmann thought, *Roger* Thornhill. *Roger?*

Newton finished his coffee. 'I think you'll be all right for a time now, sir. But best keep a weather eye open. Whatever a weather eye is. At least you know somebody wants you out of this business. Enough to kill you. A pro like you should be able to cope. Now I'll be off.'

The big man rose.

'Thank you for saving my life, Sergeant Newton,' Lohmann

71

said, and meant it. 'I shall be in touch with you and your superintendent.'

'Look forward to that, sir. Take care.'

The sergeant went. Leaving Lohmann to finish his coffee and pay the bill. Which amused Lohmann. But then he needed something to amuse him.

Lohmann went back to his bedsitter in Museum Street. It was in the news on the radio.

'An unidentified man committed suicide this afternoon by throwing himself from the roof of the *Daily Dispatch* building in Fleet Street. The identity of the man has, at this time, not been determined.'

Strange, Lohmann thought, two suicides, neither of which had been suicide.

He turned to Beth Coverley's diary.

The first part of the diary was filled with notes on what he realised was an old story about the state of unemployment among the miners of South Wales. Apart from notes, there were large segments of what Lohmann presumed was the text of the final article. This was interspersed with quotations from a young politician from the area, one Aneurin Bevan.

Lohmann skimmed quickly through this and came to a new series of notes. These consisted of names which seemed to be linked. He studied the first page.

Mussolini through Grandi to Mosley. One trail to follow...? Generally admitted by those who know.

Situation in reverse. Currency flow from Treasury. (See Rennie's notes). From private sources? From the Exchequer? Not Italy. Baldwin's attitude. Through Rue Scott-ffoliot. She might help. Considers it all a great joke. Eden's attitude? Does he know?

This was the first of two pages. Lohmann stared at the page. Baldwin, Eden, Mosley! All known. Prime Minister, Foreign Secretary, and the leader of the British Fascists. But what did it mean? A story about men in high places. Enough to get Beth Coverley killed? And did the British operate that way? He thought, all governments operate that way, if necessary.

He turned to the next page. The last page of notes.

Winston Churchill! Odd man out. (Appointment, Saturday, 10.30 Chartwell?) A starting point. Everything depends on Rennie. Would they use M's people? Says the King could be used. How? And why? Again use Rue S-f. Feeling I'm being watched. Or getting paranoiac. Imagination. How could they know? Rennie nervous. Say intelligence people knew someone had seen documents. Have they seen me with Rennie? Or are they just being naturally suspicious? Mosley's people again, maybe?

The notes on that story ended there. With questions in Lohmann's head. Who was Rennie? Who was Rue Scott-ffoliot? The last-named, he seemed to have heard of or read about somewhere. Further on, in the diary section was listed the appointment with Churchill. Saturday. The next day. An appointment she would never keep. But possibly he could keep the appointment? Winston Churchill . . . Lohmann knew little of Churchill. Except that he was a British politician. Out of favour, not in government.

He flicked through the book. No other appointments. One more note. On another story.

Wallis Warfield Simpson. M. Ernest Simpson. Previously married someone called Warfield? See foreign press clippings. Christopher thinks story must break. Can King marry commoner twice divorced? God knows?

The page ended with a two-sentence scrawl of comment.

With everything going on in the world today who cares? What a silly little man he must be!

No further notes. At the end of the book a list of addresses and telephone numbers. Not in alphabetical order. In no order whatsoever. R. Scott-ffoliot was there. An address in Curzon Street and a Mayfair telephone number. Her father's number was there, as was Joe Kahn's. And others, many others. People he had never heard of, never would hear of, the connections of a journalist over countless stories. He looked for Thornhill, Roger, but it was not listed. No need, he thought. If the man worked at Scotland Yard, the number was familiar, even to Lohmann. Whitehall 1212.

Then he found what he was hoping to find. 'Rennie, Edward', followed by an address in Hornsey Rise and a phone number. Edward Rennie? E.R. The monogrammed cufflinks. Edward Rennie would provide another step in his investigation.

A knock on his door.

'I have been calling you, Mister Lohmann.' It was Norman, the caretaker. 'You're wanted on the telephone.'

He followed the youth down to the ground floor.

'How's your mother, Norman?'

'Old,' said the caretaker. 'And gettin' older. No end to it, is there?'

Lohmann forbore to reply to the obvious. He lifted the receiver of the phone and put it to his ear.

'Lohmann here!' he said.

'It's Joe Kahn, Lohmann.'

'Yes?'

'The old man's been attacked. Maurice Kovel. Came back from the funeral to find the house had been ransacked. And the *schmek* that did it were still there. Two of them. They knocked him down and started on him. Luckily his sister came in and screamed the house down. So they bolted.'

'I will come now.'

'The old man's not too bad. A bit bruised . . .'

'Tell me when I get there . . .'

Lohmann took yet another taxi. Cursing the lack of a vehicle of his own. It was dark when the cab reached Cable Street but Maurice Kovel's house was ablaze with light.

The first person he saw when Joe Kahn let him into the sitting room was Detective Sergeant Brundage talking to Sophie Jacobs. He turned away from her as Lohmann came over.

'Well, if it isn't our Kraut friend. What brings you in at a rush?'

'I phoned him,' Joe Kahn said.

'This family seems to have adopted you, Lohmann. Or is it just your Bolshie friend there?'

Lohmann looked at him bleakly. 'What is the story here, Sergeant?'

'Nothing special,' Brundage shrugged. 'Couple of burglars. Broke in the back door. Probably locals who heard about the funeral and thought the house would be empty. So the old man came back early and they got rough. It happens.'

'So why didn't they take anything?' said Kahn with a look at Lohmann.

'The old man disturbed them . . .' Brundage took out a packet of ten Woodbine, drew a cigarette from the packet and lit it. Sophie Jacobs scowled at him. Smoking without her permission in her hall was something she did not normally permit. But Brundage was the police, the *politzei*, maybe even the Cossacks . . . he had to be endured.

'Disturbed them! Disturbed them!' said Kahn, his voice rising. 'They managed to go through every room before they met Maurice in the hall. They weren't just burglars. They were looking for something . . .'

Lohmann looked at Brundage. The sergeant's expression had not changed.

'So you say, Kahn. They took nothing. So, to me, they were disturbed. What would they be looking for in . . . the old man's house? Money, maybe? So they didn't find any. They roughed up the old man to find out where he'd hidden it.'

'Everybody in the East End knows Maurice Kovel has no money apart from what he gets out of his shop.' Kahn spoke from between clenched teeth. His face was pale, tense with irritation. 'And that, his nephews take to the bank every night. So why rob him here? Why not go for the shop and the nephews?'

There was now a small, tight smile on Brundage's face. He took Lohmann gently by the arm and led him over to the windows. Outside, Cable Street was damp under the pavement lamps.

'Look, Mister Lohmann,' said Brundage. 'They want to make something important out of a simple break-in. You know, in a city, it happens all the time. The old man's lucky they got nothing. Lucky they didn't kick him to death. So they don't want to believe the daughter did herself in, now they want to make this the crime of the century.'

'You will try and find these . . . burglars?' Lohmann asked quietly.

'That's the job they pay me to do. But who can find a couple of Spring-Heeled Jacks? There are thousands of them around here. But still we go through the routine.'

'It is interesting they took nothing. It is as if they were looking for something . . .'

'Lohmann, what are you so concerned about?' Brundage assumed a knowing look. 'You're a policeman like me. And a Kraut one. Maybe they've got the good idea back in Berlin. Who cares, they beat up an old Yid? A little harder and we'd have one less in London.'

Brundage was still gripping Lohmann by the arm. The German slid his arm from the policeman's grip and stared at him, assuming the other's expressionless look. The look policemen were supposed to practise. Blank, noncommittal, emotionless. Above personality and emotion. Lohmann knew how to simulate the look, but never, in his career, had he achieved the lack of emotion.

'Tell me, Sergeant Brundage, is it a crime now to be a Jew in England? I was not aware the Nuremberg Laws applied here.'

'They don't,' Brundage replied. 'Not yet.'

He looked at his watch. 'I've spent too long on this one. Time I was back at the station . . .'

'As always, Sergeant. You will remember to let me have the reports on Beth Coverley's death. As requested.'

'By the Assistant Commissioner? I remember. I'll have to look for them. Keep in touch.'

Brundage left. Lohmann turned to Sophie Jacobs.

'May I see your brother now?'

The old woman shrugged. 'Why not? Everybody else sees him. When he should be sleeping. Go up. The bedroom at the top of the stairs.'

Joe Kahn came into the hall with Lohmann. The doorbell rang. Kahn answered it to admit the man called Jack Comer.

'I heard what they did to the old man. I got boys out looking for the *dreck* that did this. We got some ideas.'

Lohmann, on the first step of the stairway, turned and faced Comer.

'What are these ideas, Mister Comer?'

Comer shot a look at Kahn.

'He's all right,' Kahn reassured the man.

'We think they were Blackshirts. Mosley's bully boys.'

'But an old man . . . ?' said Kahn. 'Why him? Why not me? Why not you, Jack? But Kovel . . . why?'

'I should read sick minds,' said Comer. 'Bookies, I know. Heavies, I know. All the tricks, all the boys. But these anti-Semites, who can tell what they are thinking?'

'I think they wanted something,' said Lohmann.

'What could they want?'

'When I know, Mister Comer, perhaps I'll tell you.'

'Well, I'll tell you this, mister. It won't happen again. I'm putting two of my boys, one at the back, one at the front, not twenty-four hours a day. Twenty-five hours. *Emis!*'

'A good idea, Mister Comer. Do it.' Lohmann turned to Joe Kahn. 'Joe, it would be a help if I hired a car. To be honest, I can't afford it. Can the expenses stretch to it?'

Before Kahn could reply, Comer cut in. 'I'll have a car here for you in half an hour. Won't cost anybody a penny. I got favours owed to me in the garage business. Joe tells me you was a copper. First time I've helped an ex-copper. But for Maurice Kovel . . . anything!'

'Thank you, Mister Comer. It is appreciated.'

Lohmann went up the narrow stairway and into the bedroom.

The old man was propped up by numerous pillows in a large, ancient double-bed. His forehead and eyes were badly bruised and turning purple. A piece of sticking plaster covered part of his right temple. Blinking, he squinted across the bed at Lohmann.

'So! It is the detective. You're a little late. They been and gone.'

'Have you any idea what they wanted, Mister Kovel?'

'What should they want? Nothing here for them. That policeman from Leman Street says burglars. Burglars, indeed! They knew better. Nothing here. You ask me, I think they wanted to find something . . . to know something . . .'

'About Beth?'

77

'About Becky. Looking for something of hers. When they didn't find it and I came in, they're kicking me. Saying all the time, over and over, what did she tell me? Nothing, I'm trying to say, but they're not listening. They're just kicking.'

'What did they look like?'

Maurice Kovel licked his lips, turned awkwardly to a bedside table on which was a glass of water. He took a gulp from the glass and then carefully replaced it.

'What should they look like? Do you think I'm looking? Just two men. That's all. Two men. Kicking and asking, "What did she tell you, what did she tell you?" Like I said.'

'Well, I do not think they will bother you again. Mister Comer is putting two of his . . . his friends outside to see you won't be bothered any more.'

The old man grimaced. 'Ach! All I'm needing. Gangsters around the house already! You found out anything about Becky yet?'

'Not yet. But I will, Meanwhile, you rest.'

'Huh! Soon I have all the time in the world to rest. But before that I want to know who killed Becky. So go and find out. If I'm paying you, all this talk is on my time.'

Lohmann went out, closing the door quietly behind him. Twenty minutes later he drove back to Museum Street behind the wheel of a bull-nosed Morris.

SEVEN

Later Lohmann remembered that autumn, not just for the Beth Coverley investigation, but for an impression of London that lingered long in his mind. The city was supposedly coming out of the Great Depression and certainly the West End was a dazzle of lights, a great toy shop filled with the fun and games of the wealthy. And the wealthy were very much on view, the smart set, the gay young things, the debs and chinless wonders, the Windsor set . . . now known as the King's party . . . to be seen at night, the female expensively begowned, the male in dinner jacket and black tie. It was certainly the time . . . the last time of the Prince of Wales become King. But, for a short while longer he would lead the parade. A parade unabashedly imitating most things American. Games were played, some harmless, like stealing a policeman's helmet or pouring champagne from the rooftops onto passers-by. Other games too, cocaine snorting . . . not so harmless. Also the more vicious offshoot, a small group of young so-called aristocrats who robbed jewellery shops, not without violence to those who stood in their way. Some were flogged for it . . . yes, flogging was still permissible in the enlightened English system of law.

These were some of the desperate ways the wealthy took their pleasures, possibly in anticipation of things to come, a sensing that they were living on the edge of the European abyss.

The East End was different, with a different kind of desperation. The European abyss was much more real to many of the refugee population. Already they had lost family in Germany and in Russia. And the tide that had flooded Germany was lapping at the feet of the East Enders. The Blackshirts were in evidence and planning to be even more in evidence. The death's head and the crooked cross were coming closer.

The East End too was still a dark place. Parts of it had little changed since Jack the Ripper had gone about his work. Hollow-eyed men in chokers and cloth-caps, and thin women in shawls filled the streets and alleys, struggling to keep alive. The Depression had not ended yet for them. The sweat-shops still flourished. Some, like Jack Comer, stole to live and did well as long as they weren't caught; others, like Joe Kahn, fought a different fight, the street-corner agitators, the publishers of four-sheet newspapers, politicising the poor who listened, but barely understood the words, some lost in the rattle of the passing tram-car.

Lohmann had found himself living in a limbo between both worlds. Economically closer to the East End, he was accustomed, through his previous profession, to mixing in the more expensive life of the West End. It seemed that the greater, if rarer, crimes were committed in the City of London and the West End; the petty crimes, infinitely more frequent, in the East End. What was it Brecht had said? 'What is robbing a bank compared to founding one?'

At least, he could tell himself, he was back in his old game. Like coming alive again. And being threatened with death. Rowley had tried to kill him. Why? Because he was looking into the death of Beth Coverley? If that was so they would try again. He must therefore keep one jump ahead. Knowing too he was worrying someone, otherwise why the attempt on his life? So he had to consider his next move carefully. And with the inevitable look over his shoulder to see who might be coming up behind.

The first problem was to find out what Beth Coverley had been working on. Find that and he would find his way to the motive for her killing. There was no longer any thought that her death might be suicide. There was too much against this being so. And he had committed himself to the investigation of murder. Therefore it had to be murder. There was his ego showing, he told himself, and could smile at the thought. Now he had Beth's diary, he had paths to follow, tracks to be traced.

The morning after Maurice Kovel was attacked, Lohmann lay in bed considering these options. Where to start first? Edward Rennie, he of the monogrammed cufflinks, who called himself Irving? Churchill? No, that was for the next day, when Beth had an appointment with him. He, Lohmann, would keep that appointment. Superintendent Roger Thornhill? Was he the 'Roger' of the letter to Beth Coverley? Detective Sergeant Charlie Newton had said Thornhill was out of town. Time enough when he returned.

It should be Rennie, Lohmann determined. Yet it might be better to leave Rennie to sweat for a while, see if the man he met in the flat would come after him. That was how it should read. He should leave Rennie in his rising flood of sweat for a few days. Then he might just be more vulnerable.

There was someone else. Someone who might provide an interesting story. Or nothing!

Rue Scott-ffoliot. Whoever she might be. A friend of princes, dukes and kings. And Beth Coverley. With an address in

Dolphin Square. Lohmann's memory had revived enough for him to remember where he had come across the name. In a copy of the *Tatler* magazine in a dentist's waiting-room. Viewed with an impatient eye and a nagging toothache. The Honourable Rue Scott-ffoliot (always with two small *f*'s) with Mrs Emerald Cunard . . . and further down the page, with Mr and Mrs Ernest Simpson and the Prince of Wales (it was an old magazine, eighteen months out of date).

He decided to start with Miss Scott-ffoliot.

The apartment building in Dolphin Square was six storeys high and the apartments were obviously expensive. Lohmann parked the Morris outside and walked into the entrance hall. A porter in an elaborate uniform with gold facings stopped him at a table used as a desk. The table looked like a genuine Queen Anne creation. A telephone looked out of place on the table.

'I would like to see Miss Scott-ffoliot,' Lohmann said.

'Got an appointment, have you?' Despite the uniform's splendour the accent was broad cockney, the look was arrogant. Lohmann was made aware, with that look, that his own appearance was verging on the seedy, the untidy. The hell with it, he determined. So he was a refugee. He used what he had to hand. Again he decided to utilise his old Berlin warrant card. The porter took the card, his face expressing some surprise. He went back to the table and lifted the telephone. He talked for some moments in low tones, replaced the receiver and came back to Lohmann.

'Says she doesn't know you from Adam, but you're to go up. Third floor.'

A maid in a black dress, apron and cap, admitted him to the apartment, showed him into a sitting-room and told him to wait. He stood for some five minutes looking at Louis Quinze furniture and discreet, but gold wallpaper.

Then she entered.

Early thirties, tall, slim but with a good bust, Lohmann estimated she was about thirty-two. She had a good face framed in auburn hair smoothly flowing to her shoulders. In a time of short hair, not fashionable, but right for her. She was almost but not quite beautiful; with high cheek bones and full

81

lips. She was dressed simply, in a black sweater and skirt. A single row of pearls around her neck. Her make-up consisted of a pale lipstick and a little powder. There was however a distinct aroma of Chanel Number 5.

'Inspector Lohmann!' she said. 'A Berlin policeman. How exciting! But I've never been in Berlin, far less committed any crime there.'

Lohmann explained about the card, telling her he was no longer a policeman but was now a refugee.

She gave an amused frown. 'So you're here under false pretences. I should tell you ... in case you're a burglar ... that apart from my maid, I have a very large chauffeur in the kitchen.'

'I'm not a burglar, I assure you, Miss Scott-ffoliot,' Lohmann replied.

'How disappointing! Merely a poor refugee. Collecting for charity ... ?'

'No. I wish to speak of a friend of yours.'

The lips pouted. 'I've so many. And, eh, call me Miss Rue. Scott-ffoliot is such a mouthful. My father's fault, of course. But then he was clever enough to change it.'

Lohmann looked politely puzzled.

She went on, 'He was a Rear-Admiral in the navy. During the war he came to an agreement with Lloyd George. He would be kept away from battleships and the actual fighting, remain on land as commander of shore establishments. If he was a good boy they'd make him an Earl. He was a good boy. He's now Lord Innerleithen. What did you want to see me about, Herr Lohmann?'

'You knew a Miss Beth Coverley?'

'Yes, I do. What has Beth been up to?'

Lohmann took a deep breath. She didn't know of the girl's death. He would take his time telling her.

'That is what I hoped you might be able to tell me.'

The thin eyebrows were raised. 'Shouldn't you ask her?'

'I would prefer asking you. Would it be wrong to say she is outwith your usual friends?'

'You mean, because she's a working girl on that newspaper? But I have a very catholic circle of friends, in all walks of life.

82

I'm not a snob, Herr Lohmann. I like people.'

'How did you meet her?'

'You *are* inquisitive! However . . . she came to see me . . . said she was writing an article on great war heroes and wanted to do a piece on Daddy. I must admit, that made me laugh. A war hero! My father? Never heard a gun fired except on the grouse moors, I shouldn't be surprised. Oh, he was a friend of Douglas Haig's . . . but more a friend of the family product. But, y'know, I never did really believe Beth. And she never did write about Father.'

Her voice dropped and she gave a small throaty laugh.

'I liked the girl and we became friends. But . . . eh . . . I always felt she had gone out of her way to know me.'

'Why would that be?'

'Because . . . because little Beth is a snob.'

Lohmann hesitated, surprised.

The woman went on. 'She always wants me to introduce her to people. Rather important people.'

'Who would these people be?'

'I suppose there must be some point to all these questions?'

'I suppose there must be or I would not ask them of you. Please tell me, who?'

The smooth brow furrowed.

'Just . . . just everybody. Oswald Mosley, she wanted to meet. We haven't got round to that yet. And the Mitfords. But Diana and Unity were in Germany at the time. She did meet Jessica . . . they got on like a house on fire. Silly expression! How do people get on like houses on fire? Oh, and she was very keen on being introduced to a lot of very old, very dull politicians.'

'Can you remember which politicians?'

She pouted. 'You're very persistent. I suppose policemen are. And ex-policemen can't get out of the habit. She wanted to meet Baldwin, of course. God knows why? And Eden. Well that's understandable. Anthony is rather a dish. And Chamberlain.' She gave a delicate shudder. 'Yes, she wanted to meet people like that . . .'

'And Winston Churchill?'

'I don't know if she actually mentioned Winston. Oh, and she wanted to meet your ambassador, von Ribbentrop.' She grimaced now. Can't stand him myself. All that "*Heil Hitler*" business. They say Hitler insists on it. He can't surely say "*Heil Myself*", can he? Oh, I forgot, you're German. I'm not insulting you, am I, Mister Lohmann?'

Just then Lohmann received the very strong impression that that was exactly what she was trying to do.

'Not at all, I have met Hitler and I share your dislike of him.'

Her eyebrows arched with some deliberation.

'God. A sane German. Are you Jewish?'

'Lutheran. By upbringing. Not now.'

She smiled with some degree of warmth. 'Such a stupid little man, I think.'

'Lethal, Miss Scott . . . Miss Rue. Lethal and dangerous.'

She took a cigarette from a silver box on a side table and, as an afterthought, offered him one.

'Thank you,' he said, taking one from the box.

She lit his with an ornate silver lighter beside the box and then inserted her own cigarette into a minute tortoise-shell holder before lighting it.

'You know,' she said inhaling deeply, 'I'm beginning to feel a little uncomfortable, answering all these questions about a friend. Why don't you ask Beth herself?'

'Because she would be unable to answer them.'

'What's that supposed to mean . . . unable to answer them? What has the girl done?'

'Been murdered. Yes, she is dead,' he said very quietly.

Lohmann heard the sharp intake of breath. It had taken her off guard. For a moment she seemed to sway and he stepped forward, thinking she might faint. But she regained her momentary loss of composure almost at once. But when she spoke now, it was in a different tone, all affectations gone. She was revealing another persona; under the slow drawl and the languid stance, there was an intelligent, alert woman.

'I didn't know,' she said. 'I've been out of London. In Scotland. Stupid shooting party. When . . . ?'

'A few days ago. The inquest was yesterday.'

'And the police . . . ?'

'Will do nothing. The verdict was suicide. But it was a wrong verdict.'

A touch of the original Rue Scott-ffoliot. 'You seem to dismiss our police with ease, Mister Lohmann.'

'There were many things that would mitigate against such a verdict. Her father and her friends saw these. I was asked to investigate . . . to try and find the truth.'

'Despite the inquest?'

He answered her with a question of his own. 'You knew Beth Coverley. Would you say she was the suicidal type?'

A pause. She drew on her cigarette, fiddled with the tortoise-shell holder.

'No! You're right. She wasn't like that.'

She paced the thick carpet for a moment, and then asked another question.

'What brought you to me?'

'Your name in her address book. It might have been nothing but from what you have told me, I think it might be important. Certainly useful.'

'What have I told you?'

'Quite a lot.'

Rue shook her head, a wave rippling through the auburn hair. 'I'm not aware of it.'

'She wasn't a snob, Miss . . . Rue. She was working on some important story. I think she wanted to meet certain people who might provide information for that story. Rather important people. Like your Prime Minister. Like von Ribbentrop.'

She nodded now. 'Yes, yes, it seems obvious.'

She half turned and faced Lohmann.

'I liked Beth. She . . . she made a change from . . . from some people I know. She had an honesty and a purpose . . . I always thought that . . . and now you come here and prove it to me. So few people with a purpose, Mister Lohmann. Beth . . . and now perhaps . . . you.'

'I do a job I was accustomed to doing. Without authority now. That could make it more interesting.'

She went to an ashtray and ground her cigarette out.

'You know why I was called Rue, Lohmann?'

'It is an unusual name.'

'My mother . . . not the Admiral, you understand, but his long-suffering wife, my mother . . . to escape a conversation consisting mostly of nautical terms and naval estimates . . . read Shakespeare. Became a Shakespearean scholar really. My elder sister is called Rosemary. "For remembrance". *Hamlet*, Lohmann. What's the next line of Ophelia's speech? "And there's rue for you." Inevitable. I was called Rue.'

'I see,' said Lohmann, who didn't.

'One's name follows one around. Why I'm telling you. Rue. Regret, sorrow, pity. I hide from these emotions. Give myself cause for rue and then run away. Too often. But not this time. I said Beth was my friend. Becky, that was her real name. Rebecca. She should have used it. I'd like to help you find whoever killed her.'

He said nothing. Waiting. The moment was hers. Then she tried to dismiss it, reverting to the other Rue Scott-ffoliot.

With a laugh. 'And it might be fun. Like playing the game of Murder at parties.'

He ignored that. It was for herself to play the flippant young woman.

'You may be able to help me,' he said, seriously. 'But it could be dangerous.'

'Oh, I like that. When do we start?'

She obviously had no idea of danger.

'Beth Coverley was drowned in Thames mud. Yesterday an attempt was made to kill me. This is not a game of Murder.'

She looked up at him, eyes wide and round, an expression of angelic innocence assumed.

'You make it even more exciting. What do we do first?'

He had to accept the game she was playing, at least for the time being.

'You do nothing. Until I contact you. Then you will do exactly what I tell you. No more, no less.'

'Oh, but you must give me some clue. Shall I buy a gun? I know a boy who carries a pair of knuckle-dusters. Don't know if he ever uses them. But he carries them all the time. And when Daddy died . . . did I tell you he died? . . . he left a room full of guns. The house is in Buckinghamshire. I could easily pop up and raid the gun-room.'

'No guns. Not for you. You see, Miss . . . Miss Rue . . . I believe, if you carry a gun, you must be prepared to use it. And if you have to use it you must be prepared to kill.'

She blinked. Then, all affection gone, she said, 'If I came on the person who killed Beth, I could kill that person.'

He believed her. For a second, an icy look had come into her eyes, a coldness she'd not revealed before. Then it vanished as quickly as it came.

'I will tell you how you can be of help,' he said. 'You will do for me what you were going to do for Beth Coverley. You will introduce me to the people she wanted to be introduced to.'

Again she pouted. 'No fun. Just the same old round of parties and dinners.'

'I like parties. And I often get hungry.'

'Oh, all right.' Still petulant. 'But you'll need me for more than that. You just wait and see.'

She showed him to the door herself.

'You'll be in touch?' she said.

'I'll be in touch. Next week.'

'Suppose I want to get in touch with you?'

He gave her his telephone number.

'Are you married, Lohmann?' she asked at the door of the apartment.

'I was. She died in Germany a time ago.'

Her head was to one side. She was looking him up and down. A predatory look, or was he imagining it?

'I have a sixteen-year old daughter in America,' he added.

'How nice. A ready-made family. Your next wife won't have to go through all the nappy and growing up bit. I like that.'

He stepped out of the apartment into the corridor.

She said, 'Don't go and get yourself killed, Lohmann. Not yet anyway.'

He drove from Dolphin Square to the East End and parked outside Leman Street police station. Across the road from the station someone had chalked on the wall, 'Perish Judah'. Lohmann had seen slogans like that before. All over the East End. Others too. 'Yids out!' and 'Solly, go home!' He'd seen slogans like these too. In German. In Berlin. There, they were now official. Printed in headlines in Julius Streicher's own newspaper. Or screamed by Hitler at mass meetings. He could not restrain a shudder. It could happen here. Perhaps it was happening. Perhaps Beth Coverley had been killed simply because she was a Jewess.

He dismissed the thought. There was more to this business than that. But that might well be part of it.

He went into the police station and, at the desk, asked for Detective Sergeant Brundage. He was shown into a small office. Brundage was drinking hot tea from a large mug. The sergeant wiped the back of his hand across his lips before greeting his visitor.

'Ah, Mister Lohmann. Take a seat. Want some tea?'

'Thank you, no.' Lohmann sat, facing the sergeant.

'Keeps me going, a mug of hot tea. What can I do for you?'

'The reports on Beth Coverley's death. I would like to see them.'

'Oh, yes, that.' He shuffled through some papers on his desk, and selected one. 'There! Had it copied for you. Medical report. Don't see what good it'll do you.'

Lohmann took the sheet of paper. 'And the officer's report? The one who found the body?'

'That one. It just said what Ordish said at the inquest.'

'I would still like to see it.'

Brundage grinned. His teeth were discoloured. 'So would I. Again. Saw it of course. But we can't seem to lay our hands on it just now.'

'Isn't that unusual?'

'Ah, well, so much crime in this patch. So many reports. The Yids, you know. No respect for the law. I hear you met Jack Comer. Also known as Jack Spot. Don't ask me how I know. We keep an eye on everybody. Right villain is Comer. "*King of the Underworld*", they call him.'

'I've always found the Jews very law-abiding,' Lohmann said.

'Ah, but that's in Berlin. See, the government there is pretty strict about them. So I hear. But in this country, we're too bloody lax about that type.'

'What type is that, Sergeant?'

'Oh, the alien corn, you could call them.'

Lohmann reverted to his original theme. 'About Constable Ordish's report . . .'

'Oh, if we don't find it, I'll get him to write it up again. And give you a copy when he does.'

'Of course, this time, you'll make sure it corresponds with what he said at the inquest.'

Another grin, another view of the discoloured teeth. 'As did his original report. You would think otherwise?'

'I would like to have seen the original,' Lohmann said, rising to his feet.

'Well, you'll just have to make do, won't you?'

'I shall have to.'

'You'll find the medical report the same as the bloke testified to in court.'

'It wasn't the medical report I was interested in.'

Brundage rose, the smile still set on his face. 'I don't know why you bother. A Jewish girl throws herself into the Thames. That's it. Some around here would wish a few more of them would do the same.'

'You are one of those, Sergeant Brundage?' Lohmann asked with assumed innocence.

The smile vanished. 'I do my job. Fairly. I don't have to like villains.'

'Or Jews?'

'I didn't say that.'

'You didn't have to.'

Lohmann left the police station. As he went out he brushed against a man going in. The face was familiar. He'd seen it once before at the inquest. A round, bland face, with a scar ravaging one cheek. Not a policeman, Lohmann felt sure. He could always recognise policemen.

But who was he? A man who went to inquests on strangers. There was a peculiar hobby. Some time soon, Lohmann made a mental note, he must find out who the man with the scar was. And why he was so interested in a dead woman.

EIGHT

Jack Comer said: 'There's going to be trouble.'

Lohmann, who had arranged to meet him in a pub on the Commercial Road that evening, waved over to a large blonde barmaid.

'A light ale for me, please. And for Mister Comer . . . ?'

'A pint. And put it on my slate. You don't pay for drinks in my territory, Lohmann.' He grinned. 'For that matter, neither do I.'

'And he means it, love,' said the barmaid moving away towards the long, polished brown bar. 'King of the castle, him! The Elephant and Castle.'

'Tell me about this trouble, Mister Comer,' Lohmann said.

'Call me Jack. Everybody does. Even the law. Excepting that bastard anti-Semite, Brundage. He should call me Mister, always.'

'Very well, tell me about the trouble, Jack.'

'October the fourth. The Blackshirts march in the East End. Starting at the Royal Mint, the bastards will come up Cable Street. Led by the bloody grand panjandrum hisself. Sir Oswald bloody Mosley.'

'Can it not be stopped?'

'Oh, we'll stop it all right,' said Comer. 'We'll have the boys on the streets to stop it. The Reds, some of the Labour people and my lot.'

'But it is a provocation,' Lohmann said. 'Surely the police will not permit it?'

'An' have Sir Oswald screaming about being deprived of the right of free speech? No, they won't stop him. Anyway he's got mates up there in high places. But we'll stop him.'

'How?'

'You wait and see. The barricades'll be up in Cable Street. I can tell you that.'

The barmaid put the drinks in front of them, winked for no apparent reason at Lohmann, and went back to the bar.

'She fancies you, that one,' Comer said. 'You're on, if you fancy it.'

'Perhaps on another occasion,' Lohmann said carefully, being aware that he must not cause offence.

'That's the real danger,' Comer went on. 'Mosley's mates in high places. The boys who wouldn't ever be seen marching with the Blackshirts. But they'd kiss Hitler's arse in private, given half a chance.'

'You think the Blackshirts were behind the killing of Beth Coverley?' Lohmann said.

'Not directly. Not officially. They rough up people, sure, but they haven't got around to killing anybody yet. Wouldn't be good for them.'

'It has happened in Germany.'

'Well, it would, wouldn't it. Practically legal to kill Jews in Germany. Mind you, wouldn't put it past some of his bully boys. But with Kovel's daughter, there was more to it than that. Word is, they stopped her because she was on to something that somebody didn't want her to be on to.'

Lohmann sipped his ale. 'You wouldn't know what that might be?'

Comer smiled. 'I wouldn't know what that might be. And you can bet they don't like anybody digging into whatever it is. Which is why they tried to kill you.'

'You know about that?'

'I heard. Things get around. That Rowley, I knew him. A professional. Killed people for money. Maybe for fun. He's no loss. That one wouldn't take a dive off a high building for fun. Tried to push you, that was the word.'

Lohmann was surprised. And shouldn't have been. In Berlin, it had been like this. Something happened, the underworld knew about it before anyone else. An underworld grapevine ran through the city. It had to be the same in London.

'Charlie Newton saved you. Also the word,' said Comer. 'Detective Sergeant Newton. Lucky he was there, following you. I wonder why though. Also I wouldn't put your trust in

Newton. Special Branch. It suited him to save you today. Tomorrow he might be the one to push you. Depends on his orders. You see, Lohmann, nothing is what is seems, when it comes to this kind of politics. And this is the real kind. Where people get killed. Now wasn't it the same in Germany?'

It was the same in Germany, Lohmann knew.

Comer went on. 'The Mosley characters are bad enough. It's the big boys who keep hidden that are worse. You got to keep an eye open for them. But look, October the fourth, Cable Street's not going to be too healthy. I tried to get old Kovel to move out for a few days. But he won't budge. The Cossacks didn't budge him when he was a kid and no bloody Fascist's going to move that old man today. I'll be keeping my two boys there to keep an eye on him. But things can get hairy. Would you be there to help out?'

'I will be there,' Lohmann said.

'Good. Wiv you there and my two boys, the old man should be okay.' Comer glanced at the gold watch on his wrist, and then drained his pint. 'Time I was somewhere else. Got to keep the business going.'

He said nothing of what the business was.

'One thing you can perhaps help me with, Mister Comer . . . Jack. When I was coming from the Leman Street police station, another man was going in. I saw him at the inquest also. About thirty, a round face with a scar on his cheek. Would you know who he is?'

Comer nodded. 'I know who it sounds like. Going into the police station, eh? Probably going to see his pal, Brundage. See, we think Brundage is one of Mosley's lot. But he can't admit it. His bosses in the Force wouldn't like it.'

'But the man with the scar . . .'

'Sounds like Billy Joyce. William Joyce. Says he's Irish. Or American. They'd be welcome to him. Calls himself Mosley's director of propaganda. Nasty bit of work. We gave him a sore head a couple of months ago at one of Mosley's outdoor meetings. Wiv a brick. Yeah, he'd be a mate of Brundage's.'

'Why would he be at the inquest?'

'Now you got me. Wouldn't know that. He's a devious piece of *dreck*, that one.'

Outside the pub, Comer looked Lohmann up and down and gave him a wide grin. 'Funny,' he said. 'If this was Berlin and you was in your old job, you'd be trying to nick me.'

'Very possibly,' Lohmann replied.

'You wouldn't have a chance.'

'I wouldn't be too sure, Jack.' Lohmann returned the grin.

'Just remember, Lohmann,' said Comer. 'They tried to kill you once. They won't give up after just one try.'

They parted, Lohmann walking west. Again with the feeling that he was being followed. But if he was, no one bothered him further. But, when he arrived home at the bedsitter, before going to bed, he reached into the bottom of one of the two suitcases he'd brought with him from Germany, ripped the lining from the bottom of the case, and, beneath it, stared at his old Mauser pistol. It had been issued some years ago from the armoury of the Berlin Kriminal Police Department. It fitted neatly into the specially enlarged, inside pocket of the leather jacket he had also brought from Berlin. From now on he would wear that jacket.

He slept peacefully for the rest of the night.

The next morning Lohmann drove into Kent and to Chartwell, the home of Winston Churchill. He had telephoned before he left Museum Street, explaining to a rather arrogant young man at the end of the line that Miss Coverley was unable to keep her appointment and that he was coming in her place. The young man departed to ascertain as to whether this was acceptable, returning quickly to inform him that he would be expected at eleven-thirty in the morning. Lohmann did not go into details of why Beth Coverley could not keep her appointment. Time enough for that when he met Churchill.

All morning a damp sun had been struggling to break through the cloud and, as Lohmann drove up the driveway to the house, it finally succeeded. The lawn was bathed in yellow light, reflecting on the multi-coloured autumn leaves fallen from the trees. Lohmann parked his car and, getting out, rang the doorbell. A maid in apron and cap ushered him into a large comfortable sitting-room where he was greeted by a tall woman with fine features and prematurely greying hair.

'I'm Clementine Churchill, Mister Lohmann,' she said, shaking hands. 'You'll find Winston waiting for you at the foot of the garden.'

She showed him through french windows, excusing herself and leaving him to walk down the lawn. The only person he could see at the foot of the garden was a plump figure in dungarees, laying bricks on a half-finished wall. Lohmann looked around for someone resembling a politician.

'You are looking at him, Herr Lohmann.' The figure in dungarees laid down a trowel and turned to face the German.

The head was round and bald, framed by a small fringe of hair. The features were cherubic, reminding Lohmann of the first sight he had of his daughter after she was born. The plump hands clutching the trowel were begrimed with wet cement.

'You look surprised, sir,' said Churchill. 'No need. I'm building a wall. And I have a union card which permits me to practise the craft of brick-laying. It is an admirable pursuit for a rejected politician. Most constructive.'

He laid down his trowel, wiped his hands on the sides of his dungarees and, coming over to Lohmann, shook hands . . . a firm handshake from such soft hands . . . and escorted him to two garden chairs at each side of a metal table.

'Do sit, sir. I must confess to be disappointed Miss Coverley did not see fit to come. I met her once before in the House when we talked. I should have thought she would be anxious to follow up our most enlightening conversation. *And* she is definitely prettier than you, sir.'

'I'm sure she would have been most anxious to keep her appointment with you,' Lohmann replied. 'Unfortunately she's dead.'

The head came up, there was a trembling of jowled chins and the eyes stared at Lohmann coldly.

'I'm sorry. Tell me about it.'

Lohmann told him. Everything. Even the attempt on his own life. The rejected politician listened with a deepening scowl.

When Lohmann had finished, he produced a large cigar, bit the end from it and lit up.

'The British,' he said, meditatively, 'rarely go in for political

94

assassination. Except *in extremis*. Oh, we did dispose of one Prime Minister, a nonentity called Spencer Perceval, but that was the solitary act of a lunatic. When we do utilise assassination of anyone it is an act of desperation. Like the execution of Charles the First.'

He paused, staring into the middle distance. Lohmann said nothing, waiting.

'All this would undoubtedly indicate that, whatever Miss Coverley knew, it was of considerable import to some individuals. Her killing was indeed an act of desperation.'

'You agree it was not suicide?'

'I would not think the lady was suicidally inclined. But the verdict would indicate that the police in the East End preferred such a verdict. That is one of the weak points on which pressure must be brought to bear. The police in . . . in . . . ?'

'Leman Street.'

'Exactly.' He took a puff from his cigar and looked up at Lohmann, a piercing look.

'You say you are a refugee, Herr Lohmann. My study of the Nazi regime would indicate they are not above subtle subterfuges. You could be an agent of that regime, posing as a refugee. Pray excuse my stating the obvious, but all factors must be considered.'

Lohmann flushed, a rarity for him. 'You are of course right. It would be a possibility. But it is not so. How can I prove it to you? I have no way of doing that . . Unless you have access to the files of the Security Service of the SS. Or the Geheime Staatspolizei.'

The scowl disappeared from Churchill's face. He smiled, the plump cheeks rearranging themselves. 'You're an honest man, sir. I have an uncomfortable admiration for German efficiency. I'm sure, if you were a Nazi agent, you would have been provided with some substantial proof of your refugee status. You have none. Ergo you are genuine. You will lunch with me?'

'I should be pleased to. I would like to know more about your previous meeting with Beth Coverley.'

'And I would like to know more about Herr Hitler's Third Reich.'

Mrs Churchill supervised the lunch but excused herself from joining them. She had other matters to attend to in the nearby village. Churchill changed from his dungarees to a smoking-jacket and presided over the table. They were joined by the arrogant voice Lohmann had heard on the telephone who turned out to be Churchill's son, Randolph.

Over some excellent, if underdone beef, Churchill opened his inquisition on Germany.

'You have met Herr Hitler?'

'Once.'

'I made the mistake, Herr Lohmann, of greeting the coming to power of Mussolini. It was, I now freely admit, ill-advised. I have not made the same mistake with Hitler.'

'They say Mussolini made the Italian trains run on time,' said Randolph Churchill.

'Not exactly a major historical achievement. Although it might be considered so in Italy,' his father went on. 'I believe he did it by threatening to shoot the drivers who were late. I hardly think such methods would find favour in this country with the National Union of Railway Employees. However, I would be loath to make the same mistake over Hitler. Your impressions of the man, Herr Lohmann?'

'He is, on first sight, not impressive. But he is a clever orator. Also he is . . . a fanatic. That would be the right word? And uses murder as a political weapon.'

Randolph Churchill frowned. 'Isn't that a little strong?'

'His massacre of the Brownshirts without compunction . . . of his own supporters . . . is the first example.'

'Why should he massacre his own people?' the young man said.

'It was necessary to obtain the support of the Army and its General Staff. The Junkers hated the Brownshirts. They were a threat, as an alternative armed force. The army was more important to Hitler than Rohm's people. So the Brownshirts were smashed. Also his persecution of the Jews, many of whom have been murdered.'

'The Lord knows why,' said Winston Churchill. 'Some of the best brains in Germany are Jewish. He is surely lopping off his nose to spite his face. But then it is a dangerous, if effective, political move to pick on a minority.'

'It's more than that,' Lohmann replied. 'He has a hatred of the Jewish people which borders on insanity. The pogroms in Germany will get worse. As will his ambitions.'

Churchill nodded. 'Unfortunately you confirm my fears. He has expansionistic designs which would seriously upset the balance of power in Europe. Sadly we still have to deal with this man. One way or another.'

'There will only be one way in the end,' Lohmann said.

'I fear you may be right,' said the elder Churchill. 'He is already exercising a pernicious influence, even here. Von Hoesch, the previous German ambassador, went out of his way to befriend the King when he was Prince of Wales. Now I am known to be a King's man, especially if the present crisis over the American lady comes to a head. Nonetheless the King has made several ill-advised remarks expressing sympathy for Hitler's government. I would wish he had refrained from doing so. It will give Hitler the impression the King is an ally of Nazism.'

His words induced a short silence. It was time now, Lohmann felt, to turn to the subject that had brought him to Chartwell.

'You had a meeting with Miss Coverley previously, Mister Churchill. May I ask you what was discussed?'

'The young lady sought an interview with me in the House. We had tea on the terrace.' Churchill's eyes suddenly misted. 'A pleasing and clever young woman. Perhaps inclined to support the Labour Party, but intelligent nevertheless. I suppose she came to me because of my expressed opposition to the dictators. She had, it appeared, discovered some evidence of moneys being poured into Oswald Mosley's Fascists by the government of Italy.'

'Mussolini was financing the Blackshirts?'

'My dear man, it was no secret in Westminster. Oh, Oswald denied it, but then he would do so. I think Claud Cockburn in his little newsletter had already brought up the subject. But it had not appeared in the popular press. Probably because Lord Rothermere and some of his friends were prone to support Mosley.' Churchill shook his head wearily, pink cheeks trembling. 'Poor Oswald. Might have been a useful man, but he has ideas above his abilities.'

'They say the same about you,' Randolph said, an impudent look on his face.

Churchill scowled. 'I, on the other hand, have abilities beyond even my own expectations. And sadly, it would appear, not to be utilised.'

He crumbled a breadroll in his right hand and turned back to Lohmann. 'Where was I? Ah, yes, Miss Coverley. That day we discussed the funding of Mosley by the Italians. I informed her that she should write her story, provided she had the actual proof of such payments being made. Despite the fact that the thing is common knowledge, if she didn't have the proof she would be leaving herself . . . and her newspaper . . . open to a libel suit. When she left me, she said she believed she could prove her story. Had contacts in the Treasury who could possibly be aware of the moving of large sums of money from Italy to this country.'

'But how could she prove it, if it was brought in in cash by a courier?'

'Oh, it can be done. If it were brought in in pounds sterling then doubtless the Treasury might be aware of such sums being assembled in Italy. If brought in in *lire*, then it would have to be lodged and changed to pounds sterling through a bank in this country. I know banking transactions are meant to be confidential but the Treasury keep a weather eye on such large flows of money. Ably, if perniciously assisted by the Inland Revenue. Her contact in the Treasury might provide such information.'

'Are not your civil servants sworn to confidentiality?'

'Indeed they are. Under the Official Secrets Act. But there are two kinds of men who might well ignore such obligations. One, the more dangerous, might feel it is in the country's best interests to provide such information to the Press. The other . . . pernicious, but with a less worthy motive . . . payment . . . might not hesitate if the financial rewards were worthwhile. Sadly many of our middle-rank civil servants are underpaid.'

Lohmann stared disconsolately at the fragments of roast beef left on his plate.

'If Mosley is being financed by the Italians, then there would seem little motivation in killing Beth Coverley to hide something already known in . . . in official circles.'

'Oh, I agree, I agree. But there was something else. When Miss Coverley telephoned me to make this appointment, she informed me that, during the course of her investigations, she had stumbled . . . yes, stumbled, her own word . . . across something else.'

The old politician left the words hanging in the air, indulging himself in a long pregnant pause.

Lohmann felt bound to break the silence. 'Something else?' he echoed Churchill's words. 'Did she tell what this was?'

'Alas, no. That was to be the purpose of our meeting today. She paid me the compliment of believing I could advise . . . even assist her. She laid stress on my abhorrence of the Nazi regime and I can only conclude that there was yet another connection there with the evils of National Socialism.'

Again Churchill fell silent for a moment, distinctly rheumy eyes contemplating the almost empty glass of burgundy at the side of his plate.

Finally he broke his own self-imposed silence. 'It would appear to be left to you, Herr Lohmann, to ascertain what she had discovered. We can only presume at its import although it was obviously of sufficient weight to lead to her ghastly slaughter by those involved. And . . . and, when they learnt you were investigating her death, it was of such weight that they considered it worthwhile to attempt to remove you from the scene. Permanently.'

He looked directly at Lohmann now, with what might be interpreted as a benevolent expression.

'You realise you are still under threat?'

'It was pointed out to me, last night, Mister Churchill, by an East End man with the reputation in other areas of being an important criminal.'

Churchill laughed, a great booming sound. 'Then, sir, you have so been warned by two great criminals. My political opponents would, no doubt, put me in a similar category to your East End friend.'

He became serious again. 'You have a dangerous task to

perform, Lohmann. I wish you good fortune and any assistance or advice I can give you. I should be pleased to hear of the outcome of your endeavours.'

Randolph Churchill now leaned forward. 'I'd be interested in going along with you. Helping you in any way I can.'

'An offer,' Churchill said, 'which I urge you to refuse. My son has many talents and his heart is in the right place, but he has a tendency to imitate the proverbial bull in the shop full of delicate crockery. Your task, Lohmann, will only succeed if it is done quietly and with great stealth. Randolph would almost certainly create such attention as to ensure both of you fall from high buildings or meet with some other dreadful fatality.'

Randolph scowled but said no more.

Over coffee and brandy, the latter of which Lohmann refused, Churchill turned again to the subject of Germany.

'In the event of Hitler being displaced, would a more tolerant successor be found? Rudolf Hess, the Deputy Führer, or whoever?'

'Hess is Hitler's man,' Lohmann replied. 'And as such has no real power. If Hitler went, then there would inevitably be a struggle between Goering and Himmler. I think Himmler would win and the regime would continue with ever increasing horrors.'

'What of the younger men? Or the army?'

Lohmann could barely repress a shudder. Memory was a powerful stimulant to emotion. 'Of the younger men, there is Reinhard Heydrich. I . . . I encountered him. He is as evil as Hitler. As to the army, they will go along with Hitler as long as he is strong and successful. He reoccupied the Saar and the Rhineland, probably against the advice of the High Command. And your Western governments allowed him to do so. He was right that the West would do nothing. They will respect him for that.'

Churchill sighed. 'And there is no other effective opposition?'

'If there was, they now reside in Dachau Concentration Camp.'

Churchill looked increasingly mournful. He rose from the table.

'It has been good to meet you, Herr Lohmann, although I

100

cannot say that what you have honestly told me fills me with anything but dire forebodings. If you will excuse me now, at my age I have become accustomed to a post-prandial nap. As I've said, I shall look forward to hearing the results of your enquiries. And wish you God speed in safely obtaining such results. Randolph will walk you to your automobile.'

Lohmann shook hands with him, and followed the younger Churchill to the car.

'Never mind what my father says, Mister Lohmann. If I can be of help, call on me,' Randolph said with enough exuberance to prove his father's point.

Lohmann steered the Morris down the driveway and onto the road.

Some five minutes later, he was driving along a particularly narrow lane when a large pantechnicon pulled out of a field blocking the road in front of him. He braked, bringing the Morris to a halt.

And then, felt a once accustomed sensation, a chill running down his spine. It was an old warning, an anticipation of danger threatening.

Alert, he waited.

NINE

Two men jumped from the driving cabin of the pantechnicon. They were large men and they moved with deliberation towards the Morris. Lohmann glanced in his rear-view mirror, prepared to back the car away from them. But, as he did so another car, a large Austin, appeared and drew to a halt some twenty yards behind, effectively blocking any escape to the rear. He could make out two other figures in the front of the Austin. One of them, the driver, opened the door and stepped onto the road. His companion in the passenger seat remained, staring from the window as the driver strolled in a leisurely way towards Lohmann's Morris.

Lohmann thought, three to one, with another in reserve . . . not exactly satisfactory odds. The man who remained in the Austin was presumably the man in charge, leaving the activity to his minions. Lohmann found his hands, resting loosely on the steering wheel of his car, were trembling, the palms sweating. God, what he wouldn't he give to have Reiner, his old sergeant, beside him. He had no doubt he had been neatly ambushed. But to what purpose? A simple beating-up, or did they intend to kill him? The latter, probably. Making up for Rowley's failure to throw him off the roof of the building in Fleet Street. It had been quite a time since he'd been in a position like this. Ten years at least. In Hamburg, when he himself was still a sergeant. The intention then had been to beat him senseless and throw him in a nearby canal. He had taken some punishment but, on that occasion, a patrolling policeman had come to his rescue. It was doubtful if there would be a patrolling policeman in a country lane in Kent.

He needed an edge.

The engine of the Morris was still running.

The first of the men, the driver of the pantechnicon, came up to the side of the car. He indicated that Lohmann should lower his side window. Lohmann lowered it two inches.

'You want something?' he said.

'Get out of the car,' the man replied. 'We want you, Kraut!'

There was no doubt now that Lohmann was the target. He glanced in his rearview mirror. The man from the Austin was approaching at an unhurried pace, a laconic grin on his face. They obviously believed they had all the time in the world in which to take care of the ex-policeman. They were right. If they could *take care* of him.

Lohmann switched the gear-lever into reverse, took his foot from the foot-brake, and slammed it down on the accelerator.

The Morris shot backwards at speed, Lohmann steering for his target.

By the time it covered what was now about fifteen yards to the man from the Austin, Lohmann estimated he had reached over twenty miles an hour. Fast enough. The man from the

Austin suddenly realised what was happening and tried to jump aside. But Lohmann was an expert behind the wheel of a car, even driving in reverse. The rear metal bumpers of the Morris struck the oncomer on the shins of both legs, right on the bone. Even above the roar of the engine, Lohmann heard the man scream and felt the thud of contact. The man fell, disappearing from view. As he did so, Lohmann rammed his foot down on the brake. The Morris came to an abrupt halt.

Lohmann knew with certainty that he had broken both the man's legs. The scream dropped to a wailing sound just audible above the engine.

He turned his attention to the two men in front of him, now slipping the gear-lever into first gear. And putting his foot again on the accelerator. The Morris leaped forward.

It was too much to hope that he could achieve the same result with these two. They had seen what happened to their accomplice from the Austin. The men jumped, one to each side of the lane. A small embankment on the right led up to a hedge. To the left, there was no embankment but a hedge separated the lane from a field. A man could force his body through that hedge.

Lohmann swung the Morris to the right. The man who had addressed him at the car window was in trouble. The embankment was slippery, the grass damp with the recent rain and the man was large and ungainly. He stumbled trying to reach the hedge some feet above him. His feet slipped and slithered on wet grass and mud and he went down on his back, sliding towards the approaching vehicle.

For the second time, the Morris struck a human body. But the incline of the embankment and the softness of the soil lessened the force of the impact. Certainly air was knocked from the man's lungs. The wheels of the car sank into the mud pinning him effectively to the ground, the lower half of his body under the car. His arms flailed helplessly.

Lohmann tried to reverse the car from the embankment but the wheels spun uselessly, driving the car and the man pinned under it deeper into the mud.

At least, Lohmann determined, he had cut the odds in half. He opened the door and stepped onto the road. As he did so he reached into his inside pocket and felt the cold comfort of the metal butt of the Mauser pistol. He surveyed the scene.

The man on the other side of the lane was back against the hedge, glaring at him. In the centre of the lane, some ten yards away, the driver of the Austin lay on his back on the road, the lower half of his left leg at a strange angle. He was semiconscious and whimpering. Lohmann felt momentary nausea. He had done what he had to do but he did not feel happy about it. He had committed so much necessary violence but, deep down, it sickened him. Even the claim to himself that it had been done in his own defence never really appeased the deeper feelings of revulsion. He had told himself when he came out of Germany that maybe, just maybe, he was done with violence. It was not so. Would it ever be so?

The passenger in the Austin had made no attempt to move but sat, staring out through the windscreen, the face a white blur.

Lohmann turned back to the immediate threat, the man on the other side of the lane. Now that Lohmann was out of the car and on the lane, the man seemed to think he had an advantage. He was large, with the body of a wrestler. Lohmann's slim, five foot ten figure, inclined to look awkward and shambling, would seem to present no physical threat. The man moved from the hedge, towards him.

For a moment, Lohmann was puzzled. He expected the wrestling type to produce some kind of weapon, a revolver or pistol. But there was nothing. Simply large hands, clenching and unclenching. Of course, he realised, they would not want to shoot him. A bullet would ensure a murder verdict and an investigation. Almost certainly the intention would have been for him to be found in some position that would indicate accidental death. Certainly not another suicide . . . they already used that with Beth Coverley. And too many people knew he was investigating her death. No, the intention had to be the creation of an accident. They might have just got away with that. They had omitted to take into consideration the lethal potential of a bull-nosed Morris with Lohmann behind the wheel.

The man had reached the middle of the lane, his face

expressionless as he approached. Despite the lack of expression, there was no doubt of his intention.

Reluctantly Lohmann took the Mauser from his inside pocket, and shot the man in the right kneecap. And again felt nauseous.

Another scream, this time short and shrill, and the man went down, eyes rolling upwards. Disabled but not dead, Lohmann told himself.

They had obviously not expected him to be armed. No longer a policeman but a refugee, he was in a country where few carried arms. The Mauser had been an unpleasant surprise.

He turned now and walked, Mauser still in hand, towards the Austin and the white face behind the windscreen. But before he reached the car, the passenger stepped into the road, hands in the air.

He was a young man in his middle twenties, broad-shouldered and stocky. Surprisingly he was smiling, almost relaxed despite the pale features.

'We should have known,' he said, speaking, to Lohmann's surprise, in German. 'But we did not expect the gun. Or indeed your ability behind the wheel of a car.'

Then Lohmann realised the face was familiar. A young face, but in memory it had been even younger.

'I know you,' Lohmann said.

'We met once or twice, I think,' the man replied, straightened up and almost clicked his heels. 'In Berlin. At some official function. Captain Walter Schellenberg, of the *Sicherheitsdienst*. Paying you a visit on behalf of General Reinhard Heydrich who sends his compliments.'

'I thought his compliments would have come in the form of a bullet,' Lohmann said, keeping the Mauser steadily pointed at Schellenberg's chest.

The man smiled. 'He might have preferred it so. But then it is not, I believe, done in this country.'

'That is what this is all about? Heydrich's revenge, so to speak?'

'You surely don't think the General would be so concerned about you, Lohmann? You are nothing now. Except that our

British friends informed us you were interfering in matters that should not concern you. The General sent me over as an observer, purely. Of course I did not realise the incompetence of the English in such matters as this. Had we been in Germany, we would have carried weapons, shot you, and the body would never have been found. But here . . . ah, here, they insisted they had to create an accident.'

The smile was almost disarming, but Lohmann's hand did not relax on the Mauser.

'So!' said Schellenberg. 'You have disposed temporarily of my English companions, what do you intend to do with me?'

'Nothing. Unless you intend to try and finish what your . . . English companions started.'

'I only obey orders,' Schellenberg replied. 'My orders are merely to observe, to study. Of course, now that you've surfaced, Lohmann, it may be that Heydrich will have other ideas. He is, as you know, a man overflowing with ideas and innovations. But careful when making decisions. Until he does make a decision, I suppose all I can do is assist these poor fellows to a surgeon and see that their wounds are attended to. Of course they could doubtless inform their police and have you charged with assault with a deadly weapon. Such precise clichés the English have.'

'You could do that. It would result in a comprehensive investigation. Which your friends might not welcome. Especially as they almost certainly have criminal records.'

'And you . . . you have friends in high places, I understand.'

Lohmann shrugged. 'I have friends. I think you should take your companions to a surgeon and see their wounds are treated. And tell *their* friends I'm getting tired of these attempts on my life . . .'

'One of them might succeed.'

'That's what I'm getting tired of.'

Lohmann stepped up to Schellenberg and ran his hands over the man. He was not armed.

'Satisfied?' said Schellenberg.

'I wouldn't want to be shot in the back.'

'I assure you, Herr Lohmann, if I was contemplating

shooting you, you would be shot in the chest. Unless shooting in the back was expedient.'

Lohmann went back to his car, leaving Schellenberg standing in the middle of the road. The Mauser still in his hand, he inspected the mud round the front wheels of the Morris, ignoring the man pinned by his chest under the car who glared at him with with undisguised fury. Lohmann opened the door of his car, released the handbrake and moved around to the front of the car.

'I'm going to push the car out of the mud,' he informed the pinned man. 'If I were you I would breathe in. Otherwise you may have a few ribs broken.'

Still glaring, the man breathed in, pushing his body as far into the soft ground as he could. Lohmann put his shoulder to the bonnet of the car and, with some effort, exerted all his weight on the car. Slowly it slid backwards onto the road. As it did so, the recumbent assailant groaned loudly. Once the car was on the road, the man slowly pulled himself to a sitting position.

'Am I going to have trouble with you?' Lohmann asked.

'No . . . no . . .'

With a nod of satisfaction Lohmann climbed into his car and switched on the ignition. The engine spluttered to life. He backed the car for some yards, switched to first gear and drove off.

Leaving, it occurred to him, a minor battlefield behind him. His hands, on the wheel, started to tremble.

He drove towards London. Thinking of the nausea he had felt at the knee-capping and the breaking of the other man's legs. Was he indulging in a kind of hypocrisy? Soul-searching was something new for him. As a police officer he had tried to do his job with the minimum of violence necessary; and afterwards had avoided dwelling on such violence. He had never enjoyed it but never shirked from it. But was there now an excitement in the need to exercise it, even in self-defence? Was he forgetting he was no longer Inspector Lohmann of the Criminal Police but a private citizen? Not even a citizen, an alien in a strange land.

He did not like the excitement.

*

107

It was mid-afternoon when he arrived back at Museum Street. Time to consider his next move. He climbed the narrow stairway to his bedsitter, an aftertaste of Churchill's red wine in his mouth. He felt, no sense of triumph over his assailants, but only a deep exhaustion. As he reached the door of the bedsitter, Norman called something to him from three storeys below.

He leaned over the balustrade wearily.

'What is it?'

'You got a visitor.'

Behind him his door was opened from the inside. He reached for the butt of the Mauser as he turned.

Rue Scott-ffoliot was standing in the doorway.

'You do look fierce,' she said.

He let the Mauser slide back into his pocket. 'What are you doing here? And how did you find my address?'

'You gave me your phone number. I simply phoned and spoke to the caretaker. Such an impressionable boy, Norman. Gave me the address at once and, when I arrived, let me come into your room to wait for you. Actually I think Norman's in love with me. I shall have to tell him it's hopeless. He could never keep me in the style to which I'm accustomed.'

Lohmann ushered her back into the room and closed the door behind them.

'Mind you,' she went on, contemplating the tiny room, 'I'm not sure that you could keep me in the style to which I'm accustomed. It's a very small room.'

'Please sit down,' he said. 'Can I offer you some tea?'

She ignored the one armchair and sat on the bed.

'You've nothing stronger?' she asked.

'I have tea, coffee, and a bottle of beer. I intend to make tea.'

'Then I shall have tea.'

He filled the kettle and, lighting one of the gas-rings, put the kettle on the ring.

'Why have you come here?'

She pouted. 'That's not very civil. Why have I come here? Because you are a new friend, perhaps.'

He forced a smile. 'I am a foreigner and therefore, in English eyes, not to be trusted.'

108

'Oh, but I'm more Scots than English. And we Scots are very trusting. Also I have done something for you.'

'And what is that?'

'I have been invited to a reception at the German Embassy. Miss Scott-ffoliot and partner. You will be my partner.'

Surprised, he stared at her.

'Well, you wanted to meet von Ribbentrop. He was on Beth's list, wasn't he?'

'Yes, he was.' He thought for a moment. 'Yes, it might be an opportunity to get to him. Not that I'll be very welcome.'

'Oh, they have to make you welcome. You'll be my escort.'

'I shall be on German territory.'

She frowned. 'Yes, you will. Is that bad?'

'The German government does not exactly approve of me. Still, it's a chance I may have to take.'

'They don't have to know who you are. You could be my Austrian cousin. Oh, I have one. Franz Haller. You will be Franz Haller when announced. Have you a dinner jacket?'

'I *had* a dinner jacket. I left it in Berlin.'

'Never mind. There's always Moss Brothers.'

He looked puzzled.

'They hire them,' she explained. 'Of course you could be my Scottish cousin and come in full Highland regalia. Kilt and everything.'

'I shall be your Austrian cousin.' He smiled now, genuinely amused. For the first time since he'd left Chartwell, he felt relaxed. He poured the boiling water into the teapot and put in three teaspoonfuls of tea.

'There you are then,' she said. 'You see how useful I am to you.'

'I see. Thank you.'

'I shall also make it possible for you to meet the Prime Minister.'

'Thank you again. But when I am ready. When I can ask the right questions.'

She leaned forward. Her lipstick, discreetly applied, shone on her lower lip, reflecting the light from the window. She was dressed in a simple wool sweater, skirt and a single strand of pearls. The young woman about town. Except that she was hatless.

'What are the right questions, Lohmann?' she asked.

'I wish I knew.'

He poured two cups of tea, handed her one cup and sat in the armchair facing her.

'You've no idea what this is all about?'

'The story she was working on. It was obviously upsetting some people. So much, that she was killed. So far, that is all I know.'

'I thought you detectives knew everything. Like Sherlock Holmes. Pure deduction.'

'If it were so easy. Detective work is a slow process of asking questions, assessing answers. Ninety-nine times in a hundred it is routine and very dull.'

'And the other one time?' she asked.

'Anything. Someone perhaps trying to kill you. Oh, the other one time is very unpleasant.'

She leant back on the small bed, sipping tea.

'Exciting. The one time,' she said.

'No,' he replied, feeling suddenly awkward and clumsy in the presence of this strange young woman. Strange in so far as he had never before encountered anyone quite like her. The English . . . or the Scots, as she insisted . . . were different. Not like Europeans. Cosmopolitan and yet naive. Sophisticated yet simple.

'Anyway,' she said. 'I find you a very exciting man.'

The awkwardness increased. 'I am quite ordinary,' he said. 'A retired policeman. Forced out of retirement for a short while. That is all.'

She shook her head. 'Oh, no, more than that. Hidden depths and all that kind of rot. I like it.'

He gulped his tea. 'When you have finished your tea, I will call you a taxi.'

'Why?' she said. 'I don't have to be anywhere.'

'I . . . I have work to do.'

'Not for the rest of the afternoon, surely,' she said.

He wished Sergeant Reiner had been there. Reiner was a movie fan and would have instantly recognised in Rue Scott-

110

ffoliot one of the many Hollywood ladies he often talked about. Theda Bara . . . no, that was the silent cinema and Rue could not be compared to anyone mute. Mae West . . . that was closer, although Rue was neither blonde or as buxom as that lady. More like a London stage actress he'd seen on one of his rare visits to the theatre. Gertrude Lawrence, in full flood.

He laughed aloud, which slightly disconcerted her. The frown flitted across her face briefly and then she rose, stepped forward, leaned down towards him and kissed him. It silenced his laughter. He found himself responding to the kiss. He put his arms around her waist and brought her down towards him.

He had been celibate for over a year. Before that, there had been a woman in Paris, the kind the French referred to as a *demi-mondaine*, the former mistress of a minor politician who had recently been killed. There had been some question about whether or not he had been murdered by his mistress. Lohmann had proved it to be otherwise. A brief affair had followed, on the woman's part out of gratitude as well as physical attraction. Lohmann had known it could not last; her life was inevitably tied to economic considerations. These, he was in no position to satisfy. They had parted as friends and he had come to London.

Now he found himself alone with Rue Scott-ffoliot who made no secret of her interest.

They made love on Lohmann's single bed as the autumn afternoon died outside the window. It wasn't a soft considerate act but rather a frantic, wild affair. Clothes were discarded quickly and they were together moving roughly against each other. On Lohmann's part, he told himself later, there was a kind of desperation in the act, a pent-up release of physical passion. On her part there was an animal quality, a wildness in her every move. She bit him, scratched him, moaning and writhing. When he entered her, she almost screamed. And then strangely, after they came together, she wept, tears spilling onto his shoulder.

After some moments, she sat up, wiped her face with the back of her hand, looked down at him, and said, as she might have said '*Pass the sugar*', 'time I was going, I'm being taken to the theatre.'

111

She dressed quickly. Talking all the time, about anything but the thing that had just occurred.

'I do love the theatre, don't you? Noël Coward's an old friend, you know. A nice man even if he is queer. I love going out with him. After all, every girl must have a good fairy in her life at some time or other.'

It was his turn to dress. While she stood at his mirror renovating her make-up. And still talking.

'I'm not going to the theatre with Noël this time. No, it's the Duke of Ayr's son . . . what's his name? Geoffrey Forbes-Douglas. He's in the Guards, you know . . .'

'I don't know,' Lohmann said, finding the momentary break in her chatter; wondering to himself whether this was indeed the woman he had just made love to. Passion and wildness had become sudden frivolity.

She went on: 'Don't know what he's taking me to see. But still he is . . . taking me, I mean. Then to supper. Do you like oysters? Actually I don't, but I say I do. To keep them happy. Men. Who order oysters. Remember to call in at Moss Bros. For your dinner jacket. Day after tomorrow. Pick me up at eight at my place. Oh, will you need any help tomorrow?'

'Help?' He echoed her, lost in the spate of words.

'In the investigation. Phone me in the morning if you do need me. For that.' She was at the door now, a soft smile on her face.

'Or anything,' she added. 'I know. I'm talking too much. Covers my embarrassment. I don't usually jump into bed on the first meeting. Or the second. But I couldn't help it. I . . . I just wanted to. And I liked it.'

She went leaving the face and the smile imprinted on the retina of Lohmann's eyes. Like the Cheshire cat, the smile remained.

He lay back on the bed now, dressed in trousers and shirt. Feeling a sense of reassurance after the violence of the early afternoon. As if the act of making love had reassured him that he was still alive.

Then, after a time he turned his thoughts back to the investigation. To his next move.

To find the mysterious Mister Irving, also known as Edward Rennie.

112

TEN

Hornsey Rise, in 1936, was a district on the edge of falling into a decaying gentility. To the east of Archway and the Holloway Road, some streets were made up of rows of neat artisans' houses, minute gardens to front and rear. There was the gaunt grey shape of what would once have been called a workhouse, and still served that purpose under some more acceptable nomenclature. The homeless London poor passed time here, the more fortunate moving on to council houses, the less fortunate back to Rowton houses or the streets of the city.

Then came the Rise itself, with curving avenues, occasional trees on sparsely-grassed lawns behind which stood medium-sized, late Victorian houses. Many were constructed in ugly red brick, with large rooms, strangely dim considering their equally large windows. Some of these houses, three storeys in height, had already been divided into bedsitters, others, retaining their family ownership, needed extensive renovation, which the income groups of the owners precluded.

The address against the '*E Rennie*' in Beth Coverley's notebook led Lohmann to one of these houses, halfway up Hornsey Rise. The red brick facings of the house had already been eroded and discoloured by half a century of London soot. The small garden sported a solitary tree and grass cut so short as to reveal patches of yellowish, clay-like soil. The front window, to the right of the door, was apparently curtainless. The window, unwashed for some time, was dominated by a strangely contorted rubber plant held as horizontal as it could be by a displaced tree branch which it twined around like a lethargic boa-constrictor.

At ten o'clock in the morning, Lohmann parked his car at the kerb and walked up the small, gravel pathway to the front door. On a brass name-plate was etched the one word,

113

'*RENNIE*'. Lohmann pressed the brass bell-push beneath the plate and waited.

The woman who came to the door was small, in her forties, and dressed to go out in a dowdy tweed coat and a hat that might once have been midnight blue but had now faded to the small hours of a dull winter morning.

She said: 'I don't want anything today,' with a bleak stare. And made to shut the door.

Lohmann had been long enough in the country to know he was being mistaken for a door-to-door salesman. He did what he had done so often in Germany. He put his foot forward, frustrating the closing of the door.

'Mister Rennie?' he said.

'He's not in.' The mouth became small, lips tight, a prim hyphen.

'He will be back?'

'Not now. Not today. He's away.'

'You are Mrs Rennie?'

'I am Mrs Rennie.'

'I have to talk to your husband.'

'I told you. He's not here. He's . . . he's on leave.'

The sentence echoed in Lohmann's mind. *He's on leave*. Not *He's on holiday*. Unusual. Unless . . .

'Your husband is in the army?'

'No. He's . . . not well.'

'What is your husband's occupation?'

'I don't see what business that is of yours!' Suddenly indignant, and impatient.

Lohmann used his authoritative tone. Cultivated in the doorways of Berlin. He repeated the question.

The woman visibly flinched.

'You know that! The others knew.'

For the third time. 'What is your husband's occupation?'

'He's a civil servant. In the Treasury. They know it . . .'

Something, a fragment taking shape.

'Who knows it?'

'The men who came. To ask about him. I told them. I'd telephoned his . . . his department. Wasn't well. Doctor's certificate to follow.'

114

'Who were they?'

'Civil servants. Like Edward . . . like Mister Rennie. Not his department. Another one. Just asking . . . I haven't all day, you know. I have shopping.'

Behind her, he saw the suitcase standing against a wall. Women did not go shopping with a suitcase.

'You're sure he's not in the house?' he asked.

'I've told you he's away on leave,' she replied, easy in the reply. She was telling the truth. The easy reply told him that.

'Could you tell me where I could get hold of him?'

'No! He's to be left alone. He's not a well man.'

She could be right. He hadn't looked well in Beth Coverley's apartment when he'd called himself Irving. Pale and shaking.

'It is necessary that you tell me where I can contact Mister Rennie.'

'The others said that too. I don't know. He went on a walking holiday. He needed fresh air and . . . and . . . all . . . that . . . kind . . . of . . . thing.' She was faltering, looking for words.

'Do you know when he will be back?'

'A week. Maybe longer. Officially he has a month's leave. The Treasury granted him that.'

Rennie, ill, on a month's leave and she claimed she had no address. He was certainly not in the house, he believed what she'd said about that. But not the rest of it.

'Do you know a Miss Coverley, Mrs Rennie? Beth Coverley?'

Eyes narrowing, she replied. 'No. I've never heard of her.'

'Your husband, of course, knows her,' Lohmann said. Thinking to leave her with that one. Let her nurse the thought of the unknown woman . . . and her husband. 'I am sorry I have taken up your time. I will see your husband on his return.'

He gave her a curt nod as a salute and, turning, walked down the path to the road and his car. Leaving her staring after him, puzzled and, he hoped, suspicious. Let the woman worry and she might well lead him to the husband. There was also the suitcase behind her in the hall of the house. She was ready to go out and he was prepared to bet she was taking that suitcase with her.

He drove his car up the Rise and around a corner where he

115

reversed, finally bringing it to a halt at the kerb. He was able to see back down the Rise from where he had parked. He fumbled for a cigarette, took a squashed packet of Balkan Sobranies and a box of Swan Vestas from his pocket and lit a cigarette. He had smoked rarely in Germany but, since becoming an exile, he had found himself increasingly using cigarettes as a psychological prop, something to occupy the tedious times.

This time he did not have long to wait. Five minutes later a taxi drove up the hill and stopped outside the Rennie house. The driver was about to climb out when Mrs Rennie appeared carrying the suitcase and climbed into the waiting vehicle. Lohmann switched on his engine, waited as the taxi performed a U-turn and drove off back down the hill. He moved out and started to follow the taxi at some distance. But as he did so he became aware of another car behind him moving off from the kerb. He studied the new arrival through his rear view mirror. Two men behind the wheel of a Riley saloon, faces indistinguishable. So he wasn't the only person following Mrs Rennie. Unless they were following him!

Either way, he decided, it was of interest. He had to be even more alert to another range of possibilities.

The taxi was heading for Archway and the main arterial road. If it turned right, it would be heading out of town. If left, back into London.

At the Archway junction the taxi turned left.

Twenty minutes later it was in the West End, heading southwest. And, Lohmann observed, the Riley was still directly behind him. Which would indicate they weren't very experienced at following. The ideal was to keep at least one, if not two cars, between you and the quarry. Lohmann was following this procedure with the taxi. Not that it was easy as he encountered the rattling, clanging bulk of London tram-cars.

Another ten minutes and they were in the Cromwell Road. The taxi finally drew up outside the Angleton Hotel. Lohmann brought the Morris to a halt some thirty yards behind the taxi and waited to see what the Riley would do. It drove on, passing the taxi and pulled in further down the road. Lohmann smiled to himself. The driver of the Riley was not completely inept.

Mrs Rennie stepped out of the taxi, spoke to the driver, and went into the hotel, still carrying the suitcase. The taxi waited, obviously under instruction to do so. Lohmann noted its registration number '*GA 4321*'. He then climbed from his car and walked slowly towards the hotel.

The Angleton Hotel had been carved out of four large, adjoining, five-storey private houses in the same block. It was typical of so many London middle-class, middle-price hotels. No Savoy or Claridges, it was none the less fairly large and reasonably comfortable. Imposing glass doors led to the foyer and reception desk. Peering through the glass, Lohmann could see nothing of Mrs Rennie. He glanced back and along the Cromwell Road. The Riley was parked some fifty yards away, the occupants still inside the car. Turning back, he entered the hotel.

The foyer was busy, a party of tourists about to leave. One or two of them were settling bills at the large reception desk. Others were at the foot of a staircase which presumably led upwards to the hotel bedrooms. They were talking loudly. Lohmann heard his native language. German tourists, blond young men, laughing, slapping each other on the back, an unpleasant element of contempt in their voices. Secure in the presumption that they would not be understood by the English.

'. . . nation of shopkeepers . . . even Napoleon was right . . .'

'. . . the Führer's new Berlin will make this city like some provincial village . . .'

'. . . an army of toy soldiers . . . only good for marching up and down outside Buckingham Palace . . .'

Another fragment of conversation, barely heard, and this time in low tones . . .

'. . . walking in Kent and Sussex . . . listing the RAF's aerodromes . . . personal request of General Goering . . .'

Most of them, Lohmann noticed, were wearing heavy hiking boots, but at least three of them were clad in regulation Wehrmacht issue jackboots. Even in London.

Turning away, Lohmann settled in an armchair behind a pillar where he could observe the entrance and the reception desk while being comparatively well hidden. And waited, smoking yet another Sobranie. Thinking about his young fellow countrymen. They were sent on vacation, probably sponsored by the Hitler Youth or some other organisation, each with his instructions. Observe, study. Hiking holidays that just happened to go by military bases. A kind of tourist espionage, but to what end? Certainly not defensive.

Mrs Rennie walked down the stairs past the reception desk and out into the street. Lohmann was faced with a question; to continue to follow her or to stay and find out whom she had been visiting in the hotel. She had not been carrying the suitcase. So presumably she had left it with the person she had been visiting.

He went over to the reception desk and stood, waiting, as a young German in a Tyrolean hat settled his bill. Finally the male receptionist turned to Lohmann.

'Can I help you, sir?'

He was taking a chance now. 'Have you a Mister Rennie staying at the hotel?'

'Oh, yes, sir. Do you wish me to phone his room?'

'I'd like to go up and . . . and surprise him.' Forbearing to say it might not be a pleasant surprise.

'I'm afraid I have to announce you. Policy of the hotel. Your name?'

'Tell him a Mister Lohmann would like to see him. Regarding the matter of Miss Coverley.'

'Certainly, sir. Mister Lohmann regarding Miss Coverley.'

The man withdrew behind a screen at the back of the reception area. Lohmann heard a telephone being lifted. He waited. So much waiting in detective work.

A moment later the receptionist reappeared.

'Mister Rennie will be right down.'

Again Lohmann waited. Watching the stairway. The Germans moved off, haversacks on backs, cases in hands, out into the Cromwell Road and a waiting charabanc which Lohmann could see through the glass doors. As the charabanc moved away, yet another drew up, unloading yet another company of tourists onto the pavement. As they flooded into the foyer it was apparent from their voices they were Americans. *Doing* Europe, as it was called. Though God knows why they should wish to at this time of the year. Probably less expensive than the summer months.

A tall, balding figure in a crumpled, shiny, dark suit came down the stairs and to the reception desk. A tired-looking man in his early fifties with a none-too-clean white shirt.

'Someone wantin' to see me?' the man said to the receptionist.

'Ah, yes, Mister Rennie, this gentleman.' The receptionist said indicating Lohmann.

Lohmann stared at the new arrival. Not the man in Beth Coverley's apartment. Not that man he'd believed to be Rennie, with the 'E.R.' cufflinks. This was a complete stranger. And, it would appear, part of his progress on the case had crumbled.

The stranger faced Lohmann. With a distinct odour of whisky on his breath.

'I'm Rennie. You are . . . ?'

'Lohmann.' He had not recovered from his surprise.

'What can I do for you, Mister Lohmann?'

Lohmann took a deep breath. 'Are you acquainted with a Miss Beth Coverley, Mister Rennie?'

A flood of new arrivals swirled around them at the desk. The man who purported to be Rennie opened his mouth to reply. And choked. A deep, agonising choking sound.

He reached out and gripped Lohmann's shoulder. Then he fell forward, still choking, struggling for breath; his hand ran down the front of Lohmann's leather coat, and he fell to the carpeted floor, face downwards.

The jostling crowd of arrivals were forced to part, making a space around the fallen man.

A woman screamed.

Lohmann stared down at the knife protruding from the back of the man who called himself Rennie. Then he looked around at the milling crowd of new arrivals. Any one of them could have stepped forward, stabbed the man and stepped back, losing himself almost at once.

Kneeling, Lohmann took the man's wrist, feeling for a pulse. It was there, weak, erratic, but beating.

'Get a doctor,' he said. The crowd now shuffled backwards and then parted as an elderly man in a checked shirt said, with an American accent. 'I'm a doctor.'

He knelt beside Lohmann, the victim's pulse was again taken and the American doctor studied the wound. he looked across at Lohmann and shook his head mournfully.

'He's dying.'

'The knife . . . ?'

'Don't touch it. Not until the wound can be dressed. And by that time . . .' the doctor shrugged.

The man who called himself Rennie suddenly squirmed onto his side and stared up at Lohmann. Then he seemed to try to speak.

Lohmann leaned down, face close to the other's face. There was no time for gentle methods.

Lohmann said: 'You're dying. You've been stabbed in the back. I want you to tell me, are you really Edward Rennie?'

The lips twisted into what might have been a smile.

'Funny . . .' the man said. 'Two hundred . . . two hundred pounds . . . to take his place . . . here. Never . . . told me . . . had to . . . die for him . . .'

He smiled, coughed, and blood came out of his mouth. Not just the trickle down the side of his chin as in the movies, Lohmann thought. It didn't happen that way. A great gout of blackish blood came out over his lips, covered his chin and flowed onto the white shirt and tie.

The man shuddered and died.

'Now, clear the way. Move back, all of you.' It was a uniformed London policeman pushing his way through the crowd. At his side was the receptionist.

The receptionist pointed at Lohmann. 'That's the man. He asked for Mister Rennie. And then he must have stabbed him.'

Lohmann straightened up to his full height.

'I asked to see him. I did not kill him.'

'We'll soon see about that. You'll just stay there and not move. Not until the Flying Squad get here.'

The Flying Squad arrived some fifteen minutes later, in the person of a plain clothes police inspector, a sergeant, and two more uniformed men. They were followed by an ambulance, more plain clothes men and a police doctor.

The plain clothes men proceeded to take statements from

everyone in the foyer who claimed to have seen anything. They spent some time with the receptionist and then the inspector asked Lohmann to accompany him back to Scotland Yard. It was a request he could not refuse, or indeed would not be allowed to refuse. He handed the keys of his car over to one of the detectives and was driven in a police car to Cannon Row police station. There he was cautioned and fingerprinted and then escorted the few yards across to the main Sotland Yard building.

He was seated in a grubby interview room lit by a solitary, unshaded light bulb. Then the Flying Squad sergeant who had appeared at the Angleton Hotel faced him for over an hour, asking questions he did not choose to answer and telling him how much easier it would be if he simply confessed to the killing now.

'Save so much time. Be a help to us. Noted when you go to trial. Gave every assistance to the law . . .'

'I repeat, I did not kill him,' Lohmann said coolly. He knew the techniques used by policemen all over the world, knew them too well to be bothered by them.

The sergeant consulted his notebook. 'Name of Lohmann. German alien. That won't go down well. Don't like aliens much in this country. And you said you were an ex-policeman.'

'That is so. Former Inspector, Berlin Criminal Police.'

'Then you should know the ropes.'

'I also know I did not kill the man.'

A uniformed constable came into the room and whispered something to the sergeant.

The sergeant looked at Lohmann. 'Think about what I've said. I'll be back.'

He went out, leaving the constable with his prisoner. He did not come back. Instead, twenty minutes later, the door opened and Detective Sergeant Charlie Newton came in.

'Well, Mister Lohmann, we meet again. Oh, you can relax now.' He turned to the constable. 'Away down to the canteen, Wilson and get us two large mugs of hot tea. Sugar and milk, Lohmann?'

'Please.'

'You hungry? It's past lunch time.'

'Not at present.'

Newton nodded to the constable who went out, shutting the door behind him.

'You were looking very serious,' Newton went on, sitting on a wooden chair facing Lohmann. 'No need. Despite the enthusiasm of Sergeant Lomax of the Flying Squad, we're not intending to charge you with murder. Apart from anything else your fingerprints don't match those on the knife.'

'I'm surprised the killer left fingerprints on the knife,' said Lohmann.

'You shouldn't be. You should know even the cleverest of villains do stupid things. Anyway the fingerprints we have got don't check with yours . . . or indeed anybody's we have on file. A pity. Everything would become so much easier.'

'I never found it easy, Sergeant,' Lohmann replied, remembering his years in Germany.

'You're probably right, sir.'

The door opened and a man came in. He was about the same age as Lohmann. Over six feet tall, the new arrival was still a good-looking man, his face tempered, perhaps bruised, by life. Dark hair was greying at the temples, blue eyes were set above dark inverted half moons. The weariness in the face, however, only added a depth of character to the good looks. The man was dressed in a smart, beautifully cut Savile Row suit.

Newton rose to his feet. Addressing the new arrival deferentially. 'This is Mister Lohmann, sir.' And, turning to Lohmann. 'This is Superintendent Thornhill.'

Roger Thornhill gave Lohmann a formal nod as Lohmann rose to his feet.

'Heard a lot about you, Inspector Lohmann,' Thornhill said. 'Do sit down. Read up a lot of your cases in Germany, with some envy. You were very good.'

'It was said,' Lohmann replied. 'I was also fortunate.'

'And now you are looking into the death of . . . of Beth Coverley. At the request of her father.'

'Your Assistant Commissioner Emerson expressed no objection to my doing so.'

Thornhill sat in the seat Newton had occupied. The Sergeant took up a stance behind him.

122

'We have no objection to private investigators here,' Thornhill said. 'Provided they don't impede our own investigations. *And* provided that they keep us informed.'

Lohmann said nothing. Thinking if there were policemen in this country like Brundage, he had reason not to inform the police.

'Of course Miss Coverley's death is not my investigation. Indeed the verdict being suicide, there is no further official investigation. Although I gather her father and friends do not accept the suicide verdict.'

'That is so.'

'And it is interesting that since you took up the investigation, an attempt was made to kill you. Which Newton here frustrated.'

'I was grateful for his . . . his help. Though why, if you people were not investigating the case, was he following me?'

It was Thornhill's turn not to answer. Instead he changed the subject.

'The man who was killed . . . Rennie . . . where does he come into this?'

Lohmann hesitated before replying. He had no wish to inform the police of Beth Coverley's diary. If they were not investigating the case, the diary would be of no interest to them. If they were like Brundage, it would disappear. Certainly Newton had saved his life but someone . . . wasn't it Comer . . . had said he would as soon have done the opposite if he had been so ordered. No, the diary he would keep to himself.

'I found Rennie's name and address on a piece of paper in Beth Coverley's apartment,' he said.

'You have this piece of paper?'

'No. I memorised the address and . . . disposed of it.'

'But you traced Rennie to the Angleton Hotel?'

Lohmann described his visit to Mrs Rennie and the route to the hotel. Here, he knew the police might be of help to him. He also related again . . . as he had done to Newton . . . the story of the man in Beth Coverley's apartment with the '*E.R.*' cufflinks. The man who was on sick leave from the Treasury. And who had been visited by so-called Treasury officials. To check on his absence.

'And this was the man who was stabbed?' Thornhill asked.

'No!' Lohmann went on to tell Thornhill of his surprise at the stranger who called himself Rennic and of the dying man's last words.

Thornhill looked around at Newton. 'Check. With the Treasury. And see if you can get another identification of the corpse.'

Newton went out and Thornhill turned back to Lohmann.

'We'll have to wait and see now. I have been out of London on another investigation. A matter of espionage. German tourists showing an interest in our military establishments. Of course it goes on all the time. And not just Germans.'

Lohmann thought of the young German tourists at the Angleton Hotel. Walking holidays with ulterior motives.

Thornhill rose to his feet. 'Come and have a bite. And tell me how the police in Germany are surviving the Nazis.'

They walked from Scotland Yard onto Whitehall and lunched on chicken sandwiches in a small, dim eating-house and pub. With the sandwiches Thornhill drank ale while Lohmann tried to explain how the police in Germany were not surviving the Nazis but were being taken over as another arm of the mechanism of the totalitarian state.

'Could never happen here,' Thornhill insisted.

'You think?' Lohmann replied. 'It can happen anywhere. It can happen quickly as in Germany. Or slowly without the people noticing. Watch for the signs. When the government gets secretive, when only supporters of the government get appointed to key positions. Then one morning you wake up and the totalitarian state surrounds you and controls your life. It could come in England. You already have Mosley and his Blackshirts . . .'

'Thugs playing soldiers.'

'Maybe, Herr Thornhill. But in Germany the same kind of thugs are ruling the country now. And is it just Mosley? Haven't some of your press barons, like Lord Rothermere, already expressed admiration for Hitler?'

Thornhill took a long draught of ale. 'And we have other journalists working against . . . against Fascism. Like . . . like Miss Coverley.'

'Who ends up in the River Thames. Is it coincidental? Unless you really believe she committed suicide.'

Thornhill suddenly looked pale and tired.

'I . . . I can't believe it. But, damn it, Lohmann, there's no investigation. Verdict, suicide! Case closed!

Lohmann was surprised at the intensity of the man's emotion. It was . . . how would he put it to himself? . . . unprofessional for a police officer.

'You are in the Special Branch, Superintendent Thornhill. Can you not open it up again?'

Thornhill ran a hand through his dark hair. 'I've tried. Last night when I got back to London. Not in the public interest. A waste of public money since the inquest's verdict was suicide.' He drained his glass with some impatience. 'Let's get back and see what Newton's got for us.'

On the walk back, Thornhill changed the subject.

'Funny report on my desk this morning. Someone drove two men into a Sussex County hospital late yesterday. One had badly smashed legs, the other had been shot in the kneecap. The men are saying nothing. You wouldn't know anything about that?'

Lohmann tensed. Was he being lured into some kind of admission? For all Thornhill's strange, if seemingly genuine, interest in the death of Beth Coverley he was a high-ranking police officer. And such men could be devious. Lohmann himself had been one of such men.

'Why should I know anything about it?' he asked blandly.

'No particular reason. Although the man who deposited the two wounded men had a German accent.'

'One of your German espionage people?' Lohmann suggested, aware that he could be close to the truth. Walter Schellenberg was almost certainly in England for such reasons.

'Possibly,' Thornhill replied. 'Not that I thought for a moment it might be you. The description by the hospital reception people was that of a much younger man. Very blond. And military in bearing. Pity they let him go.'

'The wounded men were also German?'

'Oh, not they were English all right. One of them had a police record. For assault and battery. And both of them were members of Mosley's Blackshirts. Not nice people. I expect they asked for what they got. And, if they don't talk, there's nothing much to be done.'

They had spent nearly two hours over lunch. Back in the interview room, Newton was waiting.

'Mister Lohmann was right,' Newton said on being asked to report. 'Bloke killed in the Angleton wasn't Rennie. We checked his fingerprints and came up with . . . guess what?'

'We're not playing games, Sergeant Newton,' Thornhill said, scowling. 'Tell me . . .'

'Name of Hugo Richards. Did nine months in the Scrubs for walking away with the funds of a Twickenham tennis club where he was unpaid secretary. Stupid man with expensive tastes. Played the gee-gees and liked to dole out money for favours received . . . to guardsmen and young lads he picked up in pubs and less savoury places. Been out a year, living on God knows what.'

'Go on.'

'Mister Lohmann's statement about his last words are probably dead right. It seems before he walked off with the tennis club funds he worked in the Treasury.'

'Civil servant.'

'Middle rank. I was on to the Treasury. The real Edward Rennie is Deputy Assistant Director, handling all the records of the whole place.'

'What would that mean?' Lohmann said, forgetting he was at the most a visitor. At the least, a suspect.

Newton looked at Thornhill who gave an almost imperceptible nod.

'Simply means he had a middle rank in the department which has files on all government financial transactions. And those that need approval of the government. Must be one of the biggest record offices in government . . . linked to Customs and Excise and Inland Revenue. But here's the interesting thing. Hugo Richards worked side by side with . . .'

'Edward Rennie,' said Thornhill.

'Dead right, sir. It looks as if Rennie took off and paid Hugo Richards to impersonate him and throw anybody who might be looking for Rennie off the track.'

'Myself included,' Lohmann said. It fitted. Two hundred pounds to a one-time colleague who was now an ex-jailbird. Only Richards certainly hadn't realised how dangerous it was. Possibly neither had Rennie. Or possibly he was too desperate to care.

'I phoned Mrs Rennie's house,' Newton went on. 'I spoke to a charlady. Said Mrs Rennie had gone out, didn't know when she'd be back. Thought she might, in fact have gone to join her husband on his walking holiday in the Lake District.'

'I'd like to know what she would have said about visiting the Angleton Hotel?' Thornhill said.

'God knows,' said Newton. 'But if she has joined her husband we're looking for a couple now.'

'Not us,' said Thornhill. 'Flying Squad, Murder Squad. Still, looks as if she thought her husband was in danger and went to warn him.'

'Or simply join him,' Newton chimed in.

Again the right hand ran through the dark hair as Thornhill looked across at Lohmann.

'If we knew what they were afraid of, we might know what this is all about. And we might know why he was in Beth Coverley's apartment,' Lohmann said.

'As you say, Lohmann.' Then turning back thoughtfully to Newton. 'Go up, unofficially, and chat with the charlady. You know the technique. Be nice and sympathetic. See if she knows anything. But no official report. Remember, we're not on this case. We're not investigating the murder of Richards or Rennie. That's the CID's job. Let Inspector Anstey and his sergeant find their own way around.'

'Except we've told them to lay off Mister Lohmann here,' Newton seemed to be reminding him.

'That stands. Mister Lohmann is not involved in the Rennie, Richards case. Special Branch . . . official!'

'Right, sir.' Newton moved to the door of the room; and stopped. 'One other thing. Mrs Rennie told Mister Lohmann two men came from the Treasury, checking up on Rennie's being ill. Not true. Rennie was an important and trusted civil servant who, if he became ill, would easily be granted necessary sick leave. They wouldn't check up . . . her phone call and the medical certificate they received was all they needed.'

'They got a medical certificate?'

'Yes. GP's opinion. Seriously run-down and in a nervous state. Recommended a vacation.'

Thornhill looked at Lohmann. 'So who were the two men who purported to come from the Treasury?'

'I think,' said Lohmann. 'They could be the two who followed Mrs Rennie and myself to the Angleton Hotel. And very possibly one of them stabbed Richards under the impression he was Rennie.'

'Interesting, isn't it? Go away, Sergeant, and talk to the charlady.' Thornhill now turned back to Lohmann.

Newton went out.

'You can go now, Inspector Lohmann,' Thornhill went on. 'But I want to know everything you find out in your investigation of the death of Beth Coverley.'

He'll know everything I want him to know, Lohmann determined. And asked himself, why a Special Branch superintendent was so concerned. Were there other ramifications he, Lohmann, knew nothing about? One way to find out. Ask.

He said: 'Why are you so interested in the death of Beth Coverley, Superintendent?'

Thornhill looked away, his face ashen. Looking over Lohmann's shoulder into the middle distance. Again revealing emotion.

'You want to know why? All right, you're investigating, you're entitled. Beth Coverley and I were . . . were to be married.'

ELEVEN

The police had brought Lohmann's car from the Angleton Hotel to Scotland Yard and Thornhill escorted the ex-inspector to the Embankment where the car was parked. Both

128

men maintained a thoughtful silence until they reached the parked vehicle.

Lohmann was the first to break the silence.

'I'm sorry about . . . about Beth Coverley and yourself.'

'Thank you.'

'If there is anything I can do . . .'

'You're doing it. Finding out who killed her and why. I can do so much myself, but it can't be official. There are other things I have to do.'

Lohmann nodded. 'I understand.'

'And even if there was an official investigation I would not be permitted to undertake it. The personal interest precludes my taking over enquiries. But, if you find out anything, I want to know.'

'Of course,' said Lohmann, climbing into the Morris.

Thornhill gazed at him in silence again for a moment. Then the Special Branch man gave him a curt nod as if of dismissal and, turning, walked quickly back towards Scotland Yard.

It was now late afternoon. Lohmann drove back to Museum Street. Wondering why he had not told Thornhill everything: had not told him about Beth Coverley's diary and notes: had barely touched on his distrust of Detective Sergeant Brundage; and had not mentioned Rue Scott-ffoliot. But then Thornhill had mentioned only once the attempt on Lohmann's life. Had their positions been reversed, Lohmann would have suggested some form of protection for the other . . . at least one detective to keep an eye on him. Thornhill had not suggested this. Indeed the Special Branch superintendent seemed, despite his apparent command of the situation, to be somehow confused. Surely he could have put his suspicions regarding his fiancée's death to a higher authority? Or was the confusion attributable to the shock of Beth's death? It was something to think about.

There was a postcard waiting for him at Museum Street. Scrawled in an almost childish hand.

Don't forget Moss Bros for Monday,
   R.

He smiled and drove to the shop behind Covent Garden where he was measured for a dinner-suit. To be picked up the next morning. He drove back to Museum Street and made a phone call from the phone in the hall.

'Assistant Commissioner's office,' announced the voice at the other end of the line.

Lohmann identified himself and asked to speak to the Assistant Commissioner. He was connected to Charles Emerson.

'What have you been up to, Lohmann?' said Emerson. 'I have on my desk a report which puts you on the scene of a stabbing at some hotel on the Cromwell Road.'

'I was at the wrong place at the wrong time, Charles. Your officers have already cleared me . . .'

'Yes, I see that . . . But has this anything to do with this woman's death you're investigating?'

Lohmann hesitated. If Emerson thought his enquiries were leading to other crimes, then the Assistant Commissioner could make it difficult for him to continue. Yet again, Emerson was his one friend in this country, his sponsor in being permitted to stay in England. He was not happy to deceive the man.

'It is possible,' Lohmann said. 'But not certain.'

'You'll give my people every assistance then? Irrespective of your investigation. Remember, you have no authority here . . .'

'I remember.'

'I hope you do, Ernst. We don't like characters being stabbed to death all over London.' Emerson was speaking in his civil service tones, with all the pomposity of his rank. Lohmann came back quickly.

'We never did like it in Berlin either.'

The voice was grudging now. 'Well, give my people all the help you can. But you were phoning me. What can I do for you?'

'A minor matter, Charles. I left something in a taxi the other night.' The lie came easily. To be a good police officer you had to be a good liar. It went with the job and the rank. 'I have the registration number and I was wondering if your records people could trace the taxi?'

He expected Emerson to put him on to the Traffic Branch but, no, the Assistant Commissioner was even more helpful.

'Give me the registration number and I'll have my secretary telephone you back.'

'GA 4321. If she'll phone me back as soon as possible at my bedsitter . . .'

'I'll see she does. Within the hour. Take care, Ernst.'

'It is an occupational habit to do so. Thank you, Charles.'

He climbed the stairs to his room and, once inside, took off coat and jacket and lay on his back on the bed. He felt suddenly exhausted. Ouside the greyness of the autumn Saturday was turning into a drizzled darkness interspersed with the yellow lights of the city. Gaslamps flared, electric lights sparkled. And, as in many previous evenings, Lohmann drowsily wondered what he was doing here in London. He should be in Germany running a police department, keeping the Brownshirts and the Communists from confronting each other in the streets, preserving the peace of a Weimar republic which had gone, its place taken by Hitler's Reich. And, in that Reich there was no place for Ernst Lohmann. In this mood he would think about those he had left back in Berlin. There was his old chief, Murnau, an honest one-time liberal, forced to join the National Socialist Party in order to keep his job and his livelihood. There was the girl, Lucy, he had loved in his own way, despite her profession. Lucy, the whore with the heart of gold. A living cliché, she had refused to come out of Germany with him. Not because she didn't want out, but for his sake, Lohmann had long suspected. And Madame Kitty who ran the house Lucy had worked in, also a friend. Strange that most of his friends were on the wrong side of the law. Not that there were so many left. Magda his wife, so long dead . . . there was only her grave in that cemetery in Berlin. And Anna, his daughter, was in America learning, he prayed, that all she had taken in at school in Berlin was part of Hitler's colossal lie.

Despite everything, he missed the linden trees in the summer, the *bierhaus* where, before Hitler, political arguments had been heated but amiable. He missed Wannsee, going on the lake, walking holidays in the Tyrol, always with Magda before her death.

He slept. In dreaming, Lucy's face changing into that of Rue Scott-ffoliot; Sergeant Brundage's face becoming that of Reinhard Heydrich . . . no, that wasn't right . . . more like a dead SS man called Zoller. And there was the sinister little

Doctor Paul Josef Goebbels, like an evil troll from Wagner's *Ring*. All of them coming and going, flowing in a thick mist, the Mall becoming the Unter den Linden, London merging with the Berlin he once knew . . .

Then he was awake and Norman was knocking at the door of the room.

'Telephone call, Mister Lohmann!'

He went downstairs, strands of sleep still clinging to his mind.

The voice on the telephone was female, cool, English, reserved.

'Mister Lohmann, this is Assistant Commissioner Emerson's secretary. The taxi registration number you gave us belongs to North Thameside Luxury Cabs Limited, of two hundred and fifty five, Cobden Lane. That's just off the Holloway Road.'

'Thank you. Please thank Mister Emerson for me.'

He replaced the receiver and looked at his watch. Six thirty. He lifted the telephone book which hung from a string beside the phone. He had to peer at the book in the dim light of the hall . . . Norman believed in saving electricity costs for the owner of the building . . . but he finally found the number of the taxi-cab company.

A cockney operator connected him to a regional accent at the cab company.

'You have a cab with the registration number, *GA 4321*?'

'What's it about? 'As he been in an accident? We take no responsibility . . .' The tone of the girl's voice indicated she came from somewhere in the north.

Lohmann cut in. 'There is no accident. I want that taxi and driver to come to this address as soon as possible.' He gave her his address.

'Hold on a minute, mister.'

There were muttered sounds of conversation in the background and then the girl came back on.

'That cab is on a job just now but we can send you another . . .'

'It has to be that one. I'm prepared to wait.'

'Oh!' She was obviously unused to requests for specific cabs.

'Well . . . if you want to wait . . . don't see the point . . . it might be an hour . . .'

'I'll wait. You have the address. The name is Lohmann.'

'If you don't mind. Museum Street, Mister Lomond.'

'Lohmann.'

'That's what I said. Mister Lomond.'

He left it at that. Hanging up he went to his room and waited. Ready in his leather coat and a black hat. And the Mauser, cleaned and reloaded, in his jacket pocket.

The taxi arrived seventy minutes later.

The driver was a small fat man in his thirties, with a moon-like face and cratered skin. Lohmann came out of the building into Museum Street.

'Where to, mister?' said the driver.

'Early today you picked up a woman at Hornsey Rise . . .'

'That's the taxi business for you.' A quizzical look on the cratered surface.

'You took her to the Angleton Hotel in Cromwell Road . . .'

'Wait a minute, wait a minute, what is this? Sherlock Holmes lives in bloody Baker Street . . .'

Lohmann took a five pound note from his wallet and handed it to the driver.

'So I took her to the Angleton Hotel . . .'

'She asked you to wait and then you took her somewhere else. Where did you take her?'

In the light from the street-lamp it seemed that the round face tightened up and grew pale. Lohmann could see beads of perspiration appear on the man's upper lip.

'I don't know that this is right, mister. Even for a fiver. I mean, taxi-drivers should be like doctors. Don't tell other people about . . . other people's business, you might say.'

'I want you to take me where you took the woman.'

The driver looked at his feet, shuffling them awkwardly.

'I suppose I can do that. I suppose that would be all right. But . . . but what's this all about?'

'What's your name?' Lohmann asked pleasantly.

'Jimmy. Jimmy Gorman. James. Gorman.'

'How much would you charge to take me to where you took the woman after she left the Angleton Hotel?'

'Ten . . . twelve bob. Maybe.'

'Take me there, wait for me, bring me back and you will earn another fiver.'

The moon face nodded, sweat still on the face despite the damp chill of the evening. Lohmann wondered why. Perhaps he was one of those people who sweated a lot.

'Okay, get in,' said James (Jimmy) Gorman.

They drove west from the museum to Hammersmith, through the garish lights of a London Saturday night. Halfway along Hammersmith Broadway, Gorman turned the taxi down a side street and, some fifty yards along he swung into yet another street. It was a narrow thoroughfare of dim, dark houses huddled shoulder to shoulder as if seeking heat and physical support. There were two breaks between the houses, the first being a public house, aging, ill-lit, and with an inappropriate sign above the door, The Great Goat's Arms — Free House. At the second break in the houses, Gorman brought the cab to a halt.

Behind bent and rusting railings was a small patch of soil, bare of grass, and indeed of any vegetation whatsoever. Beyond the patch was a two-storey building.

'This is it,' said Gorman.

Lohmann stepped onto the kerb and stared at the building. It was built from large slabs of grey to soot-black stone. From a solitary side-window issued a dull, yellow light. The roof was of corrugated iron, sloping on either side. A gate in the railings was open and just beyond the gate was a notice board –

HAMMERSMITH CHAPEL OF CHRIST
EVANGELIST.

The lettering had once been in gold paint but now the paint had peeled and some letters had been overpainted in ordinary white paint. Even this was soot-begrimed.

Lohmann turned to Gorman. 'This where you dropped her?'

'This is where I dropped her.' Gorman echoed his words.

Lohmann went through the gate and walked towards a small wooden canopy under which he could see a door. There was a sound from beyond of voices singing and an organ playing. Surely not on a Saturday night, Lohmann asked himself. But it was so. The door was ajar and light filtered through into the dimness of the street.

The ex-detective pushed the door open and stepped into an ante-room. The only light filtered through the sides of yet another, ill-fitting door to the right. Lohmann could make out a notice board with two notices on it but these were unreadable in the dim light. The sound of singing was louder now. It was coming from beyond the inner door.

'By cool Siloam's shady rill, How sweet the lily grows . . .

Lohmann was about to move towards this door when, from behind him, he heard the sound of an automobile engine starting up. He turned on his heel and was in time to see Gorman's taxi moving off.

The taxi performed a U-turn and went speeding back in the direction of Hammersmith Broadway. What the hell was Gorman playing at? He had been instructed to wait. He had not yet even received the promised second five-pound note.

Puzzled, Lohmann turned back into the ante-room and walked towards the door and the sound of hymn singing. He felt for and found the handle of the door. It was sticky to the touch, as if a child who had been eating some sugary sweet had then put her hand to it.

He turned the handle, pushed the door open and stepped in.

The light caused him to blink. The hall was lit by four large uncovered electric bulbs. As his eyes focused the smell of the place hit him. An odour of sour human sweat combined with that distinctive aroma found in a second-hand bookshop; and under this, a tinge of carbolic. Not unlike the smell Lohmann had come across much more potently in the narrow area of a prison cell.

The hall was fairly large, with only two windows, each high on the side walls. And each covered by dusty curtains. There was no resemblance to a church but rather the place was like an assembly hall. There were some rows of old, battered pews, and these were at the front before a raised platform. When the pews ran out there were several rows of collapsible seats and what looked like old cinema seats. The platform was only two feet higher than the main area. It was bare but for two more chairs, kitchen variety, a small organ at one side and, in the centre of the platform, a lectern.

Despite the seating, the congregation was sparse. Eight elderly women, one in a shawl, the others in shabby dark coats, were on their feet singing. Five old men, three of them carrying cloth caps, the other two with bowlers, – also all rather shabby – were dotted around the hall and, surprisingly, there were four young men, quite smartly dressed in sports jackets and flannels. Two youngish women, in sweaters and skirts, completed the congregation. On the platform was the organist and from where he was standing Lohmann could only see his head and shoulders, a large head, thick neck surrounded by a celluloid collar and, incongruously, an electric-blue tie. The other figure on the platform was standing at the lectern, a tall thin man, cadaverous features ending in a lantern jaw which twisted and writhed as if he was chewing something. In fact, he was singing. The man was dressed, also incongruously, in a tweed jacket with leather shoulder-facings, the kind of jacket worn on grouse moors. Beneath this were plus-fours cut from the same cloth and below the plus-fours, leggings around spindly legs.

As Lohmann came in, the singing came to a climactic *'amen'* and the meagre congregation sat down. The cadaverous man assumed a stance at the lectern, gripping the sides of the wood with long, thin fingers and staring into the middle distance over the heads of his audience. Staring indeed directly at Lohmann.

His voice boomed out. 'We are met this evening as we meet every evening to celebrate the saving of our souls through the intervention of Jesus Christ, the first and greatest of the evangelists.'

Lohmann stood, momentarily uncertain about whether or not he should sit or remain where he was. The question was answered for him.

'We have, I can see, a new arrival with us,' the cadaverous man said without altering his tone. 'Yet another stranger seeking solace. Come among us, brother, sit and learn the truth.'

Lohmann sat. Uneasily and in the nearest seat on the back row. The seat squeaked ominously under his weight.

'I will speak to you of our truth at the end of the meeting,

136

brother,' said the preacher, and went back to his peroration.

'It is only by turning to Christ and his spiritual followers that we will save ourselves. We must beware of the evil doctrines spread by the Roman Church and its offsprings, the reformed churches who merely adapted the Roman doctrines to their own profit. We must be on our guard against the evils of Israel, who have sold their own souls and would sell ours in the market-places of the world.'

His voice rose and fell, he emphasised certain phrases, shouted certain words with a kind of contempt. He reminded Lohmann of another orator he'd heard some years before, in another place with a bigger audience.

'The purity of our race must not be marred by association with the lesser beings. That is the law of God and man . . .'

He'd managed to lose Christ somewhere along the way.

'The thunderbolts of heaven will fall on those who penned the infamous Protocols of Zion outlining their plans for the destruction of the Anglo-Saxon race. Those very protocols have proved the Jewish conspiracy to enslave the pure races of the world. Until the mongrel Semites recognise the supremacy of the white Anglo-Saxon whom God has destined to rule, we must fight and strive and struggle to eliminate this evil among us.'

Somewhere Lohmann had heard it all before.

'Our day will come,' the man boomed on. 'And when it comes we will be ready . . . others have shown the way . . . and we will follow them in the cleansing of the streets as Hercules cleansed the Augean Stables.'

Suddenly the voice dropped, changed to a quieter more business-like tone.

'There will be the usual two meetings tomorrow, Sunday, tea and cakes will be served to the needy, and the usual week-night meetings will be held as ever. The young people's instruction classes will take place as usual in the afternoons and evenings listed on the notice board. Bless you all.'

He stepped back from the lectern and lowered his head, the bishop of God-knows-what bidding farewell to his congregation. The old people in the body of the hall rose and shuffled back to the door, passing Lohmann without acknowledging the

137

presence of a stranger. The four young men and the two women came together at a door at the side of the platform and moved through this door to the nether regions of the building.

On the platform the organist rose to his full three feet in height, and Lohmann realised he was a dwarf with the features of a prize fighter. The little man gathered together sheets of music almost as big as himself, and followed the young people through the door at the side of the platform.

The preacher straightened up, watched the organist depart and then, with a surprising degree of athleticism, sprang down from the platform and strode energetically towards Lohmann. The German rose to his feet as a thin hand, the skin punctuated with liver spots, stretched out towards him.

'Welcome to our congregation, sir,' said the preacher dropping for the time being the fraternal address he'd used from the platform. 'My name is Raven Marshall. Doctor Raven Marshall.'

'Lohmann,' said the ex-policeman tersely. 'Ernst Lohmann.'

'Always glad to see a new face seeking Christ. But you are not English.'

'German.'

'Then you are thrice welcome. As one of our great Anglo-Saxon brotherhood.'

'Thank you. But I am here looking for someone.'

'Perhaps you have found him.'

'Not yet,' Lohmann was suddenly curious. 'You're a doctor of divinity?'

'I am a doctor of the evangelistic philosophy of the Anglo-Saxon Christ.'

'I always thought Christ was a Jew,' Lohmann said quietly.

'He worked among the Semitic races to bring the truth to them,' said Doctor Raven Marshall smugly. 'But the Jews, Peter and Paul, lied about his origins, distorted his philosophy and created that great abomination, the Church of Rome. Would you care to come to my chambers at the back and have a cup of tea? We might discuss this person you are looking for.' Marshall gestured towards the door at the side of the platform.

Lohmann thought, this man changes the subject without drawing breath.

He said: 'Yes, thank you. But will I not be intruding?'

'Oh, you mean the young men. They talk with me . . . religion, philosophy, the search for truth. I call them instruction classes but they are really just informal discussions. The young have to be shown the way. I try to . . . show them.'

'By teaching them about the Protocols of Zion?'

'Among other things.'

'I always understood the story of the Protocols of Zion had long been exposed as a forgery.'

Raven Marshall smiled, the cadaverous features twisting into valleys and craters. It was a smile without humour.

'That is the genius of the Semitic race. To outline their plan for world conquest and then, when it was discovered, to provide false evidence indicating it is a forgery.'

'I think I've read something like in Germany. In *Der Sturmer*, Streicher's newspaper,' Lohmann said, face expressionless.

'Yes, yes, indeed. Julius Streicher, a man I admire. An important member of the German government. Come in. My . . . my young men will be most interested.'

Lohmann followed him down the centre aisle and to the side of the platform. At the door, Marshall stood to one side.

'By the way who were you asking about?'

'A man called Rennie. Edward Rennie.'

'Ah, yes. Edward Rennie. Please, go in.'

Lohmann went through the door. The room was different from the hall. It was furnished with deep leather armchairs. Against the wall at the back was an open roll-top desk. Beside the desk was another door. The walls were covered in floral paper. Above the desk was a framed photograph of Marshall surrounded by a group of young men. On another wall was a print of an oil painting. It was a bad print of a bad painting. An idealised Hitler in armour, on horseback, carrying a lance. Lohmann had seen it before. It had made him laugh. Having met the reality, he found the representation ludicrous; but, in Berlin they said the Führer approved.

The four young men and two women were standing, as if waiting for Lohmann. Certainly waiting for Doctor Raven

Marshall. The dwarf was perched like a doll on the desk, legs swinging in the air.

Behind Lohmann, Marshall spoke.

'This is Herr Inspector Lohmann, formerly of the Berlin Police, who is looking for Edward Rennie. We can now tell him, he has come to the wrong place.'

The six young people were smiling, unpleasant sneering smiles. The dwarf gave a braying laugh and jumped from desk to floor. They had been expecting him. Marshall had known who he was. And the taxi hadn't bothered to wait. The driver hadn't been expecting his passenger to reappear.

Lohmann spun around to face Marshall who was blocking the doorway. Marshall, still with an amused look on his face, stepped aside. Behind him a new arrival had appeared, a man with a scar on his face. The man who had been at the inquest on Beth Coverley, the man who had gone into Leman Street Police Station. The man Comer called Joyce.

'We all seem to be looking for Mister Rennie,' said Joyce, his accent a mixture of Irish and American.

Lohmann took a step forward, ready to push past Joyce. Out in the hall, he had a chance. and he had the Mauser pistol. But something stopped him, something twisted between his feet and he fell forward, tripped by the moving body of the agile dwarf. As he fell, another something hit him on the back of his head.

Falling, he embraced blackness.

TWELVE

He'd been dreaming. He'd been back in Berlin. Being pursued by a blind man selling balloons. There had been such a man but he'd been dead for some time. Yet, still he came after Lohmann, milk-white eyeballs searching within their own darkness, one hand stretched out, the fingers clawed, seeking something to grasp on to; other hand clutching the strings of multicoloured balloons. Lohmann was running along familiar streets, yet there were strange distortions in the buildings. There was the Reichschancellery, the walls leaning downwards towards him. The Reichschancellery, home of the Ogre-in-armour carrying a spear, swastika banners hanging from the windows and reaching out like tentacles to wrap themselves around Lohmann, stop him, prevent him from fleeing further.

He forced himself up, out of the dream, out of sleep, his body damp with perspiration. It took him some moments to force his eyes open. It was if there were weights on his eyelids. When he finally succeeded he was staring at a bare electric light bulb. Why was it nobody used lampshades around here? The bulb cast a circular ring of light. Lohmann turned his head with some effort and a stabbing pain ran down the back of his neck. He moaned softly, complaining to himself. And he thought he should be asking, 'Where am I?' But he knew he was still in that building, The Church of Christ Evangelist . . . something like that . . . should be The Church of Christ Anti-Semite, from all the preacher had said. He was lying on a mattress on a bed. It was an old-fashioned steel bed frame, and the mattress was striped, although the stripes had faded and the surface of the mattress was stained and torn, steel springs protruding.

Turning his head seemed to ease the pain. His eyes focused on the dwarf who was squatting on a chair on the edge of the ring of light, grinning at him. The dwarf had a face that resembled the surface of a walnut. A young, old face. Ageless.

'Should be surprised, so you should,' said the dwarf.

'Why . . . why . . . should I be surprised?' he croaked, his throat dry as sandpaper.

'To be still alive,' the dwarf replied and chuckled. 'You shouldn't be alive. They should have killed you straight away. I said that. Nothing personal but I told them, in books people are left alive for a time for no reason and then they become awkward and escape and things like that. It's very stupid of them. They don't read books much. Except for Doctor Marshall. Not that I like the killing bit.'

Lohmann didn't know what to say. The dwarf was right, of

141

course. Anyway they'd tried to kill him twice before. Now they had him why not do it and get it over?

He voiced the thought. 'Then why am I still alive?'

The dwarf shrugged. 'Something to do with the man, Rennie. They're looking for him. But they want to know whether you've told anybody about him. So, before they kill you, they want to find out. That's what I heard. Must be important, this Rennie. Anyway they have to ask permission to kill you.'

'Ask who?' said Lohmann, suddenly finding it difficult to move. He looked down and found his hands were tied together.

The dwarf's eyes followed his look. 'They tied you up. Because you're bigger than me, they didn't want trouble. They would have left some of the others only they had to go to one of their stupid meetings. So they gave me this.' He brandished Lohmann's Mauser. 'I'm supposed to use it if you try and attack me. I've never done it before but . . . but I will. I think I will. Anyway I don't like big people getting rough. What were you saying?'

'I wanted to know who they had to ask permission from, to kill me.'

'Oh, they don't tell me things like that.' Then he added mournfully. 'They don't tell me much at all, not really. But I don't care. Not interested. They pay me to play the organ and do odd jobs. So it's okay, really.'

His expression indicated it wasn't in the least okay. He was a sad little man and he couldn't help showing it, despite the grins and chuckles. Sad at himself? Or at the world? Lohmann tried to move again, despite the bound hands, and found it wasn't only his hands that were tied. One foot was tied to a rail at the foot of the bed.

'What's your name?' he said to the dwarf, more to give him time to think than from any real interest.

'I shouldn't tell you. But, as they will eventually kill you, it doesn't matter much. Archie. Archie Dafoe. Archibald Aloysius Dafoe. There's a name for you. My mother had big ideas. And that's funny, considering I didn't grow very big. Didn't like her much. And she didn't like me. Wasn't big enough for her.' Archie Aloysius Dafoe was obviously an inveterate chatterer.

Lohmann squirmed. Thinking. Time to think. How to get out of this. He curled his body into the foetal position so that Archie couldn't see the hands. He tested the rope around his wrists. Could he move his hands? If he could do that, he could loosen the rope. He moved his hands. That was something. Although it would take time and he was under the eye of the dwarf. And the dwarf had the Mauser. Second question, would he use the Mauser?

'I'm a good organist,' said the dwarf. 'Did you hear me playing?'

'You're very good.'

'I know it. Hands is the trouble. Stretch isn't long enough. I was all right as an organist in a picture palace. Yeah, I was that for a time, until the talkies came in. But if I'd had the stretch in the hands I might have been a concert pianist.' He giggled. ' 'magine me in Albert Hall in a nice little tailcoat. What my ma wanted. But the old cow didn't get it. Serves her right.'

'Why do you work for people like Marshall?'

The dwarf's expression changed. He glared down at Lohmann. Then suddenly leaped from the chair and brought his face close to Lohmann's. The bound man became aware of the acrid odour of garlic on his face.

'I don't work for people like Marshall. I work for Marshall. And you, you heard of the depression?' Archie Dafoe spoke vehemently now. 'Heard of the slump? You foreigners, you don't know nothing. The big slump. The Depression? There's millions. Millions out of a job. Big lads. Navvies, miners... and cinema organists. All of 'em over five feet tall. No jobs. What chance does a three-foot dwarf have with that lot out? Me! In case you hadn't noticed I am a three-foot tall dwarf. Not a midget, mind. A dwarf, three feet in height ... all right, wiv a perfectly formed body. But what can I do against that lot looking for work? So when Marshall offers me three quid a week, I'm glad to take it. To play the organ and do a few odd jobs. I'm more than glad. I'm bloody grateful.'

Lohmann exerted pressure on the rope with his wrists. Had to keep the little man talking, that was essential.

'We had the depression in Germany also,' he said.

'I don't give a tosser about Germany. Full of foreigners like you, Germany is.'

'So you like working for Doctor Marshall?'

'I like the three quid a week.'

'But you agree with what he preaches?'

The dwarf's mouth turned down at the corners. 'I don't listen to what he preaches. So he doesn't like the Jews, doesn't mean I have to not like 'em. Once worked for one when I was a cinema organist. He was a Jew and he was okay. Said I was a double attraction, a dwarf organist.' Suddenly he giggled. 'Had to put special blocks in to elevate the pedals. Same thing here. When the organ came up in the cinema they could only just see the top of my head.'

'Then you don't agree with Marshall's politics?' Lohmann imagined the rope was slackening, however infinitesimally.

'Politics!' said Archie and turning, climbed back onto his chair. 'I don't give a fuck about politics. Politics are for big people with full bellies. Me, I don't know and, I told you, I don't listen.'

'You heard enough to know he attacks the Jews.'

'So does your bloke in Germany. What's his name? Herr Hitler. What the BBC calls him. Herr Hitler.'

'Not every German supports Hitler. But I think your friend Doctor Marshall does.'

'Nuffin' to me.'

'Isn't it? You should listen to Hitler some time. He doesn't like dwarfs very much. Or midgets. He doesn't like little people.'

Archie wriggled. 'You're just saying that to get at me.'

Lohmann endeavoured to shrug. It gave him an opportunity to put even more pressure on the rope.

'Maybe,' he said. 'But it's true.'

'I'm not listening.' The dwarf became petulant now.

Lohmann changed tack. 'Three quid a week, Marshall pays you?'

'It's enough. Big people around would slit your throat for thirty bob a week.' Archie giggled again. He was quite a giggler.

'It's not very much considering you may become an accessory to murder . . .'

'I'm not going to kill anybody!'

'But am I not to be killed?'

'Not by me! Unless you get rough. Then it would be self-defence. Anything else, *they* can do . . .'

'You're still an accessory. Makes you as guilty as if you had pulled that trigger.'

The dwarf looked at the gun, pointed it away from Lohmann, and started to perspire.

'And all for three quid a week?' Lohmann said.

A gleam appeared in the little man's eye. 'I could ask for more. If I have to be what you called it, an accessory, the Doc would have to pay me a bit more. Sure, he would.'

It wasn't quite the reaction Lohmann had expected. Also it showed something of a lack of morality in Archie. Lohmann shifted as far as he could on the bed and looked down at his wrists. If he had succeeded in loosening the rope around his wrists, there was no sign of it. The fibre was still biting into the skin. It would take him hours to wriggle free of the rope, if ever. There had to be another way.

'I'll ask him for twenty quid,' Archie went on. 'Twenty quid would be good.'

'Cheap rate for murder,' Lohmann said and had an idea.

'You think I should ask for more?' God, he wanted to know the going rate for murder.

'Archie, can I have a drink of water?'

The walnut face became suspicious.

'Why?'

'Because I am thirsty.'

'You'll try and escape.'

'I am still tied up. How do I try and escape?'

The dwarf considered the question. 'You promise you won't try?'

'I promise.' At least not until you come back, Lohmann told himself.

Archie dropped from his chair again. 'I have to go to the bathroom anyway,' he said. He walked with a rolling gait out of the ring of light. Lohmann slid down the bed and then, with some effort forced himself into a sitting position. The rope that tied his foot to the bed-end bit into his ankle and he winced. Waiting.

Minutes passing. Then there was the sound of a flushing lavatory, followed by the sound of a running tap.

The dwarf came back into the light carrying a cracked cup with no handle.

Again, suspiciously, he peered at Lohmann. 'You're sitting,' he said.

'I can't drink lying on my back.'

This seemed to satisfy Archie. He came to the side of the bed, holding the cup out.

'I don't think I can hold the cup, tied up like this,' Lohmann said.

''Well, I'm not untying you,' Archie replied, squinting. 'Here, I'll give it to you.'

It was going to work, Lohmann told himself. The dwarf had the cup in one hand, the Mauser in the other. The problem was, would he use the Mauser if he was able to do so? The dwarf brought the cup to Lohmann's lips. Lohmann raised his arms and clamped them around the dwarf's neck squeezing as hard as he could, barely managing to get his arms over the large head.

Archie squealed and dropped the cup. 'What you doin'? You're hurting me.'

'That is the intention,' said Lohmann, exerting pressure. The dwarf's eyes bulged.

'You . . . you . . . promised . . .' he said, choking. 'Not to try and . . . escape.'

'That was while you were away. You're back now.'

The dwarf still had the Mauser in his right hand. And the right hand was free. The little man brought the Mauser up and pressed it into Lohmann's side.

'I . . . can . . . shoot . . . you!'

'Yes, you can. That would be murder. You would hang for it.'

The bulging eyes were close to Lohmann's face.

'And I might not let go, even if you killed me. You've heard of the death grip?' He was improvising now. 'The victim, even in death, doesn't let go. You'd be stuck here, held in the embrace of your victim.' To Lohmann the image he was creating suddenly seemed almost comical. A dark humour he had to resist, by keeping his face straight.

146

'I wonder when they last hanged a dwarf in England,' he went on. 'I think it was nineteen twenty-six in Germany. They had to build a special gallows.'

He increased the pressure on the dwarf's neck. He felt the Mauser digging into his ribs. But the small hand that held it was trembling.

'I . . . I'll shoot . . .' Archie managed to gasp. 'Let . . . me . . . go . . .'

'You'd better shoot then. Because, if you don't, I shall strangle you.' Lohmann felt suddenly afraid. If he'd misjudged the little man, if Archie was capable of killing . . .'

'All right, all right,' Archie managed to get the words out and the Mauser fell away from Lohmann's side. 'Wha' . . . what d'you want me to do?'

'Put the Mauser in my hands. Then I let you go and you untie me.'

'What if I don't untie you . . . ?'

'Even with my hands tied I can shoot you.'

'You wouldn't . . .'

'Do it!'

Archie reached behind his neck and put the pistol in Lohmann's bound hands. At once Lohmann relaxed his grip, lifted his arms from around the dwarf's neck, and pointed the pistol at him. The dwarf staggered back, gasping for air, and found himself staring at the pistol.

'Be very careful,' he said, small hands in front of him as if to avert a possible bullet.

'Untie my leg.'

Archie did so. The small body was trembling.

'Now stand directly in front of me and untie my wrists.'

Again he did as he was told, the Mauser at his chest. As the ropes were loosened, Lohmann felt the blood rush into the constricted palms and fingers. The sensation of pins and needles took over one hand. He managed to hold the Mauser without trembling. Archie backed away.

'You're not going to shoot me now?'

'I'm not going to shoot you now,' Lohmann reassured him. 'Provided you don't make a move against me.'

'I won't . . . I won't. But they'll be back soon.'

Lohmann rose from the bed. There was the usual dull ache at the back of his head, where he'd been struck down. Momentarily he felt the room swim around him. He forced himself to stand erect, head high, and gradually the room settled down.

'Where are we?' he asked of the dwarf.

'Attic room of the church.'

A compliment, calling it a church, Lohmann thought. He looked at the sloping roof, the underside of corrugated iron. From beyond the door and below there came sounds, voices and the noises made by boots on a wooden floor.

'They're back!' said the dwarf, eyes expanding, circular universes about to explode.

'Another way out?'

The dwarf's head went from side to side. Searching.

'There's a window back of the bathroom. A metal ladder down the side of the building. Like a fire escape.'

'Show me.'

He followed the dwarf into what the little man had called the bathroom. He shut the door behind them. If Marshall came in and found the attic empty he might presume the escape had been effected down the main stairway some time before. It might give them a few precious extra seconds. He looked around the so-called bathroom. There was a washhand basin and a cracked lavatory bowl with a broken wooden seat. No sign of a bath. Behind the lavatory bowl was a half window of frosted glass edged with cobwebs. To reach it you would have to stand on the bowl.

'Get up and open it,' Lohmann told the dwarf.

Archie tried. He climbed onto the bowl, teetering on the edge and tried to reach the window catch. His arms weren't long enough.

'Can't reach!'

The voices below seemed to be getting louder. He had the Mauser certainly but Marshall and his friends might also be armed. Certainly they outnumbered him. He lifted Archie from the edge of the bowl, placed him on the floor, and, jumping up, took his place. The catch on the window was old and rusted. His first attempt at opening it was unsuccessful. The rusted catch didn't budge. He took the butt of the Mauser, slipped the safety-catch on with his thumb and, using the butt as a hammer, hit the catch hard twice. The catch gave. He forced the window open. Cold, damp air struck his face. He reached out and felt the top rail of a metal ladder. And felt the rust come off on his hand.

Then he remembered the dwarf. He turned expecting Archie would have scuttled away. But Archie was still there, standing, walnut features screwed up as if he had been willing him to open the window.

'You did it!' The voice hoarse. 'Take me with you!'

'What . . . ?' Lohmann, surprised.

'You leave me here, they come up and you're gone, I get hell. I know Doctor Marshall. He's crazy. He'll kick me. He's done it before. For three pounds a week, I took it. But now, he might not stop. Kick me. To death maybe.'

Sounds from below seemed to be coming nearer. Coming upwards.

'They're on the stairs.' Archie said. 'Please . . .'

'Yes. Very well. Climb up.'

'Have to lift me out of the window.'

Archie climbed onto the other side of the bowl. Lohmann lifted him up and out of the window. Thinking to himself, Ernst Lohmann was out of practice at his job. A dwarf who'd held him captive, he was helping out of the lavatory window of an evangelical chapel near Hammersmith Broadway. Life was both dangerous and farcical.

'Don't let go until I tell you I'm on the ladder,' Archie's voice came from outside in a whisper.

Then, another whisper. 'I'm on the ladder. Climbing down.'

Behind Lohmann, in the attic room, he heard the door open. He put the Mauser in his pocket, scrambled up and out the window. Feeling for the ladder. He could hear Archie below him climbing downwards like a monkey. He followed him down, praying the ladder was not too rusted.

Faintly, from above, he heard, a shout. His absence had been discovered. Under his feet the ladder creaked its protest at the unaccustomed weight. At least Archie hadn't added much more weight to the rusting iron.

Only one storey and the attic. Not far to go.

149

Then he was on the ground at the rear of the building. He became aware only then that it was raining. Archie was standing, a diminutive gnome, shivering.

'Now we run,' he said.

A plaintive groan. 'I'll never keep up. Legs . . . too short . . .'

Only one thing to do. Lohmann reached down, lifted the dwarf, tucked him under one arm and ran around the building onto the street. And kept running in the direction of Hammersmith Broadway.

THIRTEEN

Lohmann said: 'What time is it?'

His wrist-watch had gone, probably taken by one of Marshall's people when they'd tied his wrists. Under his arm, the dwarf wriggled, and pulled a silver pocket-watch from his jacket.

'Stop running a minute,' the dwarf said.

Lohmann stopped, grateful for the opportunity to catch his breath. Archie peered at his watch.

'Twenty to three,' he said and replaced his watch in his jacket. 'Better keep moving.'

Lohmann started to run again, Archie Dafoe still under his arm. A surrealistic picture. An alien ex-police inspector running towards Hammersmith Broadway at nearly three o'clock on a damp morning, with a dwarf tucked under his arm.

Archie somehow managed to turn his head, looking back along the street.

'They're not following,' he announced. 'But best to keep going until we get to the Broadway.'

Lohmann moved on, half running, half stumbling. Not because of Archie; the dwarf wasn't too heavy but he was an awkward shape. It was the aching pain at the back of his head

150

that was making him stumble. People should not, he told himself, be struck heavily on the head.

At last they reached the Broadway and the Underground Station; which was of course dark and shuttered.

'Have to get a taxi,' Lohmann said and gratefully stood the little man down on the pavement.

Gravely Archie smoothed down his jacket and readjusted his clothing. Lohmann stared along the road. There was nothing in sight, no cars, no taxis, no pedestrians.

'Might get a late-night bus,' Archie suggested.

'We stand, waiting for a bus that might not come for hours, while your friends look for us?' Lohmann said, feeling distinctly weary.

'Not friends of mine now. After all I helped you escape,' said Archie.

'You helped me escape? You had no choice.'

'I *did* help! You want a taxi, I'll get you a taxi,' the dwarf said, scowling. He put his fingers to his mouth and emitted a screeching whistle.

They waited.

Still nothing in sight.

Then, to Lohmann's astonishment, a taxi came around the corner and drew up at the kerb beside them.

'Drop me off at my place?' said the dwarf, looking self-satisfied.

'Get in!' The self-assurance of the little man astonished him. 'Where do you live?'

'Old Compton Street,' Archie informed the driver, giving him a street number.

'And then on to Museum Street,' Lohmann added.

The taxi moved off. At the corner of the Broadway Lohmann thought he saw figures running towards them. If it was Marshall and his friends, they were too late. He leant back on the cool leather of the back seat. Archie produced a battered packet of Gold Flake, took a cigarette from it and was about to put it back in his pocket when he seemed to realise he wasn't alone.

'Want a fag?'

Lohmann took one. The little man grinned. 'What would you do without me?'

151

'I'd have been out of that attic a great deal sooner.'

The walnut face glowered. 'You just don't appreciate me. Now I'm on your side, you'll see. You won't be able to do without me.'

'I hope that is not a promise,' Lohmann said. The idea of Archie Dafoe as an assistant was not to be thought on. If he changed sides once, he wouldn't hesitate to change sides again.

'You live in Soho?' he asked Archie, grateful he'd thought of another subject.

'It was near the cinema I used to work in. Anyway I like Soho. People accept me there. They do! And . . .' A peculiar look appeared on the surface of the walnut. '. . . I have a lady friend there.' The look was Archie's attempt at indicating lechery.

'She pays half the rent too,' he added with some pride. 'When I've been skint, she even pays my half as well. You'd like her. If you're interested I can fix something up.'

It was said with a strange kind of naivety. Lohmann knew he shouldn't be surprised . . . in Berlin, he'd known all kinds . . . criminals, perverts, eccentrics . . . but Archie Dafoe, all of three feet tall, was unique. Cinema organist, church organist, associate of a right-wing group that would not hesitate to kill . . . and now a procurer, a pimp who ran at least one girl on the streets.

'I think I can find my own women,' he said.

Archie shrugged. 'Maybe it's better. See, I'm good and, knowing that wouldn't be good for your ego.' He grinned. 'Anyway, she really loves me. Anything else is just business. But I can be a help to you, Mister Lohmann. In other ways. Like I said.'

This time Lohmann said nothing. He settled against the seat and studied London in rain and darkness. Finally the taxi pulled into Old Compton Street and drew up outside a narrow doorway between a continental newsagent's and a baker's shop.

'Take my friend to Museum Street,' Archie said to the driver, and turned to Lohmann. 'What number?'

Lohmann gave him the number. Archie repeated it to the driver and grinned back at Lohmann. 'See! Now I know how to get hold of you.'

And finally, to the driver. 'He'll pay and give you a nice tip. Good night.'

Lohmann slept until midday. Without dreaming. The result of the blow to his head? He slept through the Sunday morning sounds of church bells as if he'd been drugged, which he hadn't. The pain in his head had gone, thanks to aspirins and sleep. But the back of his head was still tender and he could feel the rising swelling above the hairline.

He made coffee and went back to bed. To think. Rennie was the key. Something, verbal or otherwise had passed between Rennie and Beth Coverley. Beth had died because of whatever had passed between them. And Rennie had gone on sick-leave. After searching Beth's apartment. And paying Hugo Richards to take his place at the Angleton Hotel. Richards had been killed because whoever was after Rennie had thought Richards was Rennie. They knew otherwise now.

Mrs Rennie had deliberately led those who were following her to the Angleton. That was Lohmann and the men in the other car. Why the hell had he not taken the registration number of the other car? He was slipping, he told himself. In Berlin, he would have noted that registration number, as well as the taxi's.

Mrs Rennie had then driven on. To where? Not the Church of Christ Evangelist in Hammersmith. Marshall and his people were still looking for Rennie. So the taxi-driver, Gorman, had lied; probably been paid to lie. Had known Lohmann wasn't coming out of the church so he hadn't bothered to wait.

Lohmann determined he had to visit the Rennie house again. Mrs Rennie might have returned home to Hornsey Rise. He might yet find out where Rennie was. One thing was certain. He wasn't hiking in the Lake District for his health. Also, following the visit to Hornsey, he had to pay a visit to the taxi-driver, Gorman, again. He finished the coffee and rising, washed, shaved and dressed. Going out into the London Sunday, he found Norman brushing the front hall with the door open and sunlight outside.

'Nice day, Mister Lohmann,' said the caretaker. 'Makes a change.'

153

Lohmann noted it was a nice day. 'How's your mother, Norman?'

'Just the same. She's always the same. It's monotonous. A man was asking for you this morning. I told him you wasn't in.'

'Why did you tell him that?'

'Didn't like the look of him.'

Lohmann opened his mouth to protest at Norman making judgement on his visitors and then stopped himself. Under the circumstances it might be a good idea not to be in to visitors.

'The man left his card,' Norman said, handing Lohmann an oblong of pasteboard.

On one side was printed:

Dr Raven Marshall.
Pastor, First Church of Christ Evangelist.
Hammersmith.

Lohmann turned the card over. On the reverse was a scrawl in pencil.

As Mister Coward wrote, 'We'll meet again!'

He looked up at the caretaker. 'Thank you, Norman. You did the right thing. In future I'm not in to anyone, unless I tell you.'

Norman grinned lop-sidedly. 'Right you are, Mister Lohmann.'

How had Marshall known his address, Lohmann asked himself. He wasn't in the phone book. Only friends and the immigration people knew his address. And the little man who had heard him give it to the taxi-driver last night; Archie Dafoe, maybe, returning to the fold?

He walked in the unexpected sunlight, through damp, dead leaves to the parked Morris. He climbed in and drove to Hornsey Rise and the Rennie house.

He rang the doorbell and waited. A strange woman in her fifties, hairpins protruding from a scarf around her head, came to the door.

'I'd like to see Mrs Rennie,' he said.

'Out of luck, mate. Gone to join her husband on holiday. Walking holiday. As if people don't get enough walking just doing it every day.'

'I see. When did she leave?'

'Day before yesterday. You're not the police again, are you? Sent a man the day she went.'

'I'm not the police.' He found it strange saying that. Too many years of announcing he was the police.

'Thought you might be. They was looking for her. Some friend of her husband's was done in, in some hotel or other. Not that they thought he'd done it. So they said. Well, he couldn't, could he? Him being in the Lake District, walking.' The woman was, to say the least, garrulous. 'I told 'em, me, I know nothing. I'm the char. Just paid to come in and keep the place tidy.'

'Thank you,' said Lohmann, stepping back.

'And then there was the other lot asking for them.'

Lohmann stopped. 'When was that?'

'Just this morning. 'Course they was just like them Witnesses.'

'Witnesses?'

'You know. Religious lot. Jehovah's Witnesses. Tells you they'll be the only ones get into heaven. I always say, if them's all that'll get in, I'd rather go to the other place. Not that this lot were Jehovah's Witnesses. This was another lot. Church of something evangelic . . . something like that.'

The ubiquitous Doctor Marshall on the trail as ever.

'You're not that lot?' the woman asked.

'No. I am just . . . a friend. Thank you.'

He went back to the car and drove towards Archway. Thinking that Mrs Rennie had gone directly from the Angleton Hotel to join her husband. Wherever he was. And wherever the taxi-driver, Gorman, had taken her was not her final destination. Otherwise Gorman would not only have taken Lohmann to the church in Hammersmith but also told Raven Marshall where he had taken Mrs Rennie. But Marshall was still looking. Lohmann had no doubt he'd even sent his people . . . the charlady's *evangelics* . . . to try and find out where Rennie was.

He drove down the Holloway Road to the offices of North Thameside Luxury Cabs Ltd, in Cobden Lane. The offices consisted of a large wooden hut at the edge of a yard in which

155

were parked a number of taxi-cabs. He went into the hut. Behind a counter a large man in a short leather coat was sitting eating a thick sandwich, a mug of tea in his hand. Behind him was an ancient telephone switchboard and on the wall above the switchboard was a chart listing cabs by number and their availability.

'Want a taxi, mate?'

'No. I want to see one of your drivers.'

'Ah, well, it's Sunday, you see. Half of them is off.'

'I spoke to a young woman on the telephone yesterday . . .'

'Ah, well, she's off too. Sunday. See.'

'Gorman,' Lohmann said. 'James Gorman.'

'Oh, Jimmy,' said the man. 'He's off too.'

'Can you give me his address?'

The man rubbed his chin with the edge of his sandwich. 'Naw. Can't do that. Not allowed to do that. I mean, that's personal, in't it?'

Lohmann sighed inwardly, took out his wallet and put a five pound note on the counter.

The man rose to his feet and placed his sandwich and the mug of tea on top of the switchboard.

'I shouldn't be doin' this,' he said, and Lohmann knew he would do it.

The man lifted the fiver, crammed it into an inside pocket of his coat and, going over to a side table, took a well-thumbed ledger and brought it over to the light on the counter. He thumbed through it.

'Here we are. Flat eight . . . that's top flat . . . Shaftesbury Buildings, Camden Town.'

'Has Gorman a telephone?'

'Oh, yeah, we all have. The firm insists. 'Case they need a driver in an emergency. Not in the phone book though. They won't have that. 'Case we do private hire work. Fair enough. They own the cabs.'

'You know his telephone number?'

'No, but it'll be in the book there.'

The man moved to the ledger but Lohmann reached out and, taking it from the counter, looked down at the open page.

There was the name, 'James Gorman'. He ripped the page from the book.

'Here, you can't do that!' the man protested.

'I've done it,' said Lohmann. 'You can replace it tomorrow.'

'But what did you have to . . .?'

'Because I'd rather you didn't phone Gorman and tell him I'm coming.'

Lohmann placed the ledger, minus one relevant page, back on the counter, nodded an acknowledgement to the man and went out of the hut.

Shaftesbury Buildings was a block close to Camden Town. It was a tenement like so many other London tenements in a narrow street like so many other streets in London. A common entry led to a stairway. Each landing had two doors leading to two apartments. Gorman's was indeed on the top storey. There was no bell but a discoloured brass knocker in the centre of the door. Lohmann knocked.

Gorman opened the door, moon face and craters collapsing into fright as he saw his visitor. He tried to shut the door but Lohmann pushed his way inside. Gorman backed away.

'What do you want?' he said.

'A word with you,' Lohmann replied.

'I . . . I got nothing to say to you.'

'I asked you to wait for me last night.'

'Didn't hear you.' Still backing away against the wall of the tiny hallway. Dressed in a discoloured undervest and crumpled trousers, held up by braces over the undervest, and with the top fly buttons undone. The garb for a restful Sunday.

Lohmann looked around the hallway. Two other doors, two other rooms.

'You heard me,' Lohmann went on. 'Let's talk.'

They went to the door on the left. Into a kitchen-cum-sitting-room. With a kitchen range, once black-leaded, now just black and stained. A fire in the grate. A table with a mug and a half empty milk bottle. Under a window, a sink. And a woman of indeterminate age bending over a gas cooker. She looked up, straggling hair over a tired face.

'What is it, Jimmy?'

157

Lohmann answered. 'He has a visitor. Asking questions about last night.'

The woman's face twitched nervously. 'It's that hundred pounds. You nicked it.'

'Shut up!' said Gorman.

The woman scowled. She was used to being silenced. But Lohmann didn't think she was the type to be silent for long.

'Someone gave you a hundred pounds, Gorman?'

Gorman who was bending, cowering, tried to straighten up. 'So? My business. Services rendered. Big driving job.'

The woman's scowl turned into a sneer.

Lohmann said: 'I asked you to take me where you had taken the woman from the Angleton. You didn't. You took me to that church in Hammersmith. Why?'

The woman couldn't keep silent any longer. She addressed Gorman. 'That's what you got the hundred quid for. To take him to the wrong place.'

'Told you to shut up!'

'Told you, you were up to no fuckin' good!' she retorted triumphantly.

'One hundred pounds,' Lohmann said coldly. 'Not much when it leaves you open to a charge of attempted murder.'

There was a silence. Finally broken by Gorman.

'I never attempted to murder no one! Look, you trying to fit me up? You try telling that to the police. They won't listen to you. A bleedin' foreigner.'

A barrier he had never faced in Germany; no official status and an alien into the bargain. He was getting used to bluffing it out.

'Telephone?' he said.

'What makes you think we got a telephone?'

'Your company installed one. Where is it?'

Gorman flushed angrily. The woman answered. 'It's in the other room.'

Lohmann walked through to the other room. Followed by Gorman and the woman. The woman seemed to be enjoying herself. The room consisted of an ancient carpet, two arm-chairs, the stuffing protruding from one of them, and a large wireless receiver, the frontage designed to look like the façade of a picture palace in miniature. There was also a large bed, unmade, in the corner of the room. At the side of a fireplace, the grate filled with ashes, was a small table on which stood the telephone, upright in the fashion of the time, like an ear, listening.

'Wait a minute!' Gorman, behind him, said. 'You ain't got my permission to use that telephone.'

Lohmann lifted the telephone and waited. The operator's voice came on the line.

'Number please?'

'Whitehall one-two, one-two.'

'All right, all right . . . what do you want?' Gorman crumbled, indicating Lohmann was to hang up the receiver. He did so.

'First . . . the hundred pounds you were paid.'

'Aw, look . . .'

'The money, please.'

Reluctantly Gorman reached into his back pocket and produced a wad of notes. Lohmann took it from him.

'Thank you. Now you will please inform me of the man who gave you this money and told you to take me to Hammersmith.'

'Don't know his name. Honest, I don't. I'd tell you if I did.'

'You get ten pounds of this money back if you tell me his name.' Lohmann held up the wad of notes. Gorman stared greedily at the notes.

'I'd tell you if I could. I can use that money . . .'

The woman cut in. 'Oh, sure he can. At the pub every night.'

'Look, I don't know his name. Never saw the man in my life before,' Gorman said desperately. 'But he had a scar down one side of his face.'

The man called Joyce? It was something, and it fitted the pattern Lohmann was arranging in his head.

'Worth five pounds,' Lohmann said, placing a fiver from the wad of notes on the back of one of the armchairs. Gorman moved to snatch the note.

'No!' the German said sharply. 'Leave it there.'

The taxi-driver stopped.

'Second question . . .'

'Go on.'

159

'Have you any idea how the man with the scar knew I was proposing to look for the woman?'

Gorman shook his head. 'Don't know nothing there. Just this bloke coming up and telling me, if anybody phoned and asked me to take them to where I took that woman after the Angleton, I was to direct . . . or take . . . them to that chapel in Hammersmith.'

That, Lohmann knew, was his difficult question. There was no reason why Gorman should know, or even ask. Not with a hundred pounds under his avaricious little eyes.

'Third question.'

'Yeah, yeah, go on.'

'Where did you take the woman after you left the Angleton Hotel?'

'You wouldn't believe me.'

'I'm a trusting man. They'll tell you that in Berlin.'

Gorman started to laugh. 'Won't do nobody any good. Told the character with the scar. Didn't do him any good.'

'Where?'

'Victoria Station.'

Lohmann stared at him. Gorman's laughter dried up. 'It's true. Honest.'

The woman said: 'It's true. He hasn't the nerve to lie now.'

Lohmann believed both of them. It was so useless and so right it had to be true. He stood for a moment, man facing a blank wall. Nowhere to go.

'Listen,' said Gorman. 'Tell you something I didn't tell the character with the scar. You give me my money back, I'll tell you.'

Lohmann said nothing, still staring at him. Gorman twitched.

'All right, I'll tell you. The woman didn't take a train. She went to Victoria but she didn't take a train. You know what she did?'

Lohmann, waiting.

'I saw her,' Gorman went on. 'Got out of my cab, paid me and walked across to the pavement outside the station. And she climbed into another cab. She did. It just drove off. Hell, if I'd known everybody was going to be so interested, I'd have followed that other cab. Didn't even know the driver, didn't even get the number.'

The taxi-driver ran out of words. He stood, watching Lohmann. Expectantly.

Lohmann turned and, passing the woman, went out into the hall. Gorman came after him.

'The rest of my hundred quid?' he said.

At the door, Lohmann took out the wad of notes, took another tenner from it and handed it to the woman who had come into the hall behind Gorman.

'You had better keep that for him,' the German said. 'He is not good with money.'

It was the woman's turn to laugh. Loud and piercing. She enjoyed it.

Gorman said: 'That's my money!'

Lohmann shook his head. 'You sold me for that money. Now you're buying me back. Also I lost my wrist-watch. I can now buy a new one.'

He went out, closing the door of the apartment behind him. The moment the door was closed he heard Gorman shout at the woman, and the woman shouted back. She was the louder of the two. He went down to the street and the parked Morris.

Behind the wheel, he thought, something he'd never have done in Berlin. Take the money. Eighty-five pounds anyway. It had come from the man with the scar, Joyce. Part of the attempt to eliminate ex-Inspector Lohmann. So they'd paid and it hadn't happened. Well, they should pay for something. In the end someone would have to pay.

He drove back to Museum Street and his room. In the room he sat over the table with the typewriter on it, and stared out of the window at a wall of the British Museum. It was appropriate to study brick walls. And permit the occurrence of his identity problem. Again.

Once he was Lohmann, Inspector, Criminal Police. With the facilities. The police of a capital city had so many facilities. Now, the refugee, the alien, Lohmann, without even citizen-ship, in a foreign city. And he's asked to be a detective again. No status, he'd thought that before, no facilities, no aides and assistants. And one dead woman journalist, one missing civil servant and people trying to kill Lohmann because they thought he knew what he didn't know.

People trying to kill him? He presumed that was the motive. Unless they thought he didn't know, but might find out. That was more logical. But he had come to a blank wall. Where was the civil servant, Rennie? His wife had probably joined him. But where in the world?

Time to use somebody else's facilities.

He went downstairs and phoned Scotland Yard. Not Emerson this time, not to bother Charles too often. Consider what Thornhill might come up with. Give him the chance.

He was connected to Scotland Yard. He asked for Superintendent Thornhill and gave his name.

The operator was a policewoman. 'I'll see if he's available.'

'That is what I'm asking you to do.'

'He may not be in today. After all, it is Sunday.'

'Does crime in England stop on a Sunday?'

The policewoman had no answer to that. 'Hold on,' she said.

Lohmann waited. All detective work was ninety percent waiting. He had nursed that thought often before. From the basement below the hall, where Norman lived with his mother, there came the sound of music. Either a wireless or a gramophone. Playing 'Red Sails in the Sunset.'

Finally Thornhill came through. As 'Tiger Rag' took over from 'Red Sails'.

'Lohmann? What can I do for you?'

'I need assistance. In the matter of Beth Coverley.'

'Any developments?'

'Some. Your Treasury Department will have a personnel file on Edward Rennie?'

Thornhill laughed at the other end of the line. 'Not *my* Treasury. The government's.'

'Can you get hold of that file?'

'Possibly.'

'I'd like to see it.'

'You shouldn't. But I'll see what I can do.'

'Thank you, Superintendent. Any developments on the stabbing of Hugo Richards?'

162

'Not my case, Lohmann. Anstey's on that. I believe he has an all-points bulletin out on the Rennies. The wife hasn't returned. Not since Newton went to question the charlady.'

'I know. I went up and had a talk with her myself today. As did some others.'

'Who would that be?' Thornhill asked casually.

'I think friends of a certain Doctor Raven Marshall. I have found out, during my own investigations, that this Doctor Marshall has an interest in finding Rennie too.'

'Raven Marshall,' Thornhill said. 'Ah, yes, I've come across him. Acolyte of Oswald Mosley. A preacher, I believe. Of some pretty nasty theories. I must mention his interest to Anstey, if I can remember it.'

Lohmann felt suddenly angry. 'Do you people not help each other? You are all police officers. Yet you sound as if you are in competition with this Inspector Anstey.'

'Not competition, Lohmann. Shall we say that, in the Special Branch, we pass on information on what we British call a *need to know* basis. I may feel informing Anstey about Marshall would add too much to his work load. It might cause Anstey to intrude into investigations that are not his in which to intrude.'

'Like the link between Rennie, the killing of Richards and the death of Beth Coverley?' said Lohmann.

'Right! After all, officially there is no investigation into Beth's death. Except for your own private interest. You wouldn't want Anstey bursting in on that. A large, conscientious officer with a heavy hand and foot, not your type at all, Lohmann.'

Lohmann was partly mollified. An official investigation would put him out of the case. He would be an irrelevance, unnecessary, unwanted. And now he had a proprietary interest. Also he was doing what he was trained to do.

Thornhill went on. 'And if Beth's death became an official investigation, I would carry it out myself. For personal reasons.'

'You are working on Beth's death,' Lohmann said. 'You're using me but you are involved.'

'No, no, I'm working on foreign visitors playing espionage

163

games around our defence establishments. I told you. Also on German aliens coming into the country as refugees and, in fact still working for Admiral Canaris and the Abwehr. Know anybody that fits the description, old man?'

Lohmann thought, he's not simply using me to investigate Beth Coverley's death; he's using Beth's death to investigate me! It was clever; two birds with one stone, wasn't that an English saying?

'I think I see what you're doing, Thornhill.'

'Good. You see, I make no secret of my work. Or part of it. Just letting you know, Lohmann.' Thornhill managed to sound both affable and threatening at the same time.

'I understand, Superintendent,' Lohmann replied. 'Obviously my own assurances would mean nothing to you.'

'Hardly.'

'Assistant Commissioner Emerson's . . . ?'

'To be considered. But he may have been . . . taken in by an old friendship. Something like that.'

'Thank you for telling me. At least I know where I stand. But you forget, I was asked to enquire into Miss Coverley's death. I did not put myself forward.'

'Oh, I accept that. Until proved otherwise. But it could have been a marvellous piece of luck for you.'

Lohmann determined to return suspicion with suspicion. 'From my point of view, Thornhill, you may be a police official of similar persuasion to Sergeant Brundage at Leman Street. After all I have only your word that you were engaged to Beth Coverley.'

Thornhill laughed, a deep sound, at the end of the line. '*Touché*, Lohmann. I hadn't thought of that myself. Perfectly right. In the words of Hollywood films, neither of us can be sure who is the bad guy and who is the good guy. We are in a profession of such infinite complications, don't you think?'

'Or else we cannot see that which stares us in the face, Superintendent,' Lohmann replied quietly.

'Oh, if I do, Herr Lohmann, I will apologise to you, I assure you.' Thornhill took a deep breath. 'By the way, one thing in which you can help me. And it may be of interest to you. Have ever heard of the expression, *Tod Kommando*?'

164

He remembered. After the 'Night of the Long Knives', the night Hitler had disposed of his unwelcome comrades. The night of the massacre of the Brownshirts in 1934. The police had heard rumours of *Tod Kommando*, 'Death Squads', SS men, used by Himmler to destroy the SA. And later, when he was already an exile in Paris, stories coming from Hitler's Reich of the same 'Death Squads' used to eliminate enemies of the State. When arrest and confinement in a concentration camp was unnecessary or undesirable, bring in the *Tod Kommando*.

'Death Squads,' he said to Thornhill. 'I've heard stories in Germany. Nothing to do with the police. If they exist, they were SS or Gestapo.'

'Yes. Right,' Thornhill replied. 'I've heard the same stories. Now you know we have Mosley and his Fascists. And one or two other extreme right-wing groups in this fair land of ours. We've had disquieting rumours that all these little British parties have formed their own *Tod Kommando*. Their own . . . death squad.'

'Here? In London?'

'Hard to believe, isn't it? But, if it is so, then they would be the people who killed Beth. Who stabbed Hugo Richards to death. And who tried to kill you. That is, if the attempt on your life wasn't engineered to give you credibility.'

'You even think that?'

'I can't discount it. But if you are one of the "good guys", then there's one way I can be sure.'

'And that is?'

'If they kill you, Lohmann. You see we do believe that you might be their next target. If they succeed, then you will receive my . . . my belated apologies.'

FOURTEEN

Monday morning. That evening, the reception at the German Embassy. Lohmann wasn't even sure he knew why he was going. Certainly, von Ribbentrop's name was in Beth Coverley's notebook. But Lohmann had no idea why it was there. If Beth intended to interview the German Ambassador, she knew what questions she wanted to ask him. Lohmann did not.

Also, he told himself, he was taking a chance. The German Embassy was considered German soil. And Lohmann had considerable reason to believe that, once on German soil, he could be arrested. More than arrested; condemned and executed. Without trial. Even with a trial, the sentence would be indisputable. The former Inspector Lohmann knew too much about certain high-ranking Nazis. It was also possible that Lohmann was already considered officially dead. By courtesy of General Heydrich. A dead man cannot be executed. But he can be shot out of hand. Whether all this applied to Embassy territory was questionable.

Lohmann still in bed, contemplating death. In comfort, it was easier. And the bed was the only really comfortable place in the tiny room.

Not yet. Not yet ready for death. Too many things still to be done. Anna, in America, comes into this; he wanted to see his daughter grow up. Death squads or no death squads. And there was the killer of Beth Coverley to be found.

Regarding the investigation, there were questions at the edge of his mind. Why had Beth been killed? Why was Rennie running? What had he told Beth that caused him to search her apartment? What was he looking for in the apartment? Did he find what he was looking for, or was it simply his name in Beth's diary? How did Marshall and his friends know he had

Gorman's cab number? Where was Rennie? That was the reason he wanted the civil service file on Rennie. Thornhill had promised to try and get a copy of the file to him. There was a pattern to most people's lives, and from Rennie's pattern there just might be some clue as to where he might have gone.

The questions piled up. A distant bell rang.

Thornhill, was he really going to marry Beth? Was he investigating Lohmann? No worries there, Lohmann told himself. Unless some kind of evidence was manufactured. He'd seen police officers do it and he'd been tempted on several occasions himself when he told himself the man was guilty but he couldn't prove it. He could say smugly he'd resisted temptation.

Norman shouted from somewhere below.

'Telephone, Mister Lohmann!'

He rose. Wrapped in an aging dressing-gown, he went down to the phone. Norman was at the door, sorting out a pile of mail. He nodded to Lohmann

'Nothing for you today, Mister Lohmann.'

'Thank you, Norman.' Lohmann lifted the phone and at once recognised the voice at the end of the receiver.

'Hallo, Mister Lohmann! It's me!'

Archie Dafoe, high-pitched, over-affable. A torrent of words following Lohmann's acknowledgement of his presence.

'Remember, I'm working for you now, Lohmann. On your side. I told you. But just to prove it I went back to Hammersmith and snooped around Marshall's church. They had a service there last night. The bastard's got a new organist but I don't care. My girl says I shouldn't care. I say I shouldn't care. Anyway they had a meeting after the service . . .'

'Archie . . .' Lohmann tried to cut in but it was to no avail. The dwarf was in full spate.

'. . . and I got into the building. I know that chapel, I know so many ways of getting in, 'specially if you're my size. So I listened in to their meeting. You were right, they're not very nice. They're going to kill other people . . . not just you. And . . . there was another man there, I think he was the big chief. So I got to thinking, apart from helping you, I got information worth money. Since you lost me my job . . . okay, okay . . . they

167

were a nasty crowd . . . and, for now, I have no money coming in, if I told you about this man it might be worth something to you. I mean, you wouldn't want me to live off my girl, not all the time, would you?'

The flow came to an end. Lohmann was momentarily silent, trying to assimilate the words. At the other end of the line he could hear the little man breathing heavily.

Finally Lohmann spoke. 'I told you, Archie, I didn't want your help . . .'

'You got it anyway. Come on, Lohmann, this is worth your while. Whatever you been working on, maybe I just tied it all up in a nice parcel for you. You come, meet me, I'll tell you all I heard. You think it's worth it, you pay me. If not, no hard feelings. See, I trust you.'

'All right,' said Lohmann, reluctantly. Aware too that the dwarf could be setting him up. Although he didn't quite believe that. Archie Dafoe was going to be a nuisance, but he might just be a sincere nuisance. 'Where and when?'

'My place. Away from their prying eyes. You saw the door in Soho. Climb up to the top. That's my place. And they don't know anything about where I live so, in case you're followed, go a long way around. Make sure you're not followed.'

Lohmann thought of the German Embassy and Rue Scott-ffoliot. 'I have an appointment this evening.'

'You got a social life, Lohmann? Come after. Won't take us long. Midnight. My girl'll be out working. We'll be alone. I promise, no funny business. If you don't trust me, leave word where you're going with somebody. As insurance. Go on. I could use the cash.'

'If I decide to give you any cash.' Lohmann thought quickly. 'All right. Midnight. At your place.'

The dwarf giggled. 'You'll not regret it.'

An hour later, Lohmann went to Moss Brothers to pick up his dinner suit. Afterwards, he stopped at a modest jewellery shop in High Holborn and bought a new wrist-watch. He then drove on to the West End and the Gog and Magog.

Joe Kahn was sitting in a corner with two others. When he saw Lohmann, he excused himself and joined the German in an alcove in a far corner.

'Was with Claud Cockburn,' Kahn said. 'Thinks the Nazis will use Spain as a trial run for bigger things.'

'I am sure they will,' Lohmann replied. 'But how is Maurice Kovel?'

'He's fine. Jack Comer's got two boys at the house twenty-four hours a day.'

'Good. Tell him to keep them there. The old man is still in danger.'

'Lohmann, why are they doing this? What benefit could anybody get from the death of Maurice Kovel?'

'If I am right . . . and I think I am . . . they are afraid his daughter might have told him something of the story she was working on. Whether she did or she didn't they will not take the chance.'

'Who the hell are they?'

Lohmann sighed. 'If I could be sure, I would tell you. Certainly they are Fascists. A man called Raven Marshall might be involved. Have you heard of him?'

'I've heard of him. A *meshuggeneh* minister. Supported Mosley but is even further to the right than Sir Oswald. Not to be confused with Raven Thompson. The two Ravens, somebody once called them.'

'Who is Raven Thompson?'

'Mosley's philosopher, so called. Another lunatic.'

Lohmann waved a wandering barmaid over. He ordered a gin and tonic for Kahn and an ale for himself.

'The last time I saw Comer he said there was going to be big trouble in the East End.'

Kahn shrugged. 'When is there not? But we do think Mosley is planning a big march. It will go right through Cable Street. If anything can be called a provocation, that will be it. Meetings, he has, but a big march through a predominantly Yiddish district, that will be nasty.'

'How well do you know these Fascists?' Lohmann asked.

Kahn grinned. 'Know them? I should want to know them? Bully boys. Cockney Cossacks. England for the Englanders. They're not even too happy about the Scots and the Welsh. A bit like your Brownshirts in the early days.'

'But is there an organiser there? Mosley, for example? I mean

169

a real organiser. Someone with planning and tactics and special . . . special squads.'

'That far, I don't think they've got. Mosley wants power but all he's done is collect a party of narrow-minded, street bullies . . . he has got a personal bodyguard but that's the extent of his organisation. I think he even hopes to get into power through Parliament. His candidates have lost every by-election they've stood in. Oh, he has a few sympathisers in Parliament among the Tory extremists. Like Captain Ramsey and his friends. There's not many of them. Rothermere, the press baron, is for him, that's true. But Beaverbrook and the others wouldn't touch him with a barge-pole.'

'I asked about an organiser, Joe, not a history of the Party. Is there one man who might organise them . . . like Rohm or Himmler?'

'There is one who might. William Joyce.'

The drinks were placed in front of them. Lohmann sipped his ale thoughtfully.

'Yes, I've seen him. And I saw him again on Saturday night. He might be the one.'

Kahn looked puzzled. 'The one what?'

'I'm not sure. Is he big enough to be a leader? Has he the nerve? And the money. It would take money.'

'For what, for God's sake? He's got nerve. But no money. And he's not a big chief. He'd have to be pointed in the right direction.' Kahn said, still puzzled, turning to his gin and tonic.

'Somebody else then. Above him. Have you ever heard of a *Tod Kommando*, Joe?'

'I never have.'

'A Nazi death squad. Formed and used to commit murder when the Party deems it necessary. There were rumours about them in Germany.'

Joe Kahn did not hide his astonishment. 'In Germany, sure! But here, in England, in London, that's impossible. Wouldn't be allowed.'

'Wouldn't be allowed by whom? Sergeant Brundage and his type?' Lohmann smiled. Without humour. A dry, reluctant smile. In London, they knew so little, he thought, remembering Germany two years before.

170

'I believe they'd kill all right,' Kahn said grudgingly. 'They've proved that with Becky. But an organised murder squad . . .'

'Ask Comer,' said Lohmann, draining his ale. 'Ask around. Ask anybody you know. And tell me if you hear anything. Even a whisper.'

'I will. But I don't believe it. Not here. And you'll let us know if you find out anything about Beth's death?'

'You're paying me to do that.'

'Which reminds me, I have some money for you.' Kahn took an envelope from his pocket. 'Twenty-five pounds as a start. We'll raise the rest . . .'

'It's something,' said Lohmann. 'I have to eat. But for tonight, the German government will pay.'

'What are you on about now?'

'I am attending a reception at the German Embassy. Wish me luck. On German soil, I may have trouble surviving.'

Lohmann was dressing when the messenger came from Scotland Yard. A motor-cyclist in leathers insisted on handing over the bulky envelope to him personally. In his room, he opened it. It was headed:

PERSONNEL FILE – TREASURY DEPARTMENT. CONFIDENTIAL. EDWARD GEORGE RENNIE.

He laid it aside. To be studied later. He finished dressing. So many years since he'd dressed formally for an evening out. Seven, eight years, was it? His wife had been alive then. 1929. With the Nazis still merely a noisy rabble in the streets. Another place, another time. The memory was still painful. It had to be put away, left behind. One thing remained. He fitted the Mauser pistol into the inside pocket of the dinner jacket.

He drove to Dolphin Square.

The porter told him he should go right up to Miss Scott-ffoliot's apartment, he was expected.

A maid offered him a drink while he waited. He refused. Wanted to keep alert.

Then Rue Scott-ffoliot appeared. Her hair was cut short, the ends curling up above her neck. She wore a black, sheath-like

171

dress, low-cut with her shoulders bare. In the dress she moved like a black panther. The effect, he had to admit, was breathtaking.

'Darling, you're on time.' The voice low, and a smile on her face. Should he have been late? 'Never mind, I'm ready. But, you see, one should always make a late entrance. Much more effective.'

'In my circumstances, I would rather not make the entrance.'

'You mustn't worry. Remember, you are my Austrian cousin.'

'There will be people there who will recognise me.'

'That won't matter. You'll be with me. But the invitation had to be to my cousin, Franz Haller. I somehow don't think they would have been too happy greeting the former Inspector Lohmann.'

Of course she was right. It would have alerted certain people in the Embassy, people he would rather not have alerted.

'You see,' Rue went on. 'I've been hearing about you, Lohmann.'

His turn to be alert. 'From whom?'

'This morning I met an American journalist friend. He was a correspondent in Berlin. Philip Hardacre.'

He remembered Hardacre. A decent man, and a friend. He could relax again.

'You were such a celebrity,' Rue went on. 'You should have told me. The best detective in Germany, he said. And then you fell out with the Nazis.'

'That was the easy part,' Lohmann said.

'They say you fell out with Hitler personally. And he had heard you were dead.'

'They found it easier to say that.'

She changed the subject. 'Have you found out anything about Beth's death?'

'I'm following certain leads.'

She laughed. 'Phil Hardacre also said you were like a New England clam. Getting anything out of you was always a struggle. You think you can learn something at the German Embassy?'

172

'Who knows? Unfortunately I don't yet know all the right questions to ask. Still, one has to be hopeful.'

Suddenly she became serious. 'If you are recognised, will it be really dangerous for you to be on German soil? Aren't embassies considered to be just that?'

'It is possible. But I doubt if they will want trouble in front of so many important guests.'

She was frowning. 'If only HM were to be there. When he was Prince of Wales, he was quite cosy with the last German ambassador. They wouldn't dare do anything with the King as a guest. But he's sulking down at Fort Belvedere worrying about Wallis and Stanley Baldwin. Silly little man. I think, if Baldwin sticks to his guns, HM will throw it all up for Wallis. And, you know, I think she really thought she could be queen. Never mind. George might be there.'

From the quizzical expression on his face she realised he hadn't the faintest idea who George might be.

'The Duke of Kent,' she explained. 'He likes parties. Although Noël Coward's more his type than von Ribbentrop. Time to go. I shall stay very close to you, Lohmann.'

She smiled broadly now. 'As close as I was in your room the other day. Your own personal bodyguard.'

The porter saluted them as they left the building. Lohmann reckoned it was going to be a night of saluting.

The German Embassy was ablaze with lights. Illuminating the entire embassy row, yet at the same time, throwing other embassies into shadow. The interior was also ablaze with uniforms. The red tabs of the British General Staff were much in evidence as were the high-ranking insignia of senior military attachés from other embassies. But it was the German uniforms that stood out. The devil, Lohmann thought, gave his allies the best uniforms. There was the green and grey of the Wehrmacht, the black of Himmler's few representatives at the London embassy, and the pristine, white tunics and black trousers of diplomats and dignitaries of the Reich. Decorations were worn, as Lohmann knew they would be, and he had, with humour more English than German, worn the ribbon of his Iron Cross, second-class, earned in the Kaiser's war, in which he had participated reluctantly but with distinction.

Rue had commented on it in the car on the way to the embassy.

'Is that wise? Wearing a German medal-ribbon when you're supposed to be an Austrian?'

'Hitler was also an Austrian and he received the same medal.'

She giggled. 'You're saying it?'

'I'm telling you.'

It kept her amused until they were inside the embassy. There was a strange aroma there, as of perfume mixed with carbolic. Everything well-scrubbed for the occasion.

In the entrance to the large reception-room, they were announced.

'The Honourable Miss Rue Scott-ffoliot and Herr Franz Haller.'

Ribbentrop was standing, surrounded by aides, greeting the arrivals. He was dressed in white tie and tails, the Fred Astaire of the Third Reich, Lohmann thought as he shook a damp soft hand. No, not Fred Astaire, but a plastic figure, pale face, pale hair, despite every attempt to be otherwise, still the champagne salesman he had once been. Selling Germany like he had sold inferior champagne.

They went into the reception-room, Rue clinging to his arm. A huge crystal chandelier above their heads shone and sparkled. At the end of the room, a dance band . . . was it Harry Roy? . . . probably not, but it sounded like his band . . . was playing a fox-trot. The music was almost drowned by the hubbub of conversation.

'Half of them,' Rue whispered in his ear, 'are here for the buffet. The Nazis are not so popular so they have to put on a good show with the food. I was here once before and the people at the buffet weren't too pleased when I asked if they had any *gefüllte* fish. I wanted to bring one of the Rothschilds as my escort but he didn't think it was a good idea.'

The voice cut in on them.

'Herr Lohmann, isn't it? The question came from a small, fair-haired man with a tanned face who looked vaguely familiar to Lohmann.

'Stevens,' the man said. 'George Stevens. Charles Emerson introduced us at Grey's Club last week.'

Lohmann remembered. The Arabist, the other Lawrence of Arabia. He felt relieved. If he had to be recognised, at least it was by an Englishman.

'Of course I remember,' he responded and introduced Rue. Who was wary of his being recognised. Until she recognised Stevens' name.

'Of course I've heard so many stories about you,' she enthused. 'During the war, dressing like an arab. Marvellous. Like Valentino in *The Sheik*.'

Stevens was amused by the comparison. 'Hardly. I never did meet any beautiful females I could carry off to my tent.'

'I expect you were just unlucky,' Rue replied impishly.

A large, bear-like figure was at Stevens' side. The figure coughed loudly, demanding notice.

'Oh, may I introduce Colonel Claude Dansey?' Stevens said affably. 'Miss Scott-ffoliot and Herr Lohmann.'

Despite his rank, Dansey was wearing a dinner jacket, his bulk creating the impression that the jacket did not quite fit him. His manner matched the clothes, being at once brusque and seemingly ill-tempered.

'Knew your father,' he informed Rue. 'Bloody incompetent sailor.'

'It would take an incompetent colonel to appreciate that,' she replied quickly, face flushed with annoyance.

Dansey ignored her, turning to Lohmann. 'Heard you announced as somebody Haller. You incognito or merely gate-crashing?'

Before Lohmann could reply, Stevens intervened with consummate diplomacy. 'I think Herr Lohmann has his reasons for using a *nom de guerre*. And I think I see Admiral Sinclair beckoning to you, Dansey.'

The colonel, with a surprisingly polite 'Excuse me' turned on his heel and departed.

'You'll have to excuse Dansey. He's an irascible character with appalling manners but quite sound underneath. He likes, as one of his people said, ''to scatter his venom at long range, creating a maximum of resentment to no obvious purpose".'

'Thank you for getting rid of him, Mister Stevens,' said Rue with genuine gratitude. 'He sounds like a Nazi sympathiser.'

'I don't think so,' Stevens replied quietly, and turned to Lohmann. 'Charles Emerson is here somewhere.'

'I think it might be diplomatic of him to avoid me in this place,' said Lohmann. 'He helped me to come to England and this is not the place to advertise the fact.'

'I see. Interesting. Well, I shall leave you two. Delighted to meet an admirer of sheiks, Miss Scott-ffoliot. And, Lohmann, look me up some time. If I can be of assistance.'

He moved off as a waiter offered them drinks from a tray. Rue took two glasses, handing one to Lohmann.

'Champagne of course. Do you think von Ribbentrop gets it wholesale? Let's find the buffet. I'm starving.'

They moved into a side room, where the buffet was laid out on a long table. Guests were already crowding around it.

'Now you're here,' Rue said. 'What happens? Who do you cross-examine?'

'Hardly that,' Lohmann replied. 'I would like to speak to Ribbentrop. Mention Beth Coverley. See if I get a reaction. I doubt I'll get the opportunity.'

'Shall I flirt with him? Use my seductive wiles to lure him into a side room? They say he's quite susceptible.'

'Not, I think, the correct tactics.'

Rue made a face and moved towards the buffet.

'*Guten Abend, Herr Lohmann!*'

The voice came from behind Lohmann. He turned to face Walter Schellenberg. In SS uniform. Hair slicked down, eyes gleaming with a kind of amusement.

'We meet again,' said Schellenberg in English. 'I'm surprised to find you on German soil. You must know the embassy is so considered.'

'Perhaps I felt homesick.'

'A dangerous emotion for you. Why take such a risk? We might ask you to stay.'

'I might not feel that degree of homesickness.'

'You might have no choice.'

176

'I . . . I thought I would like to meet von Ribbentrop.'

Schellenberg smiled. 'It could be arranged. Somewhere away from the crowd.'

'Not too far away.'

Schellenberg looked around. 'There is a small room off the reception hall. An ante-room. For diplomatic discussion in private. Would that be suitable.?'

'Provided it hasn't a rear door. I wouldn't want a conducted tour of the cellars of the embassy. Too much like the cellars of the building on Prinz Albrechtstrasse.'

He'd been in the building in Berlin two years before. But not in the cellars. Though he'd heard about the cellars under Gestapo headquarters.

'We don't have cellars like that here,' Schellenberg said. 'A pity really. So useful. But, if you will excuse me, I'll see if the Ambassador can tear himself away. Only for a few minutes, you understand?'

'I understand.'

Schellenberg turned and marched back into the reception hall. Rue came up behind Lohmann.

'You've been recognised again?'

Lohmann nodded. 'An old acquaintance. But he may just arrange for me to speak to Ribbentrop in private. In that room off the hall.'

'You're mad. They'll try and trap you. Why else should they let you see Ribbentrop?'

'Possibly to find out what I know. They think I know more than I do. And it seems to worry them. Why should that be?'

'I haven't the foggiest idea. But I'm not going to let you go into that room. You might not come back. They might keep you here. They can. You're still a German citizen.'

'And I can still create a row. Which they will not want to do, close to the reception hall.'

Rue persisted. 'They could . . . they could knock you out. Drug you . . . anything like that . . . they could!'

'A chance I'll have to take. Part of a policeman's job. To take chances.'

'You're not a policeman any more! You're a bloody refugee . . .'

Schellenberg was returning. Marching across the hall towards them.

'If I don't come out,' Lohmann said. 'Ask the little man, Stevens, to look for Charles Emerson and tell him what has happened. Emerson is an Assistant Commissioner at New Scotland Yard. Not that he'll be able to do much on German territory.'

Schellenberg reached them. The heels clicked. 'The Ambassador will see you now.'

Rue made a gesture as if she was about to grip Lohmann's arm. Then she turned away. Resigned, it seemed.

The ante-room was quite large, the walls lined with books. Above a large ornate fireplace was a portrait of Hitler in oils. Taken from a familiar photograph showing him in a plain, uniform jacket with Sam Browne belt. No decorations, no medals. Simply the belt, the swastika armband and a faraway look. Staring off into the picture frame as if inspired. A fire was burning in the grate and there were several deep, comfortable armchairs and a long table. The room was empty.

'He will join us in a moment,' Schellenberg said.

They waited. As if representing two aspects of Germany. The old Germany, Schellenberg would have considered Lohmann: he himself would be the new Germany. That was the Germany that killed people as a political tactic. Lohmann was grateful he was not part of that Germany. Waiting, he studied the leather-bound volumes on the bookshelf nearest him. Goethe, Schopenhauer, Nietzsche and some minor German philosophers. Several copies of *Mein Kampf*. Bound copies of the Führer's speeches. A life of Frederick the Great.

Von Ribbentrop came in. Pale, bland features, small eyes peering at Lohmann.

'This is the man?' In German. Mouth contemptuous.

'This is the man, Herr Ambassador,' said Schellenberg.

Now the address, direct. 'You are Lohmann? I believe you are known as a traitor to the Third Reich.'

'Not so. As far as I have heard, I am considered a man who died carrying out a mission for Hitler.'

He heard that was how Heydrich had covered up his departure from Germany. An automobile accident. The neatly typed report of his investigations discovered in the car on his body. Heydrich's report. But that was an old story.

Ribbentrop stomped forward into the centre of the room. 'I can give you two minutes. I have guests. What do you want?'

'A lady called Beth Coverley wanted to interview you, I believe.'

'Many people want to interview me. I am the Ambassador of the Third Reich.'

'Very well. But why did this particular journalist want to interview you, Herr Ambassador?'

Ribbentrop paced the centre of the room. 'How should I know. She was killed before she did the interview.'

'Killed?' Lohmann said.

Ribbentrop knew he'd made a mistake. 'Died, killed, how do I know . . . ?'

'The woman committed suicide, sir,' said Schellenberg.

'Obviously an unbalanced woman. I am not unhappy about meeting British journalists. It is part of an ambassador's task to inform the people of Britain that the Third Reich holds them in high esteem.' Ribbentrop seemed to be about to embark on a routine political speech.

Lohmann stopped him. By taking a chance and a deep breath before speaking.

'I think she wanted to talk to you about information supplied by a British Treasury official.'

The Ambassador stopped pacing. His head came up.

'I know nothing about this!' he shouted. 'Nothing at all.'

He was too quick, too definite. Lohmann could see the lie at once.

'That was not the belief of Miss Coverley,' he said.

Schellenberg was quicker and cleverer than von Ribbentrop. 'You cannot hold the Ambassador responsible for the strange misconceptions of a British journalist,' he said smoothly.

Ribbentrop looked uncertainly at his aide. And then nodded. 'Exactly so. And now I will return to my guests.'

He went out. Still uncertain. Nervous. Face even paler than it had been. Glad to be gone.

Schellenberg said: 'Satisfied, Herr Lohmann?'

'You wouldn't expect me to be, Captain Schellenberg. At least I've learned what I came here to learn.'

'And what is that?'

'That you people have something to be afraid of. Now, if you will excuse me . . .'

'I think not, Lohmann.' Schellenberg was in front of the door. 'You have said you are aware that you are on German territory. I don't think you really believed we would let you out.'

The door was shut behind Schellenberg and he was standing in front of it.

'You are going to produce a gun?' Lohmann asked.

'Is it necessary? And we won't have to go out through the reception hall. The bookcase at the end of the room is false. Two of my men will come through. We may not have cellars like the Prinz Albrechtstrasse, but we have comfortable attics. General Heydrich wants you back in Germany. We will find a way of sending you back.'

Lohmann glanced behind him. A section of the bookcase had moved backwards on a pivot revealing an entry. Two large men in dinner jackets came out. Lohmann felt the comforting shape of the Mauser under his jacket. Be quite a sensation, he thought. *Refugee shoots his way out of German Embassy.* An interesting headline for the British press. Of course, if anyone got hurt, they would turn the truth on its head. Like the assassination of a German attaché in Paris by a Jewish refugee. *Another refugee emulates Jewish assassin in Paris. Ribbentrop saved from assassination attempt.* That was the way they would play it. Lohmann might even find himself being dubbed Jewish.

The problem was, could he reach the Mauser before the two men behind him produced weapons?

Then the door behind Schellenberg opened.

Rue Scott-ffoliot came in, carrying two glasses of champagne. She was followed by two men Lohmann had never seen before. They were young, fresh-faced, very English looking and possibly slightly drunk.

'Franz!' She greeted Lohmann, crossing the room to embrace him. 'I've been looking for you everywhere. I want you to meet Charlie Wykham and Johnny Causton.'

180

She made a face, nose in the air. 'Actually Lord Causton. Thought that would impress you. I'm sure your friends here will excuse us.'

FIFTEEN

It was time to go. Rue had calculated that the Embassy people wouldn't dare try and restrain Lohmann from leaving against his will. Especially in front of two guests, one of whom was a Peer of the Realm. The Nazis had an inordinate respect for titles, possibly a heritage from the old Junkers.

Charlie Wykham and Lord Causton, both of them pleasant if rather effete young men, accompanied them. Rue had given a brief explanation of why Lohmann had to get out of German territory; she doubted if they really understood the real reasons; to them it was a game and they enjoyed 'cocking a snook at the Boche', as Charlie put it.

Once outside the Embassy, Rue suggested they go to a night-club.

'It's early and the German Embassy isn't much fun.'

Lohmann could only think of excuses. 'For me, it is late. And I have to visit a man in Soho. You will excuse me . . .'

'We will not!' Rue insisted. He'd been learning she was accustomed to getting her own way. And, after all, she had pulled him out of a tight spot. Whether he could have escaped himself was problematic. He might have used the Mauser but Schellenberg and his companions would almost certainly be armed themselves. They would not have hesitated to use guns, and these would have been fitted with silencers. He might have managed a couple of shots with the Mauser, but then they would have produced some plausible explanation for two gunshots.

He went with them to the Kit-Kat Club.

It was a cellar, low-roofed, the atmosphere hazed by

cigarette and cigar smoke. The tables were small and cramped. The dance floor was a large postage stamp. The dance band clowned between and during numbers. Dancers, the women chic and elegant, moved around the postage stamp as if overcome by terminal boredom. Their partners, ranging from young to ancient, all impeccably dressed, appeared only fractionally more animated. At first the place reminded Lohmann of some of the cabarets in Berlin before the Nazis objected to the political satire which was part of their being. The English, Lohmann decided, took their pleasures as if they were at a funeral. World-weary and without joy. There was little of the unabashed lechery of the Berlin clubs. Here, lechery was muted, hidden, clandestine fumbling under the tables, or in dark corners. A few of the younger males, like Wykham and Causton, could strive to attain a noisy ebullience but this was frowned upon, an eruption of high-spirited youth, not to be encouraged.

Rue, however, appeared to be having a marvellous time. She went from table to table at first, greeting friends and even casual acquaintances with rapturous embraces. She danced first with Charlie Wykham, then with Tony Causton. She dived across the room to embrace a new arrival, an actor of small distinction. Finally she demanded that Lohmann, who had been sitting sipping champagne . . . according to her the only thing worth drinking in the place . . . and looking rather morose, must dance with her. He tried to avoid this, explaining truthfully he was no dancer, but she was insistent.

It was a fox-trot and he acquitted himself passably well, causing her to remonstrate with him.

'There'd nothing wrong with the way you dance. You're sulking. I don't know why. You should relax and enjoy yourself like everybody else.'

He almost smiled. He was surrounded by bleak faces.

'You try too much,' he informed her.

'What's that supposed to mean?'

'You force yourself to look as if you enjoy all this. But I don't think you do. You're as bored as I am.'

'I couldn't aspire to such heights of boredom. Trouble with you, Lohmann, is, you don't like people.'

The trouble, he told himself, was that he could recognise the false and the fallacious too easily. Part of the perception attained in his profession.

'I do like people,' he tried to defend himself. 'But I don't like tailor's dummies. Especially those with too much money.'

'You're a socialist? And an inverted snob.'

'Yes.'

'You're a Communist?'

'No. But this place could edge me towards the Communists.'

'You're a bloody German.'

'Again, yes.'

'Which means you're anti-social and impossible . . . and easily regimented.'

'No to the first, yes to the second. As to third . . .' he shrugged and glanced at his new wrist-watch. 'I have to go. I've to meet this man at midnight.'

'Another stupid policeman, like yourself!'

'On the contrary, he is a dwarf and probably has a police record.'

She stared at him for a moment, stopping at the centre of the floor. 'You're serious?'

'Positively grim.'

Her attitude changed at once. 'I'm coming with you.'

'I don't think that would be a good idea.'

'I'm still coming.' She turned back to the table and retrieved her gold evening bag. She wished Charlie and Tony goodnight with an embrace for each of them. Lohmann thanked them formally. They barely acknowledged this, being lost, heads together, in some private joke. Rue led the way out.

In the street, the night was cold, with traces of mist. Around them were car salerooms, their windows displaying large expensive automobiles. The headlamps of Hispano Suizas glared contemptuously at them. It was that kind of district. The bull-nosed Morris was looked down on by an ocean of Rolls-Royces and Mercedes-Benzs.

At the door of the Morris, Rue, champagne-tipsy, looked at him, an unsteady look, the unsteadiness coming directly from her legs.

183

'A dwarf with a criminal record? You are kidding me, aren't you? I mean, who ever heard of it?'

'He's an acquaintance of mine. And claims to have important information for me.'

Still incredulous. 'A dwarf?'

'About three feet tall.'

Rue giggled. 'They're supposed to be very sexy.'

'Doubtless you could find out, if you so wish.'

'I've never been to bed with a dwarf. He'd be nice and cuddly.'

She was beginning to irritate him. He climbed into the Morris.

'Get in!' he said harshly. She got in, pouting.

It was five minutes to midnight when they reached Old Compton Street. The shuttered continental newsagent was dark. As was the surgical supply store, its dusty, almost empty window displaying a small 'Durex' sign. There were splashes of garish light along the streets. From cafés, a snack-bar and the entrance to a few basement clubs, all still open and hopeful of entrapping the night-bird and the lonely tourist or commercial traveller. A few girls were on the pavements, in doorways or leaning against damp walls, shrapnel-eyed, lipstick-bright, alert for the solitary prospective customer.

Lohmann parked the car on the opposite side of the road, some yards away from the doorway into which he had last seen the dwarf disappearing.

'Wait here,' he said to Rue. 'And keep your door locked.'

'I'm coming with you. I want to meet the dwarf.'

'Later. If he wants to meet you.'

He climbed from the car, shut the door and crossed the road, walking slowly towards the doorway. A girl stepped out of the shadows in front of him. She wore a tight skirt, an artificial-silk blouse cut low, revealing half of two large, fleshy orbs. She was swinging a small handbag.

'Hello, dearie, like a short time?'

'Thank you, no,' he said, stepping around her.

'You don't know what you're missing,' she called after him.

'He has a good idea and is on to better things.' Rue, ignoring his instructions, was running past the girl to catch up with him.

184

'I told you . . .' he said irritably.

She was at his side. 'You must know I never do what I'm told.'

He sighed. She was a woman who made one sigh frequently.

'Very well. But stay behind me. There could be trouble.'

'Always behind you, *mein kapitan,*' she said, giving him a mock salute.

They went into the entry which led to a narrow wooden staircase. A lone bulb, somewhere above, was the only illumination. Dimly, Lohmann could see the walls of the stairway were covered in unreadable graffiti. Obscenities mixed with exhortations to telephone certain numbers. On the first landing, the solitary door was decorated by a sign, *Mandel Amusement Corporation.* Another floor up, a door with yet another sign, *Ernie Hovic* – Theatrical and Variety Agent. Below this, a further enticement, *First Class Variety and Cabaret Acts.* The third-floor door was presumably the first of the private residences, if they could be thus called. A cardboard sign, pinned to the wood, said simply, *Josette – French Lessons.*

The stairway became even narrower as it led to the top floor. Here the solitary light burned, and here, as he climbed the last few stairs, Lohmann felt the hairs rise on the back of his neck. It was an old sensation which he had experienced in the past, a warning of danger. He stopped, and drew the Mauser from his inside pocket.

Rue, behind him, prodded his back. 'Go on,' she said impatiently.

'Be quiet! Something is . . . not right.' He found himself whispering.

'What?'

'Just stay behind me.'

He reached the top landing. One door, with a piece of paper pinned to it. On the paper, 'A. A. Dafoe', and a smudge.

Lohmann went slowly and silently to the door. It was ajar, creaking slightly.

'What's the matter?' Rue said, her voice now dropping to a whisper.

'I don't know. Something.'

He pushed the door open and stepped through it. Into a tiny, square box of an ante-room. Four wooden walls and inset in one of them, a wooden door. No light except that which filtered through from the landing. A trace of the aroma of cheap perfume. And fried onions. He almost smiled. A comical combination of odours. Rue came into the ante-room and made a face.

'Fried onions,' she said. 'And *Evening in Paris* from Woolworths.'

Ignoring her, he opened the inner door. An entrance to absolute blackness. He groped at the side of the door for a light-switch. After a moment, found it and pressed down the switch.

The room was flooded in light. Three lights to be exact, hanging from a high ceiling, each enclosed in a kind of Chinese paper lantern. This giving the long room a colourful, almost kaleidoscopic effect. Splashes of red and amber and yellow and blue. It was a long room, a one-time artist's *atelier*, with a skylight. Now it was cluttered with objects. Inevitably a small, aged organ in one corner. A rail from a dress shop, holding a number of dresses at one end and three small suits, jacket and trousers, like clothes for a large doll at the other. A table, with two ordinary kitchen chairs and a three-step ladder from a library, a wooden back hammered to it to make a third chair for the little man.

Against the wall to the right was an artist's easel, probably abandoned by a previous tenant. A cheap wooden bookcase, three shelves empty, the fourth holding a few cheap, yellow-covered editions of popular thrillers. Against another, a deep sink, the kind found in wash-houses. Beside the sink, a gas cooker, stained with use. Two armchairs, tenth-hand, the stuffing oozing out from all sides. On the floor, various segments of carpeting, none of them matching. An old, full-length mirror propped up against the wall, zinc or silvering showing around the edges. A number of wooden boxes in the room, placed at random sites.

Over much of everything, there was a patina of dust. Above, around the skylight and in the corners of the ceiling, spiders had been busy creating elaborate webs.

At the far end of the room was a curtain, stretched on what

might have been a clothes-line, shutting off part of the room.

Behind Lohmann, Rue said: 'What a mess!'

Lohmann did not reply. He was puzzled. Signs of living but no sign of life. No Archie Aloysius Dafoe. Or his lady friend. Unless . . .

He crossed the room, a zig-zag progress through the clutter and pulled back the curtain.

Here, there was a difference. Not dusty. A large double bed with a frilled counterpane and deep, clean, frilled pillows. Bedside lights on either side of the bed on small, antique tables. At the side of the bed, a dressing-table, polished and spotless, dotted with bottles, and jars, face-cream, perfume, rouge and powder. The bedlights were lit. He looked on the bed and could not restrain a sharp intake of breath.

Rue came up to the curtain.

'What is it?' Trying to peer over his shoulder.

'Stay back!' he said loudly, pushing her away.

The woman was on the bed, sprawled back, head on one pillow, right hand reaching out, gripping the edge of the counterpane. A blaze of scarlet at her throat and running down over the front of nightdress and dressing gown. One breast protruding from the nightdress, also spotted with scarlet.

Blood.

On the woman who had presumably been Archie Dafoe's lady.

At first he thought her throat had been cut. But as he came closer, he saw one entry hole amid the blood. She had been shot in the throat. He felt her wrist for a pulse. Nothing. She was quite dead. A time ago, but not too long. The blood was still damp. She had been dead, he estimated, about half an hour.

But where was Archie?

He was, Lohmann thought, hardly the type to have killed someone to whom he had referred only two nights ago with such joyousness.

Lohmann walked around the bed and found the dwarf.

Archie was sitting on the floor, the small legs stretched in front of him, his back against the side of the bed. He was staring straight ahead, dead eyes examining a section of wall.

There was a small dot on the centre of his forehead. There

187

was a tiny ring of dried blood around the dot. The back of his head was splashed on the side of the bed, blood, bone and brains in a kind of horrendous stain among the over-hanging frills. He had been dead about as long as the girl on the bed.

Behind Lohmann, Rue, unable to restrain her curiosity, stepped through the break in the curtain. And screamed.

SIXTEEN

After a moment, when he gripped Rue by the shoulders and shook her, she stopped screaming. He managed to get her to sit down on one of the old armchairs and he closed the gap in the curtain. She went on moaning quietly to herself. He looked around, found a cracked cup, took it to the sink, washed it out and filled it with water. Finally, after a few sips, she stopped moaning and appeared to make an effort to pull herself together. She did continue to shiver, a spasmodic series of barely controllable tremors.

'Are they . . . they both dead?' she said. It was a rhetorical question.

'They're both dead.'

'She looks as . . . as if . . . as if her throat's been cut . . .'

'No. She's been shot in the throat.'

After a moment she said; 'You're so calm. How can you be so calm?'

'I've seen it all before. And worse. Dead women. Dead children. Mutilated bodies. Too often. You get used to it. After a time, you put it away.'

'You're saying you get used to it,' she nodded towards the curtain. 'How can you get used to . . . to that?'

He took the cup from her and gulped a mouthful of water from it.

'You see it often enough, you have to put it away. Out of

mind. Otherwise . . .' he rubbed his hand across his forehead. 'Otherwise you don't sleep.'

There'd been a lot of sleepless nights at the beginning. So many nightmares in the back of his mind. Kurten, the Düsseldorf murderer, who killed helpless servant girls and then raped the dead bodies; Karl Denke, a lodging house keeper, who murdered thirty men and women . . . there was evidence he'd cannibalised the corpses . . . Von Glauber, who killed young boys while he sodomised them. All these and others. Despite his having put them away, they came back in the dark hours, at the black moments.

'What do we do now?' She broke into his thoughts.

'What did you say?' He shook his head, coming back to the moment.

'I said . . .' She shivered convulsively. 'I said, what do we do now? Call . . . call the police?'

Call the police? The right thing to do. Inspector Anstey and his sergeant facing Lohmann again at the scene of the crime. Hours of cross-examination; explanations as to how he knew the dwarf. His entire investigation opened up, and the alerting of the people who had done this. It would certainly be all of that. Otherwise . . . say nothing, go now and the police would be investigating the murder of a dwarf and his woman, a pimp and a whore. A vice killing in Soho, not so unusual.

He went over and looked behind the curtain. The work of the *Tod Kommando*. Death Squad, London. With a mental apology to Archie Aloysius Dafoe and his woman. But he would find the murderers. There was a promise to the little man.

He turned back to Rue, suppressing the rising phlegm in his throat.

'No! We won't call the police. We're leaving now.'

'But . . . !'

He cut off her protest. 'Do you want to be linked with this kind of thing? A whore and her pimp shot to death in Soho. Society woman finds bodies and is being questioned by the police. Do you want that?'

'But we had nothing to do with this . . .'

'Tell that to the newspapers.'

'Max Beaverbrook is a friend. He wouldn't . . .'

Lohmann looked at his watch. Twelve-thirty. They had to leave quickly. In case . . .

'I know enough of your English papers to know that what Beaverbrook may not print today, Rothermere will take pleasure in printing tomorrow. Come on.'

She rose unsteadily. He took her arm and helped her out of the room and down the stairway.

When they reached the car, she shook off his grip, turned her back on him and vomited on the pavement. When she had finished, she straightened up, and faced him.

'You can take me home now.'

There was nothing about the killings in the papers the next morning. Not that Lohmann had expected anything. The bodies would probably not be found until later in the day. He'd reckoned on that the night before. When they'd left Soho he'd deposited Rue Scott-ffoliot at Dolphin Square. She had seemed calmer then, insisting he come in for a drink. He'd accepted the invitation to assure himself of her well-being. He'd stayed for half an hour, during which she'd gone through further spasms of shivering. However a large brandy seemed to help and, with a wan smile, she'd gone to bed and he'd driven back to Museum Street. He finally got to bed at two in the morning. Thinking as little as possible about Archie Dafoe.

Now, awake, he was studying the personnel file on Edward Rennie.

. . . born, 1896, at Mullion, Cornwall. Attended village school where he had won a scholarship to Winchester. Leaving school in 1914, he had served in the West Sussex Regiment, risen to the rank of Captain, been twice wounded on the Western Front, awarded the M.C. and been invalided out of the army because of wounds. Had spent a year convalescing at Mullion before taking up a bursary at Balliol College Oxford from where he had graduated in 1921 with first-class honours, reading economics, political economy and history. Worked for two years for a firm of Merchant Bankers, Lazar and Brockton, before entering the Civil Service . . .

Then followed a series of posts as he had moved up the ranks of the Treasury. An assessment note was amended to the *curriculum vitae*.

. . . despite the excellence of his degree and an industrious application to tasks set before him, Rennie shows a lack of flair. He has the mind of a competent accountant and, as such, is completely reliable on the middle ranks of the service. but it is doubtful if he will go further . . .

This was dated, 1935. At this time, he was in charge of the department whose function, it seemed to Lohmann, concerned the movement of currency overseas.

The final part of the report was personal.

. . . married, 1928 to Marion Elizabeth Trevallion, only daughter of Colonel George Trevallion, Cornish Rifles, at the Parish Church, Helston. The marriage has so far been without issue.

There followed a final note.

Hobbies: Reading, walking and rock climbing, sea fishing.

That was it. A man's life in cold facts. An assessment that indicated a mediocre career. And now he was running. From what? A death squad? What could he know that would make him a target for these people? Archie Dafoe had died because they realised he had betrayed them and changed sides. Rennie was hunted because he knew something and had almost certainly passed on whatever he knew to Beth Coverley. Who had died because of this.

Lohmann went through the report again. He was sure Rennie was not in the Lake District. That had been said too often. A man running would go as far as he could but would not advertise where he had gone. Lohmann tried to put himself in Rennie's place. Where would he have been running to?

He saw the possible answer. No guarantees, but surely the man would head for some place he knew; a place for which he had affection.

Norman's voice, a shout from below. 'Telephone, Mister Lohmann.'

He rose reluctantly and went downstairs.

Rue's voice was at the other end of the line.

191

'I just wanted to speak to you.'

'How are you?' he asked.

'I'm all right now. There was nothing about . . . about it in the papers.'

'Too soon. They wouldn't be found until this morning. At least.'

'I suppose so. Is this to . . . to do with what happened to Beth?'

'I believe so.'

There was a pause. He could hear her take a deep breath at the end of the line.

'You have to find them, Lohmann.'

'I intend to.'

'What do you do next? Because I want to help.' Something about her voice, a kind of angry determination.

'It would be better if you kept out of it,' he said evenly.

'Beth was a friend of mine. And when I saw these two poor souls last night, I knew I couldn't keep out of it. What are you going to do next?'

'I'm going out of London.'

'Where? I want to come with you.'

'It may be what you call a wild-goose chase.'

'I'm coming with you.' Her voice seemed cold now. 'Where are you going?'

'The West Country. Look it would be better if you kept out of . . .'

'No! You're going to the West Country. In that old Morris? It'll take you ages. We'll take my Jaguar. It's an open sports. Brand new. Ten times quicker.'

She was right about it being quicker, he had to admit. But to involve her . . . ?

'If you don't take me I'm going to the police. I'll tell them about last night. You won't be able to get out of London.'

Blackmail. He was amused. It was typical of her. Getting her own way using any method to hand. It might not be a bad idea, having her with him. If he was being watched by Marshall and his people, she might provide a cover. As if he were going away for an illicit few days. Not that they would be put off by that. They would be hoping he might lead them to Rennie. And if they did follow him, the fast car would be useful.

'You could lend me the Jaguar . . .'

'I go with the car. Or . . . no car.'

He told himself it was stupid. He would be endangering her. Also she would be a distraction, an unnecessary burden. He would have to concern himself with her safety. But the fast car . . .

'Yes. Very well,' he said. 'But you will do exactly as I say throughout the journey.'

'*Ja, Mein Kapitan*! When shall I pick you up?'

'You won't come here. These people are very thorough. This place is probably being watched. Park outside the Imperial Turkish baths in Russell Square at one o'clock. I shall go out shortly and shake off anyone following me. I shall come out of the Turkish Baths exactly at one. You will be there.'

'I'll be there. It's like going away for a dirty weekend, isn't it?'

He ignored that. 'You will not be late!'

'I will not be late. One other thing. How long will we be away for?'

'Does it matter? Two, three days.'

'Well, I have to know what clothes to bring . . .'

He replaced the receiver. English women! Especially English women like Rue Scott-ffoliot! What clothes to bring, indeed. As if she were going away for a vacation in the Counties.

Back in his room, he studied a road map for some minutes. Then he placed a clean shirt and his shaving kit in a small briefcase; made sure the Mauser was in its place in his jacket; donned his leather coat and went out. The briefcase gave no indication to his watchers that he was going any distance. He took a taxi to Piccadilly, paid the man and jumped out at Leicester Square, taking another taxi to Baker Street. Here he went in the front entrance to Madame Tussaud's, paid his entrance money and went out a side exit. He then took the underground to Oxford Circus and there, mingling with the crowds milling around, exited into Regent Street, doubled back into the Underground again and took another tube train to Euston Station. Convinced now that, along the way, he'd shaken off anyone who might be following him, he walked along several back streets until he reached the Imperial Turkish Baths in Russell Square and went in.

He stayed in the steam room until twelve-thirty, observing every new arrival. He recognised no one. Finally he showered and dressed and at exactly one o'clock came out into Russell Square.

It was a Jaguar convertible. Small, sleek, yellow in colour, the hood up, the engine running and Rue behind the wheel. She moved off at once into the flow of traffic.

'I'm heading for Salisbury,' she said. 'But where exactly in the West Country are we going?'

'Cornwall. A village called Mullion. On the Lizard peninsula. About ten miles from Helston. I will drive if you wish.'

'You'll sit there and be driven, Lohmann. When I feel tired, I might let you drive.'

In three quarters of an hour they were out of London, on the road to Salisbury. A grey morning had given way to an afternoon of intermittent sunlight. He felt relaxed, almost in a holiday mood, and, for this, was grateful after the events of the previous night. He had not yet been able to put away the image of the dead dwarf. But now it was going. Now he had to concentrate on finding Edward Rennie. There was no certainty that he would find the Rennies in Mullion. But it was a chance he had to take. If he had been Rennie, it is where he would have gone. The place in which he had been born, presumably been happy. Rennie had married there, his roots were in Mullion. The place to run to, when in trouble.

'Why are we going to Cornwall?' Rue asked. As if she could read a part of his thoughts.

'To find a man who may not even be there. Edward Rennie. A civil servant.'

She made a face. 'A civil servant? How very dreary that sounds.'

'He gave Beth Coverley information. I think this is the story. That information led to her death. And now he is a frightened man. If I'm correct, he will have been running back to what he might believe to be a place of safety.'

'Is it? A place of safety?'

194

'Perhaps. For a time. Until they find out where he has gone and come after him. I have to hope they haven't already done so.'

'You want to get there tonight? It'll be a long drive.'

'Tomorrow morning will do. As early as we can.' Early enough to catch Rennie and his wife off guard, he thought. The early morning was the ideal time to face anyone. Something he'd learned early in his career. Also the Gestapo always made their arrests at dawn.

'We could stay the night in Helston,' she suggested.

'We will stay in Helston.'

It was after nine o'clock in the evening when they reached Helston. It was a small market town, the main street sloping down, in a steep incline towards a valley. Lohmann, who had taken over the wheel crossing Dartmoor, brought the Jaguar to a halt outside the only hotel he could see, a small grey commercial establishment. Before he could even apply the hand-brake, Rue leaped from the car and disappeared inside the hotel. She booked the only double room available without consulting him, signed the register 'Mr & Mrs Scott-ffoliot', and when he finally arrived at the reception desk, grinned at him.

'All booked in, darling. This gentleman will show us to our room.'

The gentleman was an aged little man with a seamed face and trembling hands. He appeared to be of such antiquity that Lohmann returned to the car and brought to the room his own small briefcase and Rue's over-large suitcase.

The room was large, simply furnished, with a huge double bed. Rue grinned at him immodestly.

They made love for the second time, she with an even greater wildness than before. It was as if the sight of death the previous night had brought out in her a desperation to assert her own awareness of being alive. Afterwards she clung to him for a long time, talking about the dwarf and his woman.

Who was the little man? She wanted to know. What age was he? Had Lohmann met the girl before? Why were they killed? A flood of questions, some of which he could not answer.

'Look,' he tried to reply to some of her questions. 'He was

195

almost certainly a minor crook. But he did not deserve to die like that. Nobody does. He fell among greater criminals than himself. Probably the same people who murdered Beth Coverley. I intend to bring whoever killed him to justice. If it is possible.'

He was aware he must sound very correct and very pompous. Perhaps, in English eyes, very German. But she seemed to accept what he said, wept a little, and finally fell asleep on his shoulder.

They had asked to be wakened at six o'clock in the morning. The same old man roused them with a knock and brought them cups of tea. An hour and a half later they had breakfasted, enquired as to how to get to Mullion and started off on the road to Lizard Point.

It was a ten-mile drive and Lohmann took it slowly. He kept an eye on the rear-view mirror, still aware of the possibility that they might have been followed from London. An expert in a car could have been behind them, keeping out of sight most of the time, appearing only on rare occasions on their tail, checking their direction. There seemed to be no one behind them.

Some miles before Lizard Point, they turned off a side road and drove to Mullion.

It was a small fishing village, little more than a harbour and a cluster of houses in a cove surrounded by sea cliffs. Above the village, the cliffs were dotted with a few cottages and a couple of newly built bungalows, a symptom, perhaps, of future development. The solitary road leading to the tiny harbour was so narrow as to make parking impossible. Lohmann was forced to drive onto the edge of the harbour, turn the Jaguar around and drive back to park in a field at the edge of the village.

'How do we find out where this man lives?' Rue asked, sleep still marked on her face.

'We ask,' Lohmann said. 'There should be one of your very English sub-post offices.'

On foot they went back into the village. They found the post office by the harbour, an ancient, sagging building, leaning seaward. Beyond the sea wall was the English Channel, grey and becoming turbulent as the morning wind rose. Behind and below the post office building was the harbour; a number of fishing boats were riding high in the darkening water.

Lohmann had to duck to enter the small door of the post office. Thinking Cornishmen must have been tiny to live in such low-ceilinged cottages. Behind a counter, a round-faced woman with apple cheeks greeted him.

'Good morning, sir!'

'Good morning. I hope you can help me. I'm looking for a Mister and Mrs Rennie. I believe they may occasionally spend a vacation here.'

The apple cheeks divided into a wide smile.

'Oh, Teddy Rennie! He's not a tourist. He was born here. Lives in the old cottage where his parents lived. Well, when he's not living in London. He works for the government there. My sister-in-law, she keeps an eye on the cottage for them. And of course Marion Rennie is a Helston girl. I remember her as a little girl in the Floral Dance at Helston . . .'

'Are the Rennies here now?'

'You're from London. Of course. You surely wouldn't have come all this way if they hadn't been here?'

'We thought they might be. Could you tell me how to get to their cottage?'

'Rose Bush Cottage. On account of the rose bushes of course. You have to go to the other side of the harbour. Back up the road and you can cross the river there. Then down towards the harbour again and you'll see the path leading up the cliff. It's the first cottage on the cliff top. You'll not miss it. There's a sign, Rose Bush Cottage.'

It took them half an hour to reach the cottage. The cliff path was longer than it looked and steeper. When finally they reached the garden gate of the cottage, they were both breathless.

'Wait,' said Lohmann. 'We get our breath back. Otherwise we are at a disadvantage.'

Rue regarded him with a curious look. 'Everything you do, you've thought out. Everything has to be . . . just right.'

'It is called professionalism. I've seen men who forgot their professionalism. I've identified their bodies and attended their funerals.' He lit a cigarette and, as an afterthought, offered her one. She refused, still trying to regain her breath after the climb.

197

'It depends on the way you smoke it,' he said, looking at the cigarette. 'If you're nervous, it is a sign. Not nervous, it gives the impression of being casual. We are . . . for now . . . casual visitors.'

He opened the garden gate and went in. She followed him. From the path the cottage had been obscured by the rose bushes but, a few steps beyond the gate, it came into view. It was a long, one-storey building, old but recently renovated. A pleasing house, and quite large, it stood out on a bluff, commanding a magnificent view of the sea at both the front and the rear. The stout wooden front door, painted green, was on the side of the building. When they reached it, Lohmann drew on his cigarette and moved forward to lift a brass knocker at eye level. But Rue stopped him, she had glanced around the side of the cottage.

'Is that your man?'

Lohmann followed her glance.

The man was standing at the end of the garden, separated from the edge of the cliff by a waist-high hedgerow. He was clad in a polo-necked sweater and grey flannel trousers and was staring out to sea. Lohmann knew then his trip to Cornwall had not been wasted, his deductions correct. He knew the man at once even from behind. The same man who had called himself Irving in Beth Coverley's apartment. Edward Rennie.

Motioning to Rue to wait at the door, Lohmann walked slowly around the cottage and across the garden towards Rennie.

He was within ten yards of the man when Rennie turned around and faced him. In Rennie's hands was a double-barrelled shot-gun.

'You will stand still,' said Rennie. 'And do nothing. Otherwise this thing can blow your head off. Twice. I may do it anyway.'

SEVENTEEN

Lohmann thought: 'I've been here before.'

Staring down the black muzzles of a number of guns over the years; trying to assess where the wielder of the weapon would use it; seeing the finger on the trigger whiten as pressure was brought to bear. Also able to tell from the man's eyes whether or not he had determined to kill. Lohmann felt an old wound in his shoulder ache. And another in his side.

He said: 'I wish you no harm, Mister Rennie.'

Rennie, strands of hair blowing in the breeze from the sea, kept the shot-gun trained on the detective.

'So you say. You have an accent. You're German.'

'I am German.'

'That's one strike against you already. You notice I'm not asking what you want here. Because I know what you want. To put me . . . out of the way. Hence the shot-gun. To prevent you.'

'You would use it? That would be murder.' Lohmann felt his mouth dry up.

'Self-defence. If you were ever found. I would ensure you weren't found. I have a boat down below. In the cove. Weighed down by a rock, you would never be seen again.'

Rennie sounded nervous but determined.

'But I would be in your mind, Mister Rennie,' Lohmann said. 'I don't think you are a natural killer. I've met a few. Press the trigger, and you will have something in your head tormenting you for the rest of your life.'

The man laughed. Without humour, harshly.

'You think I would have a conscience about your kind?' Rennie said. 'I've been in Germany. I've seen what's happening there. The end justifies the means. Torment the Jews, torture the socialists, murder your own people when it is necessary. Oh, I've seen the National Socialist party at work.'

199

'So have I,' Lohmann answered quietly. 'That is the reason I left Germany. My name is Lohmann. I was a police officer in Germany. I could still have been a police officer there. If I had agreed to work with them. I didn't.'

'You're very good, sir. But you expect that to convince me?'

'I expect you to convince yourself. And it will take a great effort to fire that gun. Because you'll never be sure you were right. You'll wonder whether or not you should have kept listening to me. Also, though you think it may be easy to dispose of a corpse you'd be surprised how often it rises up to haunt you.' He was talking quickly now, intent on any kind of delay, of sowing any kind of doubt in Rennie's mind.

'You talk well. But then you'd have to. To save your life.'

Lohmann shrugged. 'There is another thing too. Your wife is in the cottage. You fire that gun, she'll hear and see. So then there are two minds to hold the memory. It's very stupid killing me. All you have to do is hand me to the police. Tell them I threatened your life. Tell them why too. Tell them you were responsible, indirectly, for Beth Coverley's death.'

'No! No, I wasn't . . .!'

'You put her on to investigating, I think. You told her a story. You knew, as a journalist, she would dig deeper. That's why she was killed, isn't it? Because of what you told her?'

The shot-gun wavered.

'That's why you think they'll try and kill you,' Lohmann went on. 'Isn't that so? Because you found something you weren't meant to find?'

'No. I didn't find it! It was there. I only asked questions. And . . . and they told me to forget it. Go to the police, you say. How can I do that? When the whole thing is to do with the government. I don't know who's on what side. I don't know if there are sides.'

'There are the people who killed Beth and the people who would like to bring them to justice.'

'Easy to say, Herr Lohmann. The heroes and the villains. Only there aren't any. It's all mixed up . . .' Rennie shook his head as if to negate his thoughts.

There was a silence. Broken only by the sound of the sea-breeze going through the whin and rose bushes.

Lohmann broke the silence after a long moment. 'I told you my name is Lohmann. I was asked . . . because of my previous experience in Germany . . . to investigate the death of Miss Coverley. Her father and friends did not believe it was suicide. That is the official verdict.'

'Of course it's the official verdict. They have to make it so,' Rennie was staring down at the gun-barrel. Then he looked up at Lohmann. 'That's what you were doing in Beth Coverley's apartment?'

Lohmann nodded. 'Trying to find a reason for her murder. All I came up with was you . . . and her address book.'

'You found the address book?'

'I found it. That is presumably what you were looking for?'

Rennie's turn to nod. 'I didn't want any link between myself and her. Not after they killed her. You came to see my wife?'

'They came too. They are looking for you. They already knew about you, Rennie.'

'I was afraid of that. It wouldn't have been hard for them to narrow down the civil servants who knew. And the Coverley girl may have used my name . . . I asked her not to, but it would have been difficult for her.'

'Rennie, who are ''they''?'

'Your countrymen. Or interested parties here, who sympathise with your countrymen.'

Above them, the sky was darkening. A huge rain-cloud was moving in from the sea. Below the cliff the sound of surf on rocks was growing louder.

'Have I convinced you, Mister Rennie, that I am not one of ''them''?' Lohmann asked.

A weary look of dejection came over the Englishman's face. 'I don't know. You sound all right but . . . then if you were one of them, you would, wouldn't you?'

'If you kill me,' Lohmann said. 'You will also have to kill the young woman I am with.'

He called out: 'Rue! It's all right.'

Behind him, Rue came around the side of the cottage. She had heard everything and her face was ashen.

'He is telling the truth, Mister Rennie,' she called out. 'Please listen to him.'

201

'This is Miss Rue Scott-ffoliot, Rennie. She was a friend of Miss Coverley's. If you did shoot me, you'd have to shoot her too. Would you be prepared to do that?'

Again a silence. Three figures on a landscape above a cliff. Frozen for a moment. Then the figure holding the gun lowered it.

'You'd better come inside. It's going to rain.'

They followed him across the garden and into a rear-entrance to the cottage. Through a kitchen, old-fashioned, but spotless. In the door between the kitchen and a small, narrow hallway, they came face to face with Mrs Rennie. She looked afraid.

'This fellow says he came to see you. That right?'

The woman surveyed Lohmann. 'Yes. He was the last one. After the police and . . . and the others.'

Rennie glanced over his shoulder at Lohmann. 'One strike for you, Mister Lohmann. Better come into the sitting-room, both of you. Marion, could you make some coffee?'

His wife nodded, still scared.

'I think it'll be all right,' Rennie said. 'Anyway I have to take someone on trust.'

She went into the kitchen. Rennie led them into a sitting-room, a long, low-ceilinged room with a newly lit fire in a wide fireplace. The suite of furniture was old but solid, wooden-framed armchairs, deep-cushioned and comfortable. He indicated that they sit. Rue sat uneasily in an upright chair at the window. Lohmann faced her in one of the armchairs. Relax while you can was an old motto of his.

'I . . . I probably wouldn't have shot you,' Rennie went on. 'I've never shot anybody. Even in the war. Not that I know of, anyway.'

'You were decorated and wounded?'

'You've been doing your homework. Because I couldn't hit anybody, doesn't mean they couldn't shoot me. The decoration? Oh, I'm not modest. I may well have been quite brave. I simply saw two of my men wounded, lying in a shell crater. So I went and pulled them out. Scared stiff every second, and drunk on army issue rum. If I'd known they were sniping at us, I'd never have done it. But I was too . . . too tiddly to know what was going on.'

'It is often like that,' Lohmann said.

'Is it? I wish I knew. This business has frightened me more than the Western Front.' A thought struck him. 'You say you are investigating Beth Coverley's death? But you also say you're a one-time policeman in Germany. But no longer. Now you're a refugee. So how come you're . . . detecting again?'

'I thought I told you. Family and friends engaged me in a private capacity. I knew one of his friends. Joe Kahn suggested I might be of help. He knew of a kind of reputation I had in Berlin. It was . . . a good reputation. Perhaps as good as your deserving of your medal in the war.'

Rennie looked confused. Momentarily he had to change the subject. 'So . . . can I offer you a drink before your coffee?'

'Thank you, it is early for me.'

'Not too early for me,' Rue said loudly from her seat near the window. 'After the sight of your shot-gun, Mister Rennie, I could use a large whisky.'

Rennie poured her a double, took a small one for himself. And, after giving Rue her drink, sat facing Lohmann and swallowed his whisky in one gulp.

'Now, what do you know, and what do you think you know, Herr Lohmann?'

Lohmann told him about the murder of Beth Coverley and the attempts on his own life.

'The indications are that I have come up against a group of British pro-Nazis,' he went on. '*Fanatisch Volk* who seem to have direct links with Germany. We know that Oswald Mosley received financial aid from Mussolini's Fascists. I know that you, a civil servant in the Treasury, discovered something which you conveyed to Beth Coverley. For this she was killed. More sinister for me is the evidence I am finding that something like the *Tod Kommando*, the equivalent of the Nazi death squads, has been formed here and is being used to eliminate those who get in their way.'

Rennie frowned but said nothing, indicating that Lohmann should go on.

'I do not know what you found that so interested Miss Coverley. I would make one guess. That Germany is training and financing the British Fascists in some fashion more serious

203

than the amounts Mussolini is supposed to have given Mosley.'

To Lohmann's surprise, Rennie burst out laughing. It was genuine, spontaneous laughter and the detective found it extremely disconcerting.

'I'm sorry if I have been so inaccurate. At least my theory seems to amuse you,' Lohmann said. 'But that is why I am here. To find the truth. The same truth that led to Hugo Richards being killed because he was using your name, Mister Rennie.'

Rennie stopped laughing. His face twitched. 'I . . . I have to live with that too.'

'Richards had to die with it,' Lohmann said harshly.

Rennie shook his head 'Christ, don't . . . don't you think I know it. Something else I have to live with. I laughed because . . . you were so wrong. I can tell you the truth, oh, yes. I can even prove it. I have copies of documents from the Treasury. All of them secret. By speaking to Beth Coverley, I infringed the Official Secrets Act. That may make me some kind of traitor. I also caused her death. I used Richards and he was killed. By speaking to you I do the same again. I'm also risking your life.' He was shaking visibly now. 'Christ, I only did what I thought was right. And already two people have died.'

'Four people,' Lohmann said. 'Two others you know nothing about.'

'When does it end? With my death? And my wife's? With your death?'

'Attempts, as I said, have been made already on my life,' Lohmann interjected, almost smugly. 'Either they think I know or they are afraid I will find out. So I am risking nothing.'

Rennie looked at Rue. 'And this young lady, are you prepared to put her at risk?'

Rue answered. 'I want to know. I've come this far, I want to know why they were killed.'

The Englishman stared at her in silence for a moment, then he shrugged.

'Perhaps more people should know. It . . . it would be like taking a weight from me. And from Marion.'

As he spoke, his wife came into the room carrying a tray with coffee and biscuits. The coffee was poured in silence. Rennie's

204

hands shook as he took up his coffee cup. When all the cups had been handed around, Marion Rennie went to the door.

'You're all right?' she asked her husband.

'I'm all right,' Rennie replied. 'I'm going to tell them.'

'You're sure?'

Lohmann cut in. 'If I can find you, Mrs Rennie, so can they. They know now that the man they killed in the Angleton Hotel was not your husband. So they are still looking for him.'

Her face went white. 'I know,' she said. And looked at her husband.

'I told Mrs Pengallion in the post office if anyone else asked for us she was not only to telephone us but also to say she didn't know us.' She hesitated and then went out.

'You see, when you asked for us at the post office, the old woman there telephoned here to tell us.' Rennie explained. 'And I brought out the shot-gun. There are no secrets in these small villages. Until now.'

He drained his coffee cup. Then rising, he poured himself another whisky.

'I was sorry about Miss Coverley . . .' he spun around and faced them. 'But I had to tell somebody. The people had to be told. Those damned hypocrites in the government, they're terrified it'll come out.'

'You are going to tell us,' Lohmann leant forward.

'But that's the fear,' Rennie went on. 'Who is killing people. They . . . they could be . . . this death squad you talk about . . . they could be my own people.'

'Perhaps you should start at the beginning,' the detective said gently.

The beginning was some weeks before. Rennie had been called to the House of Commons with his Permanent Secretary to discuss a set of trade figures with the Minister concerned. At the time, there was some kind of reception going on in one of the rooms in the Commons. The press were there. The Minister invited the Permanent Secretary to have a drink. And Rennie was included in the invitation.

He met Beth Coverley who asked him if he was an MP. He told her he was a civil servant in the Treasury. She told him she was writing a story about the financing of the British Fascists by the Italian Government. She wanted to know if the Treasury would have any record of large sums of money coming in from Italy.

'Not if it were being brought from Rome in cash,' he replied. 'Someone walks through Customs with a suitcase full of money. It's not illegal. If it were in *lire* then there might be a record of it being converted to sterling by a bank. If it was already in sterling, there'd be no way of our knowing.'

'And if it came through a bank?'

'Ah, that might be different. A very large sum would be noticeable. My job is to keep an eye on large movements of currency in and out of the country.'

She frowned. 'Is that the government's business?'

'Not necessarily the disposal of such moneys, but certainly the flow of sterling in and out of the country. Otherwise, with large sums we would have no way of working out our trade balances and currency values. That's putting it simply, but you will get the idea.'

'Could you find out about money from Italy?'

'If it wasn't in cash, possibly. I could but that doesn't mean I would. Especially to the press.'

'Not even a hint?'

Miss Coverley, he thought, could be persuasive. But he wasn't persuaded.

'I'm afraid that would be an infringement of confidentiality. Not done.'

That was the first meeting. But some time later, out of curiosity, with no intention of passing information to her, he tried to find some record of moneys coming from Italy. He could find no record of such transactions. But he found something else.

Rennie poured himself a third whisky before continuing. This time he remembered to offer a second drink to Rue, but she refused.

'First it looked like some massive discrepancy,' he went on. 'There are moneys paid out by the Treasury on government instruction, which we do not query. For example, the funding

206

of the intelligence services. It is never noted as such. We have some idea, so we do not ask questions. But this . . . this was different.'

'In what way?' Lohmann asked.

'It was much more than would be allocated to intelligence. An enormous sum of money being transferred out of the United Kingdom. Authorised, oh, yes, certainly, but with no indication of why.'

'But there was a destination?'

'Oh, yes, certainly.' He took a gulp of whisky. His hand was still trembling. 'You see, I'm talking now about a quarter of a billion pounds.'

'Million,' said Rue, who thought she had misheard.

'Billion,' Rennie emphasised. 'Over three years. 1932, 1933 and 1934. At a time when this country was in the midst of a depression, at a time when we had a severe financial crisis, we were giving away millions. And with no indication of why. Although that could be deduced. An agreement had been drawn up for the transference of this money. There were no British names but there was a name for the receiver.'

Lohmann leaned forward. 'Yes?'

'You see why I laughed when you thought this money was coming in, Lohmann. It wasn't. It was going out. British government funds.'

'Going to . . . ?'

'The name of the receiving agent was a Doctor Hjalmar Schacht. The money was going to Germany. And not to the German government. To what was then a private source. The money was going to a German political party then still in opposition.'

'The National Socialist Party?' Lohmann said.

Rennie nodded.

EIGHTEEN

There was yet another silence. While Lohmann considered Rennie's story.

'Why should they finance Hitler?' Rue asked, breaking the silence.

'To build a barrier against Communism,' Lohmann said. 'Put a strong anti-Communist Germany across Central Europe. A force to fight the Russians. Eventually. The trouble would be, if Hitler marched West instead of East.'

Rennie nodded. 'Russia has always been seen as the enemy. But the British government could never admit to financing Hitler. There'd be too great an outcry. From the Socialists, from the Jews, from the Americans . . . particularly the American Jews. And the French. Oh, there have always been people here who would support such a policy. Some very rich and influential people. But they're a minority. And now Baldwin is being forced to rearm . . . whether he admits it or not . . . because of German rearmament. Could he possibly admit a government he was part of, financed Hitler's coming to power and his rearmament?'

'Hitler has already marched into the Rhineland without a murmur from the British or the French,' Lohmann said. Hitler will not stop there, he told himself.

'Then it could be the British who are trying to keep you quiet?' Rue said. 'The British who . . . who killed Beth?'

Rennie was pacing the floor now. 'That's why I couldn't go to the authorities. This was government policy. Authorised from above. That's why I went to Beth Coverley. It seemed then I was breaching the Official Secrets Act. But nobody's life was involved. Until Beth was killed.'

'But you're not sure it is the British? You don't quite believe they would turn to murder?' An ironic tone came into

Lohmann's voice. 'It is not usually the British way. Not the done thing. Not playing the game.'

'I . . . I'm not a complete fool, Lohmann. When the power centre is threatened, God knows what can happen. Any government has to protect its secrets but . . . but . . . murder, I do find it difficult to believe. Whereas the Germans . . .?'

'Not only the Germans!' Lohmann said harshly. 'Murder as a political weapon has been used by all governments throughout history. The National Socialists have made no secret of it.'

'It's true, the National Socialists don't want this to come out any more than the British. They would have to admit they were, at least in part, financed by a foreign power.'

'The *Ubermensch* would not like to admit to such a thing,' Lohmann replied. 'There's a man called Schellenberg temporarily attached to the German Embassy. He came here with a purpose. To protect that secret. I believe he has organised a death squad here in London. He's been clever about it. Don't use Germans. Use some of the more violent of Mosley's people. Mosley himself probably knows nothing about it. But . . . somebody else does. Somebody else is behind this . . . death squad. Someone who has taken charge from the British side . . .'

Rennie was staring at the detective. 'It would work that way.'

'When I encountered a man called Raven Marshall, he was prepared to kill me. But he had to seek permission,' Lohmann smiled. 'How do you ask permission to kill? And who do you ask?'

'You know?'

There was a look of sadness on Lohmann's face. 'I think I know. Something happened a while ago . . . but I will have to be sure. However there are things I can do. This transfer of money would have been a Cabinet decision?'

'I can't be sure of that. There are quite a few special contingency-funds authorised by the government. For instance, the funding of the intelligence services is never called that. Simply an authorisation from the Minister concerned is enough. It's never questioned.'

'Quarter of a billion pounds can go through without question?'

'No. Never that much. Not without the Minister's approval. In this case, either the Prime Minister or the Chancellor of the Exchequer.'

'Could such a sum be concealed?'

'From who? The public, yes, easily. From the Governor of the Bank of England, doubtful. Unless he was lied to. Given another story. Certainly he would defer to the PM. But from a new administration, no. In time, questions would have to be asked.'

'Baldwin was not Prime Minister when this money was transferred?'

'No, but he was a member of the government. Lord Privy Seal.'

'But it would not have to be a Cabinet decision?'

'Not necessarily.'

'How was it arranged?'

'There was no clarity there,' Rennie said. 'An emissary was used. And as I said, Schacht was mentioned as the German contact.'

'The name of the emissary?'

'There was no name in my files. Simply the "Emissary".'

'So! To solve this we have to go to the top. Rue, you know people with influence?'

She shrugged. 'I know people . . .'

'I want to see your Prime Minister. Is that possible?'

'Might be easier if you asked to see the King. But I do know Lucy Baldwin. And Lucyr. The son. Not my closest friends, but I know them. I suppose I could try. Stanley Baldwin was a friend of my father's.'

'Good! When we get back to London, you will try and arrange for Baldwin to see me. And we will pray we succeed. Otherwise there will be more killing. We may have to use your name, Rennie . . .'

'Use it.'

'Baldwin should know a Treasury official has disappeared. That may provide me with an appointment. But could you not be charged with breaking your Official Secrets Act?'

'They don't kill you for that. Unless it's High Treason. They can't call it that. But Marion and I,' Rennie asked. 'We stay here?'

'You pack and move today.'

'Where . . . ?'

'Anywhere you're not known. Anywhere you have no connection with. Use another name . . .'

'Of course . . .'

'You're officially on sick-leave. So officially no one is looking for you. Unofficially you are being hunted. Otherwise it's only a matter of time until they realise you might be here . . .'

'We'll go to . . .'

'I do not wish to know where you are going. I will give you a telephone number. Telephone in a week and once every week after that. Your number, Rue?'

Rue gave him her telephone number.

'Miss Scott-ffoliot's number. My own may be . . . listened in to. When it is safe for you to return, I will leave word. *If* it is safe to return.'

'I understand,' Rennie said sadly. 'When . . . and if . . . You're going back to London?'

'At once,' Lohmann rose. And then added, as an after-thought which seemed to amuse him. 'This cottage, is it insured?'

'Yes. Why?'

Lohmann didn't answer but went on, 'And you will leave today?'

'I've told you.'

'It is very important that you do so. We'll say goodbye now, Mister Rennie. It's a pity we hadn't spoken together when we first met in Miss Coverley's apartment. We'll say goodbye to Mrs Rennie now.'

They drove directly back to London, Lohmann behind the wheel for the entire trip.

As they started off, Rue said. 'This is why you wanted to see Ribbentrop?'

'To get a reaction. Yes. I admit, I was very wrong. I thought German money was financing your Fascists. And I find it is the other way round. And a much bigger thing. No wonder Beth Coverley was excited. She had her big story. The Nazis were being financed by the British. And both sides were terrified it be known. I want you to try and get me a meeting with Baldwin

211

as soon as possible. Tell any story you like. Lie. Tell him I know everything that is going on in Germany. That will be a lie today. Tell him anything . . .'

'I will, I will,' she said soothingly. 'But . . . all this frightens me.'

'Yes, it should do so. Just pray that your government has not turned completely Fascist. Because, if it has, we could be dead very soon.'

She turned away, looking pale. 'Please, now and for the rest of the journey, can we talk about something else?'

Lohmann forced a smile. The car was now moving away from the coast, away from a sea-mist, into the damp, green countryside of Cornwall. Of course she was right. They should talk of something else. The worst was not now, here. Not yet.

'We should talk of something else,' he said.

There was a silence broken only by the sound of the car engine.

Then she said: 'You're a nice man, Lohmann. Oh, very serious, very intense. When you've nothing to say, you say nothing. I'm not used to that. Most of the people I know, they have nothing to say but they keep saying it, over and over.'

Lohmann had nothing to say. He said nothing.

'You are also good in bed,' she went on.

'I have no way of knowing that,' he said. 'No method of comparison.'

'Was your wife like me?'

'No.'

'Or any of your girl-friends?'

'Perhaps, one. In Berlin, years ago. Alike yet different.'

She changed the subject. 'You know, I'm very stupid. I brought a case full of clothes. For one night in a hotel. Where I didn't wear any.'

Again he had nothing to say.

'You're . . . you're . . . very German, aren't you?' she said.

'What does that mean?'

'Oh, in the best sense. Very upright. Very precise. A little ponderous. Like Beethoven. Very serious.'

'This is a serious business.'

'We're not talking about that. You're serious in bed. Serious

212

in love, I think. Thank God, you have some sense of humour though.'

'I have a good sense of humour,' Lohmann replied seriously. With a touch of humourless indignation.

She laughed loudly. 'That's funny.'

'I see nothing funny . . .

'I think I love you,' she said.

'That would be ill-advised.'

'Oh, I know. You're too preoccupied. Is that it?'

'That and other things. Also I am too old for you.'

'Don't agree. But anyway I wanted you to know what I think. So you'd know I didn't just go to bed with you for the fun of it. I don't do that. Despite appearances. Oh, and it was fun too. But I only said I *think* I love you.'

Again he said nothing. This time he didn't know what to say.

'I talk too much, don't I?' she said.

'At times.'

'You're lucky. Some women in this country don't talk at all Lie back and think of England, that's what they say about some women. Me, I'm different. I don't lie back. I join in and think of everything you are doing to me. I think I'll leave you to drive and sleep now. Thinking of all the things you did to me.'

She grinned, leaned back in the passenger seat and went to sleep.

It was late evening when they reached London. Lohmann drove to a street near the British Museum and there he handed the car over to Rue.

'Go home,' he said. 'I will telephone you.'

She drove off and he walked to his lodgings in Museum Street. As he entered the building he had a feeling someone was watching him.

Another morning. Early. Eight o'clock. A telephone call from Joe Kahn.

'October the fourth,' Kahn said.

'What?'

'They're allowing Mosley and the Blackshirts to march through the East End on October the fourth. Ernst, it's a deliberate provocation. There will be a riot. Comer and others are organising Jewish resistance. But the police should not allow it.'

'I see,' Lohmann said soberly. 'So it is definite. I have some contact with the police. I will see what they say. But Maurice Kovel must be protected that day. I shall be there. It would be an ideal opportunity for them.'

'I've talked to him again. He knows nothing about this . . . this story Beth was trying to write.'

'It does not matter whether he knows or not. It is enough that, in their eyes, he might know. They will not wish to take a chance.'

'And you? How is the investigation going?'

'It is progressing.'

'Tell me!'

'I'm sorry, Joe, but I am not yet ready to tell you.'

'But surely . . .'

'I am not yet ready.'

Joe Kahn sighed at the other end of the line. 'You're a difficult bugger, Lohmann.'

'Yes.'

'I hope you know what you're doing.'

'So do I, Joe. I will be in touch. Goodbye.'

He replaced the telephone and stood staring at it. October the fourth. Very close. There would be trouble. An ideal time for them to create more trouble. A riot. People die in riots.

Another thought. He lifted the telephone and was connected with the operator. He asked for the number in Mullion he had noted in Rennie's cottage. After a moment he could hear the number being rung. After some time, the operator came back on.

'I'm sorry, there's no reply.'

He hung up the receiver without speaking. No reply. He was pleased. Rennie had taken his advice and moved on. He lifted the receiver for a third time and asked for Whitehall 1212.

'Mister Lohmann,' he identified himself when he was connected. 'I wish to speak to Assistant Commissioner Emerson.'

A minute later he was connected.

'Lohmann! How are you? How is your . . . investigation going?'

214

'It goes. I want to ask you . . .'

'I rang yesterday but you were out of town.'

'Yes, I went to Cornwall. A place called Mullion.'

'What on earth did you go there for?'

'A part of the investigation. But that's not why I telephoned you. I have heard Mosley and his Blackshirts are being allowed to march in the East End on the fourth of October.'

There was a moment's silence before Emerson replied.

'Yes, that's so.'

'Is that not a dangerous provocation to the Jewish population?'

'It may be,' the Assistant Commissioner replied. 'But this is a free country, Lohmann. Any political party can hold a meeting or demonstrate or march. That doesn't mean I like it, but it's a fact.'

'There will be a riot.'

'Not necessarily. Mosley's had meetings in the East End before. Has them regularly. Oh there's a scuffle now and then, a bit of barracking, but that's about all.'

'This may be different.'

'I can talk to the officer in charge. The police'll keep things under control.'

'I hope they are able to do so.'

'Our problem. You'll keep me informed as to your investigation?'

'I'll keep you informed. But I have warned you about October the fourth.'

'You've warned me.'

Again Lohmann replaced the receiver. He had done what he had to do.

Back in his room he took his briefcase, put two clean shirts in it, and his shaving tackle. He donned the battered leather coat, ensured the Mauser was in place, and went out. He ignored the Morris and started off on foot.

Again he took a circuitous route around London. Again if he was being followed, he made sure he was rid of his followers. Then he took a taxi to Dolphin Square.

Rue was dressed in sweater and skirt although her hair was awry.

'You didn't tell me you were coming.'

'I only decided this morning. May I stay for a few nights?'

She looked amused. 'Well! Couldn't do without me.'

'Not exactly,' he said seriously. 'I think they may try and kill me if I stay at Museum Street. They don't know I'd be here. It is purely a precaution. You have a spare bedroom.'

Her face indicated mock disappointment. 'I have a spare bedroom. Doesn't mean I'll let you use it. But you can stay.'

He settled in a deep armchair. 'Good. And I would like a coffee.'

'Which is known as making yourself at home,' she said, and asked her maid to provide coffee.

'You are fortunate, having a maid-servant.'

'Hasn't everybody?'

'Unfortunately, no.' He scowled.

'Don't you scowl at me,' she said. 'I've been on the telephone all morning for you.'

'Good. Tell me.'

'I spoke to Mrs Baldwin. Lied my head off about you. Visiting German. Old friend. Very serious . . . Lucy Baldwin thinks I'm pretty frivolous. Concerned about his country's attitude to Great Britain. Dying to talk to the Prime Minister.'

'So what happened?'

'She telephoned me back. Told me to phone the Cabinet Secretary. I telephoned him. Not available, would call me back. Eventually he did so. Answer, the PM has no time. Perhaps next month. Try the Foreign Secretary.'

Lohmann swore under his breath.

'Oh, I wouldn't take that for an answer,' she went on. 'But Anthony Eden's an old friend. So I called him. Explained you had to see the PM. He was about to go into a Cabinet meeting. He called me back just before you arrived.'

'And?'

'If you go to the House of Commons at two o'clock, your admittance has been arranged and you can sit in the Strangers' Gallery. After Prime Minister's Question Time, Mr Baldwin will try and give you ten minutes. Best I could do.'

The maid brought in a tray with coffee and biscuits. Lohmann looked at his watch. It was ten minutes to midday.

216

'Good,' he said. 'We will have coffee and then you can drive me to the House of Commons.'

'We'll be too early . . .'

'Yes. Mister Churchill is not too popular with this government and his party, that is so?'

'Yes, but . . .'

'Good! I think before I see Mister Baldwin, I will be seen with Winston Churchill. It might make Baldwin nervous. Now, pour the coffee.'

She threw him a wide-eyed look. 'I'm not sure that I love you this morning. I don't even think I like you.'

They arrived at the Houses of Parliament at quarter to one. Rue drove him in the Jaguar, wanting to come in with him. It was the last thing he wanted, to be accompanied by a woman and one who was known as one of the so-called, *bright young things*. Reluctantly she drove off.

He waited in St Stephen's Hall until an usher brought Winston Churchill to him. A mild scowl was on the round face. The old politican wore a dark jacket above striped trousers and, under the double chins, he sported a crumpled polka-dot bow tie.

'Ah, Herr Lohmann again. I have just abandoned a glass of lunch to come to you, sir. What service can I do for you?'

'If I can replenish that glass, sir, we could talk.'

Churchill brightened up. 'There is a bar for members and visitors.'

In this bar, Lohmann provided a double whisky for the politican and an ale for himself. Thus appeased, Churchill settled in a deep chair.

'Pray tell me what I can do for you?'

'I have an appointment with Mister Baldwin after his . . . his Question Time. That is the correct expression?'

'I wish you well of it. But it will hardly do you any good being seen with me. Stanley and I are . . . at least politically and publicly estranged. Of course, socially, all is amiability. Rather like the married man and the courtesan. In private all is well, in public I am anathema to him,' the ponderous brow frowned

217

and he gave a mock shudder. 'Places me in the role of the courtesan. I don't think I like the metaphor.'

'I have read of it, Mister Churchill. But I wanted to be seen with you. It might ensure the Prime Minister pays attention to what I have to tell him.'

'You're a devious man, Lohmann. And you interest me. This has something to do with your investigation into the death of the woman journalist?'

'Yes.'

'You're going to tell me more?'

'No.'

The scowl returned to Churchill's face. He looked like a bad-tempered infant.

'Then why should I assist you?'

'Because, if the Prime Minister will not listen to me, I will come to you.'

'I don't like to be second-best, Lohmann.'

'I understand that, sir, but I think you are a great patriot . . .'

Churchill took a sip of whisky. 'No one dare question that.'

'Then you will please believe I am acting in your country's interests. I must go where the power is. If I tell you prematurely what I have discovered, it may damage your country. But, being seen with you may encourage Baldwin to take action. If action can still be taken.'

Churchill drew a cigar case from inside his jacket, produced a cigar, replaced the case, took a clip from his waistcoat, clipped the end of the cigar and lit it. All the time he stared straight ahead, pondering. After a time, he broke the silence.

'I believe you. And I pride myself on being a judge of character. But, when you are able to do so, I shall expect to hear the story. Even if only in confidence. Come, we will stroll through those areas of the House visitors are permitted to see. I shall point out some of the historical features. And we will ensure the Prime Minister knows you have been walking with me.'

Lohmann was given a conducted tour of the Palace of Westminster, walking side by side with Churchill while he expounded on the glories of the building.

'Of course there are those places restricted to Members only. The Chamber naturally. And the Chamber of the Lords. Much prettier than the Commons but then we had to give them a certain elegance to take the place of the power they lost.'

They were walking now along an arched corridor. A number of Members hurried by, some occasionally nodding at Churchill. A small balding man with spectacles, head down, face set, acknowledged them with a terse, 'Afternoon!'

'Major Attlee,' Churchill explained. 'Leader of His Majesty's Opposition. Elected when Lansbury resigned. Attlee is a very important gentleman, as Leader of the Labour Party, though I doubt he'll ever see Number Ten Downing Street. Too . . . too insignificant.

'The old building was burnt down in 1834 . . . only the Great Hall remains. But think of what that Great Hall has seen. Charles the First condemned to lose his head. A country murdering its monarch. An unpleasant event. Should never have happened. You see, I'm a Royalist, Herr Lohmann, as well as a patriot. The one is indivisible from the other.'

Another member in frock coat and striped trousers hurried by.

'Ah, what you were looking for, sir,' Churchill went on. 'The Prime Minister's parliamentary private secretary. Now it will be reported to Baldwin that you have been seen with the *enfant terrible*! And he will be concerned.'

They moved down to St Stephen's Hall again, Churchill still talking.

'It all started in the thirteenth century . . . of course at first it was the King and the nobility. But in 1265 the Parliament summoned by Simon de Montfort included borough representatives . . . the origins of the House of Commons. Since then, think of the great men that strode through those halls. Cromwell, Walpole. The two Pitts, Disraeli, Gladstone, Sir Randolph Churchill . . . my father . . .' For a moment it seemed to Lohmann that the politician's eyes misted up. Then he appeared to straighten up. 'I doubt, despite the high offices I have held, I shall ever equal their stature. A pity.'

'Surely there is still time?' Lohmann said, suddenly sympathetic.

'No, no, I'm sixty-two and I have . . . as we say . . . blotted a great number of copy-books in the eyes of my colleagues. No, I shall have to be content to make as great a noise as I can from the back benches. I shall still enjoy it but my day has passed. But now, I shall have to leave you. If you wait here, you'll see the Speaker's procession and then the usher will take you up to the Strangers' Gallery.'

The two men shook hands.

'I shall look forward to hearing from you, Herr Lohmann. But beware of Stanley Baldwin. He can be a wily fox despite his air of simple farmer. Believe none of it.'

Churchill went into the Chamber. Some minutes later the Speaker's procession moved through the hall, visitors standing respectfully watching. Lohmann was then shown up to the Strangers' Gallery.

Prime Minister's Question Time lasted fifteen minutes. The short, squat figure of Baldwin fielded various questions from the opposition and his own side, with studied expertise. Most of the questions seemed to be related to economic problems . . . at least one concerned fatstock prices . . . and, from a large Welshman, a question was followed by a supplementary regarding the extreme poverty of miners in South Wales. Churchill, on a bench behind the Prime Minister, sat glowering. Lohmann had the impression he would have preferred being in Baldwin's position at the dispatch box.

Finally it was over and the Prime Minister left the Chamber. Lohmann followed an usher out of the Gallery and downstairs. After progressing along various corridors he was shown into an outer office. A female secretary sat behind a typewriter at one desk, and a young man in striped trousers rose from behind another desk.

'Mister Lohmann? The Prime Minister can give you ten minutes.' The young man indicated another door. Lohmann went in.

Stanley Baldwin, in what seemed to be the politician's uniform, again dark jacket and striped trousers, this time with a wing collar and tie, was standing at the end of a large table, attempting to fill his pipe. The round face and plump body brought to mind the cartoon character of John Bull, an image

220

which Baldwin did not hesitate to encourage.

'Herr Lohmann,' he said, eyes on his pipe. 'Come in. I would like to emphasise that I am seeing you at the request of the daughter of an old friend.'

'I appreciate that.'

'Miss Scott-ffoliot informed me that you had recently come from Germany and had information you wished to pass to me.'

Lohmann took a deep breath. 'That is not quite accurate, sir.'

Baldwin swivelled around with surprising speed, to face his visitor.

'I am aware it's not accurate. My . . . my sources tell me you have not recently come from Germany. You were in France for a year and have been in London for a year. As a refugee. An alien. I am therefore wondering why you have caused Miss Scott-ffoliot to lie in order to take up my time.'

'I assure you it is important that I see you.'

'To whom, Herr Lohmann? It had best be of importance to His Majesty's Government. Otherwise, I warn you, I could have you out of this country within twenty-four hours as an undesirable alien! And would not hesitate to do so.'

NINETEEN

Lohmann was startled by Baldwin's vehemence. Possibly, he told himself, fuelled by the report he must have had that Lohmann had been seen with Winston Churchill. And Winston, as he admitted, was the *bête noire* of the Tory Party.

Baldwin broke into his thoughts.

'You see, my intelligence people can tell me about any alien in the country. Indeed about anyone in the country. But now I should tell you I *am* on holiday. At Blickling in Norfolk. I am only here for a few short hours while I answer some questions in the House. And then I intend to return to the lush greenery of the English countryside. As quickly as possible. So, Herr Lohmann, please state your business.'

'I am here regarding certain events in London. And the disposal of quarter of a billion pounds from the British Treasury.'

Baldwin's head came up. Was it Lohmann's imagination or did he flush?

'I hardly think Treasury matters concern aliens.'

'If you will permit, Prime Minister, I will tell you a story?'

'You have eight minutes left.'

'It started with the death of a woman journalist . . .'

Lohmann told his story. All of it, as he had experienced it. The only things he held back were his own deductions. Baldwin listened in silence, lighting his pipe as he did so. And puffing at it. Enforcing the image, as the story went on, of the simple man that could be trusted. As he listened his face gave no indication of his thoughts. He could use the pipe with expertise to conceal any reaction he might have felt. When Lohmann had finished, Baldwin again looked up at him.

'You are saying to me, Herr Lohmann, that people have been killed because one civil servant broke the Official Secrets Act?'

'I'm saying, sir, that one civil servant discovered something which he believed was of great discredit to his country. His conscience would not allow him to remain silent.'

'A favourable interpretation of what others might think a form of treason. However . . . supposing I told you there was no truth in your allegation that one quarter of a billion pounds was transferred from the Treasury to an alien political party, would you believe that?'

Lohmann shook his head. 'After all that has happened . . . no.'

'Even if you personally faced the prospect of being deported?' Baldwin asked, with a sidelong look at the German.

'Even if I was faced with that prospect,' Lohmann answered. 'The truth is not a . . . a *verneinung* . . . it not denied by a threat to one's own well-being.

'You appear to be either a man of integrity or a rash and foolhardy individual. I'm a politician. To a politician integrity can be an expensive virtue. If it is a virtue.' The Prime Minister took a deep breath, walked around the table and sat down, facing his visitor.

'Very well. Let us say, under the last administration . . . of which I was not Prime Minister . . . certain errors of judgement were made. Let us go further, that a large amount of currency was transferred secretly to a political party in another country. In the belief that it was in British interests to encourage that party.'

'To build a barrier against Russia?'

'To stem the spread of a detestable philosophy . . . Bolshevism . . .'

'Detestable anyway to the British Establishment,' Lohmann said.

'You are a Communist?'

'No, but does the encouragement of an even more detestable philosophy become justified by your fears of Russia?'

Baldwin coughed. A deep, racking cough. He gave a vague gesture. 'Mistakes were made. As I said, I was not Prime Minister . . .'

'You were a member of that administration.'

The cough was gone. In its place another more irritable gesture. 'I was Lord Privy Seal. An ineffectual position.'

'Which you may have chosen deliberately,' Lohmann pressed on. 'So that you could at least in part dissociate yourself from certain acts of that administration.'

Now the Prime Minister gave a wan smile. 'You've been studying British politics, Lohmann. There are . . . tactics one has to employ. But you must understand the position of the last government. Ramsey was Prime Minister. He was old . . . not in control . . . easily influenced, perhaps by the wrong people. There was a kind of senility . . . If I told you I was not aware of all his actions at the time, would you believe me?'

'If you tell me, I cannot prove otherwise.'

Baldwin ran his hand across the thinning hair on his scalp. 'Oh, I heard something of it soon afterwards. MacDonald . . . Ramsey had been used and manipulated . . . he was susceptible to . . . what did somebody say? . . . the flattery of Duchesses . . . and sets of people, perhaps not wholly admirable, some of whom I know held un-British views. There was also a rumour that a certain Royal personage was not unsympathetic to your National Socialists. And I am going to have further problems with that personage.'

'But when you became Prime Minister you must have known the whole story?'

'Oh, yes. And any further such transferences of sterling ceased. On my direct orders.'

'And the original financing of the Nazis . . . all knowledge of that was concealed?' Lohmann felt suddenly uncomfortable. As if, for the moment he held this powerful politician in his power . . . a feeling he did not seek or take pleasure in.

The Prime Minister was now on the defensive. 'What else could one do? The damage had been done. Also Sam Hoare's pact with Laval was on us. It was public knowledge we were accused of selling out Abyssinia to Mussolini. Was I also to admit that the previous government, of which I had been a member, had been financing the National Socialist Party of Germany? A Party which has now given us cause to rearm! And in a climate of pacifism. We would have been accused of financing the very guns which could be turned upon us. Supposing I admitted what had been done . . . I cannot think of anything that would have made the loss of the next election by my party more certain.'

Lohmann took a deep breath. He was moving into darkness. 'So, to prevent this fact becoming public knowledge and your losing an election, you might have been willing to connive at the murder of some of your own citizens?'

Baldwin's eyes narrowed. 'No such action was ever even contemplated! You talk of Death Squads. The British Government does not use such methods,' he said angrily.

'Beth Coverley is dead!' Lohmann insisted.

'Not by our hand,' Baldwin went on. 'I have never . . . would never issue such a directive. You are accusing this government of conniving at murder, sir!'

'Someone killed her.'

'Your German Death Squad.'

'Perhaps somebody in your administration took the authority upon himself.'

'If I found out such was the case, the individuals would be arrested and tried for murder. You are suggesting such is the case?'

'It is one of three possibilities,' Lohmann replied. 'One, that your people are killing anyone whom you think might be a threat to the revealing of the transfer of sterling. Two, that the German Government are using *Tod Kommando* to carry out the killings for the same reason. They also would not wish the transfer of money to become public knowledge. Or, three, that certain British citizens are working with the German Death Squad for the same reasons.'

'The second of your premises appeals to me,' Baldwin said. 'If killings are, as you allege, being carried out.'

'You would therefore unhesitatingly guarantee the lives of Edward Rennie and his wife are under no threat from his own government.'

'Not . . . not from us. If he will agree to keep silent . . . even discuss the matter with me. Of course a threat to Rennie's life from other sources is a problem. But he would be guaranteed police protection.'

Lohmann changed tack. 'Was there any government pressure on those conducting the inquest on Beth Coverley to bring in a verdict of suicide?'

Baldwin hesitated. 'Herr Lohmann, the stability of the land in which you have sought refuge must be maintained. You must understand, we are the least violent of nations. The sounds of England should never be despoiled by gunfire. Only by the tinkle of the hammer on the anvil in the country smithy, the corncrake on a dewy morning, and the sight of the solitary ploughman coming over the hill, the sun setting behind him. To preserve this England, I will not murder but I will not hesitate to . . . to suggest that when there is a choice in such matters as a verdict at a coroner's inquest . . . the truth being unclear . . . there is reason to consider the least traumatic of the options . . .'

The pedantic verbiage of the man nearly defeated Lohmann. This was Baldwin in full spate. It had to be stopped.

'. . . after all the girl could not be brought back to life . . .'

Lohmann stopped him. 'You have confirmed the motive

behind the murder of Beth Coverley and the others. Unless the killers are stopped, there may be more murders. I have been engaged to find the girl's killers. I mean to do so. Whatever political issues may be involved . . .'

It was Baldwin's turn to interrupt. 'Of course, of course. In the end the rule of law must be upheld. But as to the motive . . . as to the story of the disposal of quarter of a billion pounds, that cannot be allowed to become public knowledge. No word of that will get out. No paper will print that story. If you will give me your word on that, I will give you my support. My tacit support of course.'

'And if the killers or those behind the killings were agents of your government . . . ?' Lohmann asked quickly.

'Then you must leave me to deal with them. Not necessarily in a public court. In my . . . own way. But you know you have my sympathetic support. Oh, and one other thing. I believed you are acquainted with Winston Churchill.'

'I have met Mister Churchill.'

'On the matter of the quarter of a billion pounds, that is an official secret. Winston can be difficult, much as he is both a friend and an old colleague. You will not tell him of this matter. You understand.' There was, somewhere deep down in the request, the suggestion of a threat. At this time Lohmann knew it would be politic to agree.

'As long as I have your undertaking, Prime Minister, to prosecute those involved when they have been caught, I see no reason to involve Mister Churchill.'

Baldwin rose, taking a gold hunter from his waistcoat and studying the dial. He gave Lohmann a tight smile denoting frankness and honesty.

'Time to be moving on. I think you've had a little longer than ten minutes. But I will say I have heard that in Berlin you were a fine detective. We are glad to have you in this country, Herr Lohmann. Knowing that you appreciate the problems of government. Even the errors. Perhaps there may be something we can do to expedite your nationalisation as a citizen. If you so wish citizenship.'

To the affectation of understanding, followed by the assurance of a kind of support, was now added the suggestion of a bribe. For all the wiles, the tactics, the manoeuvring, there was, in the end, something almost naive about politicians. Perhaps, Lohmann told himself, it was their patent dishonesty and their own belief that they were successful in hiding that dishonesty.

'Thank you for seeing me, Prime Minister,' he said. The thanks were as false as Baldwin's assurance of support. They were merely part of the protocol.

Baldwin followed him to the door. 'Where else in the world can a citizen . . . or even a refugee . . . seek audience with the chief minister of a great power and so easily have that audience granted? You will inform the police authorities of any outcome to your investigation?'

'I will do so, Prime Minister,' Lohmann replied and was unable to resist a parting thrust. 'It is not the first time I have seen the chief minister of a country. The last time was with Adolf Hitler.'

The Prime Minister's face paled and his farewell hand-shake was limp, the palm of the plump hand clammy with sweat.

As he was coming through St Stephen's Hall on his way out, Lohmann brushed against a small familiar figure coming in to the building.

'Mister Lohmann, glad to see you again. Glad and relieved.'

The diminutive figure of G E Stevens smiled up at him.

'Mister Stevens. Why . . . why relieved?'

'You haven't been at your home?' Stevens asked, looking perplexed.

'I left early this morning,' Lohmann answered cautiously. What did he know of this man? Obviously affluent, moved in establishment circles . . . and had been a guest at the German Embassy . . . was noted as an expert on Arab affairs . . . in the war, a minor hero even. But then many such people were sympathetic to Mosley and often avowed admirers of Hitler. Treat with caution, was the thought that came to Lohmann.

'Very fortunate, Lohmann. But you obviously haven't seen the early editions of the evening papers.'

227

The small man produced a copy of the *Evening News*. The story was a paragraph in the 'stop press'.

EXPLOSION IN MUSEUM STREET!

An explosion shook Museum Street at ten thirty this morning. The blast wrecked a top flat apartment in a house facing the British Museum. The caretaker of the building, Norman Bates, (27) stated that the apartment was occupied by a German refugee, a Mister Lohmann, who is at present missing. No one else was reported injured although Mrs Euphemia Bates (63), the caretaker's mother, was taken to hospital suffering from shock. A police report suggested the explosion was caused by a leakage of gas, probably from a cooker in the devastated apartment.

Lohmann read the report without emotion. He had anticipated something. That something had happened. Though now they had resorted to bombs. Still, he could feel a mild relief that no one else had been injured.

Stevens said, 'Left your gas cooker on, old man? Very careless.'

'I do not leave the gas cooker on,' Lohmann said coolly. 'It is an irritation. I will have lost some possessions.'

'At least you didn't lose your life,' Stevens said.

'As you say. All I have lost is some clothes and a typewriter.'

'Be happy to put you in touch with my tailor. Could do something quickly for you.'

Lohmann looked at Stevens' immaculately cut suit. 'I think that would be a little more expensive than my finances would allow. Nice to see you again, Mister Stevens.'

'I've no doubt we'll bump into each other again, Mister Lohmann. Good day.'

Stevens went forward into Westminster Palace. For what reason, Lohmann wondered. He moved out into the street and, for a change, sunlight, reflected in pavement puddles.

He walked up Whitehall. Thinking on the explosion in Museum Street. A small bomb, hand grenade size, would have done the job in his small room. The job being to kill him. At least they were probably not aware of his friendship with Rue

228

Scott-ffoliot. For the time being. They might even presume the hand grenade had done its work. That, at this minute, he was being scraped from the walls of his room. On the other hand they were thorough. They might even have picked up his trail earlier in the morning, after they'd set the bomb. Let it go off to allay his own fears. Might even be following him now. There was that feeling again. Of a watcher somewhere behind him.

From Whitehall he went up Charing Cross Road, stopping occasionally at shop windows, seemingly staring at the contents of the windows, in fact using them as a mirror to observe anyone behind him, and then moving on. As he walked he managed the odd backward glance. It took him some minutes and some two hundred yards before he identified the follower. By this time he was on the north side of Cambridge Circus. Each time he had glanced behind him, there was a tall young man following his example, staring in a shop-window or browsing at a shelf of books outside the inevitable bookshop.

The question was, how had the follower picked up his trail? Had he been followed since he'd left Museum Street early this morning? It was possible, despite his diversions before going to Dolphin Square. It would have been no problem to an experienced shadower. It was also possible that the man had picked up his track at the Palace of Westminster. Under the instructions of the Prime Minister? It was a thought he did not relish; that Baldwin would have him followed. Then another idea occurred to him. The ubiquitous Mister C E Stevens might have set someone on his track. Was Stevens involved? He had no reason to think so. Yet the man had been at the German Embassy. No, that meant nothing, so many people were at the German Embassy, a cross-section of London society.

At Foyle's bookshop, Lohmann turned and retraced his steps, moving south again. Passing the man who was taking an inordinate interest in the entrance to St Martin's College of Distributive Trades. The man was dressed in a raincoat over a sports jacket and wide flannel trousers. With a dark shirt. Recrossing Cambridge Circus, he saw the man again, reflected in the side-window of a men's outfitters. The follower too had changed direction and was still behind him.

Further down Charing Cross Road, Lohmann turned and

walked along into Leicester Square. And into a large cinema on his right. A poster proclaiming *Bullets or Ballots* was one of the two features. Hopefully, his shadow would presume he was aware of being followed, and go through the cinema and out, through one of the rear emergency exits. But this time Lohmann decided on a change of tactics. He went down one of the aisles of the stalls and in the darkness, seated himself under the screen. Waiting.

Above him, on the screen, the huge round face of Edward G Robinson confronted a snarling Humphrey Bogart. Lohmann turned so that he could view the aisle behind him. The raincoat, flannels and dark shirt came into the stalls and, ignoring an usherette, peered through the light cast by the glare from the screen. Lohmann was hopeful he might go to one of the emergency exits. But the man was good. His eyes ranged along the rows of seats. Late afternoon, the cinema was far from busy. Patrons were dotted around the stalls, eyes riveted to the screen. Lohmann knew he'd made his mistake in looking back away from the screen. The man's eyes seemed to settle on him for a moment, then move away. He came down the aisle and sat some three rows behind the detective, eyes fixed on the giant cringing features of Bogart.

A kind of relief, Lohmann thought. Directly behind him, in a packed and darkened cinema, the man would have represented an imminent danger. Lohmann had seen it before in Germany. Once before, with a knife through the back of a cinema seat, and a dead man who hadn't even cried out. At least he was not in that kind of danger. So, it would appear, the man was simply under orders to follow him. Lohmann stared up at the screen watching but not seeing. Thinking about his next move. Leave, knowing he would still be followed? Try to shake the man off in another way? Or face him. The unexpected element.

Lohmann rose, walked two rows back. 'Excuse me,' Lohmann squeezed past and sat on the seat next to him.

'It would be easier if I told you where I was going next,' Lohmann said.

'But not as interesting, chum,' the man replied.

'Why do you follow me?'

'I'm being paid. 'Course I knew you'd cottoned on back

230

there. Good film, this. I seen it before.' Not a cockney accent, probably Irish. But a professional, certainly, with all the coolness of the professional.

'Being paid is your reason. Whoever pays you, they also have reasons.'

'Aw, now it's them wants you dead, see.'

Lohmann felt cold. Icicles on the spine.

'They missed you at your room,' the man went on in a low tone. 'They'll not be wanting me to miss you this time.'

Lohmann thought, in a West End cinema, he was discussing his own murder. There was a kind of surreality in this.

'With gun or knife?' he asked.

'No, no, not here, mister. One's noisy, the other's messy. I don't want to get messed up. Can get caught that way. An' they've been telling me you're the lucky one. Rowley tried it and got himself killed. And Rowley was a good pro. But, me, I'm better. Careful. I'll get you, when you're not looking, like.'

'Again, why?'

'How should I know? I just take the money. It's nothing personal . . .'

'I have heard that before. It is personal to me.'

'Sure, it would be.'

'Also I am getting tired of being a target for assassination.'

'Assassination, is it? And me thinkin' it was just plain old murder. See, it happens when you get involved in other people's business. Now a man like you would be fine, if you didn't interefere. It's always the way.'

Geschwätzig, the Irishman was, Lohmann told himself. Garrulous, that was the English word. Enjoyed talking.

'You are one of a *Tod Kommando*.'

'Now what the fuck would that be?'

'What you call a Death Squad.'

'Aw, that rubbish! I heard them talkin' about it. Bloody amateurs. Me, I work on my own. Under contract, you might say.'

'It would be interesting to know who was going to murder me. Your name, perhaps,' Lohmann said.

'I've a number of names. Have to, in my business.'

'Yes, you would have to.'

'Houlihan. That good enough? I can see it might be a comfort, knowing the name of the man who did it. Afterwards. If there is an afterwards. Anyway it's been nice talking to you. I'll surely have to see you again, maybe.' Houlihan rose quickly and nodded. 'Told you I'd seen this film anyway. 'Bye for now!'

He went. Back up the aisle. One row back, he seemed to hesitate and stoop. Something on the floor of the cinema. And then he was away quickly, taking long strides towards the back of the cinema.

Lohmann suddenly and inexplicably felt fear. Again.

Twisting in his seat, peering into the dim light where the man who called himself Houlihan had stooped.

Something glinting in the reflected light from the screen. Like silver paper. But not silver paper.

Lohmann reached down and felt a roundness of metal.

Remembering.

In the war.

The shape of a hand grenade.

Without the pin.

TWENTY

The newspapers the next day reported the explosion in a West End cinema as having been almost certainly carried out by the Irish Republican Army who had been occasionally active in such matters during the early thirties. The woman in the pay-box at the cinema had reported selling a ticket to a tall man with an Irish accent some short time before the explosion in the cinema. She had also seen the man leave the cinema some minutes later, just before the bomb . . . it was presumed to be a bomb . . . had exploded. There was also a telephone call to one newspaper from an individual calling himself the representative of the Anarchist Workers and Provident Society of Western

232

Europe who claimed that his Society had been responsible for what became known as the 'West End Bomb Outrage' and their next target would be the East Cheam Public Library (this was discounted by the police as a hoax).

Lohmann did not see these newspapers. He was in a private room in the Charing Cross Hospital where he remained for two nights suffering from mild cuts and abrasions. The only reason he was detained was the insistence by the registrar that he wanted to be sure the German was not suffering from concussion or the effects of shock. Three other patrons of the cinema were also detained for the same reasons.

It was considered, by the police and the press, fortunate that the cinema had been almost empty (a report which did not please Warner Brothers, the makers and distributors of the film).

At first Lohmann did not remember exactly what had happened, when he had discovered the hand grenade. Later he remembered, he had gripped the metal casing and thrown the grenade, at floor level, towards the large screen. This seemed sensible as it propelled the grenade away from the audience. Indeed the principal casualty was the image of Edward G Robinson, whose face on the vast screen was torn apart when the grenade exploded, as he talked to Joan Blondell.

Lohmann was struck on the head by a segment of wood torn from a seat in the front row of the stalls. He was knocked unconscious and only came around on the ambulance taking him to the hospital.

Later, lying in his bed in the hospital, he was interviewed briefly by the police, in the person of an Inspector Corby from Bow Street investigating the outrage. He told Corby nothing, considering further involvement with yet another police officer would only complicate the situation. He was a patron in a cinema and a bomb had gone off. He did not mention the hand grenade or Houlihan. Or throwing the bomb towards the screen. He was fortunate in that no one had seen him throw the grenade.

He received no visitors until the next day, when his name was printed in the newspapers with the other three casualties.

His first visitor was Superintendent Thornhill who sat at the end of his bed with a wry look on his face.

'An extreme form of film criticism,' Thornhill said. 'Must have been a rotten movie.'

'I didn't see enough of it.'

'I take it you and not Edward G Robinson were the target?'

'What would make you think that?'

'They did blow up your bedsitter. Just as well you are staying somewhere else.'

'As you are saying.'

'Anything you want to tell me about it?'

Lohmann thought for a moment. Whose side was Thornhill on? Was he another Brundage, a Mosleyite sympathiser? There was every reason not to trust the police in this affair. And yet it could be a test of the man's honesty.

'An Irishman called Houlihan. But not your Irish Republican.'

'Houlihan? I think I've heard of him.'

'Another professional. Like Rowley. I was the target. After he was gone I saw the grenade and threw it towards the screen. Away from the people. Myself being one of the people.'

'We'll give you a medal. You've not told me everything, Lohmann. As an ex-policeman, you should know that it would be wise to do so.'

'If I did not think some of your police were on the other side, I might have done so. And not just the police. There is a certain . . . zweideutigkeit . . . ambiguity . . . in their attitude.'

'The PM?'

Lohmann nodded.

'Try me,' said Thornhill evenly.

'Convince me,' Lohmann replied.

Thornhill sighed. 'It's as if they've just discovered bombs, these villains of yours.' He reached into his pocket and producing a sheet of paper handed it to Lohmann.

It was a short, typewritten report.

Cornwall County Police Department.
Re: Report, Helston Police Office. Sergeant Veillon.
An explosion last night completely wrecked Rose Bush Cottage, Mullion. Cottage owned by Edward Rennie, permanent domicile, Hornsey Rise, London, who was

apparently not in residence. No casualties reported. No indication of whereabouts of said Edward Rennie.

Lohmann handed the paper back to Thornhill. 'Wasn't he supposed to be walking in the Lake District?'

'We've been trying to find him.'

'To arrest him?'

Thornhill sighed. 'You're a suspicious man.'

'Like you, I was trained to be.'

'He would assist us in our enquiries.'

'Some people would assist him into his grave.'

'It would appear so,' Thornhill hesitated. 'Tell me about your Death Squad idea.'

'You've been talking to Baldwin.'

'Listening to him. You don't talk to the head man. You listen. Unless you're a former Berlin detective with a brass neck.'

'What is the *brass neck*?'

'An expression. Like *chutzpah*. I had a Jewish grandmother.'

'So had Reinhard Heydrich.'

Thornhill winced. 'Don't like the comparison. Come and see me. Soon.'

'Perhaps,' Lohmann replied. And decided to test Thornhill. 'I heard Mosley is organising a march in the East End. October the fourth. Can you stop it?'

'In two days. I can't stop it. Too low in the pecking order. You should have asked Baldwin. Anyway they tell me it's supposed to be a free country. It's a pity.'

'That it's a free country? Or that you can't stop Mosley?'

Thornhill rose from the end of the bed. 'A bit of both. After all I am a policeman. A free country can be very irritating at times. Think about what I've said. My door is always open. It's draughty. But we can talk.'

He went to the door of the room and stopped. 'Mister Emerson, the Assistant Commissioner, sent his best wishes. Couldn't come himself as he's attending a Chief Constables' conference in Manchester for a few days. You're pretty thick with Charlie Emerson. Why not me?'

Lohmann shrugged. 'Why not? He is of a higher rank than you. Still all things change in time, Mister Thornhill.'

'He's going higher still. The word is he's in line for a big intellegence job. Nobody'll say what it is, but the head of MI5 has just retired. Thought that might be of interest to you.'

'It is, indeed.'

'Might enable him to help you a great deal more in this business.' Thornhill suggested. 'MI5 will possibly have records of all these people who are trying to kill you. He would have access and power to release them to you.'

'You are cheering me up considerably, Mister Thornhill.'

'Good. He might even let me in on it. I'll tell him you're improving rapidly. 'Bye!'

That was in the morning. In the afternoon, Rue Scott-ffoliot came to visit him. Almost in tears, mixed with anger. He was dressed and sitting, reading, when she arrived.

'You could have been killed,' she said.

'Are you disappointed?'

She made a face. 'Don't be horrid. I was frightened. And here you are, sitting reading a book.'

'*Vile Bodies* by Evelyn Waugh. Strange people, your English aristocracy. And I think I was frightened too. While I was conscious.'

She sat on the edge of the bed and produced a large box of chocolates and a small mountain of grapes.

He said: 'I will never eat this much. They're letting me out tomorrow.'

'Then give them to the deserving sick.' She became serious. 'How did you get on with Uncle Stanley?'

'With who?'

'The Prime Minister. I used to call him that when I was small. And he wasn't Prime Minister. Tell me.'

He told her everything he had discussed with Baldwin.

'But if Baldwin can stop the publication of anything about this money going to Germany, why was Beth killed?'

'I'm sure now she wasn't killed by any direct action of the British government,' he replied. 'And they would not want Rennie dead. They could prosecute him under your Official Secrets Act. Or they could give him a warning and agree to hush it all up.'

236

'Then it's the Nazis who are killing people. And trying to kill you and Rennie.'

'And Beth's father, Maurice Kovel. In case Beth told him anything. But I'm not even sure it is the Nazis. I think the man who organised the transfer of the money to Schacht is behind it. He's using the Death Squad idea to protect himself. And recruiting from Mosley's people to provide his Death Squad. If such knowledge became public, the Nazis would survive, your government might fall, but it would be re-elected again. But this man . . . this go-between . . . it would be his disgrace. And ruination. So he organises killers to protect him.'

'Mosley!' she said. 'Oswald himself. Paying off and in the pay of the Nazis . . .'

'Possible but too obvious. And why should he hide it? He praises Hitler already.'

'But . . . but then how do you find out who he is?'

Lohmann put the book down on the bed, 'Oh, I know who he is. The problem is proving it. And, once proved, seeing what your government will do about it. If anything.'

'But, if you know, tell me!' she burst out.

'When I am ready. And have the evidence.' He hesitated now, brow furrowed. 'I've been thinking all morning . . . it's interesting . . . your *Uncle* Stanley said something very . . . *neuierig*. How would you say it?'

'Curious,' she supplied the word.

'*Ja*! Curious. As if a certain Royal Personage . . . that's how he put it . . . could be involved. Now if that were so, this Royal Personage might well know our man.'

'But who . . . ?' Rue burst out, and then stopped, face suddenly becoming pale. 'Oh, God, there's only one person . . . The Prince of . . . the King now! It can't be. I've heard him . . . oh, I know he's got some funny ideas and . . . and Wallis hasn't helped . . . but . . . oh, no . . . And I've been invited to dine at a house he's coming to tomorrow. Or is it the day after. The third of October.'

'You must go.'

'I turned down the invitation this morning. I have to nurse you.'

237

'I do not need to be nursed. You will telephone now and accept this invitation.'

'If it's still open.'

'Also would you not be expected to be partnered?'

'Well, yes, but . . .'

'You will be bringing me as your partner.'

'Lohmann I'm not sure if . . . you see, when a private hostess has a dinner like this, all the guests' names have to be submitted to someone at the Palace. For approval.'

Lohmann rose to his feet, albeit rather unsteadily. 'You will submit, as your partner, the name of Inspector Ernst Lohmann of the Berlin Police, visiting this country.'

'I'll have to telephone Madge . . .'

'Who is Madge?'

'Madge Van Essling. She's an American. A friend of Wallis Simpson. Rich as Rockefeller. She might even be related. You see, with Wallis abroad, discreetly waiting to see, as Madge says, which way the cookie crumbles, the King's been hiding himself away in Fort Belvedere nursing his adoration, presumably to keep it warm. He daren't go out. If Wallis knew he was on the town, there'd be hell to pay.'

'I do not understand all this . . .' Lohmann said.

'Then listen! Wallis is out to sit up there next to HM. She won't take a chance on losing him. So he daren't go out. But she'd let him go to Madge's for dinner. You see, she's no threat.'

'This Madge is so ugly?'

'Oh, she's beautiful. Also likes other girls. Made a pass at me once. But hasn't everybody? Wallis knows she's a lesbian so David can dine there. You see, just as much as he misses her, he needs company. He's not very much at the best of times, and nothing to himself. So he asked Madge to throw a little dinner party for him. Of course nobody will know about it. He'll come incognito. Mister Smith or Jones, or Cornwall or something . . .'

'I still do not understand. But find out if you can bring me as your escort. Now, Rue! Telephone now.'

She did so. Returning some ten minutes later.

'The invitation was still open. I accepted. For both of us. But you have to be cleared by the Palace.'

'Sounds like I have to take a purgative. When will you know?'

'By tomorrow.'

'Good. Now I have no clothes and no place to stay.'

Rue grinned. 'I knew you'd need me. You're staying in my apartment. As for clothes, leave that to me.'

'You will need measurements . . .'

'You got your dinner suit from Moss Brothers. They'll have your measurements. Now I'll collect you here tomorrow morning . . . you'll have a day to rest in my place . . .'

'I do not need to rest!'

'But you will.'

She left. Lohmann sat thinking. If the Palace approved, he would meet the King of England on the third of October. And the next day he had to be in Leman Street. Where Mosley's people would march. He had a feeling that the march could lead to a kind of climax. But what kind?

Rue collected him the next day and took him to Dolphin Square. He was docile and did as he was told. Resting. On the surface. Underneath, his mind was active. He telephoned Joe Kahn.

'Thank God you phoned. So far the old man is fine,' said Kahn. 'But I wanted to try and get him away from Cable Street.'

'He should go.'

'He won't go. He doesn't care about his life now Beth is dead. And Jack Comer's taken his men away.'

'What!'

'Says he needs them for tomorrow. Has to brief them on how to tackle the Blackshirts. And other things. God knows what.'

'Then the old man is . . . unguarded?'

'Except for me. Comer thinks, if they were going to try and kill the old man, they'd have done it by now.'

'They've already tried once and failed. They will wait for the right moment. That could be tomorrow. Then, if he is killed it can be attributed to the violence that will happen during the Blackshirt march.'

'Are you sure they still want to kill him? I genuinely think he knows nothing.'

'They cannot take that chance. Joe, we are dealing with a meticulous, if frightened man. If he believed there is the slightest chance of Beth having said anything to her father that might indicate his identity, he must eliminate that possibility.'

'Okay, okay. I'm on your side.'

'Stay with the old man. Have you a gun?'

'This isn't the Wild West, Ernst. Where the hell would I get a gun?'

'Never mind. Probably nothing will happen until the Blackshirts march. When do they start?'

'I don't know. Late morning, I suppose. But they may try and infiltrate people into the district beforehand. That's why Comer needs his men. They're going around pubs sniffing out unsavoury characters.'

'Very well. Wait! I will come as soon as I can.'

He replaced the receiver. It was all too possible, he thought. The march on the East End by the Fascists could be used to cover any action against Maurice Kovel. And himself, if they knew he would be there. But there would then be the opportunity for him to face those who had actually killed Beth Coverley. The Death Squad would show itself. He felt a sense of excitement. Now he would be acting as the policeman again. But alone. Also, there was the man behind the Death Squad. Who would be as far as possible from the East End tomorrow. That Lohmann would have to work out on his own. Later. No suspicion would be attached to that individual. Also he would be unaware he had already given himself away.

And now the night before the Fascist march, Lohmann would meet the King. Edward the Eighth. Known as David. The boy David. Formerly the Prince of Wales. *The little Prince, the dream Prince . . . danced with a man who danced with a girl who danced with the Prince of Wales . . . great grandson of Victoria . . . House of Windsor, formerly the House of Saxe-Coburg-Gotha . . . the caring Prince . . . 'something must be done' said to the Welsh miners . . . nothing was done . . . rumour that his father King George had told him . . . 'You dress like a cad, sir. And you are a cad' . . . something like that . . . with the mistresses behind him . . . Mrs Dudley Ward . . . Emerald Cunard . . . and others . . . all married, some older than him . . . 'the boy needs mothering' . . . and then Wallis Warfield Simpson . . . twice-*

divorced, once recently, now abroad and waiting. For what? 'David would know that'. David, formerly Prince of Wales, Duke of Rothesay, Duke of Cornwall, Lord of the Isles, God knows what else . . . now King Emperor, Defender of the Faith . . . what faith? . . . and so much else.

And friend or sympathiser to Oswald Mosley and who else? Adolf Hitler, so it was said.

The telephone rang again disturbing his train of thought. He'd been pacing Rue's sitting-room. He would allow her to answer it this time.

Two minutes later Rue came into the room.

'The King would be pleased to meet Mrs Van Essling's guest, Herr Ernst Lohmann,' Rue announced triumphantly. 'All thanks to me.'

'Thank you,' he said. 'May I now have a coffee?'

'You may. Your dress suit has arrived. 'And other clothes.'

'What other clothes?'

She showed him, while he drank coffee. She had bought him five silk shirts, several pieces of underwear, socks, etc. A sports jacket, two pairs of flannels, two suits, and one dinner suit, shirt, tie and cufflinks. None rented. All purchased.

Lohmann's face was pale. 'I cannot afford . . .'

'But I can,' Rue replied.

'I cannot accept . . .'

'Then you will be very cold. And as the clothes you are wearing get dirty, which they are already, you will be a nudist.'

'I will not be a . . . kept man.'

'You can pay me back then.'

He examined the clothes. 'It will take me ten years.'

'I can wait,' she said.

October the third. Seven o'clock precisely on a dull evening, Rue parked the car in Eaton Square. The house was in front of them, large, elegant, rented for a period of two years by Madge Van Essling.

'Not worth buying,' she'd said. 'Be a war in Europe in a coupla years. So, rent a house, have some fun and then back to Washington DC. That's where the action'll be then, honey.'

She'd not only rented the house in Eaton Square but redecorated it. Not in the style, as the owner had expected, of a

241

New York penthouse but in what Madge Van Essling considered to be traditional English style. The result was a ponderous Gothic . . . even to two suits of armour in the hall, a chandelier worthy of the *Phantom of the Opera* (The Lon Chaney version), and a dining-room table which had once graced a medieval monastery. Incongruously, the paintings on the wall were all modern, including a Dali and a Modigliani and canvases by a number of unknown painters. It had always been Madge's ambition to discover an unknown prodigy who would later be hailed as another Van Gogh, ensuring a return on her modest investment.

Lohmann followed Rue into the large hall where a butler relieved them of their coats and escorted them into the oak-panelled dining room. The hostess greeted Rue enthusiastically, kissing her on both cheeks, complimented her on her gown and then turned to greet Rue's escort.

'Herr Lohmann, great to have you here. The King was most innerested when he heard you were from Germany.' Her voice dropped almost to a whisper, an unnecessary precaution since all her other guests were aware of the information she was about to convey to Lohmann.

'Of course, HM is here incognito. As Mister Rothesay. And no word of his being here is to reach anybody. Particularly the press. Between you and me, Herr Lohmann, the little man is scared Wallis gets word of his outing and thinks he's two-timing her.'

'Miss Scott-ffoliot told me of the circumstances.'

'Rue knows the score. Come and meet people.'

He was introduced to a smallish man with a moustache and a statuesquely beautiful wife, Duff Cooper and Lady Diana. There was a Mrs Seely, seemingly unescorted, a Henry Channon with an American accent, a giggle, and a vaguely precious manner. Somehow, despite the accent, more English than the English. And addressed by the hostess as 'Chips'. After that, Lohmann lost track of names and titles and was relieved when he was given a cocktail and rejoined Rue.

"We wait now for *Mister Rothesay*. Everything waits for the little man.'

Mister Rothesay finally arrived. Late.

TWENTY-ONE

He was small, of sandy complexion, with the air of youth still about him. Yet he was forty-two and his age was beginning to show around the eyes. The crow's feet were there, and the darker, deeper lines below. The eyes themselves had a dull look belying what might otherwise have been considered an intelligent face. When he finally came closer to Lohmann and Rue, Lohmann could see the twisted look, so apparent in newspaper photographs, as if the face were sloping to one side, sliding like a mask from the skull underneath.

He entered, followed by an aide, a tall man, with the bearing of a Guards officer or, in Lohmann's eyes, the stiffness of a Junker. This was Major Metcalfe, addressed by the women as '*dear old Fruity*'. Behind them, in the hall, they left a third man, HM's detective.

At the door he was greeted by the hostess. Despite the talk of his being incognito, Madge Van Essling gave a deep curtsy and the King, in his turn, kissed her hand.

'So glad to be here, Madge,' he muttered. 'At this time we're grateful for a little company.'

Madge Van Essling then presented the other guests. With some there was yet another muttered greeting, with others, he stopped, a brief pleasantry was exchanged, there was a ripple of laughter and he moved on. Finally he came to Rue and Lohmann. Rue curtsyed, and Lohmann, following the example of the other male guests, inclined his head in a short but formal bow, managing to restrain himself from clicking his heels. Mister Rothesay addressed Rue as an old friend, kissed her hand and enquired of some mutual acquaintance. Then he turned to Lohmann. Following the bow came the handshake.

'Ah, Herr Inspector Lohmann. From Germany.' Spoken in good German.

'From Berlin, sir.' Lohmann replied in English.

'Always wanted to visit Berlin,' the King replied, now in English. 'I have had an invitation from Ambassador Ribbentrop. But my Prime Minister insists this is not the time. Of course I told him, what better time? If there are problems they can be solved in a civilised manner over a table. Herr Hitler is a reasonable man.'

It was obvious the King had never met Hitler. But now, when Lohmann spoke, it was to make his first move in what might be the most difficult, certainly the most oblique interrogation he would ever make. And always, he told himself, remembering he was meant to be a Nazi official.

'I understand, sir, you have already been of considerable help to us in the past.'

The King looked up, one eyebrow raised. 'Ah, you do. We'll perhaps have a moment to talk about that later. You see, I am very interested in how things are going in Germany today.'

He moved on, eyes steady, expressionless. Yet there had been a reaction. That was enough for now, Lohmann told himself.

Some moments later the King and his hostess led them into dinner. Lohmann to his surprise found himself separated from the King only by Madge Van Essling on his left. On the King's right was the quiet, gentle Mrs Seely.

At first, conversation flowed around Lohmann. And he was seated too far from Rue to seek help. The company was made up of old friends talking on familiar subjects. Major Metcalfe, sitting next to Rue, laughed and joked with the studied familiarity of long acquaintance. The King chatted amiably with Madge Van Essling on one side and Mrs Seely on the other. Despite an appearance of ease, there was an undercurrent, as if the two women and, indeed, anyone else who joined in conversation with the Monarch was being very careful of the subjects that they broached. It was not until some way into the dinner that the King himself mentioned the name everyone had avoided.

'Of course Wallis adores France. The Riviera and Paris actually. She always says, between Paris and the Riviera there is only a desert. Or was it Jimmy Donahue who said that?'

This permitted Madge Van Essling to enquire of Mrs Simpson's health.

'Fine,' the King replied, and then a vague look came into his eyes. 'Lonely too, of course. We . . . we both are . . .'

On Lohmann's right, a bright woman, daughter of a patrician family whose name he had not caught, seemed to take pity on his isolation and began to question him about Berlin. She was, he learned later, despite her titled connections, a novelist of growing repute.

'I've heard so much from my sisters about Berlin. They visit all the time. And Chris Isherwood goes on and on about it. Of course that was before the present regime. Is it as decadent as they told me?'

'That would depend on how decadent they described it. But now the decadence has taken a different form. On the surface it is not permitted. Perhaps it is a pity. At least there were voices in the decadence crying out. Today there is only one voice.' Then he added hurriedly, remembering his masquerade, '*Naturlich*, that is as it should be.'

'But of course socially and economically things are better, surely?'

Lohmann had to be careful now. Avoid the truth, his truth.

'For many people, yes.'

'And all this talk about the Jews being persecuted, isn't it exaggerated?'

'Perhaps, not to the Jews. But it would depend on what is said about the state of the Jews,' Lohmann replied diplomatically. Ignoring the truth of old men being forced to scrub pavements because they were Jews; of disappearances at dawn as Jewish families were arrested and disappeared into Dachau. There were rumours too of other camps being built, of even more arrests to come.

'Such a contrary people, our Hebrew friends,' said a man across the table. 'Apart from their preoccupation with money, they're definitely pushy. Of course, I'm no anti-Semite.'

Lohmann waited for the expected line. And it came.

'. . . Some of my best friends are Jews,' the man went on. Further down the table, Duff Cooper frowned. 'Some of mine

245

are even human beings,' he said acidly. Lohmann decided he liked Duff Cooper. But he said nothing. Anything he might say could only reveal his true feelings. He had no wish to destroy the image he was intent on building in the King's mind.

Madge Van Essling was a stickler for protocol. As the dinner ended, the women withdrew, leaving the men to port, brandy and cigars. The King moved around and sat next to Lohmann.

'Madge should know better,' he said, lighting a large Havana cigar. 'Can't be bothered with this brandy and cigar ritual. Half the women in London smoke cigars anyway.'

His voice dropped. 'You seem to be quite knowledgeable, Herr Lohmann. In certain areas.'

'I worked for a time closely with Doctor Schacht.' The lie came easily.

'Yes, yes, the banker fellow. I trust discretion is one of his assets. And yours.'

'Essential to the Führer's supporters, sir.'

The King gave a crooked smile. 'I put all my influence behind the transaction. Without disconcerting the Treasury too much. I put a deal of pressure on MacDonald. Of course my name could not be associated with it. My father was still alive. He believed in leaving it all to the politicians. The constitutional way. Not that he ever knew a thing about it. But even after all I saw in South Wales, when I voiced the opinion that something should be done, I was told I was constitutionally out of order. Then I began to hear about Herr Hitler. I said to myself, this is the man to tackle the problems of our time. And when we saw what was happening in Germany, well, we felt, at all costs, the Bolsheviks must not be allowed to return to power. Herr Hitler and the party were obviously the only method of combating them.'

'Most perceptive, sir. And the Führer was most grateful.'

'Of course, personally, I could do little but exert pressure. Fortunately there were those in the Treasury who listened. I fancy I had some influence.'

Lohmann sipped his port. He disliked port.

'So the offer was made,' he said.

'And I did want Herr Hitler to know I approved.'

'Oh, he was very much aware of your support. Especially in such a practical manner.'

246

'We must be careful, of course. Ramsey and some of his people could be swayed. Now, under the present administration, nothing could be done. Baldwin is . . . not so amenable. An unsympathetic man. The details of the original transaction were kept from him. Of course now, as PM, he will know. Not my part of course. Probably, deep down he agrees with the whole business. But he is so old-fashioned. In so many ways.' He was staring into space now, a mournful, faraway look in his eyes.

'They don't understand,' he went on. 'This is the twentieth century. There have been changes. In morality, in the balance of power. Europe needs a . . . a new order. Yes, a new order. As we do here. Oswald . . . he had the right idea. Oswald Mosley. We're in touch, if only by correspondence. I cannot be seen to support his movement. Trouble is, he insists on working from the outside. I sometimes think he should have stayed in one party or another and worked from within. Just as Hitler did when he courted the favour of Hindenburg.'

'You are most perceptive, sir,' Lohmann repeated the compliment with unctuous flattery.

'I'm delighted you see that. I believe it's time for the Monarch to play a greater role. Not that the government will see it that way. Won't even allow the King to make his own decisions about his personal life.' Again the faraway look.

Lohmann twisted his glass of port in his hand, turning the subject from the general to the particular.

'The envoy who arranged the . . . the transfer of funds, I think I met him at the time . . . in '32 . . .'

'Oh, I believe it was done in a most convoluted manner. An envoy to Germany and then the transfer of funds through Switzerland,' the King replied. 'As to who arranged it, I believe it was some enthusiastic civil servant. He had to be sympathetic of course but with a very low profile at the time. And not directly connected with the Treasury. Or the government. Didn't dare use anyone too much in the public eye.'

'Of course.'

'And I had to distance myself. But I have an ambition, Herr Lohmann. If and when other matters can be resolved, I intend

247

to bring Germany and this country closer together. As my grandfather did with France and the *Entente Cordiale*.'

His voice suddenly dropped. 'Duff Cooper is coming over. Like Winston, he doesn't appreciate what we are trying to do. But I'm glad we've had this talk. You'll convey my good wishes to Herr Hitler.'

Duff Cooper came around the table, hesitated, as if awaiting the Royal acknowledgement of his presence. The King rose and greeted him with assumed affability.

'Herr Lohmann was telling me of conditions in Germany.'

'I doubt, sir, if he would tell you of the debits in their national account.' Duff Cooper turned a bleak eye towards Lohmann. 'I hear the Jews are having an increasingly difficult time.'

The King sighed and answered on Lohmann's behalf. 'The Jews . . . the Jews . . . we keep hearing so much about the Jews. I'm sure Herr Lohmann would confirm that those who have been . . . detained . . . they are Bolshevik sympathisers.'

Duff Cooper assumed an air of mock puzzlement. 'Isn't there a contradiction in Hitler's attacks on the Jews? One minute they are part of a Bolshevik conspiracy, the next they are part of an international capitalist plot. He really can't have it both ways.'

Lohmann's liking for Duff Cooper increased. Yet he could say nothing. He was still playing the part of a visiting German official. The King however frowned. Not pleased.

'You really mustn't quibble, Duff. Herr Hitler obviously knows more about Germany's internal problems than you do. Shall we join the ladies?'

He was indicating the regal prerogative to change the subject. They joined the ladies, Duff Cooper with a small shrug at the rebuff. They moved into a large, opulent, if rather chilly drawing-room. The King, sensing the chill, established himself in front of the fireplace, the warmest spot in the room, and became engaged in a deep conversation with Mrs Seely. Lohmann joined Rue in a corner of the room.

'Well?' she said in a low voice.

'Mister Rothesay and I had a talk.'

'And?'

'He knew what we were talking about.'

248

'The stupid little man!'

'Does not that remark come close to high treason?'

'Doesn't his knowledge come even closer? Did you get a name?'

'I don't think he knows any useful names. We did talk about an envoy. Responsible but low profile. And no names.'

'Pity.' She lit a cigarette, inserting it in a long holder.

'At least it proves he was involved. Even if only in encouraging the principals. When can we leave?'

'Not until Mister Rothesay leaves.'

The King stayed until after one o'clock in the morning. During the course of the evening he disappeared into a study to make a telephone call to France. He returned happily and when it came to one o'clock, seemed reluctant to leave. Finally, with Major Metcalfe and his detective trailing behind him, he said goodnight to his hostess and her guests and went out to be driven back to Fort Belvedere.

There was almost a sense of relief after his departure. Madge Van Essling provided coffee and last drinks for her guests and everyone relaxed.

'Naturally he was telephoning *her*!' Madge said. 'And, since he was cheerful, I imagine all is well. She'll make it yet, y'know.'

'Make what?' Rue said with an affectation of vagueness.

'Aw, honey, you know she's hell-bent on sitting up there on that big throne next to him.'

'It won't happen,' said Duff Cooper.

'But why not? What would cement an Anglo-American alliance more than a good old Yankee girl as consort?'

Diana Duff Cooper stared down her nose at Madge. 'After two . . . or is it three divorces, and God knows what else, they'll never accept her, Madge, darling. The consort must be above reproach.'

'Oh, Wallis won't accept that,' Madge insisted. 'After all, he is the King. And she has him exactly where she wants him.'

'The days of the Absolute Monarch have long gone. He has to follow the advice of the Cabinet. If he doesn't . . .' Duff Cooper shrugged. 'He's not indispensable. He has a brother . . .'

249

'We can go now?' Lohmann whispered to Rue.

'We can go now.'

She was mildly drunk and he drove the Jaguar back to Dolphin Square.

'So Herr Inspector Lohmann, you have this night dined with the King Emperor,' she said as he parked the car.

'Another step in the investigation,' he replied. 'Not that I interrogate kings every day. It is an experience. Especially when he does not realise he is being interrogated.'

She climbed unsteadily from the car. 'Well, I'm glad it's over. I'm tired. And you must be too . . .'

'I have to go to Cable Street.'

She looked up, surprised. 'That's . . . that's tomorrow. Mosley's people don't march until tomorrow . . .'

'Some of them may arrive earlier than expected.'

Something in his tone of voice seemed to sober her. 'The same people again. The . . . the Death Squad.'

'Beth's father will be a target.'

'You could . . . could be a target too.'

'I am aware of the possibility. Which is why I shall come up to your apartment for the Mauser.'

'You could take the Jag . . .'

'I will take a taxi. I don't think it would be wise to take your new car to the East End tomorrow.'

The taxi deposited Lohmann at a shuttered Aldgate East Underground Station. He had decided to walk to Cable Street. A taxi arriving there in the middle of the night would serve notice to any observers that he had arrived. At least on foot he might conceal his arrival.

He walked down a black, deserted Leman Street. Somewhere a clock in the city tolled three. A cold breeze blowing from the river caused him to shiver. Only two days from a bomb-blast and possible concussion, he pulled his coat collar up. Becoming aware he was still in dinner jacket and black tie, an incongruous garb for the East End.

Small, dark shops were on either side of him. A narrow alley on his right ran into blackness. Jack the Ripper country. Only fifty years since the Ripper had wandered these alleys on his insane and bloody business. In Berlin, Lohmann had studied the accounts of the Ripper murders with the fascination of a professional. Now, he was on these same streets on his own murder hunt. The cobbles and the houses around him were even older than the Ripper murders. The poverty, less visible now, almost as harsh as it had been then. Perhaps today there was little actual starvation, but there was still dirt and squalor and malnutrition. And crime. Not so different from many parts of Berlin. Only there, the crime had moved from the mean streets to the Reichschancellery.

He thought, only a few hours before, he had dined with the King in a fashionable house in Eaton Square. Now he was in the slums of the East End. There was an incongruity. Eaton Square and Cable Street connected by murder and politics. Also perhaps not so different from Berlin.

He walked on, past the blue lamp above Leman Street Police Station. Passing the CWS Buildings and under the railway bridge, he came into Cable Street. In the dim light from the flickering gas-lamps it appeared at first the street was deserted but for himself.

Then the figure materialised out of the darkness. Lohmann tensed, feeling in his jacket for the comforting butt of the Mauser.

'Well, well, if it isn't Mister Lohmann?' Brundage, in a trench coat, collar pulled well up around his neck, soft hat pulled down over his forehead, a humourless smile on his lips.

'What are you doing, wandering around in the small hours of the morning?'

Lohmann relaxed his grip on the Mauser. 'Could I not ask the same of you, Sergeant Brundage?'

'Ah, well, you see, this is my patch. I like to keep an eye on how things are going. Promises to be an exciting day later on. I just want to make sure nothing is going to spoil that.'

'Herr Mosley's march?' Lohmann said.

'Exactly. A good lot of boys they are. British, you see. And there's too many foreigners living around here. Too many Jews and . . . and refugees.'

'That would of course include me.'

Brundage's smile broadened. 'Oh, I'm not worried about

251

you, Lohmann. You'll be taken care of, one way or another. I hear tell there's a deportation order just waiting at Scotland Yard to be issued. With your name on it. Ernst Lohmann. Oh, yes, you're to be sent back to the land of your fathers.'

The smile disappeared. 'To Germany. Tomorrow. If you live that long.'

The icy breeze from the river seemed to rise and bite deep at Lohmann. Through flesh and into bone marrow. He shuddered. To Germany. Tomorrow. If he should live . . .

TWENTY-TWO

Lohmann knocked on the door of the house in Cable Street. Still thinking of all that Brundage had said. If he was deported, he would inevitably be sent back to Germany. In Germany he would not live more than twenty-four hours. Heydrich would make sure of that. Lohmann knew too many secrets; knew where too many bodies were buried.

He was still shivering as he stood outside Kovel's house. Brundage was gone. Back into the darkness. The man was at home in darkness. As were those in Germany who would be waiting for him.

He knocked on the door again. Suddenly afraid he might be too late. But his fear was at once alleviated.

'Who is it?' Kahn's voice from behind the door.

'Lohmann.'

He heard a lock being turned and the door opened. Joe Kahn was behind it, in his hand a heavy metal poker.

'You're . . . you're late. I . . . I was dozing . . .'

Lohmann entered, and Kahn locked the door behind him.

'Come into the sitting-room.'

They went into the small front room. Heavy curtains were pulled across the window.

'How is the old man?' Lohmann asked.

'Upstairs. Asleep. His sister's gone to stay with her sons. I thought that was best. I should have asked the sons to come here. They might have provided a useful bodyguard. But Comer's men were still here then. I didn't know he was going to take them away. The bloody fool said he didn't think the old man was in any danger . . .'

'You told me on the phone.'

Kahn rubbed his hand across his forehead. A thin film of sweat ran down from the hair-line.

'We should have got him away from here.'

'The house is being watched,' Lohmann replied. 'Brundage is on the street outside just now. The house almost certainly has been watched since the inquest.'

'But the police should be guarding him,' Kahn insisted.

'Sergeant Brundage?'

'All right, not Brundage. What about your friends in Scotland Yard?'

Lohmann stared down at the fireplace. A small coal fire was struggling to stay alight.

'We do not know who is on our side and who is on theirs. There are people in Scotland Yard who have been told what has happened. A certain Superintendent Thornhill. And others. But, as Brundage is sympathetic to these people . . . so may some be at the Yard.'

'For God's sake, Lohmann, we're talking about the possible murder of an old man . . . !'

'In their eyes, dispensable. We are all dispensable, Joe. These people have allies in very high places . . .'

. . . thinking of Mister Rothesay. Of the King who was foolish enough to believe in a new order in Europe, led by Hitler; and by all the other imitation Hitlers. Mussolini, Franco, Mosley. And the acolytes. The Raven Marshalls, the William Joyces, the Brundages.

'So we wait here until they come?' Kahn said.

'It is, *vielleicht*, the one way we can stop them. One way we can perhaps eliminate the . . . the death squad.'

Kahn stared at him, wide-eyed. 'You . . . you're using the old man. Using him as bait. You want them to come here . . . !'

Lohmann took off his coat and sat wearily in one of the

253

armchairs. He took the revolver from inside his jacket and placed it on his lap. Kahn looked down at the weapon.

'One revolver!' the journalist said. 'And a poker. Against a fucking death squad. That's what you call them. A death squad! Two of us. Against how many of them?'

'Five I think. Led by a man called Raven Marshall.'

'What chance have we got? Five against two. Or perhaps you imagine the old man will join us?' Kahn's face was twisted in anger. 'He won't. He'll do nothing to help, even if he was able to. He wants to die. He wants to follow his daughter . . .'

'I had hoped Comer's men would be with us . . .'

'Comer's men'll be out there, throwing stones at Blackshirts.'

'We may hope when they hear what might happen in this house, they will help.'

'You're joking! Their enemy is out there.'

Lohmann rubbed his eyes. He felt suddenly weary.

'You are surrounded by your own people, Joe. Marshall and his death squad will be in enemy territory. We have to use that . . .'

'And risk Maurice Kovel? And ourselves . . . and you, dressed like a tailor's dummy . . .'

Lohmann smiled. He had forgotten he was still in the dinner suit. He was so very tired. That was what it was about now. His own exhaustion.

'Joe, I have pursued these people.' He was trying to explain the weariness. 'They . . . they have pursued me. They want me dead, as they do Herr Kovel. They've tried to kill me several times. I can go on running from them . . . you see, I have no need to pursue them any further. I know why Beth Coverley was killed. I know the people who executed the killing. I believe I know who is behind the killing, the one who ordered it . . . oh, he'll stay away from Cable Street today . . . but if I can destroy his death squad, then I can force him to act alone. And I can get to him. That is why I am here. Why I have to take this chance.'

Joe Kahn shook his head. 'It's still insane.'

'Also, outside just now, Brundage informed me that there was a deportation order waiting to be issued against me. Another reason why this has to be finished. While I am still here.'

'But they can't deport you! You've been admitted as a refugee . . .'

'That can be . . . what is the word? . . . *aufheben* . . . to rescind . . . rescinded . . . at any time.'

'But you have friends. Up there. High places. All that . . .'

'And they have friends in higher places. Joe, if you feel you cannot stay, I will not think less of you . . .'

Kahn stared at the poker. 'Where else will I go? But you . . . you'll have to tell me what to do when these people come . . .'

'There is another entrance to the house?'

'Back door. From the back court into the kitchen.'

'We can do something there. There is some string or cord?'

Joe nodded. 'There's a ball of string in a drawer . . .'

'*Gut!* Something else. *Bleichmittel?*'

'Bleach?'

'The bottle of household bleach?'

'I don't know. I suppose if it's there, the old woman would have kept it in a cupboard.'

'Stay here. I will be back.'

Lohmann went into the kitchen. He was there for half an hour. Finally he came back and sat down again. There were smudges of grime on his dress shirt.

'So?' said Joe Kahn.

'So now you make us some coffee. But don't go near the kitchen door. For what it's worth, a small booby-trap.'

'And after the coffee?'

'We wait.'

Kahn made coffee. And they waited, taking turns to doze in the armchairs. About six o'clock in the morning, the street outside came awake. Lohmann opened the curtains fractionally and looked out. A number of youths were collecting, gathering together in what seemed like a desultory manner. Hands in pockets, leaning against walls, collecting in groups, they were soon joined by older men. Cloth caps or bare heads were prominent, although there were a few instantly recognisable figures. Long black hair hanging down, curled into ringlets, black beards under black hats, these were Hassidic Jews, moving not in a group but in pairs, like the others, waiting.

255

Two hours later, Maurice Kovel came down the stairs from his bedroom, face still marked with sleep. He was dressed in an old jacket, an equally old pair of trousers and a collarless grey shirt.

'Nobody bothers to wake me, in my own house,' he addressed them both.

'We thought you needed the rest,' Joe Kahn said.

'First you drive my sister away, who looks after my house, then you ignore me. Strangers in my living-room.'

Lohmann could wonder, here was an old man whose life was threatened and he was unconcerned. Still mourning the death of an only daughter, anything else was unimportant.

'Is daylight,' he said. 'You're not going to open the curtains?'

'Not today, Mister Kovel,' Kahn replied. 'There may be trouble outside.'

'Ach, when is there not trouble? Even when the Cossacks were riding into our village in the old country my father would open the shutters and let in the daylight.'

Kahn changed the subject. 'Would you like some breakfast?'

'I will take a glass of tea.'

Kahn went into the kitchen to make the tea. Carefully avoiding going near the back door. Kovel turned to Lohmann.

'So you are here, Mister Lohmann.'

'I'm here, Mister Kovel.'

'You have found out something about . . . Becky's death?'

'It was not suicide.'

The old man sat heavily. He nodded. 'I never thought it was. That sin would not have been hers. Those who killed her, they will be punished? An eye for an eye.'

'I hope they will be.'

The sound of raised voices came from the streets.

'They sound as if it is a holiday out there,' Maurice Kovel said.

'They mean to stop the Blackshirts marching.'

'Have they no work to go to? They want to fight? Ach! *Kvetchers!* Better they go to work and ignore the *shmek!*'

'There are some people and things not to be ignored.'

The old man shrugged. 'So they have to make noises outside my window?'

He looked around, found what he was looking for, a Yiddish newspaper, and, ignoring Lohmann, started to read. Joe Kahn came in, carrying a mug of tea. The old man glared at the proffered mug with distaste.

'We no longer use cups? You think I am a navvy that I drink from that?'

Kahn returned to the kitchen and came back a few moments later with a cup of tea on a saucer.

'Is better,' Maurice Kovel said grudgingly. And, sipping his tea, turned his eyes back to the newspaper. As Kahn joined Lohmann at the window, there was a loud crash from outside.

'What the hell was that?' Kahn exclaimed.

'They've turned a lorry, or a cart, over on its side down the road. The barriers are going up,' Lohmann replied.

In the street, the young men had been joined by other figures, some of whom were haranguing the crowd. And now there were weapons in evidence, pickaxe handles, sticks, and half bricks in damp, nervous hands.

'The CP boys,' Kahn observed, peering around Lohmann. 'The Communists will be out there in front.'

'I've seen it all before,' Lohmann said. 'In Berlin. So very familiar.'

'Well, maybe Comer was right. With all that going on, maybe they're going to leave the old man alone.'

'No. They'll come here. When the trouble is at its peak, they'll come. When they hope we are all distracted by what is going on out there.'

'You seem so sure.'

'It is what they would do. *Taktik*. That is it. Tactics. You wait. I want to use the telephone.'

In the hall, Lohmann lifted the telephone and asked for Rue's number. She answered quickly.

'Lohmann! You're all right?'

'I am all right. Do something for me. I have heard there is a deportation order issued for me . . .'

'They can't deport you!'

'They can. Find out. Your friends in the government. Someone will know.'

'I'll telephone Baldwin . . .'

'He is on holiday in Norfolk now.'

'Anthony Eden will know where. I'll get the deportation order stopped, Lohmann.'

'That will depend where it comes from. If it comes from Baldwin, you will not get it stopped. From anyone else, who knows?'

'I'll get it stopped,' she insisted. 'If Wallis Simpson can believe she could reach the throne, Rue Scott-ffoliot can get a deportation order revoked.'

'Such influence,' he said mockingly. 'Governments may totter. See what you can do. I have no desire to go back to Germany just yet.'

He replaced the receiver and returned to the sitting-room. There were now shouts from the street.

'The police are up the street. Behind the overturned lorry. This is going to be very ugly.'

'It always is,' Lohmann replied. 'All we can do is wait.'

Again they waited. While outside the crowd grew larger. Waiting, they lost track of time. The street was now filled with a milling mob. Tense and expectant.

Then through the curtains, Kahn caught sight of a familiar figure.

'There's Jack Comer!'

Comer was in front of the house surrounded by a group of large men. The pickaxe handles were again in evidence. Other weapons too, Lohmann was sure. Hidden under heavy jackets. The weapons of the streets.

'I will go out and speak to Comer,' Lohmann said.

In the street, as he approached Comer two large young men who looked like prize-fighters appeared in front of him.

'You wantin' something, guv'nor?' The larger of the two spoke.

Then Comer saw Lohmann. 'That's okay, Den. He's kosher. What can I do for your, Mister Lohmann?'

'You can tell me what is happening.'

'Nothin' yet. Mosley and his boys got together down at the Royal Mint.' A short laugh. 'Where the money is, you might say. Anyway the coppers got nervous. Told him to call off the march. Official request. So he called it off.'

'Then nothing will happen on the streets?'

Comer laughed again. 'Don't you believe it. The march may be officially off . . . Mosley can trot home and complain about free speech . . . but unofficially some of his bully boys will march. Others'll come around behind. And the police'll march up to move us on. That's when the fun'll start. We'll show these bastar'ing anti-Semites.'

He looked Lohmann up and down. The dinner jacket was crumpled, the black tie askew.

'I see you dressed for our little party, Mister Lohmann.'

Lohmann felt awkward. A rare emotion for him. In Berlin, he would have been unconcerned. Especially knowing that Comer might be considered an old . . . what was the word in English? . . . an old lag. In Berlin too, he would have considered Comer as being on the opposing side. Here, he was an ally of a kind. This was something he was not used to; but then here he had to be grateful for any allies at all.

He nodded and went back to the house.

Comer was right. A short time later it started.

Riot.

Something he was accustomed to containing. Now he was on the other side. Supporting the rioters.

The noise outside rose. Shouting, screaming. Glass being smashed.

From the window, he could tell himself he was an impartial observer.

The police came up to the barricade created by the overturned lorry. Their batons were drawn. Bricks were thrown.

The police charged. The crowd broke and then reformed.

Then a group of men in black shirts came down behind the barrier. The Jews and their supporters clashed with the Blackshirts. It became hand to hand combat. The pickaxe handles rose and fell. The Blackshirts had brought their own clubs. These rose against the pickaxes. The police came over the barricade and charged. Behind them were mounted policemen, also wielding batons.

A small dark man fell in front of Kovel's door, two large, black-shirted youths kicking him. Blood flowed over the kerb.

Two of Comer's men came to the rescue of the small man. Across the road, another Blackshirt was cornered by two young men, his shirt almost torn from his back. Somewhere a razor flashed, and there was more blood on the tarmac.

Lohmann's view was narrow, taking in only the section of the street in front of the house. But from the noise and the commotion, he knew the fighting was spreading along the length of the street and into lanes, alleys and side-streets.

They were standing back from the window when the police charged – horses, riders, and men on foot. It seemed then to Lohmann that the uniformed men were concerned more with rescuing the Blackshirts than with what should have been an impartial subjugation of the riot. Now it was the police batons that rose and young boys and men in cloth caps were knocked down and beaten on the ground by the police.

Lohmann and Kahn were standing some feet back from the window. They watched with a sick fascination.

Kahn said, 'We should do something. People are being hurt out there.'

'What should we do? Call the police?' Said Maurice Kovel who had risen from his seat and his newspaper, and was beside Kahn. 'The police are part of it. This is what you want to protect me from? Gangsters in the streets, in and out of uniform. Jewish gangsters too, make no mistake. Fools, all of them. But they are happy to maim each other on the streets. They won't come into the houses.'

Then Lohmann saw the man on the other side of the road. He was tall and fair and wore a white shirt under a checked jacket. His face was familiar. From the night in the chapel in Hammersmith. One of Raven Marshall's men. Standing now staring across at the row of houses . . . no, not just at the row, but at Kovel's door and window.

The man's hand came up, almost in slow motion. The half brick was thrown with consummate accuracy at the window.

Lohmann pushed Kovel back towards the sofa; as he did so, shouting a warning at Joe Kahn.

The window shattered, glass spraying the room.

The noise from outside increased.

'You are all right?' Lohmann turned to Kovel.

The old man looked up from the side of the sofa. 'A little *gless*, so what's that? I have to pay for a new window.'

Lohmann looked over at Kahn who was flat against the wall at the side of the window, brushing glass from his clothes. He had a small cut on his forehead.

Kahn looked at Lohmann. 'That's all? A brick through the window?'

Lohmann knew then. The brick was thrown with deliberation.

'It's a signal. Now they come.'

His words were confirmed at once. There was a crash of more breaking glass, but this time from the rear of the house. The kitchen door.

'Take the old man upstairs,' Lohmann said to Kahn as he drew the Mauser from his pocket.

As he went into the narrow hallway, there was another crash from the kitchen. The door being opened. This was followed by a curse.

'Fuck it! What the hell . . .'

And then almost a scream.

'What is it? . . . God, it burns!'

'Leave him! Raven Marshall's voice. 'Get on!'

Lohmann's lips twitched, a grimace of satisfaction. The bleach in a basin over the door. A schoolboy trick. But the stuff was corrosive. One of the intruders would be out of action.

Joe Kahn pushed the old man upstairs, ignoring his muttered protests.

Lohmann took up a position at the foot of the stairs and, with his thumb, switched off the safety-catch on the side of the Mauser.

A figure came out of the kitchen door, crouching, weapon in hand. A shot-gun. Another of the men from the church in Hammersmith. Lohmann could see the crouched figure through the balustrade but the man could see nothing. Lohmann was concealed by the stairs.

With a shot-gun facing him, Lohmann could take no chances. He would aim for the head.

He swung around the balustrade and as he fired, the figure straightened up.

The man took the bullet in the throat and was thrown back against the wall, blood spurting, making a ghastly choking sound. The body slid down the wall, the shot-gun falling from the dying hand.

Another shout from the kitchen. They would not have expected a gun against them. At least they knew now they couldn't simply charge into the hall. And one, possibly two of them, were out of action.

Joe Kahn appeared at the top of the stairs, this time carrying, not the poker but what looked like a chair leg. Useless against shot-guns, Lohmann thought.

'Stay with the old man!' he shouted. Kahn withdrew back into the bedroom.

Then, for a long moment there was silence, but for the sounds of conflict from the street. In the distance, police sirens were sounding. Somebody blew a police whistle at the end of Cable Street.

It was Lohmann's turn to crouch as he ran along the narrow hall and picked up the dead man's shot-gun. As if he was back in the war. 1917. The trenches in Flanders. The body trembling, the smell of cordite in the air. He flattened himself against the wall at the side of the kitchen door. And found himself staring at the eyes of the man he had just killed. It wasn't a new sensation to Lohmann, having to kill. But afterwards, there was the sense of revulsion, the knowledge of the futility of killing. He'd thought when he left Germany, he would leave that behind him. Yet now he was staring at the body of a man he had just shot. In another place, in another country. Outside there were men trying to kill or maim each other in the name of opposing political philosophies.

There was still no sound from the kitchen. Lohmann pocketed the Mauser and gripped the shot-gun. No precision but the twin barrels sprayed a wide angle of death. It was a smoothbore with automatic repeating action.

He turned into the kitchen, finger on the trigger.

One man, on the floor by the sink, holding his face and moaning. The recipient of the bleach on face and eyes. There was no one else in the room.

Then he heard Joe Kahn shout from upstairs. The shout was

followed by more smashing of glass. Gripping the shot-gun, Lohmann was on the stairs when he heard the shot, followed by a cry of pain.

At the top of the stairs, Lohmann stopped. There were two doors, two bedrooms. The sound had come from the old man's room to his right. He moved to the door which was shut. No sound now, except from the street.

Always the worst moment in his career. Facing a closed door, behind which was at least one man . . . probably more . . . with at least one weapon. The time you needed back-up, at least one other officer. Where, oh where was Sergeant Reiner now?

Then another sound from behind the door. A low moan.

Lohmann took a step back and kicked out at the door.

It flew open with a crash and he stood for a fraction of a second before jumping forward to the side of the door, shot-gun in hand, and froze, finger on the trigger.

He took in the scene in the room at once. Joe Kahn was on the floor in front of him. The moans were coming from Joe. In his shirtsleeves, back against a fading floral wallpaper, he was clutching a blood-soaked arm. He had taken a bullet just above the elbow.

Maurice Kovel was sitting on the edge of a large bed, brass bed-ends, polished and gleaming. Standing over him, a large revolver pressed against the old man's forehead, was the preacher from the chapel in Hammersmith, Raven Marshall. Staring at Lohmann, a cold grin on his face. By the window was another of the men from Hammersmith; and in front of him was the Irish grin of the man called Houlihan.

'We've been waiting for you,' Marshall said. 'I was afraid you might take the two downstairs. But it's our turn now. Even if you fire that shot-gun, I'll still manage to blow the old man's brains out.'

Maurice Kovel was gazing straight ahead, his face expressionless. Ready to die. Perhaps even wanting to die.

'And, of course,' Marshall went on. 'The other two would kill you at once. Not that it matters whether you fire or not. We're going to kill the three of you anyway.'

TWENTY-THREE

Lohmann had faced the muzzles of guns before. Too often. Never could get rid of the sick feeling in the stomach. Or the sensation of tense muscles as if they hardened to withstand the impact of a bullet. He'd been lucky in the past; one bullet in the shoulder and a number of near misses. And guns pointed but not fired. The old adage was there, in his mind; if you point a gun, be prepared to fire it. When endangered, fire at once.

Possibly Raven Marshall's mistake. He was enjoying the situation, a kind of sadistic enjoyment, with his gun at Maurice Kovel's head. Lohmann had seen his type before. Relishing the moment of power. Would make a good Gestapo man. The pain of others, and the power to cause pain, serving as an aphrodisiac.

'Now you'll put the shot-gun on the floor at your feet, Herr Lohmann. Or else the old man'll die at once.'

Lohmann put the shot-gun on the floor.

'Good! See how precious life is, that you do what you're told, to last a minute or two longer. But I want you, Lohmann,' Marshall said. 'The old man may or may not know something, but it's Lohmann that's important.'

He was getting no satisfaction from Maurice Kovel, Lohmann could see. The old man sat, expressionless, no sign of fear. Uncaring as to whether he lived or died.

'Let the old man go,' Lohmann said. 'He knows nothing.'

Saying it was pointless. But saying anything gave him another few seconds. Between life and death seconds were an infinity.

'Not possible,' said Marshall. 'Houlihan, take the old man. Your job to finish him. I'll take Lohmann.'

Then the unexpected happened.

Houlihan said, 'No!'

Marshall's head came around to glare at the Irishman.

'I'm saying it . . . !'

'I'm not bein' paid to kill no old man,' Houlihan said. 'I was hired by himself to kill Lohmann . . .' A glance at Lohmann. 'Told you before, nothing personal. A matter of business.'

He looked back at Marshall. 'So I don't kill any old man.'

Marshall said, 'I give the orders here!'

'Not to me, you don't. I'm not one of your political playboys in your schoolboy death squads. I'm a professional man, so I am.'

It was ridiculous, Lohmann thought. But then, even in Germany, no matter how deadly, how obscene, they were always ridiculous. And now Marshall was distracted. Lohmann's hands were at his sides. He slipped his left hand into his jacket pocket, feeling the butt of the Mauser.

Marshall still staring at Houlihan. 'Do as you're told or you'll fuckin' well join the three of them!'

Lohmann fired the Mauser through the cloth of the dinner jacket. A difficult shot. Risking Kovel's life. Better the risk than the certainty.

The bullet hit Marshall's gun. Knocking it from his hand and across the wall behind him. Lohmann turned at once and shot the man at the window in the chest. The man went backwards, through the already broken glass of the window, and out.

Marshall was gripping his wrist in pain. Although untouched by Lohmann's bullet, the force of it hitting his gun hand wrenched his wrist back.

Houlihan was the only one who had maintained a professional calm. He turned his own revolver towards Lohmann and fired. But he was fractionally too late. Lohmann had thrown himself to the floor where he had dropped the shot-gun. As he went down, he felt the heat of Houlihan's bullet as it ripped through the fabric of his jacket at the shoulder.

Before Houlihan took aim again, on the floor, Lohmann grasped the shot-gun with his right hand and, swivelling round in Houlihan's direction, pressed the trigger of the shot-gun at floor level.

Houlihan howled as the gun sprayed shot into his feet and legs. Letting go his revolver as he fell forward.

Another barrel left, Lohmann turned again to Marshall who started backing away from the muzzle of the shot-gun which was aimed at his chest. Lohmann eased himself up onto his knees.

'Come, Mister Marshall, give me a reason to shoot you. You enjoy inflicting pain. We can see if you enjoy receiving it. At this range the second barrel would take away most of your chest and lungs.'

'Don't shoot . . .'

'Consider. You could be a martyr to the cause. Another Horst Wessel. Of course he wasn't a preacher. He was a pimp. But they might write a song about you.'

'Lohmann!' Behind them, Joe Kahn cried out. Houlihan was crawling, hand outstretched, towards his fallen revolver. Lohmann reached over and, picking up the revolver, threw it to Kahn. Turning back as Marshall leaped over the window sill and disappeared.

Lohmann, on his feet now, ran to the window. Below it, was the roof of what had once been a small washhouse. The way they had broken in, the way now Marshall was getting out. As Lohmann brought up the shot-gun, Marshall disappeared under the side of the washhouse.

'Keep your eye on Houlihan!' Lohmann called back to Kahn and then vaulted the window sill to land on the washhouse roof. As he did so, the shot-gun barrel hit the side of the window and fell from his hand.

Below him, Marshall ran across the back court and disappeared into the lane. Lohmann leaped down onto cracked stone and went after him. Didn't need the shot-gun. Still had the Mauser.

Running now. Along the lane, into an alley, Marshall a hundred yards in front. At a corner of the alley, Lohmann's shoulder hit the side of a brick wall. He bounced off it onto the wall opposite. And kept going, lungs heaving as he drew in gulps of air. Out of training, years since he'd pursued a wanted man. In Berlin. Along the Wilhelmstrasse. 1930. A younger and fitter man then.

But then Marshall was no fitter. At the end of the alley, he slowed down, twisted around and saw Lohmann still after him. He started to run again. Across a road, littered with the refuse of the street fighting which was still going on sporadically nearby.

Lohmann following, legs cramping, but still moving. Along another alley and a high brick wall. Decreasing the distance between himself and his quarry. Seventy yards now, Marshall stumbling, running in a zig-zag movement.

Towards the river. Probably not by choice. Running in a random direction, afraid Lohmann still had the shot-gun.

Certainly he still had the Mauser. As he ran he reached into the pocket and brought out the Mauser.

'Stop or I shoot!' The warning before using the weapon. Old habits dying hard.

One shot at the fleeing man, aimed at the legs. Missed. Throwing up chips of stone from the cobbled alley.

Then Marshall crossed another street into another alley. Leading downwards. Steps down towards the river.

Lohmann reached the head of the steps. An ancient crooked sign on the high stone wall. *Dutch Lane Old Stairs.* Marshall, near the foot of the stairs, disappeared around a corner onto the wharf. Lohmann followed, slowly now, lungs still straining to gain air. Ahead of him, the flowing brown water and sludge of the river. Deep, dark, the tide in. Going down towards this, wondering what he was doing pursuing this man on his own to the edge of the Thames. Would not have happened in Berlin. There, he would have had junior detectives and uniformed men chasing the fugitive. While he made a leisurely progress towards the scene, and waited for the man to be apprehended.

Yet Raven Marshall was evidence of the existence of the death squad; evidence that the squad had murdered Beth Coverley; and he almost certainly knew the man behind the transfer of money from London to the coffers of the National Socialist Party of Germany.

Lohmann reached the foot of the steps, Mauser in hand, in front of him, an old wharf, a structure of aging wood, and rotting timber.

He stepped onto the wharf. And knew he was too quick, too careless.

The iron bar came down on his wrist. Marshall had been waiting, against the stone wall at the corner of the wharf. A streak of pain shot up Lohmann's arm and the Mauser flew out of his hand across the timbers to the edge of the wharf.

The iron bar rose again ready to fall, this time on his neck. But, despite the pain, Lohmann, head down, charged into the midriff of the man with the bar. Marshall collapsed forward, folding up with a loud gasp as air was expelled from his body. Yet he folded on top of Lohmann and the two men fell onto the wooden timbers, each struggling to gain a grip on the other. Then Marshall was on top and his hands went out to Lohmann's neck.

As he struggled to free the hands at his throat Lohmann realised that Marshall was determined to kill him and, without a weapon, meant to do it with his bare hands. Also, amazed that he could think clearly while struggling for his life, knowing he might well have to kill Marshall to survive. Everything seemed then to be moving in a kind of slow motion. Like an under-cranked film. Choking and somehow managing to ease the man's hands away. Knowing too how difficult it was to kill a man without a weapon. Life was too precious to limit resistance.

He brought his knee up sharply against his assailant's groin. Marshall gasped and his grip became weaker. They rolled over, legs and arms flailing. Marshall grasped at Lohmann's hair, pulling his head back and attempting to butt him on the throat with his head. Lohmann twisted downwards and took the head-butt on his forehead. Using the other's tactics and lashing out with his own head, striking Marshall hard on the bridge of the nose, hearing a crunching sound of bone breaking. And over and over they rolled.

Now hands grabbing and clawing. Then fists clenched, striking, scratching. The dampness of warm blood on Lohmann's face. At first thinking it was his own; then knowing it was Marshall's blood streaming from his broken nose.

Images now. The iron bar a few feet from them. Marshall's arm reaching out to grasp it. The bar rising in the air and descending. The sky moving as Lohmann thrust his body to one side. The bar striking the timbers, gouging a white scar on the sodden wood. Splinters of wood on his face. Marshall's hand letting go of the iron bar. The side of Lohmann's hand smashing into the area of Marshall's kidneys. The man's face contorted with pain and exertion.

Then they were apart and on their feet, God knows how. Marshall kicking out at Lohmann's groin, missing and striking him on the edge of the thigh. Coming towards him now, hands outstretched, thumbs going for his eyes. Lohmann twisted away. And they came together, struggling again. Marshall's nails and thumbs scraped down Lohmann's cheek, tearing away flesh.

They were teetering now on the edge of the wharf, Marshall pressing forward, eyes glaring. On his face the determination to kill. Lohmann felt himself tiring. He kicked out, the edge of his shoe smashing into Marshall's kneecap. Marshall fell away to one side and went backwards and down.

Over the edge of the wharf.

Head striking a protruding metal stanchion.

And into the river. Disappearing under the water.

Lohmann swayed at the edge of the wharf, staring down at the river. Where Marshall had disappeared.

The voice came from behind him.

'Looks to me as if you just committed murder, Mister Lohmann.'

Lohmann turned, body aching, head swimming. To face Sergeant Brundage. Standing with a gun in hand. Pointing the weapon at Lohmann.

He thought, British police don't carry guns. The gun looked familiar.

Brundage saw him staring at the weapon. 'Oh, it's your gun, Lohmann. A Mauser, is it? Picked it up back there where you dropped it.'

He looked down at the Mauser and went on. 'Safety-catch off. Already been used. A simple story. I arrive to see you pushing Mister Marshall into the river. I attempt to apprehend you. You then turn the gun on me. But being a brave and efficient officer, I struggle with you. And the gun goes off. I think . . . under the chin. That way through to the brain. That should look authentic.'

269

'Kahn and Maurice Kovel will describe what happened in Kovel's house,' Lohmann said, voice hoarse, swaying, feeling all strength gone from his body. 'Marshall . . . he . . . he tried to kill Maurice Kovel. And myself . . .'

'I wouldn't know anything about that. So I may make a mistake. But I saw you throw a man into the river . . .'

'As you helped Marshall and his people throw Beth Coverley in?'

'Constable Ordish helped with that one. But I haven't time to explain.' He took two steps forward, and one step to the side, bringing the Mauser up towards Lohmann who closed his eyes. He was exhausted. Brundage's appearance was too much.

The shot echoed against the stone wall behind the wharf. Lohmann was struck in the chest and stumbled backwards, opening his eyes, trying to focus.

Detective Sergeant Brundage had fallen sideways, mouth open, an expression of astonishment on his face. The bullet had struck him in the small of the back, and exited through his chest, opening up a hole the size of a fist.

The figure coming towards Lohmann was indistinct at first, as if a film of mist had come over his eyes. Then the mist cleared and he saw Superintendent Thornhill approaching. Sergeant Charlie Newton at his side. Newton was holding a regulation police Webley in his hand.

'I think Sergeant Newton just saved your life again, Mister Lohman,' said Thornhill.

'*Ja! Ich* . . . I think he did . . .'

Newton caught Lohmann as he swayed forward.

'Easy now, sir.'

'Yes . . . yes. Thank you . . .'

Thornhill was staring at him. And the remnants of his dinner suit. A large hole in one pocket, edges scorched. A tear at the shoulder and other places and a number of buttons gone. Blood on the white shirt, and mud and dirt from the wharf all over.

'I'm afraid Moss Bros. aren't going to be very pleased with you,' he said wryly.

'Why . . . why are you here . . ?' Lohmann gasped.

'Oh, we came to Kovel's house just after you left. Took us time to track you down here. But eventually we just followed

Brundage. Not a nice man. I don't like bent coppers. But you want to know why we came in the first place. Miss Scott-ffoliot told us you were here. She was worried about you. Of course we didn't tell her why we wanted you.'

'Why . . . why did . . . did you want me?'

'Oh, that! We have a deportation order to serve on you.'

TWENTY-FOUR

They took him to Bow Street Police Station. He was left for some time. With a mug of tea and a ham sandwich. And a uniformed police constable in attendance. It was late evening when Thornhill came in.

'Bow Street?' Lohmann said. 'I am not important enough for Scotland Yard?' He was seated on a hard seat in a drab interview room.

Thornhill smiled sourly. 'We don't want attention drawn to this case. Indeed, as far as everyone is concerned, this is no case. You are here because of a deportation order against you.'

'So nothing happened in Cable Street?'

'Oh, yes, the newspapers are already calling it the "Battle of Cable Street". But nothing happened in Maurice Kovel's house. As far as the world is concerned.'

'I killed probably three people,' Lohmann insisted. 'You are not charging me with that? I will of course claim self-defence.'

'Then you'd have no worries. But what three people? Raven Marshall fell into the Thames. His body has just been found. Verdict, death by drowning. Bruising caused by body bashing against stanchions under the pier.'

'You can get away with that?'

'Special Branch can get away with . . . murder. Not that it does. Very often.'

'The men in Kovel's house?'

'Another man was certainly found dead in the house in

271

Cable Street with a bullet in his throat. Severed the carotid artery. And destroyed the third cranial vertebra. If there is a verdict, we can blame the man with chest wounds we found in Kovel's garden. Below a broken window. He fell out of the window. Probably trying to escape. And his shot-gun went off accidentally.'

'You do it well, Thornhill.'

'Merely illustrating what is possible. If we so decide.'

'And my friend, Joe Kahn . . . ?'

' . . . is in Charing Cross Hospital. He'll recover. From a minor accident. Also, nobody heard any gunshots. Ergo, there were none. Oh, Maurice Kovel is fine. He's at home with two detectives looking after him.'

'A little late surely?' Lohmann squirmed in the hard chair. His body ached all over. The fight with Marshall was beginning to have its effect.

'Perhaps, if you'd told us more . . .'

'Perhaps you might have been another Sergeant Brundage. How do you explain away his death?'

Thornhill looked mildly embarrassed. 'Ah, yes, Brundage. Fortunately he has no family to ask awkward questions. Except for a cousin in Hounslow who didn't like him. I'm afraid he'll have to have had a heart attack. So all this would dispose of . . . what did you call them . . . ?'

'A death squad.'

'Wouldn't want to admit we had one of those in London. Or that a police sergeant was involved with them. Why, it never happened, Lohmann. You understand?'

Lohmann thought for a moment. 'What about the Irishman?'

'What Irishman?'

'Houlihan. He was one of them. I . . . I think I shot him in the legs in Kovel's bedroom.'

Thornhill frowned. 'There was no one else in the house when we arrived.'

'That is very nice,' Lohmann said. 'He was especially employed to kill me. And he is still free.'

'Houlihan. Houlihan.' Thornhill said meditatively. 'Yes, I think he was in our IRA files at one time. You say he was there?'

'And he would be limping. I fired the shot-gun at his legs.'

'There'll be a lot of people limping in Cable Street today. Still I'll put out a call for him to be brought in.'

'If you can find him.'

'As you say.' Thornhill was relaxed. At ease. No Irishman at loose, employed to kill him. 'Of course it's academic. Remember, we have a deportation order against you.'

'That is genuine?'

'It would seem so. Appeared on my desk at Scotland Yard. After the events of today, possibly justified. You have, after all, created all this mayhem we have to conceal. I gather Miss Scott-ffoliot has engaged a solicitor on your behalf. She's here, by the way. Brought you some clean clothes. You'd like to see her?'

'I would like to see her.'

Thornhill nodded. 'Then you shall.'

He went out and a few minutes later Rue was ushered in. She was carrying a suitcase.

'God, what a mess!' she said, gaping at him.

'There was some activity. But I am quite well.'

She started to laugh. 'You look as if you've been in an earthquake.'

'A very small earthquake. How did you know I was here?'

'That man, Thornhill, telephoned me. Told me you might need some clean clothes. I've got them in the case. And . . . and he thought . . . he thought it was all over.'

'He is wrong. It is not all over. Part of it is over. The man behind it is still to be found. About the deportation order, what is happening?'

'I got hold of our family solicitor. Sammy Wallace. Sir Samuel Baird Wallace . . .'

Lohmann smiled. It was painful to smile. He couldn't keep it up for any length of time. Marshall had loosened one of his teeth and bruised his jaw in the fight on the wharf. He also had a sore throat.

'I'm impressed,' he said.

'He's at the Home Office just now. I'm also going to try to get the Prime Minister on the telephone. He's in . . .'

'. . . Norfolk. I know.'

'Sammy says you can't be deported right away. He can appeal against the deportation order . . . didn't they give you a chance to clean up?'

'Perhaps they thought, in this condition I was an item of evidence.'

Rue turned to the uniformed constable. 'I wish to see Superintendent Thornhill. At once!'

She saw Thornhill. And a few minutes later Lohmann was taken to a washroom. Soap, shaving soap and a razor were provided. Afterwards he changed into the clothes Rue had brought for him.

When he returned she was seated in the interview room, chain smoking. He sat, facing her.

'You look much better now,' she said. 'Still a little battered, but better. Oh, I forgot to tell you. Mister Rennie phoned this morning.'

'He and his wife are safe?'

'Both fine. You want a cigarette?'

'Thank you, no. I have a sore throat. They got away from Mullion all right?'

'They're still there . . .'

Lohmann looked startled. 'They are still there!'

'Rennie told me, before the cottage was blown up, they got away. As you advised. Told everybody in the village they were going up north. But instead of doing so, Rennie thought it would be clever if they appeared to leave and went to a place about half a mile along the cliffs. Big house called Wintershill. Owned by his wife's sister. Right on the cliffs. No one except the sister-in-law knows they're there, he assured me of that.' Rue shrugged. 'I think he thought he was being rather clever. And he wants to know when it will be safe to come back to London.'

Lohmann seemed mollified. 'As long as no one knows where he is. But safe to come back to London . . . no, not yet . . . he should stay where he is . . .'

'He was trying to phone us last night. When we were at dinner. When he couldn't get through to us he phoned Scotland Yard . . .'

Lohmann's head came up, face ashen, bruises livid.

'What did you say?'

274

'He phoned Scotland Yard . . . he wants to come back as soon as it's safe and talk about the documents he saw at the Treasury.' Rue seemed surprised at the expression on his face. 'What's wrong with that? The man wants to clear himself.'

'Who did he speak to?' A terrible urgency in the question. 'Was it Thornhill?'

'He didn't say. Someone high up at the Yard. He said, they were very reasonable. Told him to stay where he was just now.'

Lohmann was on his feet now. Tense.

'Well, they only told him to stay!' Rue was puzzled. 'That's what you said he should do . . . ?'

'I have to leave here! At once. There might just be time . . .'

'Thornhill won't let you go. Not with the deportation order. Sammy Wallace says it can be appealed. And while the appeal's being heard, they may let you out on bail. But you won't be in court until tomorrow . . .'

'Tomorrow will be too late. Did you telephone the Prime Minister?'

She shook her head. 'I told you, I was going to. But there's no need, now I've got hold of Sammy. He said, in his judgement, they will not deport you to Germany if we can prove your life is in danger if you go back. But, Lohmann, it has to go through the courts . . .'

'I have to speak to Mister Baldwin. You have the number of the place where he is staying in Norfolk?'

'Yes, but . . .'

'Find Thornhill. Bring him here.'

There was no arguing with him. Indeed, there was now a sudden authority not only in his voice, but in his whole demeanour. As she imagined he had been back in Berlin. She left him pacing the interview room and went to look for Thornhill. She found him about to leave the building. He accompanied her back to the interview room with some reluctance.

'It is necessary that I telephone the Prime Minister at once . . .' Lohmann insisted.

Thornhill smiled drily. 'I hold a senior rank in the Special Branch, Lohmann, but that doesn't entitle me to ring up Stanley Baldwin whenever I feel so inclined . . .'

'She . . . Miss Scott-ffoliot will telephone him. She has a personal acquaintance . . . it is most urgent!'

'You better come to one of the offices,' Thornhill sighed.

They found a vacant office and Rue made the call. It took some ten minutes until she got through and had the Prime Minister at the other end of the line. She handed the telephone to Lohmann.

'Sir, this is Ernst Lohmann. We met the other day . . .'

'Herr Lohmann,' said the Prime Minister ponderously. 'For the second time, you are presuming on a personal relationship between myself and Miss Scott-ffoliot's family. Over a matter of some delicacy. If, by a certain knowledge which you have obtained, and which I have never acknowledged to be either true or accurate, you have some kind of motive . . . possibly blackmail . . . I can assure you, I will not tolerate further such . . .'

'Mister Baldwin, only last night we dined with the King . . .'

There was a pause. Of considerable duration. Then Baldwin spoke again, in a more subdued tone.

'You discussed with His Majesty the matter you discussed with me?'

'Yes. It was . . . of interest.'

'Very well. We had better talk. You will come to Norfolk.'

'I would wish to do that. But I am detained by a Superintendent Thornhill under a deportation order.'

'Put the superintendent on the telephone.'

Lohmann did so. And waited while Thornhill listened, speaking only to interject the occasional, 'Yes, sir' into a one-sided conversation. Finally he replaced the receiver and turned to Lohmann.

'You seem to have some influence with the PM, Lohmann. I have to provide a car and an escort. Sergeant Newton can go with you . . .'

'And Miss Scott-ffoliot,' siad Rue.

'Miss Scott-ffoliot will go to her apartment and bring me an overnight bag,' Lohmann said.

'You can collect that en route. If you'll excuse me,' Thornhill said, not without a touch of irony. 'I'll have to lay everything on for our distinguished visiting German.'

He left them alone. 'You have a revolver?' Lohmann asked Rue.

'Not something every woman in London keeps in her home.'

'I need a weapon . . .'

'To see Baldwin?'

'No. Before that. For Cornwall. Then Norfolk.'

She looked surprised. 'You're going to Mullion?'

'To finish it. Hopefully. The weapon will be necessary.'

'There is an army major in the apartment next to mine at Dolphin Square . . . he would have something like that.'

'Beg, borrow or steal . . . but get it and put it in the overnight bag.'

'If I do, I'm coming with you.'

'What else? You may be useful.'

Charlie Newton sat behind the wheel of the unmarked police car, Lohmann at his side. They were waiting at the entrance to the apartment building in Dolphin Square. They had been waiting for twenty minutes. Outside it was dark and raining.

'How long does it take Miss What's-her-name to pack an overnight bag?' Sergeant Newton said impatiently.

'Perhaps she is not used to doing such things herself. And it is possibly her maid-servant's evening off,' Lohmann suggested.

'Servants. eh? One of the undeserving rich, that one.'

'Sergeant, you sound like a communist.'

Charlie Newton shook his head violently. 'Naw, naw, none of that. I'm not a subversive type. Just think things in life should be organised better. Fairer, like.'

'Dangerous talk for a Special Branch sergeant, surely?'

'It's a free country, so they say. Of course some of us know better.'

Rue came out of the building carrying a small suitcase and climbed in the back of the car.

'Sorry I was so long,' she said. 'Had to call on my next-door neighbour. Army type.'

With a sidelong glance at Lohmann. 'Asked him to keep an eye on my apartment while I was away.'

'Very wise, miss,' said Newton, starting up the engine of the car. 'Lot of villains around these days. Housebreaking's becoming a national pastime.'

He depressed the handbrake and steered the car away from the kerb.

'Norfolk, is it? Very flat, Norfolk.'

Rue smiled in the darkness as she quietly opened the overnight case and took a package from its interior. 'Didn't you give that line to a playwright friend of mine, sergeant? A Mister Noël Coward.'

'Don't know the gentleman, miss. But he probably knows Norfolk just as well as I do.'

Rue reached over and handed the package to Lohmann. The movement caught Newton's eye.

'What's that, miss?' he said.

'Something for the journey, sergeant.' Lohmann replied, feeling the shape of a service revolver through several layers of brown paper wrapping. He proceeded to unwrap it on his lap. He could feel the cold, slightly greased shape of the weapon in his hand. Gripping it, he turned the barrel towards Newton.

'We are not going to Norfolk at once, Sergeant Newton. We have to go to Cornwall first.'

Newton took his eyes momentarily from the road and stared down at the revolver. His eyes widened. The car swerved and he turned back to correct the steering.

'I'm not going to argue with a loaded revolver, Mister Lohmann, but don't you think you're being a little unwise?'

'Cornwall, sergeant. A place called Mullion. A house called . . .?' Lohmann looked at Rue.

'Wintershill. Owned by Rebecca Trevallion.'

'I shall be in a lot of trouble with Superintendent Thornhill,' Charlie Newton said, his face like a mournful bulldog.

'I will take the responsibility,' Lohmann replied.

'You don't pay my pension, Mister Lohmann.'

They drove west.

Eight hours to Mullion. Along narrow roads, through sleeping towns. Rue, dozing, half asleep in the back of the car; Lohmann trying to stop himself from falling asleep in the front; and Charlie Newton driving steadily, eyes on the twin beams from

278

the headlights. The windscreen wipers moving nonstop, the rain getting heavier and heavier as they moved nearer to the West Country.

'You should sleep, Mister Lohmann,' said Newton. 'I don't think you slept much last night. You're not having any tonight. And it was quite a day yesterday.'

'Cannot afford to sleep. I have to get to Cornwall. Before Edward Rennie is killed.'

'You think this character is still in danger? I thought we'd destroyed their little death squad yesterday.'

'But not the man behind it. Rennie is still his biggest danger. Rennie was in the Treasury. He, above all, can prove what this man fears.'

Newton ran his hands over dry lips. 'All double-Dutch to me. But I have to take your word for it.' He changed the subject. 'I stopped smoking a couple of months ago, do you know that? Well, actually I stopped buying cigarettes. I still smoke other people's now and then. When I'm offered. You don't happen to have a cigarette on you?'

Rue, who had momentarily come awake, produced a silver cigarette-case and offered it to Newton who took two cigarettes.'

'Save me waking you for one later, miss,' Newton explained, placing the second cigarette behind his ear. 'Now, Mister Lohmann, you take a sleep. I'll take you to Mullion. As long as you remember to tell Thornhill you had a gun on me all the way. See, I'm taking you on trust. Which is very nice of me.'

'You're good, Sergeant Newton. As good as my old sergeant in Berlin. A man called Reiner.'

Lohmann closed his eyes. He found it almost impossible to keep them open.

Lohmann came awake as they reached Mullion. He was stiff, his body aching and cramped as he peered out of the car window up to a heavy, clouded sky streaked with the early light of dawn.

'We're here, sir,' said Newton, second cigarette between his lips, seemingly unruffled after the eight-hour drive. 'Where to now?'

279

In the back, Rue was awake, also smoking. She was no longer using a cigarette holder.

'I think Wintershill House is up on that bluff overlooking the sea. On the way to the Marconi monument,' she said.

Charlie Newton drove the car around the edge of the village towards the bluff. A wooden sign, 'Wintershill', hand-painted, sagged at the beginning of a narrow track. Newton swung the car onto the track. The car bucked and jumped over potholes. To the south, below them, was the sea, blackness crested by white horses, the dawn mirrored roughly on a surface of angry waves.

They came to the house through a clump of trees. It was a large, impressive, eighteenth century building, now showing every evidence of being run down. On one wing the windows were shuttered. The gardens in front of the house were unkempt, overrun with weeds and bracken. On a gravelled area before the entrance a Mercedes-Benz was parked.

Seeing the Mercedes, Lohmann was seized by a kind of panic. Was he too late? Had his antagonist already arrived? He leapt from the car and, running towards the large oak front-door, grabbed a bell-pull at the side of the door and pulled. He could hear the bell ringing faintly somewhere in the depths of the house. He was vaguely aware too, of Newton and Rue coming from the car behind him.

He waited, finding himself trembling not only from the chill of the morning but from an inner coldness, an icy fear emanating from the very marrow of his being.

A gale of sleet blew in from the sea. The door opened and he was facing a strange woman. Behind the woman was Elizabeth Rennie, a slightly younger version of the woman at the door.

'It's all right, Rebecca,' Elizabeth Rennie said. 'This is Mister Lohmann who came to warn us . . .'

'I have to . . . to see your husband . . .' Lohmann gasped.

'Gone for his walk,' she said. 'Only time he goes out. Before people are up. In case anyone sees him. Said he thought you'd approve, this early . . .'

'Where has he . . . ?' The panic rising in his voice.

She cut in, pointing before he could finish the sentence. 'Over that way. The cliff path. Up by the Marconi monument.

280

But it's all right. The man from Scotland Yard just arrived five minutes ago. He's gone after Edward to make sure he's all right.'

Then she saw the expression on Lohmann's face.

'I told the man where he'd gone,' she went on, suddenly the words crowding on top of each other. 'That was all right, wasn't it? He said he knew you . . . said you'd sent him . . . I didn't mean to do anything wrong . . .'

Lohmann turned, staring towards the bluff high above the sea. More light in the sky now. He thought he could imagine a figure nearing the monument . . . and further down the path, another figure. Or was it a distortion of the light?

'Rue,' he said over his shoulder. 'Wait with Mrs Rennie. He could come back for her. Newton, go with me . . .'

And he ran over the gravel, pain racking the muscles of his legs, towards the cliff path. Newton, without questioning, followed.

TWENTY-FIVE

The path, rutted and uneven, had been created over years by the feet of thousands of cliff-walkers. At first it led sharply upwards, the ruts becoming like uneven, pitted steps. It was never meant for running on, but for slow, patient plodding. Yet Lohmann, despite weariness and pain, ran, gulping air as he did so, knowing that, if he delayed, Rennie would be a dead man.

Charlie Newton stumbled on behind him. A policeman, accustomed to city streets, he found the going hard. And the breeze from the sea was becoming stronger, wilder, an icicle blast of sleet and rain, numbing their faces, freezing their hands. Two hundred feet below, the sea, stirred up by the wind, crashed against the ragged, serrated teeth of the rocks in an unreasoning fury.

Ahead, Lohmann could now clearly make out two figures, the furthest nearing the base of the small plinth that commemorated the place from where Guglielmo Marconi, in Newfoundland, received his first transatlantic radio signals. Behind this figure, climbing up steadily towards it was the second man, Lohmann's quarry.

The ex-detective thought, 'please God let me reach them in time.' Strange how at some moments, one muttered obeisance to a deity whose existence, at other times, one doubted. Despite his Lutheran upbringing, Lohmann had seen too much horror in his life to be certain of any belief in an omniscient being.

He was climbing higher, closer to the two figures. A stabbing spasm in his side had added itself to the aching bruises on his body. Sharp pains ran up his legs and his lungs strained for air.

Then suddenly, behind him, he heard Charlie Newton fall, with a faint cry, almost lost in the gale. Lohmann stopped, and turned, using the pause to gain a second wind. Newton was lying on the ground, face contorted, reaching towards his right foot.

'Never mind me . . . keep going . . .' Newton said. '. . . I think I've broken my blasted ankle . . .'

Lohmann took a step towards the sergeant. 'You will be all right?' He shouted into the wind.

Newton shouted back. 'No! I'm not all right. I may even die of exposure. For God's sake, go on! Before that bastard gets to Rennie.'

Lohmann turned and pressed on. Upwards towards the memorial. And beyond the memorial, the sheer cliff that fell down to the rocks and the maelstrom. He ran easier now, as if he had gained his second wind. Behind him, Charlie Newton produced a handkerchief from his pocket, a large bandana-type square of cotton and, doubling up, face contorted with pain, tried to secure the material around his ankle.

It was daylight now and the first figure, that of Edward Rennie, had reached the memorial plinth and was standing on the flat turf at the peak of the bluff, staring out to sea. The second man was still climbing steadily. Behind him, Lohmann was catching up, unseen as yet by the pursued.

Rennie turned from his view of the sea, face soaked with rain, the taste of salt on his lips. He moved into what small shelter he could obtain from the memorial, leaning wearily against the damp stone. Trying to relax. Ever since he and his wife had left the cottage and later heard it had been blown up, this was the only time of day he had permitted himself to leave Wintershill House. To breathe fresh sea air, to escape the fear that he had lived with for so long. The destruction of the cottage had proved that fear was justified. But now, he could believe in an end to it. When he had tried unsuccessfully to telephone Lohmann, he had determined it would be better to contact Scotland Yard; to tell his story, find a way to communicate with the higher echelons of government. After all, what had he done? Spoken unwisely to Beth Coverley who was now dead. Certainly a breach of the Official Secrets Act. He would probably have to resign. But the matter was so delicate, he doubted they would risk prosecuting him. It might even be that there were those in power who were not fully aware of what had happened . . . there was a new government now . . . he could be performing a necessary act . . .

The man appeared over the rise. The tall, slim figure was wrapped in a heavy raincoat. Greying temples under a soaked golfing cap pulled down over the face. Long, delicate hands in leather gloves. The right hand gripping a walking stick.

'Mister Rennie?'

Rennie tensed, alert, the adrenalin of fear flooding into his blood. He straightened up, leaning away from the memorial.

'I'm Rennie.'

The newcomer must have been at once aware of his fear. 'It's all right, Mister Rennie. We spoke on the telephone last night. I'm from New Scotland Yard.'

Relief was visible on Rennie's face. He relaxed, leaning again on the stone plinth. 'I can't tell you how glad I am you're here.'

'The feeling is mutual. We have unfinished business.'

'Yes, of course. We can go right back to the house. My wife and I'll be happy to come back to London with you. As I said on the telephone, I want very much to get this business off my mind. I want to make a statement . . .'

'All in good time, Rennie.' The man came closer.

'Of course. Sorry you had to come all this way up. You could have waited at the house.'

'I was anxious to meet you.'

'Yes. Well. We should go . . .'

The man turned and stared out to sea. 'Quite a view.'

'If you like the sea . . .'

'And the cliffs are quite impressive.'

Rennie straightened up once more. 'Yes, they are. I was born quite near here. It's part of my childhood, you might say.'

'I might, if I'd known. I should have known.'

'I tried to get hold of Mister Lohmann first but I couldn't contact him . . . that's when I decided to telephone Scotland yard. By . . . by the way, I don't even know your name. Or your rank.'

The man turned from the sea and faced him. But the reply, when it came, did not come from him but from behind them both.

'Emerson. Charles Emerson,' Lohmann said. 'Assistant Commisioner for Crime, New Scotland Yard. Soon I believe to be offered a senior post with Military Intelligence. MI5 or MI6, Charles?'

Lohmann, at the top of the path, was facing them both. But his eyes were on Emerson.

'You don't seem surprised, Lohmann,' said the Scotland Yard man.

'Oh, I am not surprised. I have known for some time.'

Emerson, back to the sea, swayed in the wind. 'Indeed. Since when?'

'The taxi-driver, Gorman. Through him I was taken to Raven Marshall's chapel in Hammersmith.'

'So?'

'You found the owner of the cab number for me. The one Mrs Rennie used when she left the Angleton Hotel. *GA 4321* . . . Gorman led me to Marshall's chapel. Later, when I found him again . . . after I escaped from Marshall . . . Gorman told me that he was . . . what is your British expression? . . . *got at* . . . by William Joyce, I think. He was paid a hundred pounds to take me to Hammersmith. How did Joyce know I was looking for Gorman? You were the only person that knew. So you had to have passed Gorman's name to Joyce.'

'Hardly evidence. The people who killed Richards could have noted the cab number . . .'

'A slim possibility. Still I might have allowed you the benefit of the doubt. But again you were the only person I told that I had seen Mister Rennie here in Mullion. Of course I didn't tell you I'd warned him to leave. But after I did tell you, his cottage was blown up. That confirmed all I had suspected.'

Rennie, back against the monument, was staring from one to the other.

'What the hell is going on?'

Lohmann turned to him. 'One mistake, Mister Rennie. You should not have telephoned Scotland Yard. You told the one man who was looking for you where you were.'

'Isn't it all rather academic now?' said Emerson. 'At this point I have to behave like the villain in a lurid melodrama and draw a revolver from my coat.'

He did so. A Webley automatic. He held the weapon flat in his hand, contemplating it with a rueful expression.

'I should have guessed earlier who was behind the entire affair,' Lohmann said, his voice shrill against the wind. 'The courier. The middle-ranking civil servant who came to Germany to study police methods. All you wanted to do when you were with me was see the night-life of Berlin. The rest of the time, you were supposed to be seeing civil servants. And bankers, Charles? Like Schacht.'

Emerson grinned crookedly. 'And Hitler. I saw him, you know. After all, he couldn't ignore the man who was carrying authorisations for the financing of his party. And of course, I don't like the . . . *middle ranking* . . . civil service bit. A better description would be someone on his way up . . . ?'

'And if the story came out, you would be on your way down. That was why you had to have Beth Coverley killed. Why you have to kill Rennie and myself.'

'Stupid, isn't it? Self-preservation.' Emerson looked sharply at Lohmann. 'More than that of course. I believe. In the philosophy. Fascism. Planned control. The only way. The iron fist. It wasn't just for personal advantage, you must understand

285

that. Hitler . . . Hitler was visionary. A new order. If . . . if only enough of them would listen to Mosley . . .'

A gust of wind took the hat from his head, spiralling it up into the air and away over the cliff. The smooth dark hair was ruffled, blown over his forehead.

Lohmann stared at the revolver still flat on Emerson's hand.

'Why did you bother getting me . . . a refugee from your . . . your new order . . . into this country? Why encourage me to investigate Beth Coverley's death?'

Emerson shrugged. 'Getting you into this country . . . why not? You were misguided but I liked you when I met you in Berlin . . .'

'And you could always claim you had helped a refugee from Nazi Germany.'

'Oh, yes, that too.' The smile returned. 'An asset on the other side if I needed it. And of course, what was I to say when you asked my advice about taking on the investigation of the Coverley woman's death? I could always keep an eye on you. So I thought. I was . . . mistaken. Otherwise, would we be here today?'

Rennie, wiping the rain from his face, said, with a kind of desperation, 'So what happens now?'

'Mister Emerson has the gun in his hand. It would seem to be his move,' Lohmann replied. 'Could you use that gun, Charles? You have no death squad now. You have to do the killing yourself. Not pleasant, having to kill someone. Ugly and messy. So much blood and fluid discharges. *Übelkeit*. Nausea. I know. I have killed.'

'If it has to be done . . . why not?' Emerson squared his shoulders. As if readying himself to make a decision.

'And not just us,' Lohmann went on. 'There are three women back at the house. Mrs Rennie, her sister and Rue Scott-ffoliot. And on the path a Special Branch officer with a broken ankle. Six people, you'd have to kill. A small massacre . . .'

'For God's sake . . . !' Rennie exclaimed.

There was a pause. Broken only by the ever-present wind, rising and falling. Emerson stared down at the Webley. His face was pale, tense.

286

He broke the silence. 'Of course you're right. Can't see myself perpetrating a massacre. But . . . but if I had time . . . to get across the Channel.'

He looked up at Lohmann. 'Would you allow me time?'

'Drop the gun!' The shout came from behind Lohmann. He turned to see Charlie Newton who had crawled up onto the bluff, and was kneeling on the grass, some thirty yards from them, police revolver pointing at Emerson.

The Assistant Commissioner looked up, startled, and grasped the butt of the Webley.

'Don't shoot!' Lohmann shouted to Newton just as the wind rose with a loud howl.

Charlie Newton never heard him. He fired, not to hit but to frighten. The bullet thudded into the turf at Emerson's feet. Emerson jumped back, dropping the Webley, and his feet then slipped. He fell, sliding backwards on sodden grass and mud towards the edge of the cliff. His hands opened, grabbing at grass and rock and barely finding purchase as his body slithered over the bluff.

Lohmann ran forward, dropping to his knees at the cliff-edge. Emerson was hanging by his fingertips, body suspended over the void. Some two hundred feet below were the jagged teeth of rocks surrounding a small strip of sand.

Emerson's face, racked with shock and terror, stared up at Lohmann who reached forward with his right hand. 'Can you grip my hand?'

'Can't . . . let . . . go!'

Lohmann gripped the sleeve of the man's coat just as the fingers of Emerson's left hand slipped from the rock. His body was now suspended by his right hand and Lohmann's grip on his coat.

'No . . . use . . . no point . . . any more . . .' Emerson gasped.

His right hand came free from the rock, and he was hanging only by Lohmann's grip on his coat. His arm was starting to slip through the sleeve.

'Better . . . this . . . way!'

The arm slipped through the sleeve and he was supported for a moment by the coat around his body and his one-handed grip. Then the sleeve started to tear away at the seam.

Lohmann stretched forward, left arm flailing the air, trying to grip another part of coat or man.

The sleeve tore away.

Emerson fell. Without a sound.

His body struck an outcrop of rock, bounced from it and onto yet another rock and then down to the jagged teeth of stone by the strip of sand. And then Emerson was lying still on his back, face a white dot staring up at grey clouds.

Lohmann rose to his feet and backed away from the edge of the cliff. Shivering. Knees weak. Ignoring the slanting rain, the driving gale. Taking a deep breath as if fresh air in his lungs would wash away the image behind his eyes of the body at the foot of the cliff. He turned to Rennie.

'Take Sergeant Newton and help him back to the house.'

'And where do you think you're going?' said Newton, on his knees in the grass.

'Down there. He could be still alive.'

'After that fall. No chance. Still, I suppose you're right.'

'There's a track down to the sea over that way,' Rennie informed him, pointing to the left of the memorial. 'But you have to be careful. If you slip on the wet rock . . .'

'I will not slip on the rock,' Lohmann said quietly and moved off in the direction of the path.

It took half an hour to reach the strip of sand and the rocks on which Emerson's body lay. A twisted shape, a broken doll in a crumpled business suit and torn raincoat, one arm under the torso, one leg terribly broken and attached to the upper leg by only a strip of flesh. Dead and cold. Yet above the tidal mark, the body could be recovered later. Lohmann determined. Not that it mattered. It was over. The affair, the case, the killings. Lohmann stood staring down at the dead man, no longer hearing the wind or the sea crashing onto the rock. Unaware of the salt spray on his face. Under his clothes, his skin was damp with perspiration. The search for Beth Coverley's killers passing through his mind. Some moments magnified, others distorted. Archie Dafoe, dead on the floor of his room, small legs stretched out and out until they were no longer small. The man with the bullet in his throat in Cable Street, name unknown. Member of a death squad. Organised murder.

Schellenberg with his men on the road from Churchill's house. Incidents becoming artefacts considered without emotion. No feeling left but a grey weariness.

'I can see I'm a wee bit late.' The voice broke in on Lohmann. An intolerable intrusion on his thoughts. Irritated, he turned.

Houlihan, standing on the sand, was hunched against the spray, awkward, leaning on a walking stick, feet splayed out, swollen to larger than normal. Both legs bound in bandages. The instinct for self-preservation came to Lohmann and he reached in his pocket for the Mauser. To come all the way, finish it, and then be endangered by the small-part player, Houlihan; it was not right, not fair.

His emotion must have shown in his eyes. Houlihan leaned heavily on his stick.

'Aw, it's nothing to be worrying about, Mister Lohmann. See, that fellow there, he's the one paid me to kill you.' He pointed to Emerson's body. 'Half payment on contracting me, other half when the job was done. But he'll not be able to pay me the second half. So there's no point, is there? Now, if I'd been earlier in getting here, it might have been you lying on the rock there, life punched out of you. But, since he can't pay, you're in no danger from me now. Only fair to tell you. Wouldn't want you to go through life looking over your shoulder for old Houlihan here.'

'I should be relieved,' Lohmann said.

'Indeed you should. And I wouldn't shed any tears for Mister Emerson there. He wasn't a nice man. They never are, the ones that want folk killed. Mean and connivin', I'd call them. Now, with me it's just business. But, with them, it's greed or fear or hate. Now, all that's dead with him. I thought, since I'd come this far, I'd at least tell you that.'

Houlihan looked down at his legs. 'No hard feelings about the old legs. You were only defending yourself, and any man's entitled to do that. But I'll ask you as a favour to be giving me your assurance you'll not come after me. You've slowed me up a bit and I wouldn't want to have to try and run. So, if it's all right with you, I'll be off, peaceful like.'

Lohmann nodded, a sidelong glance at the body on the rock.

There's been enough killing. He watched the Irishman limp away, turn at the end of the strand, give him a wave with the walking stick, and disappear around a clump of rock.

Twenty-four hours later, Lohmann was in Norfolk. From Wintershill, they had gone to the cottage hospital in Helston, where Charlie Newton's ankle had been put in plaster. They had then driven back to London accompanied by Rennie and his wife. Depositing them in the house in Hornsey, Lohmann and Rue had at once set off for Norfolk, and Lohmann's meeting with the Prime Minister.

By the time they reached Norfolk it was morning. The interview took place in the library of the large house in which Baldwin was vacationing. At first there were only three of them present; Baldwin, Lohmann and the tall, angular figure of Neville Chamberlain, the Chancellor of the Exchequer. Stern, grey and sharp-edged, Chamberlain stood aloof as Baldwin, in checked jacket and leggings, his customary guise as country squire, listened to Lohmann tell the whole story. All the while the Prime Minister stared out at a green expanse of damp lawn, sucking his pipe in silence. Chamberlain, in plus-fours, assumed a grim expression at the story-teller throughout Lohmann's discourse.

When he'd finished, there was a pause before the Prime Minister turned and cast a cold eye on Lohmann. But it was Chamberlain who broke the silence.

'The Exchequer knows nothing of this matter!' the one-time mayor of Birmingham said coldly.

'Don't bother to prevaricate, Neville,' Baldwin cut in harshly. 'An examination would show the money was filtered from the Treasury through the contingency fund to Germany.'

'Five hundred million . . . ?'

'Over three years. Oh, I know you did not authorise it. Neither did I. It was under another Prime Minister. Herr Lohmann's story is true. Emerson was used to make the arrangements. He was a misguided man with aspirations above his station. And he was supported and encouraged by fellow fanatics. But all this must never be known.' The Prime Minister swung around and faced Lohmann. 'You understand that?'

'I understand it,' Lohamnn said. 'But there are conditions.'

Baldwin flushed. 'Conditions? You're in no position to make conditions. The press in this country would never release such a story. Would never be permitted to . . .'

'The French and American press would not hesitate. The damage to your country, Prime Minister, if the American newspapers published such a story, would be considerable. Especially when the then Prince of Wales is shown to have been sympathetic to Adolf Hitler . . .'

'Are you presuming to blackmail the British Government?' Chamberlain said without apparent emotion. Yet there was something behind the tone, an implicit threat delivered in the only way this colourless man could suggest such a thing.

'No, sir,' Lohmann replied. 'But to ensure silence, certain things must be guaranteed.'

'Name them,' Baldwin growled, the country squire image giving way to that of the cold, calculating politican.

'There should be no charges against Edward Rennie under your Official Secrets Act. Such charges, even if held *in camera* would only call attention to the matter. Rennie himself would be happy to take early retirement on full pension.'

'Agreed,' Baldwin said without hesitation.

'And Beth Coverley's father should be officially informed that his daughter did not commit suicide . . .'

'That is a triviality . . .'

'Not to Maurice Kovel.'

Another pause.

'Very well. He shall receive such a letter from my office. If he will undertake not to publicise the matter.'

'I don't think he has any interest in publicity. Simply the fact.'

Baldwin nodded. 'What else?'

Lohmann rubbed his hand across his forehead. 'One other matter. Of interest only to myself. The order for my deportation. I have no desire to return to Germany while the present regime is in power . . .'

Baldwin stared across at Chamberlain.

'The deportation order,' said Chamberlain. 'Was recommended to the Home Secretary by the Assistant Commissioner, New Scotland Yard. That is . . . or was . . . Charles Emerson.'

'That order has no longer any validity,' said the Prime Minister. 'Anyway I'd rather you stayed in this country, Lohmann. Where we can keep an eye on you. Is that satisfactory?'

'It is satisfactory, sir.'

'Good! Neville, will you leave us a moment? And send in the two gentleman waiting outside.

Not entirely pleased, the Chancellor of the Exchequer withdrew. And a moment later two other figures came into the room.

'I believe you have met Stevens and Dansey?' Baldwin said.

C E Stevens gave Lohmann a tired smile. 'We've had a job keeping up with Herr Lohmann.'

'These gentlemen are members of British Intelligence,' Baldwin explained.

'Fellow's been doing our job for us,' said Dansey dourly.

'You see, Lohmann,' Baldwin went on. 'We were not entirely unaware of the situation. These gentlemen had the task of ensuring that this matter be explored thoroughly.'

'You made our job easier,' Stevens smiled.

'Perhaps more to ensure it would not be made public,' Lohmann replied.

Baldwin coughed loudly. 'Yes, well, that will be all, gentlemen. I intend now to resume my holiday without further interruption. Thank you, gentlemen. And thank you, Lohmann.'

Baldwin turned to the window again, to contemplate a cypress in the garden, sad in the chill air. The three men moved to the door, Lohmann bringing up the rear. But, as he reached the door, Baldwin called him back.

'Lohmann, a moment alone.'

Lohmann closed the door behind the two Intelligence men. 'Sir?'

'I suppose we owe you thanks.' The words and the tone were grudging.'

'If you think so, sir.'

'The matter of the financing of the National Socialists I would rather had been left buried. However you have agreed to help us re-inter it. For good and all.'

'Yes.'

Baldwin turned from the window, brow wrinkled. The simple country squire confused by events. Lohmann thought, 'he turns it on and off at will but it is a clever performance.'

'In the matter of a certain personage . . . The King's ideas may be well-meant.'

'If you say so,' Lohmann replied icily. He'd had too much experience of those in Germany with whom the King's sympathies appeared to lie.

Baldwin went on, 'And he had corresponded with Sir Oswald Mosley. We know that. All this casts doubt on his suitability to continue as Monarch. And of course there is the business of the woman, Mrs Simpson.'

He took a deep breath and stared fixedly at Lohmann from under his eyebrows. 'He will have to go. Mrs Simpson makes it doubly desirable. You have furnished me with another reason and another weapon, Herr Lohmann. In the event that he tries to form a King's party, your discoveries will be useful as yet another lever. For that I owe you thanks. It will be my final act as Prime Minister to ensure his departure.'

'Your last politician to achieve that was Oliver Cromwell. I think, sir.'

'A historic precedent, Lohmann. But I will not, thank God, have to go to such extremities as Cromwell. Still, I will be equally effective. And after it's done, I will be able to retire and leave Neville to handle Hitler. God help him.'

Baldwin turned again to contemplate the cypress.

Five minutes later, Lohmann climbed into the car beside Rue.

'Since I am no longer to be deported,' he informed her, 'I shall have to find a new place to live.'

'Why bother? My place is big enough for . . .'

' . . . for the time being. Until you find another interest.'

'But I shan't . . .'

'You shall. But, until then . . .' he shrugged.

She smiled. 'If you think so. But, until then . . .'

They drove off towards London. There were consequences. There were always consequences.

Emerson's transfer of moneys to Germany contributed to

Hitler's coming to power. There followed Lohmann's investigation and its conclusion. And the further consequences thereof.

On December the tenth 1936, after a reign of three hundred and twenty-five days, Edward VIII abdicated.

In January, 1937, Sir Oswald Mosley, having been married to Diana Mitford in Germany, with Hitler and Goebbels as guests at the wedding, was again speaking at a Fascist rally in the East End of London. At his side was William Joyce.

On the third of September, 1939, William Joyce was in Berlin when war was declared. Rue Scott-ffoliot was married to a banker in the City of London and living in Buckinghamshire. Ernst Lohmann, former Inspector of Berlin's Criminal Police, was living in London, still a refugee from Nazi Germany. He had applied for British citizenship and was working as a translator and announcer in the German section of the overseas service of the British Broadcasting Corporation.

5204 009